ADVANCE PRAISE FOR YOU WILL KNOW VENGEANCE

"WA Pepper writes a new techno-charged version of The Shawshank Redemption *for the 21st century.* You Will Know Vengeance *is the first part of a fresh, new techno-thriller trilogy by author WA Pepper. Set within the confines of a prison, and the wilderness of cyber space, the two disparate worlds collide in a tense, gripping drama. It is a fast-paced, high-energy novel, that will keep readers on the edge of their seats. Whilst this book will certainly appeal to techno-thriller junkies, it is an easy-to-read novel for neophytes, providing a fascinating insight into the hidden world of hackers, cyber criminals, and the dark web. A FINALIST and highly recommended."* - Readers' Choice Book Awards (5-starred review)

***

"W.A. Pepper pulls no punches in sounding out the adversity and conspiracies affecting the world, and so readers will find this scenario as familiar as it is frightening...Those who pursue realistic thriller stories without being torn over man's inhumanity to man will find You Will Know Vengeance *a powerful saga which promises (and delivers) a fast-paced, action-packed*

series of changing scenarios. *Part of what gives this story an especially vivid "you are here" feel in comparison to the majority of thrillers is Pepper's descriptive prowess, which reaches out to grab readers with sights, smells, and sounds...From dark web routines and Hackers' Haven to a gritty, streetwise analysis of social, political, and legal dilemmas, the story evolves on different levels to reflect the narrator's power and force...Re aders seeking a thriller steeped in too-possible worlds, undercurrents of society that exist today, technological conundrums, and the added overlay of interpersonal relationship challenges affected by conspiracy will find all these elements and more in* You Will Know Vengeance. *This book belongs on the shelves of any library devoted to building a solid, exceptional collection of thriller novels, and is highly recommended for readers who can absorb trigger subjects in the interest of a complex, thoroughly absorbing story packed with surprises." – D. Donovan, Senior Reviewer, Midwest Book Review*

★★★

"*Pepper deftly amps up his engaging prison tale with perpetual threats.. .The author's crisp writing smoothly clarifies technical jargon with no sign of condescension; this creates a protagonist/narrator who comes across as an endearing, sympathetic journeyman more than a highly skilled ha cker... An absorbing, tech-smart tale that unfolds in a tense prison setting.*" – Kirkus

★★★

"*Readers will relish the ins and outs of Pepper's well-crafted dystopian prison society, swarming with cutthroat miscreants who will stop at nothing to dominate... Pepper's true talent is in scene development, and his pages are permeated with dark, gloomy tones... readers will be ab-*

Thrillers by W.A. Pepper

Tanto Thrillers

- DoGoodr (a Tanto Prequel)

- You Will Know Vengeance

- Running on Broken Bones (coming September 27, 2023)

- Burn It All Down (coming September 27, 2024)

You Will Know Vengeance

A Tanto Thriller

W. A. Pepper

W. A. Pepper

Hustle Valley Press

Print and eBook cover design by Damon Freeman and his team.

Formatted by W.A. Pepper.
Published by Taddy Pepper (Publisher) at Hustle Valley Press, LLC.

Author photo by Taddy Pepper.

Danger's photo permission provided by his people.

ISBN 978-1-958011-00-3 (Ebook)

ISBN 978-1-958011-01-0 (Paperback)

ISBN 978-1-958011-02-7 (Hardback)

LCCN 2022914819

OCT 0 9 2022

To Frank Darabont and Stephen King, two visionary greats whose inspiring stories, as suspenseful and dark as they might be, often leave us, the lucky ones, with one undeniable feeling: hope.

Disclaimer and Trigger Warning

Some advance readers were concerned about certain elements in this book, while others were not. To handle any potential concerns, this trigger warning is here to point out that certain elements exist, but not to assess (or guarantee) the impact they will have on the individual reader.

While this thriller is a work of fiction, it contains many of the dark things that, unfortunately, exist in our world: physical, emotional, and mental violence, discrimination, sexual assault, suicide, intolerance, drug abuse, and neglect. Further, the sentence above is not an all-inclusive list of the potential triggers in this book.

This book is not a call to action to hurt people, pets, or even yourself, whether that hurt is physical, mental, emotional, or spiritual.

This book is about overcoming those horrible obstacles, about diligence and resilience in your life, and about how evil will never triumph over good.

Finally, please don't cause yourself or anyone else harm. Love people and love yourself.

Taddy and W. A. Pepper

For assistance, there is a glossary containing technical terms used in this book at the end for your convenience.

Table of Contents

Pages were numbered according to the Paperback Print Edition of this book and may vary from various e-readers and formats.

Chapter One

Ice Cube on the Sun

The Feds give you zero notice when they kick in your door. There is no warning siren. There is no knocking on your door, which is soon to be shattered by a battering ram. There is only silence before the calculated chaos.

A loud crash awakens me, followed by what sounds like the rolling of tin cans along my hardwood floor. I jump out of bed just as a flash-bang touches my big toe. Out of the corner of my eye, I spot a drizzle of gray emitting from the smoke grenade atop my dirty laundry pile.

My thudding heartbeat fills my ears right before the explosion of the holy trinity of SWAT hand grenades—equal parts phosphorous, lightning, and thunder—floods my one-room apartment. I scream, but I cannot hear my own roar. Only my ringing ears, stinging eyes, and burning throat let me know I am still alive. The vibration of a stampede of footsteps shakes my body as leathery gloves assault my temporarily handicapable Helen Keller ass and shove me onto my bed, nose-first. The smells of rancid sheets and garlic fill my nostrils. A faceless assailant pins my arms behind my head and zip-ties my hands together. Then I am yanked to my feet.

The pure, white light blurring my eyes dims slightly. Through slitted eyes, I count six flashlights. Barrels of submachine pistols at the end of each beam of light are trained my way. I glance down and spot half a dozen lasers freckling my unshaven chest.

Four men rip all my electronics from the wall and bag everything. A man in a gas mask talks to me, but it's all a muffle of words, like I am talking to Charlie Brown's teacher. I nod. I do not know what I have agreed to. Soldiers exchange words. They pull something from a bag and march it my way.

The man closest to me shoves a hood over my head. My life as I know it melts away like it never existed.

I might as well have been an ice cube on the sun.

Chapter Two

Staring at a Living Dead Man

When his kingdom was under attack by a flock of Wyvern, King Arthur ordered a sealing of Camelot. The men, women, and children worked night and day to fortify not only the walls but also the open roof. Their attackers, small dragons the size of children, were fierce, cunning, and, most importantly, patient. They often would lie in wait for days, not moving even an inch, to stalk their prey.

The securing of his kingdom took six days. When they had finished, King Arthur asked his most trusted advisor, the wizard Merlin, what he thought of the kingdom's protection.

"That depends, my lord."

"On what?"

"Have you considered that the monsters are already inside?"

***

2010: Eight Years After Capture

A warning siren screeches, and I clutch at my ears. It shifts from an annoying, level hum to one that screams "get off your asses or get shocked!" My fellow cubicle zombies claw at their ears because the overpowering bass frequency of the alarm is at the intensity that not only rattles your fillings but also upsets your stomach. Some people call it "the Brown Noise" because it can make you blast your pants.

I squint through the pain and spot Foshi_Taloa clinging to his keyboard. I forgot that this is his first time as a member of the welcoming committee. When he arrived seven months ago, he was as dazed as any new resident in Hackers' Haven. His ponytail whips as he pukes.

Even though his last meal is now on his Microsoft ergonomic keyboard, he knows it is better to be here than to arrive here. However, just glancing at the vomit makes me gag because I am sure it smells vile.

Vile is such a layered word. There's a solid delineation between evil and vile acts. Some would consider an evil act one that causes temporary pain or discomfort. Vile ones linger, burrowing below the skin, past the veins and under the muscle, and drill straight through until they lodge in bone. Tripping a kid who is running too fast in the playground is evil. Tripping that same kid, taking his lunch money, and then forcing him to trip others, well, that's vile.

For eight years, this place has forced me to become vile, to trap others like myself.

And despite enduring years of mind games and a multitude of tortures, buried deep within my battered shell and hardened cold exterior, one last ember burns to save people, not trap them. That warm coal reminds me of a former life, one outside of these gray concrete walls. I will not go so far to say it is a better life, but one with a better purpose. It is one that I have trained for since I could shave, a life as a Chukanbushi, a protector of the innocent, not this villain for the "greater good" that I have become. All that buried spark needs to encounter is the right catalyst. Little do I know that the fuel my soul needs is a mere two minutes away.

As other prisoners get up from their terminals and head out, I glance at the giant glass box above us. At the top of the stairs is a square office about the size of a Volkswagen bus. It consists of glass sides and one bottom of one-way glass, the kind used in police lineup identification so that only the *good guys* can see the *bad guys*. From here, Warden Cyfib runs this fiefdom with an iron fist. Among all of us indentured servants, it is known as the Cube of Death.

A buzzing hits my ears and it's as if a beehive flew in my left ear and paraded out the right. Quick, shallow breathing speeds up my heart as a moment of panic floods over me. Maybe it is my anti-conscience kicking in, the brainwashing we all experience daily here in Hackers' Haven. *My target's freedom always equals my incarceration*, I think. With enough captures or, as our warden calls them, "kills," you can buy almost anything in this place . . . including your freedom.

My shoulders loosen as I pause, close my eyes, and force the outside world out of my head. Throughout history, it was not uncommon for a Bushido warrior or Bushi to enter a meditative trance in the heat of combat. So respected were these swordsmen that their enemies not only refused to attack them during these moments of tranquility, but most took this unflinching gesture as a chance to retreat.

"Get moving, inmate."

I stumble as a guard shoves me, interrupting my thirty-second breathing mantra. I march past our War Room's line of workstations and enter the blindingly bright hallway. Harsh fluorescent bulbs assault my black-and-white-monitor-accustomed eyes. Each inmate already has his hands and nose against the cold, concrete wall, because we always fear the disciplinary shock. I join my fellow docile prisoners.

The sirens cease. Pulses of a phantom base-beat echo in my ears as my head adjusts to the silence. Then, for what feels like an hour, none of us utters a word, a grunt, or even breathe audibly. Anything less than total submission would inflame the warden.

Next to me is Lance-a-Little, a hacker ten years older than me. He reminds me of the actor Sam Elliot, more in his demeanor than his appearance. His brown eyes shift from a spot under my feet, then to my eyes, and then back to the floor.

Between my feet are drops of crimson, almost like someone took an eyedropper of red Kool-Aid and dripped it over my shoulder when I wasn't looking. I touch my hand to my pencil-thin mustache and look at my fingers. I have been so distracted that it's only just now that I notice the smell of copper that floods my nostrils. I rub blood between my thumb and index finger until it seeps into my skin.

Nosebleeds are common in a profession where "Nintendo Time" exists: the brain completely skews the world's normal clock, where what you think is merely twenty minutes has been, in actuality, six straight hours. Through intense training, a warrior could focus his *zanshin,* his "mind without remainder," on any task and ignore the world around him until completion and victory. Of course, victory and perfect health rarely are bedfellows. During "Nintendo Time," you don't eat, drink, or piss, which usually means that it will all come back and bite you in the ass later: migraines, nosebleeds, and UTIs, oh my!

The march of the guards as they enter our wing of this clandestine prison sounds like a herd of Clydesdale horses. The rattle of chains, and squeak of prison-issued flattop shoes on tile in little, geisha-length steps means that my fellow inmates and I are about to meet a newly convicted and processed hacker. If I wasn't so terrified for the rookie, I'd chuckle. In a traditional prison, you start out a criminal and come out a torn-up towel: useless yet harmless. Here, the processing results in people above the warden's pay grade going through your body and soul with surgical precision.

Sure, they stretch your psyche and beat your body, but in the end, they never fully shatter someone's mind or spirit. After all, a broken tool is worse than not having a tool at your disposal.

And just like a puppy enters the world confused, with closed eyes, the processing's impact on an individual varies from mere shock to sheer insanity. After all, the rookie just finished days of experiments, surgeries, head shrink torture, isolation, sensory deprivation, and possibly sterilization. Who among us captives really knows? I can't remember much except for flashes of pain. Then, at this prisoner's lowest point, he also would've signed his prison contract that a U.S. government's genius lawyer filled with ironclad thirteenth-grade words. These commitments require the rookie to achieve five hundred captures. Until such time, he has zero shot at parole. Until then, under our Constitution, he is not even considered human.

It doesn't matter what the convict's state of mind is when he signs away his soul. Finding oneself "under duress" means bubkes to us domestic terrorists.

To anyone who hasn't set foot in this hellhole, it is impossible to describe the damage the rook just went through. In here, the powers that be drop the broken at our feet. While it is unwritten, it is up to me and my gang to dust a rookie off, gather up his broken pieces, reassemble him into a functioning trapper, and keep him alive.

Even if we patch up the damage, this new guy might bail on my group. I have invited many a wounded warrior into my clan. Few have stayed. Most found a life of discipline and focus unappealing when they could just follow the warden blindly and "kill" anyone in their path. Sadly, they are right. That is the easier road. A Bushi's life is full of failure. It requires a quest for pure equilibrium, like a trapeze artist holding a long stick for balance, with pride at one end and shame on the other. Too much or too little of one and you plunge because, without the yin, there is no yang.

The footsteps stop. A squawk of a radio precedes a guard saying, "Turn." As we rotate toward the two guards and the poor sap under a black hood, I shudder and my toes curl. No matter how many times we get a new guy, I always remember my time in that darkness and everything that came before it: the extreme fatigue, a desert's dryness in my entire body, a seasick-worthy dizziness, and confusion that borderlines on insanity.

Hell isn't a place; it is a state of mind.

The taller guard, a new baby-faced giant that I've never seen before and wearing a name tag that reads Stevens, stands next to the hooded prisoner. The guard yanks the hood from the rook. Sunken eyes, busted nose, and purplish, baggy face. Someone did a number on this acne-covered lad. Guard Fontana, a beefcake with a body of granite, shoves his baton in the guy's gut when the prisoner lunges his way. The impact is more of a gentle reminder than a damaging impact. Fontana doesn't want to injure the kid. He just wants him to keep moving.

The push is just enough to get his train back on track. However, the rook stumbles and moves his legs too wide for the restrictive ankle chain. Fontana reaches out, but his hand misses the rook's shoulder. The rook falls face-first into the floor. He thrashes against his ball gag. Two long strings of slobber now connect his face to the floor from his mouth. He fights the handcuffs that connect a chain from his wrists to his ankles. It's a bad sign that he's fighting. It means he still thinks he's classified as "human." Sadly, he'll soon learn the error of his ways.

The problem is that the rookie is fighting a losing battle, and the only way to change that type of outcome is to change the rules. That's what Miyamoto Musashi, the only Bushido warrior to never lose a fight, did. Like me, he started his own discipline at age thirteen because he knew his life needed something more. However, his was with a sword and mine was with a keyboard. Regretfully, all I do now is lose, but I choose to lose so that others will survive.

Even after face-planting and possibly breaking his nose, the rookie is lucky. Worse arrivals here have occurred.

A half floor above us, the door to a booth opens. A chill runs the entire length of my body. My skin feels like I've just entered the North Pole.

Dreaded *cha-chings* ring out across the hallway. All other sounds cease. *The Warden.* Like something out of an old western movie, he always wears boots with damned spurs on them that herald his arrival, like he is about to kick open a saloon door and shoot everyone inside. It makes perfect sense: when you're held prisoner near Houston, Texas, you expect at least one of your captors to wear cowboy boots. *Cha-ching. Cha-ching.* Just like him, the sounds are deliberate. Hard. Efficient. And terrifying to my core.

Then it happens: I spot a reflection of light from something in the rook's hand; something that is not part of the standard check-in at Hotel Hell here. He has a weapon. It will not equal the outcome he probably expects.

I am staring at a living dead man.

Chapter Three

This is Gonna Hurt

The guardian angel, the one that sits on your shoulder and usually yells for you to not rock the boat, needs to shut the hell up and take a coffee break. It is time for less rational voices to come out and play.

The rookie is a good three steps from me. A lot can happen in three steps. He could swipe an Achilles heel. The guard would scream and fall, then the prisoner could slit his throat before the guard smacked the tile floor.

The rook could crouch and stab a guard's sweet spot, the area in the liver that is impossible to fix upon rupture, an injury that results in thirty-four seconds of pain before a sleepy death.

He could even slit his own throat.

My eyes shoot a question at Lance-a-Little. He raises his silver eyebrows before closing his eyes and sighing. "On a day I wear clean underwear," mutters Lance.

Anyone in these walls is given a chance among our brotherhood. We never have more than ten residents in Hackers' Haven at a time, and the rook would make ten slots full.

Maybe if I move a little closer to him, he will sense my good intentions. Stranger things occur in these walls.

Unfortunately, I take a baby step forward as the *cha-chings* grow in intensity. My feet root, and not even gale-force winds could move me from that spot.

As the six-foot-four muscular rock of a man crosses in front of me, his beady eyes meet mine. A white pipe, possibly mother-of-pearl or even rhino, hangs in the right crook of his mouth. I look away and retreat, placing my back against the cement behind me so hard that I probably just took some of the next floor's weight off the load-bearing wall.

The warden leans down over the rook, and a large flash drive slips from his pocket and clatters against the floor. It bounces and flips as the warden chases it, finally landing face up with the number-letter combination 5TB emblazoned clear as day across it, right before the warden snaps it up. The warden never moves fast for anything, so whatever is on the drive is important.

I didn't even know they made a flash drive that big. It would be rare to use a drive that size anywhere in the world. All *our* work is compiled and stored through a Server Room. I've heard the guards complain that they are asked to leave their cell phones, flash drives, and even their remote-access car keys at the sign-in desk. So, for the warden to be carrying around a large flash drive . . . This thought drives an itchy nail into my curiosity.

As a Bushi, I know a thing or two about keeping secrets. Before my imprisonment, I had more fake identities than James Bond. All the Bushido warriors kept their strategies secret, which was why the thousand-year-old Bushido Code remained unwritten until just before those knights faded from history.

The warden clears his throat and returns his attention to his newest prisoner.

"Who you think you are . . . is gone. You are no longer what the United States considers human. You are a dog. A dog does not have rights. A dog is not a pet. It is a tool. And a tool without a use is to be disposed of."

His clipped tone isn't the only thing precise about the warden. From his white, crisp ironed shirt and thin black tie to his perfectly creased pants, he is about as close to a robot as Agent Smith in *The Matrix*: void of personality or likability. And if he gets his hands on you, he'll either turn you into something just like him, or destroy you.

When that was me in the cuffs and bleeding on the floor, everything sounded garbled, but the warden's flat tone and enunciation of every syllable conveys his message clearly.

The warden puts his scarred left hand on the prisoner's neck and clamps down with his sausage fingers. The rookie screams; the long, blond-haired monster has found a pressure point. After one more scream, the warden loosens his grip, yet keeps his hand on the rookie's neck.

"A dog's only purpose is to kill other dogs. All that matters are the kills. Your target has taken *your* rights. Dogs, bark."

In unison all the inmates chant, "Your target's freedom always equals your incarceration."

Nausea hits my stomach and bile rises in my throat. On the one hand, the repetition of that phrase makes my brain go all Pavlov's dogs and salivate to please my master, which is stomach-turning enough. But more than that, the sickness rises at the thought of the lives I have failed to save and that I personally destroyed when I was under the warden's spell.

My mind has played that mantra over and over so many times I still hear the warden's robotic voice in my sleep. Of course, when he was proving his point those many years ago, he also blasted me with a body-crippling shock to prove who was in control, even though I had done nothing wrong.

A long time ago, I used to dream I was in feudal Japan in full battle attire, fighting legions of faceless men in armor. I was climbing a hill, my Katana drawn, and I was parrying and slicing my way through my aggressors. My battle cry was so intense that many of my enemies fled instead of daring to engage me in battle.

Now, when I close my eyes, I only see darkness. All I hear is my overseer's voice.

As the warden steps away, the Guard Fontana bends over the prisoner and unlocks his chains and removes the ball gag without a word. Were my eyes playing tricks on me? Maybe I imagined the shiv.

However, when both guards lift the rookie, I see the metal shank rotate in the prisoner's hand, the jagged edge shimmering in the light. The instrument is so sharp and his grip is so tight that the rook's own blood drips to the floor and splashes against the white tile.

Then the don't-rock-the-boat angel and the let-the-bridges-you-burn-light-your-way devil return from their coffee break and get back into my ear to battle for my soul. *If you do nothing, they'll beat him within an inch of his life. If you do something, we all get shocked. Don't get involved.* He thinks he's the hero of his story. He's not. None of us are. This rook is a pawn, like the rest of us, ready to be sacrificed for the "greater good." Don't make it worse for everyone. You don't even know him. He might be the worst human to walk the Earth since the death of Hitler and the formation of Coldplay. Do not get involved.

Then my instincts chime in. My lack of action could kill this man. As the world slows, I know my conscience has joined my shit-for-brains gut against me. I curse under my breath because this will at the very least ruin everyone's morning. At the worst, this might kill us as well as him.

Screw it. This is gonna hurt.

What happens next didn't directly kill Hackers' Haven's newest prisoner. Nope. I'd later learn that I'd already started his agonizing death a while back.

Chapter Four

Who Did This to You?

O f all the Bushido Code virtues I live my life according to, the principle of rectitude is one of the hardest. This is because rectitude requires you to analyze the world in three dimensions: past, present, and future. You learn from the past to make an unequivocal choice in the present that will set a course for the future. It includes not just justice for wrongs, but also striking down evil before it ever occurs. In today's world, people ask, "Would you kill the serial killer Ted Bundy as a baby?" Most people answer yes. Now, the problem with that arises: Bundy, a man who killed at least thirty women, volunteered at a suicide hotline when he was in college. His colleagues said his charisma calmed many a caller, and he was the best person in the station. So, if you killed him as a baby, how many lives would have been lost to suicide?

Of course, if you choose to let him live until he finishes that job, well, don't tell that to his first victim, Lynda Ann Healy, a classmate of his at the University of Washington.

When you develop a discipline, a habit, you rarely notice it once it ingrains itself to your core. I did not notice that I was already three breaths into my technique when my ears popped and my feet propelled me forward. My mind, now free from the fear of the warden's shock, has accepted the responsibility for my actions and nonactions, and moved past it. My sole focus is saving this kid from himself.

I tackle Hackers' Haven's newest inmate and twist both of his thumbs until they pop like Bubble Wrap. *Sprained, not broken,* I think. With his hands in mine, the kid's arm, full of healing needle wounds, shows his ID bracelet. *Handle: Quidlee.* Something in my mind blows dust off a long-forgotten box with the same name on it.

"I have got to get out of here!" The rook's statement does not come as a surprise. No one really *wants* to be in here. Well, except for me.

The short guy rolls with me back toward the entrance to the secure area of the prison. We simply call it the Gate, but I am sure it has an official name in some brochure or the like.

As our right legs tangle up, they swing together near the Gate's metal detector-type sensor. It emits a chirp I've never heard anywhere in the prison, and before I can even be confused by the sound, the Gate opens and shuts in a blur, under two seconds.

That's not possible, I think. *Our disciplinary chips don't work like that.*

A body-stopping shock interrupts my thoughts, pulsing through me so hard my jaw slams shut and my back teeth cut a slice out of my tongue. The electrical current from our implanted devices will overtake both of us now, as well as every other prisoner.

As I lay on the white tiles, I push the rook's shank—a sharpened, metal computer casing hinge—into the floor's air vent and play it off like an arm spasm from the shock. I hated to hurt the kid, but I had to take his hands out of commission. This way, he wouldn't have the option of attacking anyone else. I can't guarantee that the warden would have his joy buzzer/prisoner shocker on him. I ain't a saint, but I'm a not a fan of violence unless absolutely necessary. If I were a soft drink, I'd be Diet Violence or Pacifist-Lite because, despite what the movies tell you, Bushi warriors were not driven by violence. Honor guided them, and they only took a life when there was no other option.

Even in daily life, in moments that don't involve sharp objects or elec-trocutions, I think, *What would a Bushi do in this situation?* Then I think back to Mr. Perry, and the answer is almost always obvious.

Lon Perry, a man who added to my life code through his actions rather than his words or even his presence, never physically harmed a soul. He fit the mold of the average forty-year-old

'Merican at the end of his proverbial rope: a Bible-thumping, happily married, oil man with a house, a white picket fence, and two-point-something kids.

He also happened to be my neighbor when I was growing up, and he became my secret role model when I started hacking for a living. Mister Average American Male robbed more banks than Bonnie and Clyde. Mr. Lon decided that when times got tough, he'd color his white hat a darker shade. He never killed or injured anyone, yet he was a successful criminal. His strategic benevolence influenced me the way hearing the *White Album* influenced Beatles fans: it changed my perception of everything.

I am ripped back to reality by a voice void of an accent. "Dog, fighting is not permitted."

I crap my pants a little.

I've never placed our despot's accent, because he speaks in clipped sentences, like the human equivalent of a child's Speak & Spell computer toy. The words are there, just not the tone that lets you understand the *intention* of the words.

I pretend to fall as I rise so that I can topple on top of the rook. His sea-green eyes pulsate, not from the prior electrocution, but in rage.

In a whisper, I try to reason with a wild animal. "Your thumbs are just dislocated. You'll be fine."

As if his immediate spitting in my right eye wasn't enough of a response, he adds, "I'm going to kill you."

Not until you regain the ability to wipe your ass, you won't.

A zap hits us all. It is lesser in intensity and duration, which allows me to roll over to my side. From the corner of my eye, I spot a tiny piece of paper and snatch it up. It's a photo of an Asian girl, probably early twenties. She could easily be this rook's sibling because she, too, has those sea-green eyes. She is wearing a blue T-shirt, a white bike helmet, and peddles along on a yellow bicycle. Her pink hair curls up in the wind, almost dancing in the air. Someone took the shot from the girl's back, but almost at an angle. She'd been able to spot the photographer in her right peripheral vision, which may explain why her cherry-red, pencil-thin lips smirk at the photographer, a look like she knows a secret that she will never tell.

The harsh fluorescent lights brighten for a just a second; for a moment I forget where I am and how long I've been here. It is as if the light doesn't shine on her; it attaches to her. She is the most beautiful being I've ever seen.

As I pocket the photo, I glance over at the rook. I get a better look at the injuries not caused by me. There are clear bruising patterns on his face that resemble ridges of a tire. But upon closer review, they are overlapping contusions supplied by someone's knuckles. Finally, I make out the shape on his neck: one giant handprint.

A shiver goes through the rook's body, the kind you get when you leave a warm building and step directly into a blizzard. The rook's bloodshot eyes dart around the room. *Is he looking for his assailant?*

As if he's reading my mind, the rook answers my internal question of *Who did this to you?* with one word. And, out of any words that could have come out of this tiny man's mouth, he utters the one he guaranteed to make my blood pressure shoot up a hundred points.

"Barca."

Oh, my Lord, no.

Before I know it, I am on my feet and facing Lance-a-Little. He must've heard the word because his eyes widen.

Then a hand the size of a basketball lands on my shoulder, disrupting this delightful turn of events. A large-and-in-charge Samoan with a smile worthy of a Cheshire cat towers over my five-foot-eight ass with a look of concern in his light brown eyes.

"Enough, dogs," says the warden. "If you continue, you will be fined six kills and assigned evening latrine and repair duty. Dogs, make your next choice wisely."

The big guy does: the Jolly Round Giant removes his hand from my shoulder, looks me in the eye, shrugs, and punches me dead in the face.

Chapter Five

Hell Just Got Two Hundred Degrees Hotter

"I said I'm sorry," apologizes AldenSong, a jolly Samoan in the medical pod next to me. He is telling the truth, because, by my last count, he's apologized five times for almost breaking my nose. "Also, you winked at me."

"I did not wink. I *blinked* . . . before you smashed my face in."

"Again, I said I'm sorry."

There are people in this world who cause harm by accident and others who mean it. AldenSong is the type that fixes the harm that others have done. The world needs more people like him, so I cannot hold a grudge against this guy even if someone paid me a million dollars.

"Well, patient Tanto, I hate to tell you this, but we're gonna have to change your handle," Dr. Fel's voice quakes from the corner of the room as he holds back a snicker. "Your new handle is Peanut, because you just got . . . assaulted. Get it?"

I die a little every time he makes a dad joke.

Dr. Fel mutters, "Everyone's a critic," then leaves the room.

I close my eyes and try to relax. Each time I try to get some meditative sleep in this pod, the hum of the scanner keeps messing with me; just as the world fades away, a *click* or *whirl* jolts me back to the reality that I am stuck in a medical pod. Just like we run performance and maintenance software on our computers, the pods are used once a week to check for any problems in our overclocked bodies. When you spend fourteen-plus hours a day staring at a monitor while you're surrounded by machines that are putting off over one hundred watts of heat because they are constantly processing and potentially emitting low levels of radiation, you're bound to catch something.

After any level of altercation, from a single punch to a full-on stabbing, it is standard to send all convicts, or as we call ourselves, "hackvicts," to the Infirmary. We get checked out by Doc Stu Fell, a beanpole of a man. Like six-nine and a hundred fifty pounds soaking wet level of tall and lanky. It is hard not to like the guy. He always greets you with a smile and even gives us stickers that say "Got Well with Dr. Fel" when we leave. I don't care what age you are; it always feels good to get a sticker. Of course, we also get put in the pods once a week to get checked out, to make sure we "tools" aren't rusting or coming apart.

"Also," I say, holding onto the pain like it is a grudge, "how in the world does a wink mean that you should punch me in the face?"

"I feel like I'm in a Xerox copier." AldenSong, one pod away, changes the topic the way a guitarist shifts chords: with perfect fluidity. A *zip-zip-chirp* from the speaker next to me means my first hour in the pod is up. Three more to go.

"Click-whirl, click-whirl," he imitates the machine, "paper jam, paper jam . . . or maybe stuck in that casket they put Spock in on *The Search for Spock* and shot him out into space."

"Aldy, that was *The Wrath of Khan*." Blasphemy comes in many forms. "*The Search for Spock* was after the casket crashed on the planet."

"Ooooohh, look at the big Vulcan ears on this smartie."

I chuckle. Big boy can make a man, with his head stuck in the guillotine awaiting his own beheading, laugh.

"'Now I know what a microwave dinner feels like,'" I say, quoting *Die Hard*.

"I don't get it . . . besides, you'd be rotating and popping, spewing out little squirts of blood from under your plastic wrap. This could be a tanning bed. It's the right size for it. Maybe you'll get rid of that chalky exterior, get some color in your vampire-looking cheeks, Tanto."

"That's racist."

"Naw." He snickers. "That's Irish. You've got so much whiteness in you that your organs are actually just a collection of differently shaped and sized potatoes."

He isn't wrong. As near as I can tell, my family history originated from white trash in Europe who hitched a ride over the ocean to continue that pattern of bad decisions in the good ole You Es of Ay.

"T, did you see the rookie come in?"

"My guess is they took him back to evaluation since he lashed out as soon as he entered Double-H."

It isn't unusual for an arriving hackvict to rage after setting foot in here. Generally, you arrive either broken or angry. However, immediate violence usually merits further psychological examination.

"Tonight, we gather one of our sheep and protect it from the wolves." Aldy clears his throat and deepens his voice and adds a drawl to his accent, making him sound like a televangelist. "*'Be alert and of sober mind. Your enemy, the devil, prowls around like a roaring lion looking for someone to devour.'* First Peter, chapter 5, verse 8."

"Just don't go throwing holy water around because that stuff makes my skin burn."

Aldy laughs. He knows that the Big Man Upstairs and I don't see eye to eye. Aldy's upbringing was about as different from mine as Little Debbie Snack Cakes are from Cow Pies.

"I'm going to try to get some shuteye, Aldy. Just try not to punch me in the face while I'm napping."

"No promises, cause I wanna nap, too, but first I gotta pee," AldenSong moans, sounding like a dying hippopotamus. "Dr. Fel? Are you there?"

I can understand AldenSong's frustration all the way in my pod, and I feel an empathy twinge in my bladder for the big guy.

"Screw it, I'm gonna pop, so I'm going." Aldy's pod door swings up, sounding like the DeLorean's in *Back to the Future*'s opening. However, within ten seconds of opening the lid, an alarm sounds. "Well, poop."

Through my window in my pod, I watch AldenSong instinctively put his arms in the air as the voice of the security guard who watches our hallway monitors and other sensors, such as the Gate and these Med Bay pods, booms over the intercom.

"Inmate, get back in your pod."

"But I really need to pee, like I'm gonna explode and then there's gonna be pee everywhere."

There is a brief pause, and a response over the speaker of, "you have two minutes."

"But that's not enough—"

"You now have one minute and fifty seconds."

A rapid series of thuds fills my ears. For a big man, Aldy sure can sprint when nature calls.

As I shift in my pod, I grit my teeth. My jaw pops, and not in a good way. Maybe it's the sharp pain, like I've just bitten down on a Dorito and the pointy part has jammed into my gumline, but my mind jumps back to the lone word the rook had said about who beat him up and how I associate that name with nothing but pain.

Barca.

If Barca is involved, then hell just got two hundred degrees hotter.

Chapter Six

I Am the Reason

*B*arca.

It's a short word, but one loaded with meaning in the hacking community. Some think it is an organization that hires other hackers for black hat missions, the kind that are for profit or destruction only. Others think it is one guy, a well-known boogeyman.

Barca is a force of nature. Imagine you are watching a weather pattern that starts over the Caribbean Sea. It grows and darkens like a bloodstain seeping through a white shirt. The stain twirls and grows as it approaches the continental U.S. By the time the storm reaches your shores, you can't see any landmasses on the radar any longer, only the destructive storm engulfing everything.

The word *hacking* implies risk. Barca wants all the benefits of the hack, and none of the risk. He does virtually none of the work, but he has money to hire the best. With money comes power.

The golden rule: he who has the gold makes the rules.

Like the T-shirt featuring Mario the Plumber on it, I was once young, and did dumb things for the gold coins.

I took a hack Barca recruited me for.

I rarely handled small gigs like this one, but the pay was too good to walk away from. Plus, two of my favorite dam breakers, SizerKoze and RomTeagan, had signed on. Those guys were a lot like me, good at their task, and needed no handholding.

So, five others and I emptied one account at a small-town bank. The target was the largest seed provider in Tennessee. Don't let overalls and sunburnt skin fool you; there's a lot of money in farming if you do it right. The problem with the hack was, once we were through the firewall and had gained administrative access to the files, Barca raided the entire cookie jar and left no crumbs. No account was left untouched.

I was helpless to watch online as Barca used root code to drain every account. Sure, most of the money was insured, but when you have a couple who have put every penny into a CD and it was above the government's FDIC two hundred fifty thousand dollar insured rate, they lost that money.

At first, I wasn't worried about the Feds catching me. I was set up in a storage unit I'd rented under a fake name, piggybacking my jack using a hotspot backdoored through an unsecured router from the adjacent fast-food joint. The U-Store-It Depot had three viable exits, plus my pocket bolt cutters could handle any section of the wire fencing. I was ready to run if the job went south.

And haywire it went. We were midway through Barca's digital blitzkrieg when something in my stomach soured as I watched our shared-screen connection with Barca. For every withdrawal from the bank, Barca uploaded a digital packet on the bank's servers. When I tried to open one of the files, it required a password.

Just go.

I yanked the power cord from my POS laptop, flipped it upside down, and yanked out the battery. From my backpack, I grabbed two glass bottles: one with a stark white liquid and the other yellowish. First, I poured the one with bleach all over the computer, my chair, and anything I might've touched. Second, I flung the gasoline on top of the bleach and lit a match.

By the time flames emerged from storage unit 45B, I had sprinted one block away.

The police were at the storage unit before I made another block. It was not the fire that got their attention; it was Barca.

Unlike a hacker who either works for fame or a cause, Barca is a pure mercenary. While I cannot confirm what I know in my heart to be true, my instinct tells me that Barca reached out to the seed company that we raided and offered them two things. One, their money back, for a percentage. And two, the names and contact information of everyone else involved in the hack.

He must have been swift to make the exchange during the hack because the Feds found my location so quickly it was like I had a giant red flag hung outside my door. Knowing Barca, I probably did.

I went underground for a month after that. I was one of the fortunate few who worked with Barca and lived to tell the tale. A few weeks later, I tried to contact SizerKoze and RomTeagan. Their accounts sent back cryptic messages, and both handles failed my code work sniff test: they answered questions I asked that no hacker worth his salt would dare admit to, like admitting to hacking.

Barca leaves no survivors. People I'd worked with on the outside were destroyed by that man. Now, I must protect this house from him. This is my home, and if he is coming, I need to ready myself for this monster.

Though I never served in the military, I always appreciate that, when people swear the oath of their service, it is not to a sitting president or Congress. It is to The Constitution, and it includes protecting citizens from enemies both foreign and domestic. You don't get more of a domestic enemy than someone like Barca. I, too, swore an oath. No, I did not stand before a flag when I did it. There were no witnesses, no official record, but I swore to protect the people I held dear. Even if it killed me.

Let's just hope it wouldn't come to that.

It is about this time that AldenSong sprints in from his bathroom break. His labored breathing reminds me of a malfunctioning vacuum my mother had because it blew more than it sucked. However, after Aldy plops back into the pod and closes the doors, his breathing slows. I bet he is using our breathing technique to calm himself.

"Aldy?"

"Yes . . . T . . . ?"

"Did you have to hit me so hard?"

"Can't . . . hear you . . . sleeping." The big guy fakes a snore for a few seconds before he actually fades down to sleep. He has the right idea. We are here for a few more hours, so why not just get some shut eye?

Just before I am about to doze off, a last thought robs me of peaceful sleep. It jars me awake stronger than a coffee enema.

I remember where I know the handle Quidlee.

Damnation. I am the reason he is in Hackers' Haven in the first place.

W. A. Pepper

Chapter Seven

You're in Hell

later that evening, after our multi-hour scan and Dr. Fel's checkup, the second part of our punishment for fighting kicks in. While the other nine hackers and half dozen guards either sleep or hack, the rook, AldenSong, and I clean our dormitory-style bathroom with toothbrushes, mops, and sponges. Our progress is slow, what with my swollen face, the rook's bandaged hands, and Aldy's infernally cheery whistling.

AldenSong crawls to the hallway and glances around like a child about to raid the cookie jar. "The coast is clear."

"Thanks, Paul Revere," I say.

In response, the big man wipes sweat from his brow and flicks a glop of it onto my face.

The rook lies on his back a good ten feet away, struggling to clean boogers from under one of the sinks with a toothbrush.

The toothbrush slips from his hand, its plastic handle bouncing against the tile. This is the fifth time the sad sack has dropped it. Nerves and his bandaged hands keep getting the better of him for what should be a mindless job.

Watching him struggle, I'm overwhelmed with the urge to make things right. Sure, I've possibly saved his life. But, according to the Bushido Code, now that I've saved his life, I'm in charge of it until the favor is returned. Strictly speaking, he's meant to be my protégé and follow my commands. Somehow, I doubt this kid with sunken green eyes and an early Beatles haircut will be keen on *that* arrangement. Best I keep that on a need-to-know basis.

I retrieve the toothbrush for the gnome and dangle it between my thumb and forefinger. "We can't fix your hands, Rook, so trying to hold the brush like they aren't messed up is just going to mean you keep dropping the toothbrush."

I reach down and put his bandaged mitt in my grip.

Though hidden behind his long hair, his dagger-like stare warns me just before the rook lunges and wraps his hands around my neck. We land, my back to the floor and all his weight on my chest. I lower my chin to my chest, preventing him from crushing my windpipe.

A few feet away, Aldy jumps to his feet and extends his giant paw to snatch this rookie off me.

"No," I croak. The word starts so slowly in my chest that AldenSong's fingers graze the kid's shoulder by the time it crawls past my lips. Aldy removes his hand but holds his ground, just in case I am wrong about this kid's reason for lashing out or in case I don't muster the strength to keep him from killing me.

I let my attacker continue. Part of my Bushido training means compassion is always required, especially with the ignorant. Of course, compassion and self-preservation aren't mutually exclusive tasks, which is why I jammed my chin into my chest. My first day in this mind screw certainly filled me with the same rage pulsing from the rook's eyes. If it weren't for the kindness of Lance-a-Little and my training, choking the life out of someone would've been the least of my sins that day.

Of course, I am in some danger of slipping in the blood of my own bleeding heart and winding up dead. A flicker of stars enters my peripheral vision. My heartbeat pulses against my temples. My eyes move to Aldy, his giant body shuffling from foot to foot. Finally, our pack's newest puppy tires himself out on his own and rolls off me.

Gasps of air burn my lungs. My body demands oxygen, but too much of it at this point might knock me out. It is counterintuitive, but I've practiced the ancient breathing technique pranayama enough to know that if we control our breath, we control our body.

Aldy holds fingers in front of me: one on his right hand and four on his left. I nod. He joins me in the repetition. *One breath in, four breaths out.*

AldenSong breathes through his open mouth, making a noise during each inhale and three exhales. "Hip-hup-hup-hup-hup. Hip-hup-hup-hup-hup."

AldenSong thinks well on his feet, because some people who grew up in a cult can't think for themselves. It's amazing that he grew up in a commune in a secluded part of Maui, because most people I've met, whether or not they were part of a cult, couldn't react to a situation if their asses were on fire and they were handed a bucket of ice water.

"Hip-hup-hup-hup-hup. Hip-hup-hup-hup-hup." *Condition the lungs. Steady blood flow. Clear the mind.*

A few seconds later, the rook rolls to his knees, drops his hands, and screams in frustration at the ceiling. "What kind of prison is this?"

I can't blame Quidlee for asking this question. Lord knows I've asked that many a time over the last eight years.

The burning in my chest subsides. My head clears. Not even a trace of headache forms. The Samoan smiles, lifts me from under my shoulders, and helps me to my feet. I walk over to my attacker and extend a hand.

He swats it away. I cannot tell if he is upset with himself or me or both. I guess both.

"You're . . . not . . . in . . . prison . . ." The sentence leaves my dry throat almost as if words haven't left it in years. I squat down and meet the rookie's gaze.

"You're . . . in . . . hell."

Chapter Eight

Revoking Your Status as a Human Being

"Hey, it has its good days." Aldy, aka Mr. Brightside, instantly negates my dramatic line.

I shoot him a look through slit eyes. *Don't contradict me in front of the kids.* He at least has the good grace to duck my gaze.

"Check the hallway . . . Aldy." I croak, my vocal cords still hoarse from the rook's death grip.

"*Please* check the hallway, Aldy," the big lug mutters under his breath as he walks over to the lone door to the latrine, pokes his head out, and pans for guards.

"Boo!" There's no telling how long Lance-a-Little hid behind that doorframe, but I'm sure his scaring AldenSong into producing a high-pitched squeal was worth it. "I just thought I'd stop by since I was out of my cell because the good ole doc needed to run some tests on me."

Aldy punches Lance in the shoulder as he returns, shaking his head. I snatch an empty blue mop bucket and turn it upside down to sit on. Lance does the same as Aldy nervously paces.

"You boys teaching this kid about Tax Software?" Lance asks. During my first year here, Lance-a-Little told me that, in college, he used to burn all his *sensitive information* to CDs and label them Tax Software titles and things like Tax Software Patch v1.2. He did this so no one in his dorm would steal those disks because no one deliberately looks for tax software.

"Not yet, Lance. We're in the foundational part of *Imprisonment 101 for Dummies.*"

"Lovely." Lance crosses his arms and kicks his head back. "Proceed with breaking his heart, dear sirs."

When I was brought in here eight years ago, there were already a handful of others like me in this newly built facility. We were not classified prisoners, but we were not free to leave. Only Lance-a-Little has a longer residency in this resort than I do. In eight years, here's what I've assembled from stories, rumors, scraps of paper, and the occasional deep dive into the dark web.

"When something happens in our country and the powers that be cannot find a way to address it in the Constitution or Bill of Rights, they take their dear sweet time in coming up with an answer to a question. Since 9/11, people like me and Lance-a-Little here have been on the government's 'to be decided list' of how to process our crimes."

AldenSong chimes in, "What about me?"

"You've been here four years, big 'un," says Lance. "By the time you got here, well, this little prison had lost its new car smell."

"Well, even if I'm not as old-timey as you two are," adds AldenSong, "I am very much aware that we, fellow prisoners of this fine facility, do not qualify under the Constitution of the United States of America, as well as its compliment the Bill of Rights, as human beings."

"That's bullshit," counters the rook, as if doubt makes anything better.

"You're bullshit, you little shit, so shut up and listen," says Lance as he sticks his finger in the rook's face. "These two are the nice ones here, but they take forever to tell the rules, so I'm gonna tell it to you straight. I'm gonna tell it to you once because I'm not a patient man. One, you're gonna work in here. Hard. Harder than you've ever worked in your entire life. You're gonna rack up twelve-hour days every single damn day with the day shift. That's with these two angels here, Saint Irish and Friar

Fatso. You can't shift to the other shift, the night shift, so don't bother asking. Also, I hope you're not claustrophobic because you're gonna get locked up for eight straight hours every night from ten p.m. to six a.m. unless you're in the Med Bay . . ."

"What's the Med—?"

"What part of *shut up and listen* was not clear?"

Apparently, Lance takes the scowl on the rook's face as enough of an answer to continue.

"Two, there are two guards on duty at all times. One in the War Room. One in the Control Room, aka the Server Room. They are not your friends. They are men that can kill you without blinking an eye. Don't get any ideas that fewer guards means you can escape. There are a dozen different ways to die here. Three, shut the ever-loving hell up at work. I do not joke with you. You can jaw and gab like ladies at a bridge club who've consumed one too many martinis basically any other time, but don't talk at work. Now, I'd ask if you wanted me to repeat anything, but I really don't care that much. Just don't screw up."

Quidlee states the obvious by saying, "How can they treat human beings like that?"

"Um, here's some more bad news," says AldenSong in a chipper voice, trying to put honey on a turd of a conversation. "There are governmental structures in place that give corporations human rights. Under certain laws, not only are non-human "entities," such as corporations, protected, but living, breathing human beings are not, because they lose that designation after being accused of a crime. Especially a cybercrime."

I put on my best college professor cap and continue. "We, unfortunately, live in this gray area. It is called the new Section 18 of U.S. Code 2331. In it, the code roughly says that cyber terrorists are immediately guilty of performing quote domestic terrorism, end quote. Now, you might be wondering what domestic terrorism means . . ."

"I wasn't."

Smart-ass.

"Anyway, these are activities that, quote, involve acts dangerous to human life that violate the criminal laws of the United States or of any State and appear to be intended to intimidate or coerce a civilian population; or to influence the policy of a government by intimidation or coercion; or, finally, to affect the conduct of a government by mass destruction, assassination, or kidnapping, end quote."

Lance snickers. "You memorized all that, T?"

"My noggin can hold a lot of useful stuff when it wants to. So, rook, notice that nowhere did I say that these acts are committed by a, quote, human being, end quote. Nowhere in any government document that I've had the luck of getting my hands on is there a definition of a domestic terrorist. Only domestic *terrorism*."

Lance slaps me on the back and brings the whole thing home. "What all this mumbo jumbo means is that these actions, under the view of the United States of America's judicial system, can be classified as crimes committed by non-humans, such as computer programs. So, we hack-victs now have less of a voice and hope than ever. And we didn't have much to begin with. Welcome to Hackers' Haven, kid."

I wouldn't call it a blank stare on the rook's face. More one of confusion, like when your parents tell you Santa's not real. I can't blame the kid's quietness. Of course, trying to make sense out of how the government, this private prison, and what we do for both is like trying to make spaghetti out of a brick.

When the rook finally opens his mouth, the power flickers. Three, four strobes of light later and everything returns to normal.

"What's happening?" asks the rook as his eyes meet mine.

"Power surge. It's not uncommon. We're drawing enough power and bandwidth into the building that sometimes the circuits need a breather. At least that's my hypothesis."

AldenSong chuckles. "I think it's an alien invasion. They're slowly sucking all our power away, one sip at a time."

"The world's kindest conspiracy theorist here," I say, pointing to my large-and-in-charge friend, "is AldenSong."

"Howdy."

"That's Lance-a-Little."

Lance tips an invisible hat toward the rook. "Greetings and salutations, young one."

"And they call me Tanto."

"You mean like . . . your stupid handle is named after the Lone Ranger's sidekick?"

Aldy breaks into song as I roll my eyes. I owe the big lug two units anytime this happens when I say my call sign.

"I'm gonna get me a Snickers, I'm gonna get me a Snickers," sings Aldy as he shimmies his arms like he's churning butter.

"Rook, first of all, never insult someone's handle." I sigh, running my fingers through my hair.

"Why?"

"Because it's the only thing you own right now. Not your freedom. That's property of Hackers' Haven. Not your time. That's Warden Cyfib's. You're going to be hunting for him twelve hours a day, sleeping for six to eight, and eating in between, with an hour outside a day, if you're lucky. You don't even own your prisoner identification number. That's deeded to the good ole You Es of Ay. In here, all you own is your handle."

The kid opens his mouth to speak and argue. I don't wait. "Second, I'm no Jay Silverheels."

"Who?"

My second sigh is intentional and over-exaggerated because I'm a little put out that I have to explain this, like I always do. "The actor that played Tonto on *The Lone Ranger*. My handle is Tanto. What is your handle?"

"My name is Tim Wyn—"

"Enghhhh!" AldenSong chimes in with the error sound worthy of any game show. "Never tell anyone your real name in here. That's a rookie mistake, Rookie. Only your handle. No names."

"Aldy's right. Your name is Mud, as far as I'm concerned. Don't tell anyone your name. They don't need, nor should they want. That equals power over you, even to the staff. Most of us hackvicts did some mighty bad things out there in the real world. There are people who would pay good money to find us and make us suffer. Be careful and always remember, technically, you're not a prisoner, you're a tool."

"Tool?" asks the rook, confused. "Since when are prisoners considered tools?"

AldenSong and I try to keep from laughing. I might have made it if I hadn't noticed the ripple in the big guy's body, but when we made eye contact, all bets were off.

"What? What'd I say?"

Wiping a tear from my eye as Aldy catches his breath, we tell the kid what he doesn't want, but needs, to hear.

"This is Hackers' Haven, Rook—"

"It's Quidlee. My handle is Quidlee."

"Quidlee." AldenSong reaches his Samoan mitt out to our prison's newest member and pats him on the shoulder. "Starting today, you will discover the benefits that the United States government gets by legally revoking your status as a human being."

Chapter Nine

A Feature, Not a Bug

I n the movie *The Matrix*, Morpheus and his crew never freed a human past a certain age because having his or her reality thrown in their face could crash the human brain.

As much as I wanted to tell Quidlee what was going on and what to expect here, we had to parcel out the information in small amounts. Too little water for a man dying of thirst and he will fight you for every drop. Too much at once and the man drowns. No matter how many rooks I meet, the starting point never gets any easier.

Lance-a-Little puts his hand into the shape of a phone, puts it to his ear, mouths the words *call me*, and leaves us. Also, I laugh a little because neither he nor I have used a phone in close to a decade.

AldenSong asks, "Have you seen the prison movie *The Shawshank Redemption*?"

"Well, yeah, who hasn't?" Quidlee shrugs and turns to me. "So what? Like I'm Andy and you're Red or something?"

"Negative." I don't feel he is mentally ready for this talk, not this soon into his residency in here, but I go against my gut and continue. "I want you to understand that we are living in the polar opposite of that movie. Almost everything that you learned from that movie about a prison is not only wrong in here, it will hurt you and maybe even worse."

"I don't understand."

I consider what scrap of information I can give him now that he can properly absorb. "In a traditional prison, in or out of the movies, you sit still and do your time. In here, we have to *work* hard to earn parole."

"That's great!" The rook's green eyes flash like I just hit a bumper in a pinball game. "So I can get out of here quickly?"

"No." The pinball prize light in his eyes dims but does not go out. "But you *can* get out. In time. It is a lot of work, and it is more than just a cubicle clone work, like data entry or assembly line crap. We will help you learn."

"Learn what?"

I am moving too fast. He's gotta know the rules first.

"First, let's talk about some other rules here. Aldy, you want to lead?"

"Most things, like getting caught talking, or hiding food in your bunk are minor things—for which you might lose one, two units. However, things like causing harm to a guard or staff, you get punishment that goes beyond what you can buy. You get shipped out to the Bay," starts the big man.

"You get caught performing illegal activities, you get Guantanamo Bay," I add.

"You get caught in restricted areas, such as the Cube of Death . . ."

"What is that?" asks Quidlee.

"You'll see." I wash my hands in the sink and wait to tell him the last warning because it is crucial, especially for stubborn and hopeful rookies. "Any attempt at escape, or discovery of a conspiracy to escape, you get the Bay."

"Has anyone ever escaped?"

"One guy . . ."

I shoot a look over at Aldy with eyes so beady and mean it should've zapped him with lightning.

Aldy's shoulders drop as he mouths *sorry.*

Well, dammit. That kind of behavior is what we are trying to discourage. You don't go telling a fire-eater that there's a can of gasoline lying about.

"That's a rumor."

"But, Tanto, you said you were here when . . ."

I slam down my fist. "Rumor."

Silence fills the room.

Curse Aldy and his honesty. He never lies. Hacking is all about lies—the lies we tell our prey, our target, and even ourselves. We lie that we are the best at what we do, knowing that we are one bad keystroke from incarceration . . . or worse.

Sure, AldenSong jokes, but if you ask him a question, he will always tell the whole truth, not some version of it. He believes a lie by omission is still a lie. I do not know how he's made it through life. Something about his Christian commune upbringing makes him a diligent hacker, able to focus and achieve long periods of coding without stimulants, but that life also made him his own worst enemy.

He's also the only person I've ever known to get his lawyer to plead "very guilty" in a trial.

"Well, how do we get out if we don't escape, and we're nothing but tools?"

"Time is up." The voice echoes down the hallway, and it means a guard is about to enter the room. "Pack it up and get to your beds."

Putting our cleaning supplies up, I have to make time for a final warning, at least until we get back to our punishment the following night.

"Listen fast. Until you see us tomorrow night, only speak to answer questions. Only answer in the way you think they want you to answer. Do not engage in a conversation. Not to a guard. Not to a fellow hackvict. Do not give anyone an opening. Not until you know what is really going on."

"I still don't understand."

"On your feet and out the door, inmates." Guard Fontana's baton rests across his skull-sized bicep. His rolled-up sleeves reveal the same old, tiny, faded red teardrop tattoo on that shoulder. I've spent enough time with enough *unsavory types* to know that means he's killed a man, possibly in cold blood.

We march in a single file line from the latrine on the third floor of our "home" and Guard Fontana locks us all into our individual cells that are the size of a small U-Haul. Each cell door squeaks loudly as Fontana ushers us in for the night. When I first got here, I thought these doors were just in a state of disrepair. It wasn't until later that I learned the sound was a feature, not a bug.

A jarring, eternal sound, reminding us unequivocally that we are trapped here.

Chapter Ten

Trap Begets Trap

The rook isn't at breakfast, which doesn't surprise me. He isn't missing much: my bland oatmeal and a probiotic smoothie that smells like a mixture of freshly cut grass and a wet mop and tastes about the same. Together with this, I drink coffee so dark and strong the cooks probably used pieces of the warden, aka Cyfib's black soul, to steep the coffee beans.

Who am I kidding? That man has no soul.

The dining hall is unusually quiet. Part of me knows it is because Hackers' Haven's newest resident is absent. The scraping of forks on plastic trays, accompanied by the occasional grunt of someone chewing through their individualized and dietary-restricted meal, are the dominant sounds that fill the silence. Sure, we have other things to discuss, but when one of us is missing, the rest of us are on edge.

The food tastes like they removed salt from my diet. *Oh joy.* Probably from something in my recent med scan and blood draw.

I'm no killer, but right now I'd maim a fool for some Tabasco sauce.

Maybe the powers that be took the Rook's altercation with me as a sign to start his evaluation over, or at least reassess certain psychological traits and triggers. That would explain why he isn't here. Of course, they should've done this immediately. Just because someone is a hacker doesn't mean they aren't physically harmful. Then again, nothing seems immediate in a place where time is mostly irrelevant. However, if the rook fails his eval, they'll ship him out to the Bay. And no one comes back from there.

Once he gets back from evaluation, *if* he gets back, either AldenSong or I, maybe both, will give him a bit more intel about what is going on in this prison.

Lance-a-Little joins me for a bite. As he plops down and stares at his food, a small smile crosses his face.

"T, I need to talk to you about something I've . . . found out . . ."

Before he finishes his statement, an alarm blares.

I wonder what that's about?

"We've got movie sign!" AldenSong yells in homage to the *Mystery Science Theater 3000* catchphrase.

Even with the risk of demerits or extra work, every seasoned hackvict cheers. One of our new guys, SweetThree, a Dominican who joined us about a year ago, raises an eyebrow, curious about what is going on.

He's never experienced a Chicken-Choker trap, what PoBones calls it when someone sneaks through one of the select firewalls of our watched systems. Chicken-Chokers, according to PoBones, are what he calls these worms that live in the ground down in these holes about as wide as a pencil is round. They have nothing to do with chickens or choking. After a good rain, you'd take a piece of grass or straw and slip it into the hole. Then wait. If there's a worm in that hole, it'll sense the straw and climb up. The moment you see a nibble, you wait, but not too long. You yank too soon; the worm lets go. You wait too late, and the worm pulls the straw out of your reach. If you yank the straw at precisely the right moment, out flies a worm you can use to fish with.

Trap begets trap.

Let's say someone on the dark web notices a firewall or virtual private network, or VPN, that goes outside of the standard on-the-shelf box software. They often want to break through just to see what it is. They're the worm, and our firewall is the piece of straw. When they get past that first layer of our security, our alarm sounds, but we don't yank yet. We let them nibble. Now, the moment they start drilling down and going after files and running decryption software, we know it's a hacker and not an accidental visitor. Then we yank them out of their holes and into ours.

The room clears as everyone darts to the War Room. I down my coffee for the caffeine spike and sprint out with the crowd.

That alarm means we get to hack a hacker. Now we just have to figure out which hole he's after.

Chapter Eleven

The Storm Was on the Horizon

Hackvicts occupy all the terminals in the War Room, aka our Control Room, except for the one directly beneath the Cube of Death. I whip out my good luck charm from my pocket. All hackvicts have them. We tend to place them next to our temporary workstations. AldenSong's is a hula girl bobblehead. PoBones has a New Orleans Saints mini helmet with the words *Who dat?* on the side. Even Lance-a-Little kicks back in a chair and pumps his little pig-shaped stress ball twice.

Mine is an empty pill bottle, its orange exterior and white top now placed on the roof of my monitor.

You would think in a prison like this that Warden Cyfib would frown on these attachments. However, he treats us like dogs, and even caged animals get toys to keep them docile.

I press the power button and my system boots in under five seconds to our own operating system called HoneyBadger. It draws from both Linux and Windows components, so we get the best of each operating system. Each system possesses enough RAM to double as a campus server for a junior college. Every time I think about the memory hard wired in our actual servers, it blows my mind.

Cyfib is already on the war floor, standing near the coffeemaker, his spurs clicking as the four monitors mounted on the far wall light up. Each is around forty or so feet long and ten feet wide. Basically, they are the size of four vertical school buses running side by side to each other. PoBones calls them the "jumbotrons."

Only when the monitors are on do I contemplate how tall this room really is. The War Room is half of this building. At fifty or so feet tall, it runs next to the entrance and cafeteria on the first floor, as well as the administrative offices and guard dorm on the second floor, and even our dorm and latrine on the third floor. The only thing above and below it, besides heaven and hell, are the rooftop basketball court and the basement Server Room.

One monitor shows a map of the United States of America and has various blinking dots—facilities we're defending. We handle the protection of a few businesses, but mostly we protect government and government-connected facilities. Anyone who breaks through the firewall of the largest weapons manufacturers in the United States gets greeted by us kicking in their teeth during the assault.

The second monitor reveals a series of fluctuating code, showing where the attacker is pinging and bouncing his signal from. The hacker is jumping around every twenty seconds, fast enough to avoid the average trace but slow enough for us to catch him.

The third screen shows bandwidth and memory usage of our systems and servers. I don't read the exact numbers, glancing at the monitor like one would a thermometer on the wall. The numbers are blue, not red, so we are fairly under any overheating issues or system crashes.

The last screen displays a kind of filter: it takes all the data from the other systems and breaks everything down into a readable, single number. That number varies between zero, or a lost trace, and five, meaning "gotcha."

We are at a one, which is expected because I think the system caught the hack at the beginning of the attack, unless the hacker stops searching, wipes his system, and shuts off power to his origin grid, killing the power in his neighborhood for an hour. That's more than possible; that's how I used to roll.

I pan over to the corner where Guard Fontana is reading some book. It probably is a children's book because he brings those in sometimes. Today he is making notes in the columns. He once told a former guard he was rewriting the stories with better endings for his children. I like that about him: he probably is a good papa, making sure the story is good enough for story time. However, thinking about Fontana's life outside of these walls makes me uneasy.

I know what is in the other corner. The Big Gun, covered by a big red curtain. If the hacking gets exceptionally dirty, that's what we use to clean it up. And I'd be in charge of firing that cannon.

Even though there's a penalty for any outburst in the War Room, some are worth it. Lance-A-Lot throws caution in the shredder and starts our ritual, which is soon to be penalized. "Burn bright!"

Man, it's been a minute since we got fired up to take down a hack.

Despite the upcoming unit deduction for speaking without permission, AldenSong adds, "Burn fast!"

And baby makes three as I join in. "Burn down!"

"Quiet, dogs!" Even through his flat tone, it is clear that Cyfib hates camaraderie in any form. However, the joy of tracing, tagging, and bagging a hacker only occurs sporadically in Hackers' Haven. "Guard, make sure we penalize each violator one unit."

"Yes, sir," the new Guard Stevens chimes in, a little too chipper for me. Apparently, I am not the only one who thinks so because a smattering of chuckles ripple throughout the room like fans doing the Wave at a sporting event.

"Dogs, give me a system update," Cyfib barks even though he is at the front of the room, just under the damn board that gives him a damn update.

Foshi_Taloa, a Native American from one of the Colorado tribes who always speaks in a whisper, if he even speaks at all, is at the terminal next to the warden. He'll be closest to the warden's wrath, not if but when the rage comes. And it will because we've only moved to a score of two in the trace.

Truthfully, our systems and scripts actually pinpoint the attackers pretty well by the time the human equation enters. I think we started our last hack at a three. Today's is up to a two, and well, that's surprising. Apparently, the hackers are upping their game.

"Faster, dogs, faster."

A few obligatory *yes sirs* ring out. Cyfib won't penalize them for this suck-up-ery, but he also won't encourage it. I watch as our hacker's broadcasting ping, where he or she pretends to originate from, shifts from Des Moines, Iowa, and Washington, DC. If it ever gets to Texas, that'll help our trace.

Most hackers think that if they bounce from server to server or randomize their IP addresses they won't get caught. Some pros even hide behind VPNs so they probably won't get caught. For security companies, catching someone who randomizes their IP address isn't a viable option. Further, catching a ping's origin while in the act of hacking is damn near impossible for most.

But we ain't most.

Imagine you're a kid playing in the rain with your little brother. Your boots get muddy. Mama calls you to come in but warns y'all not to track mud or water into her house or else. She leaves the doorway and heads to the kitchen on the other side of the house. Little brother runs in and goes to his room.

You make it a few steps into the living room before you realize you've tracked mud on Mama's favorite rug. So, you take off your boots and throw them in the corner. You go a few more steps and then toss your rain hat, which is filled with water and lands on the wooden floor. Repeat your steps with raincoat, shirt, socks, pants, and every wet thing until you are stark naked in front of your mama in the kitchen. She looks at you and sees no immediate mud or water on the kitchen floor, even though there's mud and water in the house somewhere else causing damage.

By the time she finds the mud and water damage, you're already safe in bed and can blame it on your brother because he didn't show Mama that he was clean. Little brother will say he didn't do it, but words are just words. You appeared innocent, and little brother appeared less innocent, though not officially guilty.

In court, that's what's called "reasonable doubt." That's why the prosecution brings so few hacking cases to trial. The proof is not in the "maybes." The proof is in our tracking.

Well, by the time you're nude in the kitchen after you think you've secured your final false ping and have a little brother to take Mama's whooping, we've traced you back to where you got dirty. We found you way back when you first got in the mud, so you never get to hack the servers under our protection and dirty our house.

"He's rabbiting." AldenSong points at the map. Two new nodes light up, ten seconds apart. The hacker's line has shifted from Tulsa, Oklahoma, to San Francisco, California.

This is like a game of tether ball: pretty soon the hacker will choose a point that is so close to him we'll spike the orb and the rope will wrap right around our intruder.

"Dogs, give me a lap count."

A lap count is like when a runner makes a lap, and the coach clicks the stopwatch. A lap count for us is time between pings changes. If the laps are consistent, we can triangulate the origin. If the laps are speeding up, it means the hacker is circling the drain. In other words, he has realized we are onto him. His focus on closer ping points means he is almost done with his hack. He's just buying time before he escapes.

Now, if those pings are intermittent, say ten seconds in New York City, six seconds in Tampa, and then twenty seconds in Anchorage, Alaska, that changes the game. That takes a different, more surgical approach.

The data stream is consistent, so we also won't neutralize this hacker the same way if he is attacking with more than one infiltration packet. That kind of attack can shift into a fuster-cluck of insanity. A series of bots attempting to breach the wall, well, that requires a completely different tool.

That requires the Coffin.

"Consistent, sir."

I check the scoreboard: we are at a four. That's golden gravy right here.

Then an alarm sounds. Two pulses.

Aldy mutters under his breath, "Ru-roh Raggy."

"Dogs, where did he jump?"

"Un-un-unsure, sir," stutters PoBones.

Cyfib shoves Foshi_Taloa, snatches his monitor, and chucks it at the wall at the far right. Guard Fontana only ducks, knowing that neither the outburst nor the monitor is aimed at him. The screen shatters as a screech of plastic popping and tumbling to the ground fills the room.

The clickety-clacks never stop for a second, even when the room's forecast shifts into tornado season.

From the way the warden's posture shifted a minute ago, his legs shifting from slightly side to side to a more rhythmic movement, I sensed this storm on the horizon. At least Cyfib hasn't stabbed anyone . . . yet. The number shifts from four to three, and that's when I leave our hunting software and open my own separate file.

Then the number drops to two.

Son of a bitch.

Our prey is rabbiting.

Chapter Twelve

One of Ours

With that big number two on the systems board, we now have about a 20 percent chance we'll catch this son of a bitch before he drops his connection.

"If he escapes, I swear every dog will lose every unit it has," says Cyfib, his tone flatter than normal.

He isn't bluffing. Cyfib has bankrupted our units once over my eight years here. It was enough of a trauma to stick like a tick.

I am sixty units away from parole, give or take, depending on what our warden steals from us today. That also doesn't account for whatever the asshole deducted for Aldy punching me in the face. Just like in the real world, here in prison, you get penalized when someone else causes you harm.

I am not the best tracker in the room. And, no, even though he has more time in Hackers' Haven, it isn't Lance-a-Little either. It is Cyfib. Sure, he's the biggest bully in the schoolyard, but behind a keyboard something different, almost mechanical, occurs behind those dead eyes. His mind keeps one step ahead of mine, calculating and running scenarios of how long a ping lasts, its distance from the last ping, and a dozen other variables. He has that type of mind.

Me? Well, for the past thirty seconds, I've run our hacker's data through a piece of software Lance and I called SkipTrace.

SkipTrace, named for what bounty hunters do to apprehend bail jumpers, calculates a stronger pinpoint "guess" for the hacker's home. It takes the actual distance from the ping's source, the time at each occurrence, the bandwidth downloaded and uploaded to various IP sources, and the strength and number of Internet connected devices in a known area, as well as the draw of power from the utility company. It also takes in a few other odds and ends weighted accordingly to the scale. I hate to get technical, but sometimes that is just how my brain works. Basically, the software puts each item through an algorithm of my own design and narrows down all possibilities.

It is not a perfect program, but there is no silver bullet in software. No one knows that this program even exists, except Lance and I, because it uses the same amount of storage space on our server as that of a standard portable document format file, or PDF. The truth is this little baby, which I think was initially started by a hacker who left before I got here, latches onto our existing programs so that any memory usage or output will slip by undetected.

It is just like any other worm I've designed in my life: carefully crafted, beautiful, and virtually untraceable.

Sadly, the last thing I truly created was a monster: Gakunodo. It was something the warden forced me to design. Hopefully, my bomb will never drop on any population, digital or literal.

I glance over at the War Room as the compiler on my program runs its course. Every back is rigid; every face is glued to a monitor.

The number drops to one. Time is running out.

The SkipTrace shows me three possible IP addresses.

192.168.0.1

224.5.7.2

127.0.0.2

I automatically throw the first number out. That's a home router, not secure at all. It's a decoy.

The second address might work because it is a multi-cast designation, but this guy would've shut down any other uses of broadband such as TV or Roku, so I'm not drawn to that particular offender.

However, the third number sticks out like a big *F U* to anyone trying to catch this guy.

"Aldy, we need to change tactics because we're losing and this guy's going downhill while we're trying to ice-skate up." That gets a chuckle from PoBones. Apparently, I am not the only fan of the movie *Blade*.

"Quit pointing out problems, dog, unless you have a solution." Cyfib's no-nonsense bedside manner never fails to ruin a moment. "Time is ticking."

"Aldy, I need you to dam-break 127.0.0.2 and grab any log files you spot."

"Sure . . ." Aldy opens a new window and enters the address. "Why does that IP sound familiar?"

"Because it is one digit off of Loopback."

Loopback may arguably be the most famous IP address the average person has never heard of. Of course, that isn't most of Hackers' Haven. Unless you're a programmer or have worked testing integrated chips after you've removed them from a computer and soldered them to over-clock a system, which I first did when I was fifteen, the average Joe Schmo will never need to use this IP address.

To techies, it's different. We know our tools. Our hacker is a fellow builder. If he is going to get caught, he wants it done by someone who respects the life.

But why would he want to get caught?

"Got it. His VPN is encrypted."

"PoBones, grab the share screen."

Cyfib *cha-chings* my way. "Run point, dog."

That catches me off guard. So much so that I fail to close my SkipTrace software until the warden is over my shoulder. Maybe he didn't see it.

That's about as likely as Santa bringing us all paroles this Christmas.

I sprint to the front of the room and clap the monitorless Foshi_Taloa on the shoulder.

"Foshi, I need you on a terminal prepping, some bait and tackle. PoBones . . ."

"Already panning for gold, Tanto," says PoBones.

Good. PoBones has grabbed the screen share from AldenSong, then blasts it across all four massive monitors. We now see Aldy's command console filling with code. Once he gets through, all available log files blanket these monitors. Plus, if anyone can find the log file, the solid piece of evidence that links a particular machine to our attack, it is PoBones.

"I'm through!" Aldy glances over at me with a smile so wide I can toss a Frisbee into it.

"Din-din done serv-served, Tanto," adds PoBones.

The monitors now show all the files and sort the log files by date, time, size, and frequency of use.

From a drawer under the second monitor, I grab a laser pointer and hand it to PoBones. We often forget it's there, so I hope the battery works.

"PoBones, you point, I'll shout."

Our resident lounge-about has eyes focused to a pinpoint stare. He's ready. His head runs back and forth so fast, I get whiplash just watching him. By the time I've attempted to read one line, four more have already failed PoBones's sniff test.

I chose PoBones to skim the thousand plus files because, while his blood type might be self-identified spicy gumbo, he reads classical books faster than the average person reads a comic book: three pages a minute, and he retains every drop of it. He's a genius wrapped in an intentionally redneck life.

"Gonna be shouting out possibilities, though most might just be bogies . . . Foshi, take the lead."

Red dot after red dot flash on various lines and I can hardly keep up yelling out potential files that might have the data we need. PoBones flies through the files. I rattle off each one. My team will handle the rest.

I am sure that Foshi_Taloa already has a separate screen on his monitor keyed up.

I do not know how much time passes, but eventually Aldy's voice bursts through. "Got the golden ticket! Got it!" he shouts, practically leaping from his chair.

"On screen, dog."

With a few clicks, AldenSong's decoded Internet Relay Chat, or IRC, log file spreads out across all four monitors. This file includes home and connecting system's IP addresses, and a hundred or so fake pings. It also includes the username of the culprit.

Everything the Attorney General needs for a conviction.

With a cheer worthy of a sporting event, everyone bursts out in joy.

I go around patting everyone on the back. "Back up all files and dust off the TPS report. We've got a capture."

"Hold the capture, dogs."

The roar of excitement dies down faster than if someone had just dropped dead in front of us.

I know I'll lose units, but I have to ask what everyone is thinking. "Warden, why?"

"He's one of ours."

Chapter Thirteen

There Are Things Worse than Death

O *ne of ours?* Was this all a test? If so, who was testing us?
The thought haunts me, and several other hackvicts as well, I'm
sure, throughout the day. Cyfib will never give us the reason. No one owes
tools explanations.

Even as Aldy, Quidlee, and I work on our next mandatory task, the
questions bounce between my ears.

"Man, look at the size of my caulk!" AldenSong points at a hole in
one of our Server Room's walls that he's just overfilled with a bottle of
compressed bottle caulk. The white goo bubbles out of the hole in the
concrete wall like whipped cream from the nozzle.

From under a desk, I hear the pressurized squirt of Quidlee's can as he
says, "Hey, your caulk isn't as big as mine!"

I'm surrounded by ten-year-old boys. As continued payment for our
insubordination that arose from Quidlee's arrival, the three of us are on
hole-filling duty. Tiny holes do not matter in a normal prison. It's not like
the average prisoner is going to shrink themselves and sneak out.

But this is no normal prison, and this year we face a threat straight out
of a techie's horror movie because tiny monsters from a foreign country
are eating our electronics.

I'm talking about those crazy Russian ants everyone is reading about. Technically, their name is paratrenicha species near pubens, but since they arrived in our city's port on a cargo ship from Mother Russia, the Russian nickname stuck. The "crazy" part of these ants is not just that they love to sink their teeth into electronics. Unlike disciplined ants that follow in lines and work as a team, these ants form erratic marches, often stumbling off like drunken sailors in search of a tasty pint full of terabyte.

We've had a small invasion recently that ate a hole in two workstations, so now we must fill every single hole where these tiny terrorists might enter our home. I guess this addresses my instinct to protect our home from foreign invaders, but it still feels like grunt work.

"Hey, um, I was gonna ask about how we get mail here," says Quidlee.

"You don't," I reply.

"What's that mean?"

AldenSong cups his hands like he has caught a firefly, opens them to reveal nothing, and then sends a frowny face toward the rook.

"First of all, do you remember how you're not a human being anymore?"

"No shit."

"A simple *yes* would have sufficed," I say. "Well, second, this place, just like you, doesn't exist. At least not on any paper anyone in here can find."

"Come again?"

A deep breath later, I let my thoughts fight it out for a decent answer. "From hidden hacks by Lance-a-Little, myself, and a few others, the main thing we've found is that this building used to be owned by one of those petrochemical companies, RiterPetrol. You may remember them from the news. They caused one hell of an oil spill just south of Galveston Bay and, instead of cleaning it up, the company folded, leaving the EPA to take on the cleanup. Some part of our government took ownership of the building until they sold it off."

"So, we're in a government-owned building."

"Error. Error. Does not compute." I give AldenSong's robot impersonation and robot arm movements a B, B+ in my head. "This was right
around the time that the housing bubble burst, so about 2008, two-ish
years ago. Used to be that a person either owned their home or the bank
did. The housing bubble created a new option, and a lot of those mort-
gages went into a larger portfolio, which was then split up across different investors. That's probably what happened to this property. E'rybody
got a piece of us!"

Quidlee scratches his right arm in thought. "Hold up. What about reverse engineering some utilities, phone lines, you know?"

Smart kid.

"We've done that," I say. "Every utility bill, water bill, sewer bill—you
name it, I've seen it and they all are paid in cash."

When someone thinks like you, it is a blessing and a curse. The blessing
is that you both are trying to solve the problem in the same manner and
not butting heads. The curse is that no new solutions arise. That kind of
stalemate is enough to kill your momentum and your hope.

Silence fills the room. I should say something. A leader would, but
I'm no leader, at least in my eyes. Leaders are infallible. I'm pretty damn
fallible. At most, I'm a supporter, someone who helps those asking for
help. Maybe those two roles overlap, like how a therapist asks questions,
yet lets you answer.

So, no one speaks. No one jokes, because it is scary not knowing who
owns the place you lay your head at night.

I want to tell the rook that there are a few upsides to this type of imprisonment. We eat healthy, sleep well, the work keeps our minds active,
and we get lots of medical attention. However, when one discovers that
their sole purpose in life is functioning as someone else's tool, that one is
disposable at any time, well, there's no sugar that will sweeten that piss
tea.

I take a moment and clean the nozzle of my caulk can. It works fine. I just want it to function at its highest level, much like I want myself to hit that pinnacle.

There are many ways to honor the Bushido life, and this ritual is one of mine. The workstation, keyboard, and mouse are my Katana, the weapon of the Bushi. These noble warriors never let anyone else handle their weaponry, let alone sharpen their swords and knives.

Even though this is electronics maintenance, it makes me think about crafting a better life. Experts craft Japanese swords from *tamahagane* or Damascus-grade steel. They forge the metal in a fire so hot that it causes the steel to lose its firm structure so that they can snap it in half from its original form. Then those pieces are bent, reheated, pounded, and folded as many as a thousand times to remove impurities until the new, reformed metal reaches a level of achievement that the blacksmith classifies as Bushido warrior's-grade of Katana.

I have no traditional sword, but that does not mean that I am not a weapon. We choose to either be forged and strengthened by life's flames, events, or people in a way that often brings pain and hardship, or we choose to melt away (because it is often easier to do nothing than something) when those flames engulf us. If we keep striving, if we keep focusing on moving forward, even if we must step back and take little losses, then we are forging and honing our spirit.

Quidlee is now near the toolshed, where the staff keeps our drills, batteries, and nonkill-able or potentially break-out-able tools when he glances my way, then turns back. Gears are turning in the rook's head. I am curious to see what they come up with.

"Tanto . . ."

"Yes, Quidlee?"

"Where the hell are we?"

"Can't you see all the shotguns and see the dern steam rising offa the sidewalks, boy?" Aldy's southern accent lacks a rolling *r* and the heaviness on the throat that this area's never-ending bombardment of humidity feeds. "You're in Texas, boy!"

"I can tell *that*, fatso." Quidlee sprays a corner, then wipes it with a rag to even out the caulk. Aldy smiles. The kid is warming up to us.

"Quidlee, what're some of the things I told you about this place?" I ask.

"That this ain't Shawshank prison?"

"More than that." On a rolling cart, I slide next to Quidlee. "You have to remember that it's the polar opposite."

"You mean the prisoners are the guards and the guards are the prisoners?" He laughs, too pleased with himself.

Smart-ass. "Do you want to learn or not?"

The gnome looks at me like a hurt pup when I fail to praise his wit. I cannot blame him; he is so new here that every comment I bat back at him probably hits his already thin and damaged psyche armor. However, I also cannot indulge him—not this early in his residency at Double-H. My first months here blurred in pain and panic. If it weren't for Lance guiding me, protecting me, I'd have chased my vitamin-heavy dinner with a bottle of Drano to end the pain.

I made rookie mistakes during my first few months: poor capture attempts, snapping at the wrong times, and two stints in the Hole. I also had a . . . *bully,* for lack of a better word. I still do not know how Lance-a-Little, or whoever, got the a-hole deported, but it certainly saved my life.

"In that story, everyone starts out nude, deloused, and oriented to the way of doing things. Here we start out clothed, probably sterilized, and heavily disoriented. In other prisons, you keep to yourself. Here, it helps to depend on the other dogs, as the warden calls us. Because, if you hit zero, you get shipped outta here-o. So, we back each other up. Pack mentality, and all that."

"Woof woof!" Aldy barks from the peanut gallery for emphasis. Of course, as he did, he accidentally forgot to wipe the excess caulk from a hole he's just filled. Now he repeatedly tries to wipe away the already hardened substance but to no avail; finding out that the white bubble on the wall is here to stay. I chuckle as Aldy moves a garbage can in front of the bubble to cover up his mistake.

I sigh and get back to Quidlee. "In traditional prisons, you must always look out for yourself. Sometimes new prisoners are yelled at to kill themselves the first night. However, to the warden, you are a tool, so he needs us alive as long as we are producing results. Tools have no feelings. Only usability. The moment a tool loses its usefulness, it gets tossed in the trash."

Quidlee sprays holes and he chews the inside of his cheek. "So, you're saying that the moment I lose my usefulness, I get killed?"

"Why's everyone so worried about dying these days?" asks Lance-a-Little, his head peeping into the room. "Me, I'm just worried about living."

I reintroduce Quidlee and Lance-a-Little. They nod at each other, the lazy man's handshake from across the room. Part of me wants to ask him why he isn't locked in his cell, but I don't want to draw away from helping the rook right now.

"Hey, T, when you get a chance, I need to talk to you."

"I'm kind of in the middle of something, Lance."

He shrugs and leaves, sauntering to who knows where.

I think about immediately answering Quidlee's question; the answer might reassure him. But there is safety in being a certain level of scared, so instead of answering, I toss my now empty bottle of compressed caulk in the trash and snatch another from the toolshed.

"I'd rather just bust out of here." The words leave the rook's throat way too easily. "Can't be that—"

Aldy slaps the rook on the back and leans into his ear. "There are things worse than death." He speaks this at a whisper's volume for emphasis. "Escape would lead to one of them."

Quidlee grabs a mop and furiously scrubs the shower walls. He's taking his frustration out on the work. *Good.*

Quidlee breaks his furious silence after a moment, asking the inevitable, "Worse than death *how*?"

I finally speak, and when I do, I feel like some evil wizard in a fantasy novel standing in front of a cave, warning explorers not to go in.

Maybe I am.

"Let's talk more about the Bay."

Chapter Fourteen

Vultures Circling

"Guantanamo Bay." I put my compressed can of caulk filler on the floor and meet eyes with Quidlee. This is one of those moments where I need him to understand that I am not playing around.

"No one sent from here has ever returned," I say. "We only know rumors and, while rumors aren't factual, they get the point across. In here, you will get beat, cut, and put in isolation. There? Well, that's a whole different set of torture."

It works because he is squirming in his seat, as uncomfortable as a kid in the principal's waiting room.

I wonder if the rook is old enough to hear rumors of its horrors. The name of this place, the Bay, is a phrasing that sounds like a welcoming vacation but it is actually a place where the government sends the *combatants* they cannot legally "interrogate" on U.S. soil.

"That's bullshit."

Ah, there it is. The doubt phase. We all go through this stage. At least Quidlee has us here to crush it.

"Put your head down, do the work, and get paroled." From there, we tell the rook about how his classification in life has shifted, at least in the eyes of the United States of America's elected officials.

"Do you think you are a criminal?"

"Sure," says Quidlee with a snort. "I'm in jail, ain't I?"

"You're wrong on both accounts . . . you're a conduit of domestic terrorism."

"So, I'm a terrorist?"

"Ehh! Wrong," Aldy pipes up. "See, to be a terrorist, one must first be human, Quidlee-San."

"Y'all ain't making any sense."

Tools are to be cared for, supported, and sharpened. In prison, we choose to take new arrivals into our flock, even if they are just a new cog in the wheel. Unlike our warden, I don't view my fellow hackvicts as tools that are destined for use or disposal. That's not what I am called to do. Again, I am not a leader of men, rather a supporter of them.

"If your capture count ever goes into the negative numbers, you get shipped out."

Quidlee snatches a bucket from the corner, flips it over, and plops down on it to sit where he can watch me better.

I put the plastic top back on my can. In the distance, a guard's radio chirps, and we all jump. Someone is patrolling the halls, not that we are doing anything too illegal.

"Kills . . . or captures, if you prefer." I realize I need more words when using words like *kill*, because I hate thinking what we do are kills. We are not technically ending lives, just ruining them. "You capture five hundred targets, you get paroled to this prison's version of 'work release.'"

"What's that?"

Well, damned if any of us knew. We never asked questions. No one ever really reached back out once they got paroled. Since we're not allowed visitors or mail, we rarely hear from anyone. From traditional channels, that is.

"Just do the work, rook, and you'll be fine."

"So how long does a capture take?"

"Depends." Aldy grunts that word as he clamors to add some caulk to the metal border of a shoebox-sized air vent near the ceiling. "During the hot streak season, which is summer, naturally, a good hacker can rake in two, maybe three every three, four weeks."

"Are you freaking kidding me?" Quidlee stands and kicks the blue mop bucket across the room. "How long does it take to get your first one?"

"You'll pop your cherry soon enough." I can almost hear Lance-a-Little answering my question with that same answer eight years ago.

"I hate that expression," says Aldy.

"Everyone does . . . that's why I said it."

"It might take you a month or two to get the hang of it . . . be diligent, not dumb."

Quidlee mumbles something under his breath. I think I catch it, but I ask the rook to repeat it.

"I said I'd rather freaking die than stay here."

Right then, Guard Fontana sticks his head in the Server Room. "Warden needs to see everyone."

I swallow hard. The guard saying that Cyfib needed us just as Quidlee talked about death felt like when someone looks up and spots vultures circling them.

Chapter Fifteen

What Has He Done?

I *'d rather freaking die than stay here.*

The words still ring in my ears as we walk to the War Room.

From his ivory tower, the balcony next to the Cube of Death, Cyfib's gritted teeth and laser-focused stare forces even the hardest among us to look at the ground.

"Dogs, you are all failures."

Well, what now?

"One of you has taken the coward's way out." He holds a blue Ethernet cable, covered in red stains.

Dammit. I glance around the room and do an internal inventory. It doesn't take a spreadsheet to figure out what's happened.

SweetThree must've taken himself out of the Game of Life. *Dammit.* He hasn't even been here long. For some reason, the hippie from Seattle never took to the routine. He was constantly fighting for two kills a month, maybe less. Ultimately, he took the trip out of the Double-H in a one-size-fits-all bag.

I am not talking about body bags. Humans get body bags. We get sent next door to the funeral parlor that has a crematorium and come back in a Ziplock with a freshness seal. The next day, the funeral home next door will reduce SweetThree's body to ash. Then Cyfib will show us that bag and repeat how each one of us *dogs* failed.

Just because it is a power play does not mean it will not work.

Following the loss of one of our own, there is always a general spike in productivity, though brief. It sometimes makes me wonder if Cyfib doesn't just have someone killed to improve our quarterly numbers, but no one could be that cruel.

Right?

There I go again, lying to myself. In a world where Cyfib and Barca exist, I often wonder about the expression *God only gives what you can handle*, especially because I think that someone should remove the word *handle* and replace it with *survive.*

Then the warden points at Lance-a-Little. My heart stops. My friend, my mentor, is in the monster's crosshairs.

Oh, no, what has he done?

Chapter Sixteen

Two Devils in Our One Hell

"**A**re you packed, dog?"

"Yes, warden."

Packed? What are they talking about?

Then, without another word, Lance-a-Little walks up to each hackvict, looks us in the eyes, and hugs us.

Oh. My. Lord. He is getting paroled. How did I not see this coming?

Lance-a-Little was always ahead of me in the kill department. I knew he was close to reaching his five hundred captures. I just never expected it.

That is why he wanted to speak last night. Another opportunity missed by yours truly.

I am the last one that Lance-a-Little addresses. His handlebar mustache quivers. I'm sure my rat-haired one does the same. I cannot even meet his gaze after he wraps his arms around me, squeezes me tight, and whispers in my ear. "I don't have much time, so don't argue with me like you always do. Tanto, your beliefs make you who you are. They got you through some dark times. They fortified you. But Tanto, they can only take you so far. Something, someone, is coming. Stay strong but be prepared to alter your course. General Franks said it best: no plan survives contact with the enemy."

From his pocket, he sneaks out a blue felt bag about the size of a baseball. He presses it into my stomach, so I take my hands from my sides and cover up the present.

And then, with a nod and a tip of an invisible cap to everyone, Lance-a-Little turns and walks out, escorted by Guard Fontana.

I am overwhelmed in the moment. I know to not look at the present until later. There is no telling what's in the bag. However, in the span of two minutes, we are down one rookie hackvict, and I have just lost my mentor.

It also doesn't help that the next thing Cyfib says blows any sense of calm out of the water. "Luckily, dogs, tomorrow another joins you in your servitude."

As he walks back into his office, the chill usually reserved for my spine runs a circle around my skull and slams a migraine into my brain.

Oh no. What Lance said could only mean one thing.

Barca is coming.

Here.

Tomorrow.

If God only gives us what we can handle, then could we handle two devils in our one hell?

Chapter Seventeen

We Were Just Skimming the Surface

That next day AldenSong, PoBones, Quidlee, and I meet outside of the War Room before our shifts start at six. Quidlee yawns and rubs his eyes. He'll get used to less than eight hours of sleep. We all do, except for Foshi_Taloa. That man sleeps fifteen minutes at a time.

"Rook, grab the terminal next to me." I put my hand on his shoulder and he flinches back. I'm sure there's a story in there, but now's not the time. "Do what I do, but do not let anyone notice that you're watching me, because Cyfib might consider this education as nonproductivity."

"Wait . . . isn't there an orientation or something?"

PoBones chuckles. "Life's da orientation, rook . . . saddle up."

We grab the cubicles in the corner that's in the far left of the room. Walking to the workstation, I point out the scanners on the floor near each terminal. They are a cross between a grocery store self-checkout station and a bathroom scale, with a slot for a hackvict to place one leg. I roll up my pants leg and slide my hairy-ass leg into the slot. The computer boots up.

Quidlee takes a stab at doing the same on his machine but rolls up the wrong leg, and I shake my head.

"Why does it matter?" he whispers.

"Just do what I did."

He frowns and does so. "Ow!" Quidlee withdraws his leg and his monitor flickers to life.

I didn't tell him about the minor shock because just telling someone that they'll be shocked sometimes intensifies the sensation.

That's when he sees for the first time how the devil marks each of us dogs: the implanted microchip next to his tibia. Quidlee's eyes go wide as he runs his hand down his leg and gets shocked again when he presses down on the glowing spot on his bone.

"Son of a . . . what the holy hell is that?"

It is our own personal 666 brands, marks of this beast, implanted deep and for life.

"Shut . . . up . . . sit . . . down . . . " the words slide through my gritted teeth as I roll my eyes up to the Box of Death. The rook doesn't need an orientation to understand that the only thing worse than Big Brother watching you is getting caught by Cyfib doing anything he thinks you shouldn't be doing.

Unfortunately, common sense comes from experience, not advice.

"Naw . . ." he continues. "You need to tell me what the hell is going on with my leg."

The *cha-chings* ring out over the floor and I duck my attention to my terminal screen. The kid has no units to lose, which means he is at the end of a zero-sum game if I don't act quickly and with perceived malice. Or else it might end with Quidlee on the waterboard conveyor belt at the Bay.

"Look, rook, get the hell away from me!" I pound my fists next to the keyboard so hard my mouse bounces to the floor. "You're slowing me down!"

"Dogs," interrupts the warden, "why aren't you actively capturing?"

"Sir, this rookie keeps screwing up my kill count by asking questions."

Quidlee stands at attention, but stumbles as his leg releases from the computer's sensor. His imbalance adds to his wide, deer-in-the-headlights eyes and the confusion spreading across his face.

"I'm only sixty from parole, and I don't care if he needs tutoring . . . I'm getting out of here."

"Sir, I was just wondering about, um, how we capture, and I was only asking . . ."

"This little bastard wants some of my captures, is what the hell was happening . . ."

"Whoa! No! I was—"

"Don't lie to the warden, rook." I rise from my seat and put my finger square in Quidlee's chest. "You can't have what I've earned."

"Both of you dogs, silence."

I remove my finger and sit back down. If I make eye contact with the warden, he might see through this ruse. On one hand, he has a rookie capable of capturing hundreds of targets yet is untested and arguing with one of the most proven veterans on his team. On the other hand, he also has the opportunity to remove a potential troublemaker before he slows group progress.

My eyes don't need to study Cyfib to know his wheels are turning. He wants, no, needs an outcome that is only best for him and the corporation.

"I need him gone, sir."

Quidlee's eyes widen again, and the color leaves his face. I know my full-of-finality statement will require Cyfib to give a response greater than my command.

That's why I am not completely shocked when Cyfib's punch is fast and surgical, finding the pain center where my neck meets my skull. The quick impact sends lightning up my spine and stars through my eyes. I slouch on the keyboard before pushing myself up to attention.

"Both of you dogs need discipline." Cyfib snatches my chin with his mammoth of a mitt. The sensor for my leg chip chirps and my machine goes blank as the warden pulls me to my feet. "For insubordination, you lose ten units to this dog. Further, he is now under your care. His mistakes are now yours."

With a flick of the wrist, Cyfib releases my face before punching Quidlee in the stomach. As the rook collapses to the floor, Cyfib stands over him, whips out his dick, and pisses on him.

You don't get more primal a response than public humiliation. The rage that spreads through Quidlee's eyes is like watching water boil in a clear kettle that has no hole: roaring but with nowhere to go. His hands ball into fists as he prepares to attack the warden.

I cannot blame him. Even actual dogs do not do anything this vicious. I motion slightly with my left hand for him to *stay down*.

The beady look in Quidlee's eye and snarl on his lips says otherwise. He attempts to stand. The warden raises his right boot. He hooks the heel behind the rook's neck. With one stomp, he smashes Quidlee's face. Into the ground. Into the piss.

Quidlee struggles to breathe, yet I know what is really going on. The warden wants for one of us to jump to the rescue. It's just a big, gross game of chicken. One that may end with Quidlee's death. I want to say I know the warden won't stomp and kill the kid. I really want to say that, but I just can't.

Seconds pass. Every eye is on our struggling hackvict.

Hang in there, rook, we're almost there.

"Congratulations are in order." Cyfib removes his boot and zips up as Quidlee gasps for air. "This dog now has ten units, less the units this . . . *incident* cost him. A net five. Clean the floor, then continue your work."

The warden *cha-chings* up to the Cube of Death, no expression on his face.

Tears roll down Quidlee's face as he balls up in the fetal position in the middle of the War Room. Not a clickety-clack is heard. I've read somewhere that tears are just pain escaping the body. It does not make watching my new friend suffer any easier.

I stay in my seat as our tribe does its job. The first person to Quidlee's side is AldenSong, and somehow he's grabbed a handful of paper towels.

Quidlee knocks them away.

I drop to my knees and sit back on my heels in front of rook. The warden's warm urine soaks into my pants. I extend one hand to the rook's shoulder. He knocks it away, though not at the same ferocity as the swipe of paper towels.

PoBones must've run to his room because he returns with a blanket. This time, the rook doesn't fight our helping hands as PoBones covers Quidlee as the adrenaline leaves his body. The shakes overtake him.

Foshi_Taloa places his mitt on the rook's soaked head. The kid rolls his neck toward the quiet man's touch.

I add my hand on top of Foshi_Taloa's. Aldy puts his on mine. Then PoBones and every other working hackvict, all of us, pile on as Quidlee's tears slow, and he sniffles. I might have spotted others crying too, had I not held my eyes shut.

I try to speak, but the words refuse to come. Sadly, I understand what he is going through. The sooner you break in here, the sooner you change. It is inexplicable to someone who has never slept behind bars, but it is the only way to rebuild yourself. Sometimes the process takes days, even weeks, or months. For Quidlee, I am amazed he's letting out this pain, this frustration, so soon. I think it was a blessing.

I am wrong. Later, I will find that we were nowhere near Quidlee's rock bottom. We were just skimming the surface.

Chapter Eighteen

The Sludge in My Soul

That night's latrine duty is tense. That's the problem with showing vulnerability, whether you are confined to a prison with other criminals or in front of a loved one. You just hope they don't kick you when you're down, or worse, take advantage of the situation.

The lights flicker: some faulty breakers or the backup generator is failing to store a full charge. I've played with enough electricity and taken enough shocks from man-made lightning to know faulty wiring. Of course, it might be those damn ants. We can only caulk so many ways in and out of here, and there is no telling what damage the ones that are already in the building are doing to our home.

Quidlee mops a shower as I hand wash a sink. Aldy is plunging something foul down the toilet behind me, something with an odor somewhere between old diapers and what I assume the smell of spring break in Tijuana is.

Repetitive work like this brings déjà vu. However, the last time we did this, the rook wasn't a peed-on hackvict.

With no guards around, I glance at Aldy. "Marbles?"

"Marbles." AldenSong kicks his head back and rolls his eyes around, searching for a topic. "Two tons of fun" moves to the closest shower and plunges it with the same plunger he used on the toilet. "Most underrated Asian actors?"

"Easy . . . Toshiro Mifune. You?"

"Jackie Em Effin Chan."

"Are you kidding me?"

"Not a bit." Aldy yanks the plunger, and the same smell from the toilet rises from the shower drain.

Hurray for linked pipes.

Quidlee keeps quiet, mopping the same spot enough to wash away some of the grout sealer.

"You're focusing on *Drunken Master*, aren't you?"

"That is incorrect, dear sir . . ." AldenSong takes the plunger handle, leans over, and uses it to cut on the showerhead, spreading the filth across all the stalls. "*Police Story*."

"You cannot tell me that *Police Story*—a good movie, I'll agree—is better than Mifune's *Samurai Rebellion* or *Yojimbo*?"

"Ah-ah, we are not talking about the quality of the movie, we are talking about the range of the actor."

"Well, Aldy, who handles silence in a scene better?"

To me, there is an art to handling an acting role with just a glance. I have Big'un there. I rise to my feet, pivot to AldenSong, and he does the same. He bows in defeat. I bow in acceptance.

"What are you guys bullshitting about?"

Even though Quidlee's use of profanity in a sentence is about as accurate as a third grader when they learn a dirty word and want to try it out, I take his asking as a good sign. We'd laid out enough bait that something needed to snag him.

"We keep our minds sharp by arguing over minutia."

"Definitely better than stupid silence." Aldy plunges another shower drain. This one burps extra loudly when he finishes, and the unclogging suction downs the sludge.

Quidlee mops up AldenSong's mess. "I think those last movies you mentioned were, like, Samurai movies . . . I don't really watch those."

"They're not Samurai. They're Bushido."

"That's the same thing, right?"

My posture straightens, and I scowl. The rook's just stepped into a bear trap. Maybe if this question occurred earlier in our relationship, a kinder response would've escaped my lips.

Probably not, though.

"Not at all, you dumb little bastard. The term *Samurai* designates the aristocracy's servants. Bushido or Bushis followed a life code."

"Still sounds like the same thing."

A rage builds in me. Sure, some historians may disagree with me, but I prefer to think of the Bushis during their time before they followed governmental orders, for obvious reasons. I know it is only my pride rearing its ugly head, so I take a beat before I smile, stand over the rook, and ring my sponge out on his head. He lowers his head and chuckles, taking my response as lightly as I'd meant it. Where I could, I wanted the soap to counter the pee that had rained upon him.

We scrub for a few minutes in silence. The squeak of small tires on tile means someone is wheeling in a delivery of premade meals for the residents from the loading dock. There was a time last year, out of sheer boredom, I'd have taken bets on what was coming in, or what they claimed it tasted like. Then, when I finally accepted that whatever the slop was named it all tasted the same, the issue lost its limited interest.

"Well, rook, are you ready for another bite of this bullshit orientation sandwich?" I ask.

"Yum, yum."

I chuckle. Quidlee's sarcasm powers are impressive. "Rook, give me your leg."

I reach for it, assuming he will follow my order, until he withdraws his puppy paw and crosses his arms. "Get your own leg."

"If you're worried I'm going to go all *Stranger Danger* on you, just look at the area under your right Achilles tendon."

"Why?" comes the eloquent retort.

"Humor me."

As Quidlee pulls up his gray, standard-issue, cotton pants with his fingers and rolls down his thin white socks, he spots the culprit: a hidden scar.

"What the hell?" he asks as he runs his fingertip along an incision behind the long back tendon. He presses down, then winces when his finger finds a round device the size of a Skittle just next to the pinkish mark. "I'd forgotten all about that."

"Careful now," I say. "That's what shocked you when you were about to gut the guard when you arrived here. Though tiny, there's enough voltage in that device to fry your nervous system. If you'd have even touched a guard—"

"Buzz!" adds AldenSong, sounding like a Southerner's porch entertainment, aka an electronic bug zapper.

Like a kid picking at a scab, the rook presses on the chip again and grimaces, probably realizing that a low-voltage zap occurs each time he pushes. Of course, he pushes again to be sure.

I glance down at my own leg. From under my leg hair, I can see my Tic-Tac-shaped implant. I am one of the Original Gimps, or OGs, in here. I cannot say for sure, but I think they went to the Skittle a year after I got here.

"When the hell did they do that?" Quidlee asks.

"That surgery is standard, and the recovery includes our captors getting teeth impressions, fingerprints, blood tests, and all that fun stuff. Don't try to cut out the shocker, either. You could wind up either setting it off or severing the tendon, which makes your leg useless."

Static dances through the air. The lights dim further. Then red lights fill the room before the white lights return. Something is putting the backup servers through hell, which means it'll wind up on my to-fix list soon enough.

"How about the *Seven Samurai*?" I ask, not so subtly changing the subject.

"I've heard of that one. Isn't it, like, a remake of *The Magnificent Seven?*"

In that moment, I admit an overwhelming amount of respect for teachers of all stripes, because I want to shove Aldy's dirty plunger into the rook's face for that remark.

"Damnation, rook, you're a hard nut to crack. No, if anything, it's the other way around, except *The Magnificent Seven* is the bastardization of Akira Kurosawa's masterpiece. The movie also isn't about Samurai. It is about a Bushido brotherhood."

"So, the movie is misnamed?" asks Quidlee.

"Exactly. I have this argument with AldenSong all the time."

AldenSong interjects, "You could've just let that door stay shut . . ."

An alarm, deep and body shaking like an air raid siren, blasts, cutting off any further conversation. We heard this heralding boom not so long ago. I toss my gloves in a blue bucket, snatch the rook by his prison-issued, black-and-white striped shirt, and drag us both into the hallway.

"What's going on?"

"Rook, that siren means we've got a new hackvict arriving." All Hackers' Haven residents pile out of their rooms and join us in the hallway. "With you arriving recently, I've just never seen it happen this close together . . ."

"Oh no . . . it's him, isn't it?" The shocked look in the rook's eyes blasts exactly what worries the sludge in my soul.

Barca is no longer on his way.

He is here.

Chapter Nineteen

Never Been So Scared of Anyone in My Life

T he PA blasts the warden's command for all prisoners to face the wall. Aldy leans over and whispers into Quidlee's ear, yet loud enough for me to hear.

"If things ever seem *normal* around here, that's usually the calm before the storm."

Something in my gut knots for no explainable reason as I face that wall. Eight years. Eight years here and no one has ever arrived after dinner. Most prisoners arrive right after breakfast, giving them at least a full workday to get the hang of this place. The weather outside is calm. I was on the rooftop earlier today and didn't see any storms on the horizon. There isn't an upcoming holiday. This situation is as off as a train without a track.

The lights flicker. I can't even blame our systems' draw on the grid, because no one is working a terminal right now. It is almost as if this prisoner's arrival is sucking all the power from this place.

The outer gate opens. From the corner of my eye, I see two guards flanking the newest prisoner. I strain to see without turning my head. From what I can tell, this prisoner's sheer size makes the guards look like math geeks, and none of the men in uniform are slouches in the muscles department. It looks like horse jockeys escorting a pro wrestler.

That isn't the oddest part. What is so odd is that I can do more than just make out the outline of his body.

Our newest arrival walks in without a hood on.

That, too, has never happened. The hood is standard protocol. After intense interrogation and mind screwing and all the dysfunction that disoriented me and every prisoner, comes the hood.

I take the risk and turn my head. Worse than expecting the hood is actually seeing this guy's face. I have no idea *if* this is Barca, but I have to look. Yes, I might get us shocked, but I must see what is coming for us. I don't say *who is coming for us* because the legend of Barca makes him a *what*, something more than a man. However, never in my time here has someone with a jawline made of granite, eyes so intense they appear black, and a body built by Arnold Schwarzenegger entered these walls.

Hackers don't fit this profile. Some may look slightly muscular or toned, a keyboarding version of Ed Norton or whatever. This guy is a walking tank. Just his shadow could eclipse Cyfib.

To top everything off, this beast shows no fear. He is not even stoic. He is smiling.

With his head kicked back and straight black hair glued to his scalp with hair gel like a hedge fund manager planning to bankrupt a mom-and-pop store before his three-martini lunch, our newest prisoner is as cool as James Dean sitting on his convertible, lit cigarette to his lip, the wind at his back, and not a care in the world.

Cyfib's *cha-chings* announce his approach, yet I still cannot force myself to blink. When the prisoner turns his head and catches my stare, he tilts his head slightly, smirks, and *winks*.

Even though I've never seen him before, this man sends a chill through my body. It's like jumping into one of those frozen-over lakes in Alaska.

I break eye contact and stare down at my feet with such focus my skull hurts. The beast is ten steps from me. If he so much as steps my way, I don't know what my body will do.

The *shhhp* of scissors precedes a wristband floating like a feather toward my shoes.

Handle: Barca

Each box on his entrance evaluation procedure on his wristband is marked.

The isolation.

The medical tests.

The psy-op screening.

The surgeries.

All completed.

And yet this man smiles.

I've never been so scared of anyone in my life.

Chapter Twenty

We're Going to Be Good Friends

A pparently, I am not the only one sensing a new apex predator in our midst, because a shock blasts from my leg through my body and almost every other hackvict screams out in surprise.

Almost every hackvict.

Our newest addition merely grunts and glances down at his ankle. He laughs loudly, like Hercules mocking the old gods. This brings forth another blast of electricity that wrenches a semi-scream out of him, although it is through gritted teeth. The rest of us are crying for Mama over here.

The warden clears his throat, as he does before his introductory terrorizing speech, and approaches his newest prisoner. "Who you think you are . . . is gone. You are no longer what the United States considers human. You are a dog. A dog does not have rights. A dog is not a pet. It is a tool. And a tool without a use is to be disposed of."

The prisoner meets the warden's gaze. If this were an old spaghetti western movie, somewhere in this showdown a high-pitched whistle followed by a *wah-wah* noise would play. Instead, the air conditioner's flow through the vents and the rattle of chains are all we hear until the prisoner speaks.

"Here to serve . . . sir."

Barca will not start chaos immediately, unlike Quidlee. That's too rookie a move for someone like him. Barca is the quiet dragon drinking from our village's pond. He takes slow sips and remains still, even as the villagers approach. He might even let a few of us touch him. We, the villagers, the trusting, will relax around him, thinking this destroyer of worlds is our pet, our friend. I'm just hoping to catch the warning glimpse in his eye before this dragon turns, gathers his fire, and burns us all to ash.

Cyfib holds the remote high—a device he uses to shock us into submission before he thumbs the shock button. Out of the corner of my eye, Aldy tenses up, awaiting the pain.

The prisoner, a good foot taller than the warden, never flinches. Cyfib holds the clicker like a gun, but Barca keeps his chin high.

The warden zaps us. Again. And again.

After each zap, Barca grunts, but he never breaks eye contact with the warden. And neither of them blinks.

And then the unfortunate moment morphs into an improbable one as Cyfib aims the buzzer right at me.

"Dog, you're training one already. It takes no more effort to train two."

And, with that, he *cha-chings* up the stairs to his office and I register, for the first time, how odd it is for him to be in the joint this late.

He wanted to greet Barca personally.

Why?

The guards unhook Barca and step back. He rubs his wrists with hands the size of my head.

The giant approaches, setting off a dizzying, almost Hitchcockian effect—the room spins and the space behind Barca seems to shift backward with every step.

"So, you must be the head honcho here." His unblinking eyes scan me from head to toe. "My name is Barca."

I say my handle, or at least I think that is the word that slips from my throat. I put my hand out, but the shock of this gesture catches me so off guard that my hand flops over his like I am royalty, and he is to kiss my ring. Before I can change the grip, the man pulls my hand tight, then pushes me back and laughs.

"Get a load of this guy!" His voice is so booming it echoes and fills the hallway. "He expects me to kiss his hand like a little princess!"

Chuckles and laughs come from the other hackvicts. I even eek one out.

"Nice to meet you, Princess." Then Barca squeezes my hand so hard I hear something pop, not break, but some wounded muscle screams out in shock and pain for release.

Then Barca leans in. "We're going to be good friends; I can just tell."

Chapter Twenty-One

Oh, We're Golden, Princess

To say I didn't sleep that night is an understatement: my eyes never shut. It was like living one of those scary movies where the monster was already in the house before the family locked the front door.

Maybe this is just paranoia. I've had my fair share of that.

Just because you're paranoid doesn't mean they're not out to get you. Isn't that how the saying goes?

I gather my pre-made breakfast tray in silence, choosing not to sit with Aldy, PoBones, and Quidlee. If Barca has singled me out, I don't want him to know my comrades.

Also, I am hoping to get Barca alone. Unfortunately for me, it works.

When I sit down in the far back corner of the room, away from everyone else, Barca picks up his tray and squints over everyone's heads until his eyes rest on me. *He's nearsighted.* No clue how that'll help me, but maybe it will. Maybe the work will give him migraines, and they'll ship him to the Bay.

Of course, maybe I'm wrong about his potentially cruel intentions. That's what this breakfast is all about.

Barca tosses his tray down on the table and rips off the plastic cover with *Barca* written on it in black Sharpie.

"Morning, Princess." Barca takes not one but two cups of piping hot, jet-black coffee from his tray. I notice some of the liquid gold spills on his hand as he sets them on the table, yet he never flinches from the pain.

"Good morning, Barca, how'd you sleep?"

"Ah, it could've been better."

That's a lie. Florence Wellz, a medical doctor turned sleep-trepreneur who founded Sleep-Wellz, made our cots. The company sells customized mattresses at fifteen thousand smack-a-roos a pop that combine a person's height, weight, age, racial background, education level, injuries, the number of days you dream a week, and more, so that the buyer never has had a more restful night's sleep.

I savor a bit of joy after Barca takes his first bite of his meal and gags a bit. He is not immune to all discomforts, apparently.

"What the monkey asshole is this?" He drops his spoon and glances over at my cranberry oatmeal. "Gimme yours."

He's gone straight into bully mode. If he were more of a stereotype right now, he'd dust off his letterman jacket before shoving me into a locker.

"I'll do you one better." I reach into my pocket and withdraw a Snickers candy bar. I'd made a run by the Commissary, our candy store, and picked up the world's go-to chocolatey-nougat snack.

"That's more like it."

I slide it halfway across the table but keep my finger on the end of the wrapper. As Barca reaches for it, I scoot it an inch back my way.

"I do not want any bad blood between you and me or you and anyone in here. Some of us are . . . more fragile than others," I tell him.

A smile creeps across his face, somehow neither mean nor especially kind. It's more like he's enjoying a joke only he knows.

He slams his hand over mine, shaking the trays and rattling the metal table so loudly that all words and fork scraps stop.

"Oh, we're golden, Princess."

Barca presses down hard, popping my wrist. In pain, I let go of the candy bar. The beast snatches it up, rips open the plastic wrapper, and eats half of the thing in one bite. Then he tosses the other half across the room toward the tray drop off area.

He glares at me as he chews it with his mouth open. After he swallows, the giant points at my tray. "Now I want your oatmeal."

I'd expected this. He wants more because I want something. "No."

Barca straightens his back and leans toward me. With his elbows on the table, maybe it is just my mind, but I swear the silver metal table bends under his weight. As his eyes bore holes in my soul, it occurs to me that maybe I need more words in this situation.

"I think what you really want is to get out of here."

Chapter Twenty-Two

What Have I Done?

I slide a unit transfer card facedown his way. These bright orange cards allow us to transfer our kills, our units, to another hackvict. This is one of the few *privileges* we tools have in here.

Out of the corner of my eye, AldenSong flat out stares. I take my eyes off Barca to shoot him a tight-eyed *quit it* look. When Barca glances that way, Aldy looks up at the ceiling with wide eyes, like he's never ever noticed that it existed before now.

As Barca turns back with pursed lips, I flip over the unit card to reveal its quantity: ten units.

"What's this?"

"These get us out of here on parole. If you get five hundred units, you get out of here on parole. For every week you do not cause trouble, especially with the hackvict you got into a fight with . . ."

"What the hell is a *hackvict*?"

"That's what we call ourselves instead of prisoners."

Barca laughs and looks around the room. "If it looks like a duck and it quacks like a duck, well, then it's a . . ." However, before he finishes his cliché, Barca makes eye contact with Quidlee. The rook ducks his head, hoping that this dragon will not come for him again.

"Oh, that's the fragile little runt, huh?"

"Barca, every week you behave, I will give you ten units."

"How many units do you have?"

"Enough to make it worth your effort."

"Why don't you just give them to me now?"

"Then what incentive would you have?"

That's part of the truth. We aren't allowed that big a transfer. The key to transfers is that it forces those who produce to stay in because you're spending your parole points on someone else.

The mountain of a man picks up the card and rotates it, corner over corner, before he puts it in his pocket. He stretches his arms wide, then grabs my oatmeal off my plate. I think that if a minor wind flicked Barca's ear, he would've given it more care than the units I've just given him. He completely ignored the offer and forgot about the units like they never even existed in the first place.

It's like he didn't even notice. I am a flea dancing on an elephant.

Then Barca turns back, studies the table, my table of friends in the distance, and leaves the room.

Maybe I have won something, at least for now. Maybe he'll behave.

A few minutes pass and I enjoy the silence. As I eat something akin to chalky eggs and drink my probiotic wheatgrass smoothie, Barca returns with a handful of snacks from the Commissary: Sun Chips, Moon Pies, and a few other bags of snacks. He drops all his bounty on my crew's table.

"Hi!" he practically shouts. "I'm Barca, and I come bearing gifts!"

"Funyuns!" Quidlee squeals like a ten-year-old finding out where his mother hid the Halloween candy. "Man, this was my jam!"

Barca answers PoBones' outstretched hand for a handshake by raising his hand for a high five. After the Cajun hits it, Barca blasts, "Boom!" and repeats the instant bonding exercise with each person at the table.

Oh no. My heart sinks. Technically, he is doing what I asked, not causing trouble, but in actuality, he is worming his way into my group. He's infecting them with his virus, a false identity. Barca's first impression with them is one of kindness. My kindness. My hard-earned units.

After PoBones asks Barca to join them on the bench, Barca kicks his right leg over the side and sits on the end. As he plops down, the giant turns his head my way. His wide eyes and smile fade into an icy stare, reserved only for me.

He will not follow rules, especially mine.

Then, like a light switch flipping, he turns everything back on, rotates his head back, and starts laughing over nothing with his new friends.

What have I done?

Chapter Twenty-Three

Planning a Hack of His Own

After breakfast, Quidlee grabs the terminal next to mine. "So, what are we doing?" he asks loudly enough to be shushed by every single hacker. His potato chip breath covers my body.

"Quidlee, you need to watch out for—"

"Watch out for what?" Barca's voice booms, sending a spittle of nacho cheese and chocolate to the back of my neck.

"I was going to say watch out for the warden." I recover from the shock of Barca, and counter with some advice that's on the level of common knowledge. "Just because I'm training you two doesn't mean that anyone gets a free pass to jerk off."

"Giving out free jerk offs?" Barca laughs. "Enough about your mom, Princess."

Several hackvicts chuckle. The sad truth is that even though Barca meant that as an insult, he is completely right about my mom. However, sometimes the only way to stop a bully is to top their actions.

It pains me to do so, but to take back some of the power, I have to play Barca's game.

"Your grandma still owes my mom two dollars for letting her eat my mom's ass."

"Damn!" PoBones falls out of his roller chair, which alerts the warden and ends our back and forth.

I lurch forward. *Too much, dumb ass.* My head almost hits the keyboard. My damn pride had reared its ugly head, and I'd gone into win/lose mode with a guy who will play dirty and sacrifice anyone to win. *Curses.*

"Quiet, dogs." The warden motions to our trio in the center of the room. I've chosen those spots so that Cyfib's ever-watching eyes might catch on to Barca's manipulations. When trying to slay a dragon, you use all the tools available.

Once the warden returns to his office, I lean over to each of Quidlee's and Barca's terminals and open our private messaging app, Alviss.

Alviss was a god in Norse mythology whose name meant "all wise" and the sun was his Kryptonite. The story goes that the god of thunder, Thor, did not want Alviss to marry Thor's daughter, so he played Alviss' pride against him. He challenged the dwarf to a test of wisdom, a contest he could not hope to win. Thor started the contest late in the evening, after many drinks of mead in an open field. It thrilled Alviss to throttle the god of thunder all through the night, thinking victory was surely in his grasp.

But Thor had never planned on winning; what Thor had planned on was the sun rising before the game finished, thus turning Alviss into stone.

This program, too, is far from "all wise." It records every keystroke and interaction, saving them for our warden to peruse. However, since this is a program developed internally by us indentured servants, it has some . . . *intentional* flaws—features, not bugs. I think it was Lance-a-Little's and Hub's work, a hacker who got paroled a while back. One such flaw? Well, if you double tap the *NumLk* key, it disables the recording option for thirty seconds.

I keep that part of coding secret as I quick-key Alviss on my system, then both of theirs, and change the font to size 36 so that Barca, even with his bad eyesight, can watch over my shoulder if he feels so inclined to spy.

[Tanto]: Welcome to Trapping 101. I'll be your instructor, Professor Tanto. Today, we discuss how you will work one-hundred-plus-hour work weeks backtracking dumb people too dumb to know they are doing illegal crap and handcuffing them to your sinking ship. Open the program Omni-Viewer. It is the one with the U.S. flag on it.

Quidlee and Barca click on the icon, as do I. All our monitors appear to dim. Then, on the right side of the screen, a web browser opens. On the left side, a plain, white screen with a flashing cursor awaits instruction.

[Tanto]: When you click on that icon, it means you get access to the web. However, everything is recorded, unless you activate Alviss. This job is about bringing home trophies. Every single week you should be able to track at least one or two dumb asses on the web and assemble a report that converts their actions from illegal to convictable. You might not capture, or *kill*, them this week, but you are planting seeds.

Quidlee types in his open screen of Alviss, though with his bandaged hand he types more slowly than a child with mittens on.

[Quidlee]: What happens if you don't make your numbers?

[Tanto]: Nothing. However, if you ever drop below zero, you get deported.

Barca grunts before his surprisingly nimble ogre-sized hands add to the discussion.

[Barca]: Hold up. What's that mean?

[Quidlee]: You get sent to Guantanamo Bay.

I'm glad the kid chimes in. It adds to our team unity, if only by a sliver.

[Barca]: Princess here told me you can get these units from other convicts.

[Quidlee]: Hackvicts. In here, we are hackvicts, not convicts.

[Barca]: I don't care if you call us dancing frogs, we are convicts. How many units you got?

[Quidlee]: Only five.

[Barca]: Well, that's more than me. Give me some so I don't wind up deported.

Barca is baiting me, pushing me to give him more units without flat out asking. He doesn't like the boundary I put up for him to *not cause trouble*. He wants free rein to do whatever he wants.

[Quidlee]: I'm not going to give you any. You clearly have some because you used them on those snacks.

[Barca]: Which you ate! I didn't even get any.

That's a lie. Barca's shifting the narrative to extremes to prove that he needs the credits more than Quidlee. It is manipulation at its purest. I hold my tongue. This is not my battle. Jumping in will only show favoritism. Favoritism could result in Barca using Quidlee against me by making me concede something.

[Quidlee]: Fine. I'll give you two.

[Barca]: Four.

[Quidlee]: No! I don't want to be left with just one.

[Barca]: Okay. Three it is. You'll be able to earn those back in no time because you're so smart at this stuff, I bet.

Quidlee opens his mouth to ask me something, but I nudge his leg with my foot. I squeeze his mitten and stop him. I meet his gaze. He correctly matches my look and understands to *let this go.*

Barca just got the first hit in and kept pounding and pounding and pounding until Quidlee caved. I can't protect the kid right now because his ego is as delicate as rice paper. Barca knows that. He's utilizing it for his own benefit. There is nothing I can do about it. Not now. In this type of situation, it is best to not play at all. Quidlee lost the battle the moment he set foot on Barca's field.

[Tanto]: Now that you two have worked out a deal, open the support link and read the first two stanzas.

There is nothing of real value there. I'm just stalling to give myself time to think. *How do I stop Barca without enraging him?*

Just as I'm toying with typing some woo-woo, pep rally pump up, go team, rah-rah sport shit for both of them, Quidlee rolls up his sleeves, stretches his arms wide, revealing a spot on his arm that had been covered yesterday. I'd assumed that a blood draw or IV was the culprit for the Band-Aid, so I never thought too much about it. However, now that he has rolled up his prison-issued shirt, I spot those familiar, faint dots, like level moles; they clash with his tannish skin.

He's an addict.

Or at the very least, a frequent user. That complicates things. Enough hackvicts are on various uppers and downers, but Dr. Fel makes sure our livers, kidneys, and the other useful parts of us tools continue to work.

Drugs done incorrectly are like when you pull the pin on a hand grenade, then snag two more and decide to juggle the trio. At some point, something explodes, and everything around you gets obliterated by the fragments.

I'd dabbled in nose candy once upon a time, mainly to focus on long-term hacks, when the Adderall wasn't cutting it. But I never did it more than once a month. I knew addiction well enough; I had consistent front-row seats to two different shows growing up. While heroin wasn't my mom's favorite pastime, if someone was serving it, she wouldn't pass it up. Mom popped pills like they were in a Pez dispenser. Only when she was high as a kite dancing among the clouds did she stop blaming herself for Dad's alcoholism. Mom never lived down those six months their conversations went mute. Of course, that all was before Dad let his military-issue Colt 1911 and a single round to his brain pan speak on his behalf. Then, for close to fifteen years, no matter the medication, prescribed or otherwise, Mom told me that his voice tormented her dreams and even her waking hours. She never needed to tell me that; I saw it firsthand in the way she answered questions out loud that no one ever asked.

There is a level of damage from addiction that covers everything it touches in a vile and degenerating film. Mom frequently rambled about hearing Dad taunting her, blaming her for all the failures in her life and mine. The day I found her with vomit in one hand and a spilled pill bottle in the other, I didn't even check for a pulse. I loaded up my worn-out books, my VHS collection, a binder full of newspaper clippings, and all the cash and valuables in the house. I heard the screen door slam behind me and never looked back.

I hadn't thought about it until just now, but those old movies and the newspaper clippings gave me something my life was truly lacking at that point: Structure. Purpose. Hope.

Quidlee catches my stare and hastily covers up his arms and taps his space bar twice to get my attention.

[Quidlee]: Done.

[Barca]: Yeah, done.

[Tanto]: Good. Both of you can do this. Just watch me for the next hour, and don't put unrealistic expectations on yourself.

[Quidlee]: Thanks, old man.

[Tanto]: You do realize I'm only twenty-eight.

[Quidlee]: And I'm twenty-two, which makes you old.

[Tanto]: Then just listen to your elder and follow my lead.

I log into our system. Our software portal, aka Theia, named for the Greek goddess of sight, follows a series of well-designed scripts we run through the dark web.

I take six, seven minutes to find a likely target in the chat rooms: BigRedWood69. Anyone with 69 at the end of their handle is overcompensating.

[Tanto]: So, as you can see, from the previously recorded chat window, I chatted with this guy several times over the last few weeks. Now, he's back for more. I set my profile to public, so he can see the fake stats for my character [Lacy1]. She's thirty, single, and has a twelve-year-old daughter.

[Quidlee]: Do you always pretend to be a girl?

[Tanto]: Always.

Barca laughs. I ignore him.

[Tanto]: Now watch.

Both Quidlee and Barca lean toward my monitor as I chat about random stuff for a while. Barca reeks like stale junk food and oppression, but the focus on the hunt clears my mind of his smell. It isn't until our target asks me about porn that I know he's not on the dark web searching for completely harmless content.

[BigRedWood69] So u telling me it's free?

[Lacy1] Yep. No credit card required.

[BigRedWood69] Man, dat's sweet. Tired of PornHub and PornHole charging like twenty a month. Ain't got that kinda scratch.

[Lacy1] Money tight?

That was one of my three little questions: money, family, and intent. I am trying to decide if this perv is worth the world of hurt available at my command. Luckily, it came up naturally, because when you force the questions in, the prey spooks back into the woods.

[BigRedWood69] Uh, duh! I lost my job after the housing bubble burst, and people ain't exactly hiring realtors.

Oh, how my heart breaks for you, BigRedWood69.

[Lacy1] That sucks! I just got a new job, but it still won't pay for my daughter's braces. They're EXPENSIVE!

I have no daughter, or at least none I know of. As PoBones, our ponytail-wearing resident Cajun refilling his cup with liquid gold from the basic white Black and Decker coffeepot on top of the mini-fridge in the corner would say, "I done got enough of dat *strange* that they need to start calling it *familiar*." He's told me that joke nine times over the last six years. It gets less funny each time.

Granted, there were some wild nights after our hactivist guild, ROBIN-GOOD, brought down the servers for MCI/WorldCom, IBM, Deloitte, Wells Fargo, and any other Fortune 500 companies that were in our well-paid and world-leveling crosshairs. I'd been safe, or at least intended to be, but an incoherent mind does not make the best choices. The hardcore rocker, Rick James, said it best: cocaine is, indeed, a hell of a drug. I wasn't exactly on a sobriety high horse when I fell. More like I was climbing out on my designated limb in the family tree and, when I slipped, I slammed into all my family's bad habits on the way to the hard ground.

[Quidlee]: Does your character have a backstory?

[Tanto]: Yes. A fluid one. I always pretend to be a broke, single mom. Some of these creeps mistake someone's life situation for weakness, so I play the role and maximize the misogynists' stereotypes. That way, I get an unspoken leeway in my communications because if someone thinks you need saving, they already think you are beneath them in life.

As if on command, our target chimes back in.

[BigRedWood69] Girl, I ain't got no kids. Big swinging parties at my crib! Just got myself a disco ball with strobes, girl!

[Lacy1] Wow! That's good to know ;).

So, he's got a lavish lifestyle. Or at the least pretends to have one.

[BigRedWood69] So, how old is your daughter? She got an account on here?

And bingo. He fails two of the three questions. Even though he is broke, he has no kids and is asking about *mine.* He's passed Possible Pedophiles 101. Now to see if he hangs himself with his own intentions.

All I do is give him the link to my *daughter's* profile. Then, when he clicks on it, a new screen pops up on my system. It doesn't take three guesses to figure out who is a-knocking on my computer's front door.

As for my current conversation, it goes dead. From there, I do the same type of convo with the target, except pretending I'm the daughter now. Until he asks for pics. Then I tell him I've got some up on this site that my *mom* doesn't know about.

He asks for the link.

I warn him it is just something my junior high friends and I set up, showing us experimenting with our bodies.

He asks repeatedly for the link.

I send it to him.

And then I wrap all this up in a saved file for the Attorney General.

[Tanto]: As you can see, I followed the procedures to entice and not entrap him, and ultimately get him to slip up, producing enough evidence to capture him.

[Quidlee]: This doesn't look too hard.

[Tanto]: Slow and steady. Always remember that.

People think the dark web is mysterious and dangerous, a land where you hire hit men and buy automatic weapons. The dark web is more like a shortcut than a place. Imagine the Internet as a big city. You're in one part of the city and you need to get to the center. There are four or five routes you can take. Each varies in traffic, distance, number of lanes on the road, stoplights, and so on, affecting how long it will take you to get to your destination.

The dark web is the sewer that runs below the city. There's no traffic, however, no one maps the pipes. You must know your exact destination and how to get there before you start your trek, otherwise you'll wind up lost, vulnerable, and with shoes full of shit.

[Tanto]: Okay, now it is your turn.

[Barca]: So, if I get five hundred kills, I go free?

[Tanto]: Hypothetically, yes. They parole you. Then this place sets you up with a job. I don't know much more than that.

[Quidlee]: So if I get ten kills a week, I will be out of here in about a year.

The kid's optimism reflects in his face, a flushness in his cheeks. I tell him how lucky the hunt and capture of BigRedWood69 was compared to the daily drivel here. Even so, Quidlee wiggles in his seat, a runner waiting for the starter's pistol. I know better than to tell him that no one has ever gotten out of here that quickly. It is not my job to squash dreams.

[Tanto]: If anyone can do it, it is you. Go.

A small squeal creeps from Quidlee's throat as he pops his knuckles and dives in. He opens Theia and studies the possible targets. He ignores the small-fish targets, the ones that are downloading a single file for a few seconds and then disconnecting service. He is waiting for a whale, someone that is downloading large files, such as whole videos, and has a long connectivity.

My thoughts on this are that anyone can make a mistake. For example, I once tracked a guy who was downloading a good amount of amateur porn, then he wandered into a baited snuff porn folder. That's the videos with actual blood and gore. He downloaded one file, then went back to minor league porn.

For me, that's like drug dealing. The first one is free. For the rest, you pay full price. In other words, you're on my shit list.

I glance over at Barca to see that, instead of starting work on his own, he gets up and walks around the War Room. He examines the giant monitors, studies the Cube of Death looming over us, and then goes over to the giant red cloth covering our coolest gadget.

"What the hell is this?" Barca asks loudly while staring at the Cube of Death. Almost every hackvict braces for a shock. Speaking loudly often merits such a punishment. However, after I unclench my fist, nothing happens.

How does Barca get a free pass to speak without punishment?

Cyfib never emerges from his office. Either he didn't hear him, doesn't care, or something else entirely. Barca shrugs and yanks off the velvet sheet to reveal a clear tube large enough for a tall-ish man to stand in.

"Now, what does this bad boy do?"

No one answers. Barca is apparently immune to shocks. The rest of us aren't.

Barca opens the glass tube and steps in, leaving the door open. I stroll over to him and whisper, "Stop playing and get to work."

"First, tell me what this is, and then I'll consider it."

The bastard wants to negotiate? What the actual hell?

I lean into an empty workstation. Barca grips the lone hand-sized button in the chamber. He presses it and tosses it between his hands like he owns the damn thing. Then Barca drops it and walks over.

I whisper, "That is LODIS, or Liquid Ocular Display Interceptor System."

"What's it do?"

"It stops large malware bot attacks with visual and sensory motions."

"So," Barca rubs his chin before answering, "it is like Galaga?"

"No, well, yes, actually, it is just like Galaga."

"Ah." Barca glances back at it and asks, "What about the button?"

"It allows for the user to leave the device. Now, can we go back to our terminals? Please?"

We return to find Quidlee exploring targets by chatting with several prospects. He's a natural. The rook starts a private window with the user, something about the torrent files taking forever to download, and asks about any awesome new sites the target knows about. It is bait, hoping that a polite gag reflex will mean they will ask the same question back, meaning anything Quidlee answers isn't quite entrapment. It is enticement.

However, when I glance over at Barca's screen, it is blank. As I lean back and look at his face, he moves his head forward. He is looking past me. He is looking at Quidlee.

While Quidlee is physically hacking his target's web presence, Barca is watching the rook, probably planning a hack of his own.

Chapter Twenty-Four

The Handle

The next few days are a repeat, like most of them here in Hackers' Haven. Get up. Shower. Dress. Breakfast. Hack. Lunch. Hack. Dinner. Chill. Sleep. Lather, rinse, repeat.

It is a pleasant surprise to discover Barca keeps mostly silent during our meals. Maybe ten units a week *is* worthy of his time.

A couple of times, when I've stopped at the doc for migraine help, I've noticed that Barca chats with Quidlee while I'm away. Sometimes I'll catch Barca making Quidlee laugh. Other times I will notice Barca ignoring an apology from Quidlee for something done or said.

Whenever I am alone with the rook, I ask him what's going on. He always answers the same way. "Nothing."

It isn't until the next week when Quidlee gets his first capture that things split sideways.

The kid's target is what you'd expect: a white male in his early fifties with two-point- something kids and a marriage burning out at the end of a spent candle's wick.

It appears the guy is trying to relive his glory days, which is when he was the high school quarterback who "had more ass than a donkey farm." The target has maxed out his credit cards with the usual porn, yet he "wants those high school girls again." Not the ones about to enter college. He wants those underage ones, the innocent ones who haven't needed to be told to keep away from creeps like him. The target wants something more.

He wants it risky, and he wants it free.

When I was three years old, my mama told me that there ain't nothing in this world for free. Doesn't matter if you find it on the street. That just means someone else lost what I gained. Hell, all those free samples of random pharmaceuticals that my mother made me stuff my jacket pockets with every time I visited a clinic weren't free. They cost her body years of use. They cost me my innocence.

When Quidlee gets that creep's IP address, dark web activity log, and even a copy of two archived chat logs where he'd solicited—and was rejected by—a minor, my chest bursts with pride.

The rook opens our general Alviss chat window to share his success, as if everyone in the room cannot already hear his chirping and see his arms popping in the air, the lazy man's seated victory dance.

[Quidlee]: I got one!

[Tanto]: Great, kid. Don't get cocky.

[Quidlee]: Did you just quote *Star Wars* at me?

[Tanto]: I may or may not have.

[AldenSong]: The hack is strong with this one.

[PoBones]: Hack or no hack, there is no try.

A few others send out their congratulations. Even Barca writes the words *thumbs-up,* which is about as lazy of a supporting message as you can send.

[Quidlee]: This is such a rush!

I cannot disagree more. But we haven't gotten to that part of the rook's education yet.

And his first capture *is* righteous. A true predator. I hope he continues his focus on similar creeps and follows this same train of thought, because the temptation exists to grab the low-hanging fruit out there.

Very few people downloading illegal movies, music, and software are doing it to be vengeful. Most of these crimes that entail trying to download pirated movies and software are punishable with a fine and minimal court work. Those captures stink, but do count toward our kills, so they are a necessary evil. However, sometimes those little fish fail to impress the Attorney General's office, so they use our information about the people we catch to get search warrants for anything that ever touched a computer, such as flash drives, CDs, and more. All it takes is one minor mistake by a user to open the door to find other illegal activity—from piracy to tax evasion to flat-out murder.

[Quidlee]: I mean, that guy's so toasted! He's gonna go to jail.

[Barca]: Just like you?

[Tanto]: Thanks, Captain Buzzkill. Just remember: enticing is not entrapment. Slow, careful steps. Make sure you download the log file and store everything like I showed you.

I know I am poking a hornet's nest, but Barca needs to stop raining piss on Quidlee's parade.

[Barca]: I'm just saying I'm in here because I got caught red-handed breaking into my fifth bank in a row.

Why would Barca admit why he was in here like this? No one admits to crimes in here. Barca is up to something. He's playing a game with Quidlee; I just cannot see what the sport is. *What the hell does Barca know?*

[Tanto]: And how's that first kill going for you, Barca?

[Barca]: How'd you wind up in here, Tanto?

[Tanto]: Got caught loitering. Get back to work.

[Barca]: Quidlee?

[Quidlee]: Got busted on some false porn site. Didn't want to pay. A power user told me it was legit.

[Barca]: Yeah, I think you told me about that.

They're having conversations without me around. While that makes sense, that means Barca knows all the pieces and rules in this game, and I'm sitting here figuring it out as we're already several turns in.

[Barca]: Hey, isn't what you got caught doing a lot like what we're doing right now?

I put my arm under Quidlee's arm and drag both of us out of the War Room.

"Hey, what're you . . ."

"Shh . . ."

My grip is so tight that my fingers vibrate from Quidlee's rapid pulse. I only let go when we finish our trek to the dorm.

"Barca is messing with your head."

"Nah, man." Quidlee knocks my hand loose. "He's just being friendly."

"No, he's not." I know exactly what I want to say next, but for some reason the words lock into my throat. I have to shake my head violently to knock them out. "He's not to be trusted."

At that moment, Quidlee steps back and takes a good hard look at me. His eyes scan every inch of me and even stare straight through me. I'm too late because I know what he is going to say before he says it. "Barca said the same thing about you."

I open my mouth, but this time I have no words. The *nu-uh* defense only works with six-year-olds and drunks.

Quidlee shrugs and walks back to the War Room. I take a moment and breathe. Seven breaths. That's enough time to figure out what I must do.

When I return to my system, I chew on some Corn Nuts I got at the Commissary. I hate junk food, but snacking will throw off any suspicion that I'm forming a plan.

My Theia software's chat window timed out, so I open it back up. Whoever I was chasing got a free pass. I'm left with nothing but a blank screen.

A few crunches later, enough noise to throw off any scent of what I'm about to do, I opened the Alviss group chat.

[Tanto]: Barca, I want to apologize to you. I know we've gotten off on the wrong foot, but I want to make it right.

Give him a taste of what he wants, and I can regroup.

[Barca]: Hey, Tanto, we're all good. I think you're just like everyone else here, pretty freaking awesome.

Lying liar. Now everyone here will think he's a freaking saint and I'm the devil.

[Tanto]: Well, you're the bee's knees as well.

Play in and play up.

[Barca]: Hey, Quidlee, what was the handle of the guy who caught you?

Oh no. We've moved past this. Plus, he's doing this on the main group chat.

[Quidlee]: Man, I'll never forget it. Rosemond_McGreg. Why?

Barca smiles as he kicks back in his chair, then leans back to his keyboard.

[Quidlee]: Why?

[Barca]: Huh. Hey, Tanto, why is that the handle you're using right now?

Chapter Twenty-Five

Knows Our Systems

hat the holy hell? I wasn't using that handle under Theia earlier. Low and behold, there it is. Barca must've keyed it in.

I was completely wrong. Barca wasn't playing Quidlee. He was playing me, and I was one move from everything going ass-up.

[Tanto]: Ha, ha, hilarious.

[Barca]: What's so funny? It's the name you're using.

Quidlee snickers. He's smarter than Barca thinks.

[Quidlee]: You did that, Barca. It's not like Tanto is the douchebag who caught me.

The clickety-clacks in the room slow until the room falls silent. This entire conversation is happening on the public chat and it's all about to turn into what PoBones calls the fourth turn of the Texas Motor Speedway in NASCAR: you stop what you're doing and watch out for potential car wrecks.

Anyone with browser access could've pulled up our Dead Pool: the kills, time spent on them, who got them, and what username was used. The last part was listed so that we would retire a handle after three uses, which meant the handle Rosemond_McGreg was listed in our Hall of Fame text file and on the board.

As my fingers start to work on a lie and then I backspace, erasing it, my closest friend does what close friends do: call you on your shit.

[AldenSong]: Tell him. "And you will know the truth, and the truth will set you free—" John 8:32.

[Quidlee]: Wait . . . what does AldenSong mean?

Damn you, Aldy, damn you for doing this now and, most of all, damn you for being right.

My fingers cramp and a frog buries itself in my throat so I can't swallow. I squeak out, "Quidlee . . . I am so sorry."

He wasn't the first I'd apologized to trapping here. Hopefully, this would end better than it did when Hit-Man666 got sent to the Bay.

"Are you kidding me?" Quidlee suddenly is standing above me and shoves me out of my chair.

I hit the floor and his voice escalates.

"Are you kidding me?"

"Look, it is what we do . . ."

Quidlee grabs my hair and rams my head into my keyboard. Keys pop loose and fly across the room. While the impact sounds worse than it is, no one rises from their chair to stop this. This beatdown is merited. I just wish it was more private.

Then come the *cha-chings*. The rook is doomed.

"Unacceptable, dog," comes Cyfib's monotone voice, followed by a slam of a fist on the same keyboard my face just crash-test-dummy product tested.

A guard is already in the room, but it is Fontana. He's seen this type of altercation occur before. He knows it is justified. As long as no one dies, a beatdown is just part of the pack's mentality: one way or another, when the bill comes, you pay what you owe.

I glance up from my spot on the floor. In the rook's flushed face, there is more than anger. It is more than hurt in Quidlee's teary eyes.

Betrayal.

Cyfib turns his back on Quidlee and strolls toward the Cube of Death. "Guard . . ."

"No!" Quidlee raises a fist to strike the warden.

Luckily, Guard Fontana tazes him before the blow lands. Fontana mumbles something to himself as he zip-ties Quidlee's arms first, then his legs. Fontana is unlikely to report this *almost attack*. That new guard would've gotten Quidlee sent to the Bay and never given it another thought.

As they drag Quidlee away, he chants one line over and over again, his brain stuck in an endless loop due to an internal error. "You did this to me! You did this to me! You did this to me!"

It goes on for another few rounds as Quidlee's voice fades in the background after echoing down the hall, approaching the Hole.

The rest of the chanting resonates behind my eyes.

"Dog, report to the Infirmary." A sigh follows Cyfib's voice over the PA. The warden has just lost valuable and productive time. "You've spoiled your hunt for the day."

Before I can move, AldenSong's hands are under my shoulders, lifting me to my feet. "I'm sorry, Tanto."

I want to go off on Aldy, but I know him too well. I'd never ask him to betray who he is as a person, who he is down to his core. I merely sigh as he picks the T-key from my hair.

Then my ears catch the cracking. The popping.

There, in his seat, is Barca, chomping down on my Corn Nuts, his mouth wide open as he chews, each crack echoing in his mouth.

"That sucks, man." The giant raises the rest of the bag to his lips and sucks down the remaining dust. "I was just joking around."

He's trying to downplay this A-bomb he set off intentionally. The bastard no more guessed that I got Quidlee arrested than I was the queen of England.

Barca knows our systems.

Chapter Twenty-Six

Figure Out What It All Means

The next few days sucked more than most. Even though I was *just doing my job*, my actions led to the capture and ultimate incarceration of my newest friend. The discovery of that betrayal felt like I was sitting on the blade of a knife: if I didn't move, I'd forget about it. However, the moment I think about what I'd done to Quidlee, my body squirms and a new cut forms.

I remember the last few years of my life here in Hackers' Haven better than the earlier ones. Year one was more reactionary, followed by failure after failure. I refused help, even from Lance-a-Little, mainly because I was prideful. I robbed years two and three of any progress because I was learning under the wrong mentor: Cyfib. His mantra of *your target's freedom always equals your incarceration* became so indoctrinated in me I'd go days without sleeping so that I could capture more and more.

It wasn't until Lance took me under his wing and I stepped back and looked at our system —how we capture the uneducated and ignorant, not evil people—from an overhead and outside perspective, that I realized the system is more than broken.

It is malevolent.

Lance had already done a bit for me when I started: a unit or two added to my account whenever I was having a rough time. Lance never took credit for my assistance, even though a lesser person might've held those kindnesses over my head.

Maybe, like Lance, it *is* time for me to go. I'd sworn I'd stay as long as I was useful, guide where I can, and share kills where necessary, but maybe I am kidding myself.

What I need is a pick-me-up. Even the damned must take a breather. As I sit down at my terminal, I pull out the pouch that Lance-a-Little gave me as his going away present.

After I loosen the velvet rope, my fingers snag one of the few delicacies I let myself have in this world: Gin-Gin candies. Throughout the world, these spicy-sweet candies cure nausea and are about as healthy as a sweet tooth can get.

I unwrap one and pop it in my mouth. Instantly, the ting of ginger clears my nostrils. I wad up the wrapper and angle it for a shot at a garbage can ten feet away. Naturally, I miss completely.

"Air ball," PoBones whispers, sending a chuckle around the room.

Guard Fontana moves automatically toward the wrapper, but there's *something* sticking out of it. I dash over and snatch it up.

"Um, sorry, I'll handle my own trash." I mime throwing it away in case anyone is watching.

Fontana mumbles something under his breath, and I dart to the bathroom. I look around for prying eyes. I find none. Then I enter a stall and look at the paper.

On it, there is the letter *W*.

I hurry back to my workstation and pretend to work for five minutes. Then, I grab my bag of sweets, shove it into my pocket, and return to the bathroom. There, I open all the candies. In each wrapper, I find a single letter.

Now it is up to me to figure out what it all means.

Chapter Twenty-Seven

Nothin-What It Seems

I decode the message but cannot act on it. Not yet.

It is only after I have just wrapped up a capture of a creep snooping where he shouldn't, searching the dark web for underage amputee snuff porn of all odd topics, that I decide to do what helped me years ago: ask for help.

I leave my terminal near Aldy and stride toward the exit like I am headed to the bathroom. Before I leave, I notice no one looking my way and I angle back under the Cube of Death to grab an empty terminal.

Once there, I close my eyes and stare at my reflection in the cube's underside. There is a chance that Cyfib is staring at me right now. However, I cannot risk any other hackvict getting in trouble or seeing what I am about to do. I must work jackrabbit quick for this to work out.

I set a timer through the Stopwatch app in our system and enter the Alviss software.

Lance-a-Little left me a handwritten script that allows me untracked access to the web for six minutes at a time. I don't even need to create an executable file that the anti-virus system might discover and quarantine. It is merely a standard library file that piggybacks off our existing systems. Child's play.

Through this back door out of our system, I now go to the other piece of the puzzle: Woot.com. This site is the bomb. Every night at midnight a single item goes on sale. Almost all inventory sells out in a matter of minutes, so people will complain about how rigged the system is or how cool it is they got to buy something. Among those comments is where Lance-a-Little hinted that there was a way to contact him.

The post would stand out. This was like the children's picture game where you try to find the odd thing in an otherwise normal image. A firefighter holding a hotdog instead of a firehose. Or a police officer arresting a flower.

I don't dare use any of our software, so I use Mozilla, a web browser that doesn't track, and dive into the Woot forums. Lance would have posted under their section "Everything but Woot," an unregulated sector. At least that is what part of the code spelled.

Okay, Tanto, which of these is not like the other? Checking the timer, two minutes have flown by. Setting up took longer than I thought. I can't activate the software back-to-back without risking drawing monitoring software attention.

I scroll and scroll through threads about food, diet, word associations, word games, Pokémon, and more. Then I find it: Broken Tax Software.

Bingo. It is just like what Lance-a-Little joked about in the latrine: no one deliberately looks for tax software, especially broken tax software.

I open the forum. Each day is a post, talking about how this programmer wants to fix some software but only when the time allows. The posts themselves are around ten to twenty words, like *Version 2.1 is crap.* Also, at the end of every post is a series of numbers that look like a phone number. I double check something. Yep.

They aren't phone numbers at all. They are the reverse of an IP address. The only thing missing are two numbers, which are listed in the body of the text.

I ping the address. It is online. With just over two minutes left on my timer, I open a communication window with it and send a note out that only Lance-a-Little would understand.

[User1]: Excalibur is nice to have for a beheading . . .

Now the hard part: the waiting.

Another minute flies by. Maybe Lance isn't online. Just because his VPN is running doesn't mean he has a window open to this terminal.

Under a minute remains. I close several windows but leave this one up.

Just as I am about to close the window, the chat window flickers.

[User2]: A-daggerIsEasier4-ass-assination.

Boom. The spelling and structure are off, but it is him. Maybe he is using a handheld device. Maybe he is in a hurry.

Whatever the case, Lance-a-Little is responding to me.

Twenty seconds.

[User1]: I'm considering cashing in my units.

Nothing happens. Ten seconds until I must end this chat.

What is taking him so long?

Then something happens that turns my world upside down.

[User2]: AvoidpppParole. Stay. Nothin-what it seems.

Chapter Twenty-Eight

What We Are Trained to Do

An alarm sounds overhead. My blood rushes to my eyes.

Do not panic. Even if you're caught, cover your tracks.

I close out my window and hit CLEAR+F7+I, a command Lance-a-Little has set up to switch out those six minutes of non-Hackers' Haven work from keyboard trackers and log files with the same basic text. It represents a faux back-and-forth failure of a conversation between one of seventeen fake usernames in a hidden Dynamic Link Library or DLL file, and forty-two other fake target names. The dialogue is stilted, but anyone looking might only deduce that my ruse as WhoreyRorey failed to gain the interest of LongLarry6969, mainly because the conversation read that he was into large-and-in-charge women who were more likely to shop at Dillard's and argue with managers over expired coupons instead of tweens getting piercings from Hot Topic.

Once my heart slides down from my throat, my mind places the siren.

This isn't my fault.

We are under attack.

I dart from the station under the Cube of Death and grab a terminal closer to the front. AldenSong joins me on my right, while PoBones flanks my left. Neither speaks, but a smile crosses the big guy's lips.

Nothing brings a team together like a crisis.

After a few keystrokes, I pull up our four screens. Then they go blank.

"Da hell?" PoBones kicks back in his chair and stands. He leans behind the closest jumbotron and jiggles a cable.

I spare a glance at the Cube of Death as the new guard darts in.

I mutter, "Now where is the W—"

The rest of the words leave my body as a scream. I immediately hit the floor, along with all other prisoners, when a shock originating in my lower leg ripples through my body. From my fetal position, the new Guard Stevens, the one with enough acne to be the *Before* picture in a '90s Clearasil commercial, stands over us holding the universal shock remote. I stand and he again hits the lone button that triggers all our ankle shockers.

The room fills with screams.

"You can't touch any of those systems without alpha authorization," says Guard Stevens who, upon further review, appears just old enough to shave.

"Then get Cyfib!" I yell, half expecting another shock.

"The commander is en route."

Our Bastard-in-Chief wasn't even in the cube today.

"*En route* does absolutely jack shit right now because, to shut down our systems like this, we are in the middle of a two-pronged attack, if not more," I say through gritted teeth. I'm half expecting another shock for my smart mouth, but luckily, the guard just points the remote at me like I am a PowerPoint presentation.

Just like what had occurred a few days prior, I opened my mouth, and the words failed to form.

What is going on with me? I'd see the doc about this when I wasn't trying to protect the freaking country.

Through a throat full of cotton balls, I say, "Please . . . listen . . ." Then my body shakes for some weird reason. I stumble toward the guard. The joy buzzer shocker must've hit me harder than I thought.

"Get back and get on the ground!"

From his spot on the floor, AldenSong grumbles. "Tanto, I swear, if I blast my pants because of you, you're doing my laundry for the next month."

Then Barca stands up and raises his hands in the air. He might've meant for that to look like a move of submission. To me, it makes Barca look like a grizzly bear about to pounce on a bunny rabbit.

What the hell is he doing?

"Hey, buddy, I'd listen to this guy." The giant speaks smoothly, in a voice low and calming, taking time and space between each meticulously selected word. "I know I'm the new guy here, but this old hat wouldn't be trying to mess with your authority."

There's no way this is genuine, but I'll take my victories where I can.

"Convict, get back on the floor!"

Barca purses his lips and, instead of laying on the floor, he takes a seat in the closest chair. The guard aims the remote at him. Barca crosses his arms.

The siren's volume and intensity increase.

"Now's the time to get off your ass, Princess."

I open my mouth, but this time I hold the words back on purpose. Even a ticking clock waits between beats.

Breathe. Think. Relate. Plan. Weigh. Decide.

Even though I've just begun this quick meditation, head bowed, and palms spread wide, I can hear Barca ask AldenSong what the hell I'm doing.

"He's a Bushi."

"You say that like I'm supposed to have a damn clue what it means. Why's it look like he's meditating while standing up?"

"That's kind of what he *is* doing. Only better."

"We don't have that kind of time."

I run scenario after scenario through my brain. Doing nothing and waiting for Cyfib. Unacceptable. The hackers already have a head start. Attempting this op by myself. Untenable.

I cannot do this alone.

Then I calculate how many hackvicts it will take to handle this and who would risk Cyfib's definite discipline.

Our counter hack is occurring, one way or another. The new guard has no idea he is leaving us and all our government connections open to invasion by holding us hostage.

By the Bushido Code, we must extend kindness to the inexperienced. Our new guard is as ignorant as a monkey working a Playstation. Sometimes this kindness requires unique action, such as starting this counter hack without Cyfib present. To do nothing when action is an option would not only be to condemn the ignorant but could be viewed as taking delight in someone else's misery.

That said, now to convince the guard to let us do what we are trained to do.

Chapter Twenty-Nine

Mount Up

I open my eyes and raise my hands just as the alarm goes from a high banshee shrill to a deeper bass beat. The guard darts his eyes around the room and aims the remote at me.

"Guard, I didn't cause that frequency change, but I can be part of what fixes the problem." I carefully curate every word for this conversation, because I don't have a relationship with this guard like I do with Guard Fontana. One false move and we'll lose this chase. "Do you understand what is happening right now?"

He flicks the remote at the ground, indicating that I should get on the floor. A simple *no* would've sufficed.

Then the jumbotrons flicker. A yellow light on the third giant screen shifts to red. Now the room looks like a scene in a horror movie where the killer sneaks up on the teenagers doing it. Spoiler alert: the couple doesn't live happily ever after.

I point at the red light. "AldenSong, I need you to earworm a song."

"You've got to be frickin' kidding."

"Now." My eyes widen as I shoot Aldy a look somewhere between demanding and panic. "Please."

The Samoan takes a breath, curses something under his breath, and sings in his most soprano range, the chorus to Sir Young MC's *Bust a Move*. He hits all the notes for both the male and female parts. I am equally impressed and ashamed.

I rotate to face Aldy. He avoids my glare so fast that Aldy slaps his own forehead against the floor tile.

Thanks, fatso. I now must save the situation using the wisdom of '90s hip-hop.

"Fine. Guard, do you know that song?"

Silence.

Of course, he doesn't. He's freaking twelve. We're screwed.

Then I catch the rhythmic tap of his foot on the tile and know that the song sticks in the guard's head like shit on a shoe.

"There!" I point at his foot. "You know the song. Great song. Wonderful hit. But here's the thing. What just happened was our off-key singer's chorus got that song in your head, whether or not you wanted it to."

"Hey, Tanto! That's cold!" yells AldenSong.

"Anyway, that's like our firewall. It doesn't want a hook or song or especially a virus or worm in it. When that light flashed yellow and the alarm sounded, that meant we had the potential for an intruder. When it went red, that meant that the threat was real and we now have a hook that's infecting our entire system, like *Bust a Move* went from your ears to your feet. I can't yet say how, but somehow something or someone in this building took the bait, downloaded a Trojan horse virus, and let a fox into the henhouse. And I have a pretty good idea what opened the gate."

As a hacker, I love worms, the digital kind that is. Before my incarceration I knew that the closest thing I'd probably ever have to children were my hand-created digital worms that gobbled up the right financial information like kids demolishing a cake at a birthday party.

"Ah." I notice the bulge in the guard's front pocket. "You have your cellphone on, don't you?"

"It's not on."

"I believe you." *I don't.* "Would you please check?"

A bead of sweat trickles from his temple down his cheek acne to his chin. He wipes it away with his right sleeve as his left hand pulls out his phone.

I've never seen someone power a phone off so quickly, like he is sitting in the front row of a packed church and just got a phone call during the preacher's sermon.

"Wait!"

Too late. The guard has powered off and put the phone in his pocket. That complicates things. *Shit.*

"What Wi-Fi are you on?"

"My phone wasn't even on."

If that's true, I'm Bill Gates.

"Okay, what's done is done. Let's say that *someone's* phone, not necessarily yours, was on the Wi-Fi. Which network might it have been on?"

The guard lowers the remote and yanks at his straight black hair.

"This is bad." The guard's panicked eyes dart around. "This is bad . . ."

"This is fixable. Look, you don't even have to say anything. Just blink once for *no* and twice for *yes*. Okay?"

The kid just stares at me. We are losing time here . . .

Then he blinks twice.

"Is a particular phone set to auto-update when connected to available Wi-Fi?"

Double blink.

"Is it connected to a Wi-Fi network named Tectumque?"

Again, double blink.

Great . . . and dammit. The good news is that we know how the hacker got in. The bad news is that he went through a side door for the wireless router connected to our server. I have no idea why we even have that liability.

If he's hacked root access, that means he could set his administrative rights to God-level and cripple us with our own system.

"Okay. Now, when is Cyfib getting here?"

He checks his watch yet remains silent.

"Okay, so you don't know. Well, we're going to get to work because there is more than your job at risk here. Understood?"

He holsters the remote, which I take as a *yes*.

I turn on the closest monitor and click through our bandwidth analyzer until I find the port with the most traffic on our network. That might be the leak. I enter the kill command to close off the connection.

Nothing happens.

A few clicks later, the second monitor flashes as a blip of root kit code pops open, scanning directory after directory. Dammit. They're using that software to fight for God-like control of our computer system. Also, that gives the intruder access to every single damn thing in our databases.

And that's a whole lot of secrets.

Damn. Someone's hungry. "Alright! Heads up, people! I'm not asking anyone to endanger any units or risk discipline, but I haven't been part of a hunt this big in two years. This might be nothing, but I sure as hell hope it is something. And I, for one, really want to know who just kicked down our front door and is pissing all over our house. Anyone want to join me?"

I expected maybe PoBones and AldenSong to join me.

What I didn't expect was for every single hackvict to stand up.

"Mount up."

Chapter Thirty

Time to Drown

W hile most everyone grabs a workstation, Barca walks to the guard. I expected Guard Stevens to step back, or at least warn Barca to back off. Instead, he lets Barca whisper something in his ear. The next thing I know, the guard opens the back of the shocker remote, grabs the spring that connects with the battery for power, breaks it off, and tosses it into the trash.

What the hell . . . ? No. There's no time for speculation now. We must act faster than the Road Runner outrunning Wile E. Coyote and our villain already has his ACME traps set.

From over my shoulder, our resident Cajun PoBones whistles so loudly my left eardrum buzzes.

"Oh, I'm calling dibs on bringing da funk!" he belts out before plopping down in the closest chair and powering up his monitor.

"Good. PoBones brings the funk. Who brings the noise?"

Foshi_Taloa raises his hand. It is ironic that the quietest guy in the house also is a master of flooding a target with so much raw and useless data it could crash a network. It's like trying to take a drink from a full force fire hose: it's possible if you don't mind losing a few teeth.

As for the noise, PoBones is great at creating a force field effect for our data. He's not exactly creating an additional firewall. He's just focusing our processors on a flood of useless tasks, not what the hacker is looking at. It's like if you're watching a movie on your computer while also trying to load web browser pages. One thing must slow down for the other to work.

"I need a Dam Breaker." Before I could formally ask, AldenSong comes to the rescue.

"You can't have a party without me." He turns on a monitor and logs in.

AldenSong can break through a firewall as if someone made it out of tissue paper, so he is our best bet at cracking the hacker's protective barrier.

The problem is we are so late to this attack that it is like walking into a rock concert during the encore: our system score is at a one and the bandwidth is dropping.

"Um, Tanto, he's blocking my access to our tools," says Aldy.

Crud. Since the hacker has root access, he's shut down our defensive and offensive software.

I log into SkipTrace; it doesn't even boot. The hacker has taken our knees out from under us.

This intruder thinks he is in control, so he is in no hurry to leave. We need him to believe that for another few minutes because we have one not-so-little tool left in our arsenal.

"Can you still do this manually?"

"Such as hunting down each assaulting packet? That's damn near impossible. Plus, it'd take forever, but if everyone focuses solely on that task we might target-lock him, and maybe we have a shot. Why?"

I toss him a smile, and Aldy catches my exact meaning.

"Oh, damn . . ."

Time to drown.

"Power up the Coffin."

Chapter Thirty-One

Dark Void Before My Eyes

In the *Wizard of Oz,* the mystery was who was behind the giant curtain. Only after they pulled it back did Dorothy and her band of heathens discover that the all-powerful Oz was nothing more than a magic act, complete with smoke and mirrors.

In Hackers' Haven, we have a curtain of our own. Behind the ten-foot red behemoth in the corner is our hidden magic. Unlike Oz, the thing behind the curtain is powerful enough to kill its user.

It has before.

PoBones yanks the velvet sheet off the Coffin. To the naked eye, it looks kind of like those tubes where they freeze people in those sci-fi movies.

The latest in liquid technology interface, it is our secret weapon in fighting an onslaught of hacker bots. The theory behind this technology is that a man gets into the tube. The tube fills with some type of hydrogen hydrate, maybe a combination of H_2 and H_2O water, not H_2-O. I know next to nothing about the composition of the liquid, but I think the reason for this is that hydrogen, the first element on the periodic table, stores and delivers energy. Therefore, since computer interaction requires energy, what better way to do that than through an energy-nourishing elemental combination?

This tank's water with extra hydrogen allows for about a hundred different projectors and hundreds of motion sensors to not only transfer data but also read eye movement. Once you put on goggles that aid in capturing the eye movement, you strap on your oxygen tube and settle in as the tank fills with H_2H_2O. Water fills to the brim. The unit pressurizes. Then the user can work at the speed of sight. In theory, this is the future of technology.

Theory is one thing. In actual use, LODIS has earned its nickname the Coffin. Twice.

The first time it was used, the pressure was so intense that Lionel_Pooree suffered an aneurysm. Since those outside of the tube cannot see in, there was no way to know he was in distress. We assume that Lionel knew he was in trouble. However, if something had not disoriented him or the aneurysm occurred later, Lionel might've hit the eject/flush button on the right of the user, and we could've gotten him medical attention in time. In theory.

The second time, ArakNidKid's feet slipped from the bottom-locking grooves, and the tube for the oxygen tank wrapped around his neck and he hung himself. In here, if it benefits the job, Dr. Fel will get it for you. His *prescribed* diet of uppers and stimulants might've messed with ArakNidKid's mind, or something else went wrong to cause this. There's more speculation with that death.

Then there is me. I've used the Coffin two times, both in practice. The first time, I screwed up, lost my bearings, and had to hit the eject button. The second time, I managed a fake capture of two attempted hackers in our simulations. That trial run had only sixty bots.

That was practice.

This is real. And well over a hundred bots, beating down our walls.

I check the readout screen for the assault. Currently, there are 182 bots, little programmed coders, either attacking the firewall or already in.

What I would do in the Coffin would be like playing the old Atari game Galaga. Even better, Asteroids, except instead of starting with a blank screen, the *game* would start surrounded by attackers because more and more are entering through the firewall's weak spots. We must plug the holes in our boat before we bail out the water.

"Everybody get in spotter positions."

AldenSong is exempt from the order because he has to get me in the right head space, one where I forget about the high odds of dying in a standing bathtub.

I strip all my clothes off and put on the semi-foam, neoprene void wetsuit. AldenSong twists the knob on the oxygen, puts the tube in his mouth, and inhales, testing the oxygen flow. He's protective like that.

Yay, he's going to give me cooties.

AldenSong emerges from behind the Coffin. His usually jolly face carries a concerned frown. "Um, Tanto, the oxygen tank's empty."

Son of a bitch.

I thought we filled the tank after the last practice run.

There are too many things going wrong to rely only on manual tracking. The problem with that is so many of these bots are self-replicating and that, by the time all the human hands in this building complete all the keystrokes to remove one bot from our system, there might be four more bots in its place. Plus, none of our automated defenses are online.

I study the screen. My idea is not ideal, but it is doable. If I can take down the primary force, the team can handle the dregs. Something in my gut wants to do this.

"I can make it two minutes or more in the LODIS."

"Now hold up, T." Aldy's protective nature always runs point in his mind, which is both a blessing and a curse because it makes him more risk averse. My protective spirit usually calls shotgun to risk's driver's seat. I am just close enough to grab the wheel should we go too far off-road and approach a cliff.

AldenSong, always caring, squares up with me. I look him in his soft yet focused eyes. We have an entire conversation with just our looks before I whisper, "This is just breath control."

"In a tank that has already killed two other people, T."

"I can do this."

Aldy breaks his stare and turns his view to the ground as he chews on the inside of his left cheek. There is nothing he can say to change my mind. I don't care if it is the adrenaline leaving my body from earlier or my stubborn pride, but I want this win.

"T, the moment you get the whiff of worry, you hit the eject button, do you hear me?" AldenSong shakes his head. "I'm not speaking at your funeral."

"You would."

". . . shut up and be careful."

Aldy moves his hand back and holds fingers in front of me: one on his right hand and three on his left. I nod, roll my shoulders back, and focus. Aldy joins me in this repetitive technique. One breath in, four breaths out. AldenSong breathes through his open mouth, probably making a noise during each inhale and four exhales. I can't hear him, and he can't hear me, of course, so I pretend and prep my breathing.

"Hip-hup-hup-hup-hup. Hip-hup-hup-hup-hup."

My lungs burn, then cool, during each round. The goal of this ancient exercise is to prepare your lungs for maximum vacancy, not occupancy.

Before I enter the Coffin, PoBones yells out, "Burn bright."

"Burn fast," Aldy adds.

"Burn down," I conclude.

I stand in the tank and close the doors. I mouth the words *Yes Mother* at Aldy through the glass. He flips me off, then places his hand to the glass. I respond in kind.

The Coffin's doors latch behind me. A hiss of pressurizing fills the air. After I put the snorkel in my mouth to catch my air bubbles, Aldy points to the dangling earpiece that hangs from the side of the inner tube. I'll hear him, but he won't hear me. There's no way to communicate through the mouthpiece. Maybe someone will install that feature in the next iteration of this death trap. I put it in my right ear. Of course, the big guy talks before I am properly hooked up.

". . . dummy. Anyway, all monitors are up. We're going to be hitting you with the location, duration, and intensity of attack for every bot slamming into our firewall. Once that's done, we'll shift to detection and isolation of the bots already through the wall. We will use 76 percent of our power on all that. The rest of the juice is for you and Zeus."

Good call. Zeus is the software that weaponizes the LODIS. It pinpoints any type of enemy attack and destroys it, with human guidance, that is. Interestingly, it is not named for the father of the gods; not directly, anyway. It's actually named for the world's first battlefield laser-slash-energy weapon designed for destroying mines and unexploded missiles.

As the water fills up past my eyes, the background and all my friends fade into the dark void before my eyes.

Chapter Thirty-Two

Earn Its Name

T he first thing that occurs after the world fades out when you are in the Coffin is your ears pop, just like a deep-sea dive or when an airplane loses altitude suddenly. Your mind goes weightless as well.

Nausea is common in this sucker. It's not unheard of to puke in this H_2H_2O liquid and disrupt the entire function of this machine. You can't properly target when you're floating in a pool of your own vomit.

Everything goes from pitch-black to shades of white and black. The Coffin is still in prototype mode, so color inputs and fancy racing stripes are on the to-do list. Hundreds of points fill my view, like stars in the night sky—except each of these stars want to destroy our system and prevent us from protecting millions of people's information, power grids, and more.

Imagine functioning inside a multilevel touch screen that flows like a song. Every move forward or backward takes you either a level deeper or shallower. When I told PoBones what controlling the Coffin was like, he said it must be like living in a deck of cards, where each card is its own screen. You either move forward or backward in the deck with a millimeter of movement and you can control the power of hundreds of systems and targets. For a redneck, he's a clever cookie.

Every single way you look, a cursor follows. With the intensity of a stare, combined with the retina's reaction to a single thought, the system destroys a target.

That is the power of the Coffin's software. Some might argue that artificial intelligence could do a better job. However, with someone already through our firewall and in control of a good portion of our operating systems, the value of human decisions skyrockets.

In the right corner of my screen is a number. 432. Our computer either lied to us about the numbers or the hacker's root kit corruption is just that deep.

The bots had been entering our system through two bot-sized openings. The good news is that they're currently pinched in a data stream bottleneck, fighting each other to get through the holes and slowing each other down, so for the moment the invasion is a trickle instead of a flood.

Thank goodness AI is as dumb as we humans are, at least today.

I would breathe and center myself, but our oxygen tank is as dry as a desert. Instead, I open fire.

The biggest drawback to the Coffin—aside from the risk of death—is that when I blink, the system takes that as the command to refresh the screen, losing my place and costing me seconds each time I wet my eyeballs.

Did I mention it was a prototype?

He'd never admit it, but my Bushido focus is the main reason that Cyfib picked me to operate the Coffin. Many a warrior was trained not just in meditation, but also in spatial awareness and proximity sense. That means focusing your vision on your target, no matter what happens around you.

How Cyfib knew I trained that way eludes me.

The bots are coming in fast and furious, each bouncing off our firewall, but cracking the surface. I start with the bots located just outside of the two openings in our firewall and make sure not to shoot down the ones fighting and slowing the other bots' progress.

A dozen later, a flash goes off in my left peripheral, signaling another failure in the firewall. It catches me off guard, and instinctively I blink multiple times.

Dammit. The screen reboots, costing me precious time.

When the screen returns, I lean back to study the entire board. Three openings. Of course, they aren't near each other. It seems like a strategy designed to split our resources, and suggesting the hacker knows our system.

Leaning forward, I take out the bots hitting the original firewall perimeter. The number of bots is down into the two hundreds. We are gaining ground, but the breach still exists.

The screen flickers. But I didn't blink. A small fire starts in my lungs.

"Um, Tanto, we have an issue," comes Aldy's voice in my ear. No one ever uses the word *issue* in a sentence to mean something positive. "They're hitting our power grid."

That makes sense. If whoever is in our system can make us jump to emergency power, it would cut our speed down by 80 percent.

I wish I could let Aldy know I've heard him, but the pressure in the Coffin cuts me off completely to those outside the plexiglass.

I close my eyes, preparing to double my effort. No more blinking from now on. Time is running out. The fire in my lungs grows. With my eyes wide, I use all my focus to blast perimeter bots, minus those warring with each other.

Almost immediately my eyes sting with the desire to blink. Even though I have practiced this, my eyes burn and throb at the same time. I hold my vision tight until I take out all the bots I can see. Tears pool in the corners of my eyes. Only after I destroy the bottlenecked bots do I allow my pulsing eyes a break. After I blink, only four or five fresh bots are in the distance.

If the hacker is still sending bots, his hack isn't complete. *Good.*

I lean forward four increments in the H_2H_2O liquid. My eyes enter our network. Server after server fills my vision and I spot the bots currently in our system, causing chaos. The rectangular server boxes, all connected through nodes and links, have bots attached to them like ticks.

This is good. Since they are attacking more than one server, their target is not one particular data source. They are gathering in general.

Since fewer bots are appearing, I guess someone has fixed the firewall code and plugged the other two holes. *Good.*

The last air bubble from my burning lungs creeps past my lips, rolls up my cheek, and over my left eye. Only a couple dozen attackers left. The wrecking crew that actually has oxygen can pop those pimples.

Time to get out.

I press the eject button.

Nothing happens.

My thumb must have slipped, or maybe I didn't hit it hard enough.

I press the button again.

Again, nothing happens.

A gush of water should fill my ears.

The water stays.

I pound in anger on the glass, knowing that no one outside in the War Room can either see or hear me.

The Coffin is about to earn its name one more time.

Chapter Thirty-Three

No Longer Protect My Tribe

M y lungs burn like someone has just pissed off a family of fire ants in my chest. Over three minutes have passed since the water covered my head and I took in my last good breath. My fingers creep along the Coffin where the glass shell meets the metal construction, trying to find a way out.

Nothing.

I put my back against the wall and push with all my leg strength.

Again, nothing.

I kick against the glass and punch as hard as I can. Again, and again. My struggles fail to even make a sound.

A few drops of water creep into my lungs, the way a cockroach crawls through a crack. My body thrashes, the water an unwelcome alien invader in my body. An uncontrollable tremor shakes me.

In moments, my body will thrash and then shut down. Sleep will overtake me.

There is no getting out of here.

As deaths go, this isn't the worst. A Bushi must always not just anticipate one's passing, but welcome it. I've always feared I will go slowly, withering away in the corner of a nursing home, strung up by IVs and beeping machines designed to keep me alive but only reminding me of my fading mortality.

However, going out that way would mean I'd lived a long life. Twenty-eight years on this rock is a blip, barely over a third of what the average man gets.

I don't think about God, or whether I'll wind up in a place filled with either clouds or flames. I worry about those that I've sworn to protect. Will Quidlee still try to escape? Who knows? Maybe AldenSong will help him.

Poor Aldy. He'll take my passing the hardest. Maybe the Samoan will put in a word with the Big Man Upstairs, and I'll get to finally be at peace. Of course, if he doesn't do that, I'm going to haunt the hell out of that big softy. Out of all the good that is AldenSong, I'm going to miss his big smile and the way when he hugs you, your body basically morphs into his chest as his arms wrap you tight. He is the human equivalent of a loving beanbag chair.

A spasm shoots up my right leg out of the blue. My first thought is that this limb wants to live more than the rest of my body, but it actually comes from my implant.

Is it trying to shock me back to life?

I don't know.

I'm going to miss PoBones and Foshi_Taloa. One talks too much, while the other never speaks, but they are part of my family.

Barca.

Barca will still be here, in our home, after I die. Without me to keep him in check, he's going to run rampant. There is no telling what and how much damage he will do.

Before my eyes close in final deep sleep, a sense of regret and longing fills my brain.

I can no longer protect my tribe from this monster.

Chapter Thirty-Four

Spring

I come to lying on the floor, coughing and spitting water as the world flashes in and out of focus.

AldenSong puts his arm under my back and lifts me up to a sitting position. He wraps me in his bed comforter like a firefighter who has just saved me from a burning building.

I lean forward and cough so hard, my back spasms. Even my kidneys hurt from these violent outbursts. This must be what it is like to smoke two packs a day for fifty years.

As my lungs settle down and let me hold a breath for more than two seconds, I drink in the scene before me. All my tribe stands over me, concerned yet joyful.

PoBones nods and smiles at me. His crooked teeth are a joy before my pulsing eyes.

Foshi_Taloa sends me a thumbs-up. That is probably as close to a shout-out as I'll ever get from him. I love it.

Quidlee squints at me, almost unsure of how I am alive.

That makes two of us, Rook.

Cyfib and Barca both stand with arms crossed, heads slightly tilted back. Their eyes focus on the four screens, watching data instead of my Lazarus ass. I guess the warden had finally arrived while I was temporarily dead.

"Did . . . we . . . get . . . them?" The individual words eject from my throat after each exhale.

"Not yet, but we're close," says Aldy.

"How . . . did I . . . get out?"

"Him."

I glance over to where AldenSong is pointing and would've gasped if my lungs didn't hate me right now.

Barca.

Big bully Barca saved me?

"How?"

"Barca had some gut instinct that you were stuck," says Quidlee, sitting cross-legged next to me. "So, he hit the emergency release lever on the tank. You flopped out of the tank like a dead fish, but PoBones knows CPR and you came back to us."

The only thing more shocking than the redneck knowing a medical lifesaving technique is Barca knowing where the emergency release is on the tank.

I owe this monster my life.

Maybe to others, that wouldn't mean much. To a Bushido, it changes everything.

As I am about to push myself up, Barca's hand appears under my chin. I look up at the man's solemn face, as unemotional as an Easter Island statue. I grab his hand with both of mine. With one yank, I am on my feet and Barca's mouth is at my right ear.

Maybe this is the change I need to see this man in a new light.

"Today was nothing."

Barca's whispered words confuse me. Is he telling me that his actions of saving my life took no effort? Would I have granted this man the same courtesy? I know I could never take a life, but is inaction to save a life the same as pulling the trigger myself?

It isn't until he lets go of my hand and I stumble away that I notice what he had slipped into my grip.

It is a simple spring, silver and bouncy, one that is thinner than my pinky finger but half as long.

Something that would fit perfectly inside the eject button of the Coffin.

Chapter Thirty-Five

We've Been Played

S on of a bitch. I want to lash at the monster, but we are still in the middle of a hack. This must wait.

I clear my throat, and crawl-walk over to AldenSong's shoulder and scan his monitor. "Can you snare the worm and find the objective?"

AldenSong's hands fly across the keyboard like he is on fast-forward as he pumps all our intel and data through our system.

"Tracer bullet sent, Tanto." Aldy chews his thumbnails as one of our own designed worms follows the diagnostics scripts through our system.

"Come-on-come-on."

I am exhausted from my near death and so desperately want to take a seat. However, with Lance-a-Little gone, we need a general leading this expedition.

In my time before the Double-H, in team hacks, I preferred not to lead. The role of wrecking ball or Dam Breaker worked for me because that meant my part of the hack was getting to smash through the firewalls. It's a single task and I hate multitasking. I am even better than AldenSong. However, I am not the best in the Double-H.

With a split second to breathe, I praise the work done.

"Thank you, everyone. The bots slowed a lot, so flooding with static images worked. PoBones, what'd you use?"

"The obvious." The Cajun points at his crotch. "Dick pics."

Everyone's clickety-clacks in the room slow.

"You have over a terabyte of dick pics just ready to send out?"

"Wouldn't you like to know?"

I shake my head as he cackles.

"Da bandwidth slowed because I routed a ton of instant messaging files from some outdated Yahoo! teenagers' forum about the best angle for dick pics. Tons of useless yet high megabyte files. This jammed up da bad guy's anti-virus filter during transfer."

"But did you ever find out the best angle?" asks Aldy. "Asking for a friend, of course."

As the worm finishes its crawl, AldenSong turns his head my way. "Do you think we're too late?"

"Possible, but not likely. Results?"

"On screen."

I step back and glance at the giant screens. The output makes no sense. There was virtually no bandwidth usage attributable to anyone other than the people in this room. Everything is accounted for.

Except it isn't. Someone is showing us false data.

"We've been played."

Chapter Thirty-Six

That's How We Catch Him

We've been chasing a decoy. That is exactly what just happened. When the attack was on, my gut told me that the hacker or hackers activated a rootkit behind our firewall.

We stopped the attack, but we can't tell the damage. We cannot trust our readouts. If this hacker installed fabricated log files, we would play into his hand even further.

Damnation.

Now everyone in the room is waiting on me to jump in and save the day. I'd failed to figure out that this was a two-pronged attack, one with the bots, and the other with the hidden rootkit. The first hit was to disrupt us into protecting our base, while the second attack was the one that hurt the most.

"Aldy, force a reboot of the primary server and then put it in safe mode."

"T, that'll mean our tracking won't pinpoint as well."

"We have no choice. Do it."

A few clicks later, two jumbotrons go blank and then flash back to the main code.

"Dogs, status check?"

It is just now that I notice his gold tie and blue suit. It occurs to me to wonder what all the flash and color means, but we just don't have the time to dwell on sartorial choices. Also, his shoes are black polished leather, not his daily spurs. I log it away for later.

The new guard is standing next to him, so there is a chance the warden is up to speed on my leadership of this fuster-cluck. Instead of insulting or striking me, Cyfib merely glances at the Coffin before returning his gaze my way.

I take the initiative. "Sir, they released a rootkit within the system. A reboot should remove the executable worm."

"Dog, there is a world of difference between the words *should* and *will*. Are our firewalls secure?"

"Yes, sir."

"Proceed with the hunt."

He leans back and crosses his arms. Something is different. Maybe he's gotten promoted out of here. Maybe he's gotten laid. Whatever it is, he is letting me run the team. I will not screw up. The only thing worse than Cyfib in his general bad mood is if I ruin his current good one.

I shake my head. Time to stop filling it with thoughts that don't matter right now.

"Aldy, how many pings?"

"Give or take, ten."

That is not bad, but it also isn't good. The hacker will not make it easy on us by using a static IP.

"Is it in random flux or systematically changing?"

"Why would that matter?" he asks, but the way he shakes his head means he realizes where my mind is headed as soon as the words are out of his mouth. "Curse your scrawny hide for being right all the damn time. Checking. Checking. Okay, it is increasing each time by ten and we have evenly distributed locational points . . ."

Cyfib grips my shoulder and I tense up. However, instead of disciplining me, he points not to our system's horribly low score of one, but instead to the map of pings.

"Sir, we have multiple zones and are taking—"

"Dog, look closer."

I stop and stare. *What has the madman seen?* Then it hits me: it isn't quantity, it is quality.

"Holy cow."

Cyfib releases his grip and I swear that the faintest smile crosses his lips. *No time to dwell on it.*

"PoBones, lock in on Philadelphia and start running pentests on broadband service providers."

"Whoa, hold up . . ." AldenSong's focus on his own monitor never breaks. "Tanto, every time I get a lock on an address, it changes, but I'm not losing the guy yet."

"Save the energy." I roll Aldy away from his screen and point at our map of all the pings.

Aldy shakes his head. "Great, now we have two more pings."

"We have four more."

"No, there are two more . . ." AldenSong stops mid-sentence and his jaw flops open.

Cyfib is right. We are all staring at the forest when we should've seen the trees.

"The node on Philadelphia is larger than the rest because it is actually three overlapping smaller pings."

"Correct, dog."

I say what we all are thinking. "The hacker is bouncing back and forth from there because he's refreshing that node because it is the closest to him."

PoBones finishes my thought. "That's where his downloads are going."

"And that's how we catch him."

Chapter Thirty-Seven

Destroy Me or Save the Day

"Slow down Philadelphia."

"On it, T!" PoBones pops up a new window and is about to blast the City of Brotherly Love with enough digital noise that every service provider's bandwidth speed will be about to grind to a halt.

"What're you using?" AldenSong beats me to the question. Hopefully, PoBones won't reuse his dick pic material from earlier because that might get us in a little hot water when the data floods the general public's web browsers and bandwidth quotas.

"Don't getcha panties inna wad, ya prudes. I'm using every buy, sell, hold, and trade currently in the S&P 500. If that doesn't work, I'll open the floodgates."

Perfect. The service providers will see the bandwidth as a glitch from some hedge fund's network and not pursue it.

"Foshi, lock the grid from outgoing traffic."

The quiet man's black ponytail bobs as he nods in agreement.

The second screen to the right fills with all the numbers relating to regional raw broadband data.

"Now that we've got Philadelphia surrounded, begin filtering now. Double-check every outbound transmission and cross-reference them with our attacker's previous pings' origins."

Every single user, every single device connected to the network in the city lights up the map on the grid.

Then half fades away.

Then half of that.

We are narrowing down our perp's location.

This is too easy. Why is the guy still online? What does he need so badly that it would take him this long to find it?

"Got him! He's part of the BanLock Broadband network. Got the IP address he's filtering through. Boom! We've got a lock on their multiple transmissions. One is in DC, the main one . . . location: Zhanaul, a small town on the border of Russia and Kazakhstan. Whoever is on the other end of that transmission is sucking up a majority of the bandwidth. Downloading all log files and about to shut down all connections . . ."

Without skipping a beat, I say, "Get the files, but hold off on the disconnect, PoBones."

Everyone in the room stops typing and looks my way. Something in my gut tells me to push harder on this guy. We have only touched on the real reason behind this attack: to plant a rootkit.

What is the rootkit trying to find in our databases?

AldenSong glances around the room and takes the initiative when it appears no one else will.

"Tanto, we've got enough data for the arrest."

"We've never been this late to a party. I want to know why it was thrown."

It is a dangerous plan, and Cyfib will check me hard against the figurative and literal walls if I am wrong.

"Something in my gut says this is bigger than a cyberattack. Piggyback this guy's connection and run a relay over him."

"Well, damn, that's damn near impossible to do."

I want to say to AldenSong *that's not helping*, but his doubt *is* helping my case.

When I don't respond, he continues, "No one here has ever done that before on a live system."

"One of us has." I glance over at the warden.

Prisoners do not address the warden directly, do not speak unless spoken to.

But to demand that we follow my new plan over Cyfib's locked-in rules? That is about as close to a mutiny as it gets in here.

I've played my hand. In all my years here, this is the one thing I have on the warden. It is at this point he will either destroy me or save the day.

Chapter Thirty-Eight

Unreachable Deadline

C yfib's eyes look my way, but he does not focus on me. He looks past me. He stares my way, but his vision clearly sees something else. Behind his gray eyes that shift at times from light to dark, this man about fifteen years older than me runs scenarios.

The irony of our prison situation isn't that hackers are catching other hackers. It is that the biggest hacker out there is enslaving others to protect not just businesses, but the same department he almost destroyed.

The rumor is that Cyfib founded DISRUPT, the guild of hackers that historically and digitally gang banged the Defense Department's servers in '96 for no other reason than just because they could. They screwed with the brass for over a year without a break. And the whole time, the media made sure the world knew about our government's incompetence.

Their joyride of successful mayhem ended when the White House then created what would ultimately become the Department of Homeland Security, with a focus on IT infrastructure. Unfortunately, the initiators of this "preventative" division of the United States of America, President Bush and his posse, were John Wayne cowboys who knew how to drop bombs and provide shock and awe on a world stage but understood nothing about shutting down digital mavericks. As the comedian Dennis Miller said, "Bush played checkers, not chess." The creation of this agency probably fueled more hackers than it stopped.

The agency focused on short-term strikes. The best hacking focuses on long-term strategies.

This and a bunch of other world-news-making hacks led to the creation of our current hell: Hackers' Haven. Who better to protect the U.S.' IT infrastructure than the very people who could easily destroy it?

As for Cyfib's history, well, it's mostly rumor. But what I've seen with my own two eyes only supports those rumors in my mind. Like I said, I am probably the *second*-best Dam Breaker in Hackers' Haven.

Without a doubt, Cyfib is the best.

Very few hackvicts know how skilled he is. I hate him, and yet he gets credit where credit is due.

It was by pure chance I discovered the warden was the best all-in-one package I'd ever seen. Five years back, after completing after-hours inventory, I walked in on him in the War Room, capturing four Croatian hackers trying to breach our firewall. It was the foiled hack that inspired our current Anne-Frank-hide-the-Nazis-are-coming level of alarm system we enjoy today.

The man was bouncing between three machines. With one, he was tracing. The next he was dam breaking. The final one he was looping. Until that point, I thought looping was just a myth that hackers had made up to sound cool.

Looping is the ultimate multitask in the hacker community. It means that you ghost or copy the files of the system that you are hacking just enough to perform a live-action mirroring of it. Traditionally, ghosting works like using jumper cables on a car: you take one working battery to charge-slash-copy another battery. This process takes hours, and the copying system must be in a standby state. What looping does is it takes key components of the system and lets you interact with another system without the other party knowing you are doing it.

In comparing looping to tracing, imagine taking a piece of paper and a pencil, then putting the pencil on an engraving. If you rub the pencil across the raised print, you get a decent copy of the engraving. This is like that, but it will not be a complete copy, like with operating system files and historical data. However, it is enough that what your target sees on their monitor you see on yours.

Looping, when done perfectly, can enable you to take control of a target's system without alerting them. It will even keep you logged in even if they are trying to kick you from their system.

The difficulty—impossibility, some would say—with looping is that it requires not just intercepting the upstream and downstream files but doing so in a way that the data still arrives on the hacker's system without any screen lag or flickers. If the hacker's system flashes or there is a spike in workstation processing, you're cooked and your target will shut down their systems.

The only way to keep that from happening is to adjust your uploading and downloading bandwidth to the *exact* same frequency as the target's. This requires a person to manipulate the data transfer by hand.

I've watched enough cheesy '80s action movies to say this is like jumping an 18-wheeler, flatbed truck off a bridge and landing on the bed of another 18-wheeler below—one that is not only going the same speed but also doesn't crash when the truck lands.

Even the boys from *The Dukes of Hazard* never pulled this maneuver off.

But Cyfib could. Somehow, he managed to lay a copy on top of the Croatian hackers' system and hijacked it after he recorded their activity on our servers. Using some code that only he has access to, like a maestro conducting an orchestra, he manipulated the flow of data in and out of our servers perfectly.

It was like watching Houdini cut himself in half and never stop talking to the crowd: beautiful, sadistic, and mind-blowing.

Of course, Cyfib found me snooping and deducted twenty units from me.

Fake money well spent.

Now in the War Room, Cyfib approaches me. I have just called Odinson down from Valhalla to join us mere mortals in the fields. The least I expect is a punch in the face. Instead, he cuts Foshi_Taloa a harsh glance that our quiet man rightfully takes as a command to jump up.

After a flash of keystrokes, Cyfib enters his command system. "Dog, use your software to give me a parallel port to the target."

Shit. My knees all but buckle. He knows about SkipTrace. *Of course he does.*

If the devil is in the details, Cyfib's middle name might as well be Fine Print. I grab a keyboard, enter my commands, and get the warden what he needs: an open port on our target's IP address.

"Sent to your system, sir."

The warden never acknowledges the transfer. His laser focus is already moving forward.

At this moment, I don't feel the crushing weight of Hackers' Haven. Even AldenSong sends me the biggest smile I've seen since he found an emulator of the original Wolfenstein first-person shooter on a server.

I ping the target and filter his bandwidth spend through our access to the Internet provider's relay points. I send the info to the third screen above our heads. Cyfib glances at it and enters something into his system.

On the second screen is, for lack of a better word, the frequency that our planned looping system is on. On the third screen is the frequency of our perp. The numbers are close to one another, but not exact.

Not yet.

Cyfib's hands fly across the keyboard. The screen above him ramps up the download speed to match the target but overshoots it by four megabytes. However, he evens out the upload speed to within a kilobyte of the target's.

The warden stares at the giant screens and squints his eyes. He holds one finger over his keyboard's enter button.

Like playing an arcade game that requires you to hit a buzzer to stop at just the right moment and line up with the prize in the bin, Cyfib waits. For a second, I think the same numbers on the two screens overlap. Maybe my eyes are playing tricks on me.

I see it again. *Why is he waiting?*

Then it hits me: by the time the numbers are on the screen, it is too late. He's waiting to predict the split second before the numbers align.

Click.

He presses the button. Our four giant screens fill with media windows that are not ours.

The screens appear frozen. One shows an intersection map with dots on the buildings. The way those dots form a square it looks like a kill-box shape, meaning anything that enters the area meets four different angles of gun and/or rocket fire.

The screens aren't moving, though. Maybe the hackers had detected a change in processing speed. Tension in the room amps up as we all wonder the same thing.

Are they aware that we are watching them?

Then the screens shift from a coded window to a live traffic one of Constitution Avenue and 2nd Street in DC.

No screens shut down.

We are in.

A cheer erupts in the room like the winning touchdown thingee has happened in the World Series or whatever sport has touchdowns. I don't know because I don't watch people play with balls.

However, the warden's face stays stern and focused, his cheeks pulled in like he's just sucked on a lemon.

"Dogs, the target will notice our intrusion in under five minutes. Finish this correctly, or you all go to the Hole."

Nothing screws up a plan like an unreachable deadline.

Chapter Thirty-Nine

Unspoiled

"Tanto, you seeing what I'm seeing?" Aldy points to the live feed camera. Rather than the street and traffic, the camera focuses on the entrance and exit for LOT 48525.

"Good eye, Aldy. Someone get us a reverse lookup of what we're seeing."

"Done, son!"

Of course, I should have known PoBones would be the first Johnny on the spot with any information ammo.

"There's a motor pool for government vehicles there."

"Okay, Foshi_Taloa, get us a list of recent file downloads from the target."

"You sure we haven't missed our window?" Aldy says, tense. He has a point, but something in my gut tells me we are still in the game.

"If they'd already gotten what they needed, they would've shut everything down . . . that one, open it."

The first screen lights up with a list of coded entries, the kind that need a cypher to decrypt.

"Anyone got a clue which software works with these?"

No one answers.

"Aldy, I need you to look through the target's database for digital receipts. Look for something ending in *dot gov*."

"On it."

The big man opens the target's database and enters the search parameters. Within ten seconds, the results pop up, producing two files.

"Got it. They spent thirty-five bucks and change on some software recently."

"We need exact numbers for this to work."

"Thirty-five fifty-two."

"PoBones, cross-reference that amount with government discounts of software. Barca, can you find the filename extension they're looking for?"

It is a risk to include this monster in our search, but it is a simple task. Hopefully, the goodwill will stick.

"Dot em pee ess," says Barca.

Aldy pops open a search engine and searches for file properties before I can ask.

"Ducky says it's some type of scheduling system," Aldy says, referring to the untraceable search engine Duck Duck Go, a personal favorite of those in the privacy community.

"Ding!" chimes PoBones. "Car Renter Lite is the software. It's for checking in and out cars."

"Perfect. That's the file they're in. Someone download a demo and open the file."

Within seconds, Foshi finds the software and uploads the file to our screens. A travel itinerary pops up with a name we all know: David Masterson, the U.S. Secretary of Defense. According to the readout, he is six minutes from departure, and these hackers are setting up a kill box for him.

Speaking of time, we finished in four minutes and fifty seconds. No Hole time for us. For now.

If it weren't for Cyfib, we'd have flags flown at half-mast tomorrow.

As if the devil knows I am thinking about him, Cyfib says, "Dogs, shut down their system and get the log files on the server. I'll contact my bosses and they will contact the target's security detail."

A smattering of *Yes sirs* pop up around the War Room. The absolute best part of Cyfib's looping means we are through any and all firewalls for the attacker's machine. I send a packet into their system I call Program Lidocaine. It is a worm I invented back in the early two thousands. It shuts down a system slowly and freezes everything up to and including the BIOS system.

In layman's terms, it puts the computer in a coma.

We watch as the target's screen twitches, as if there is a serious bandwidth lag. A curser jumps across the screen. The hacker has no clue what's happening. Then the screen flickers, a blue screen of death appears, and we lose contact with the target.

Someone's pants just went brown.

As everyone cheers, the warden puts his finger in my chest.

"Dog, get to the Infirmary to get checked out and then come to my office immediately after."

No good moment goes unspoiled around here.

Chapter Forty

Blow Up in My Face

In the Infirmary, Dr. Fel touches my neck with his icy hands. A million thoughts attack my brain. They all come back to the same question: *How did Barca know how to sabotage the Coffin so that I'd be at his mercy?*

There were no blueprints outside of our servers for LODIS. As far as anyone in Hackers' Haven knew, the idea originated from some blueprints we discovered when we reverse- engineered a bunch of Latvians who attempted to break through our firewall about a year ago. The end result was we broke their wall first and found these plans among their log files. From this, Cyfib ordered us to build the prototype. Thank goodness some of the residents of Double-H have engineering degrees.

So, how did Barca know about the workings of the Coffin?

Maybe he took time to sneak in, take the thing apart, and re-engineer it.

That's what I would've done.

Did he let all the oxygen out of the tank? AldenSong and I both thought, maybe, the tank had run empty on its own with a leak or something. Now that hypothesis isn't as solid.

For every paranoid query, I have some sort of answer. Except for these two lingering questions: *How did Barca know about the hack?*

Every possible answer to that question led me to the big one underpinning it all: *Who is Barca, really?*

As Dr. Fel runs his cold stethoscope across my back and chest, occasionally asking me to take a breath, another tremor shoots through my right leg.

"Does that happen often?"

"Maybe . . . I don't know . . . why?"

"It's probably nothing."

I'd spent enough time in hospitals with my drugged-out mother to know that the words *probably nothing* were the same as *don't look down*.

"You've got one of the oldest functioning security chips in the compound, an outdated model, so it may get faulty."

Yay. Even my leg wants to punish me today.

"We're going to run an EKG and MRI on you, just to be sure."

Great. More time stuck in here while Barca soaks in his heroic accolades. He's locked in his untouchable, good-hearted status for now. I can no longer openly cast doubts about his good intentions actually being manipulations.

I have to confront him and let him know I am not afraid to die, that his scare tactics will never work on me, even if they end with my death. The best thing to do to a bully is stand up to them and watch them crumble.

Of course, there is no way to predict how badly this choice will blow up in my face.

Chapter Forty-One

Spaceship with a Hole in It

When I leave the Infirmary and head to the warden's office, my sphincter is tight enough I could rename it Jaws of Life.

The Box of Death takes no visitors that aren't guards. For him to call anyone in there, let alone me, is as rare as a unicorn riding a unicycle.

My feet move for me, taking me to the warden's mirrored door before I've half-processed what's happening.

I knock on the glass, and it produces a higher noise than I expected, almost as if I just knocked on a small, hollow vase.

"Come."

I twist the doorknob and leave reality as I enter a cyber-Neverland.

Inside the cube is the largest consecutive computing station I've ever seen. The entire room bristles with electricity and a few hairs on my head stand up.

To the left of me is a parade of input devices: four keyboards, three different types of mice, an ocular headset, and a pair of noise-canceling headphones. And next to that is a simple notepad, Bic pen, and Cyfib's white stone pipe.

On the double-sided mirrors that serve as walls are streams of data and command prompts. The warden is using the glass as monitor space as well as a view of the War Room. The floor is a clear map of the United States with flashing green, yellow, red, and black dots. Even the ceiling shows live news reports from six different channels.

Cyfib picks up the pipe and places it in the corner of his left lip. He chews it as he studies me. I don't know whether my capture of the hacker is praiseworthy or demands condemning. Either consequence is on the plate for the warden.

"I want Gakunodu operational by the end of the month."

Of all the sentences my mind predicted Cyfib would say, that was not one of them.

Gakunodu. When I first started this project, I named it Gakunodu because that is where Bushido warriors most felt safe before, during, and after a battle. It was a sacred tent where even the most battle-stressed and wounded warriors found refuge.

In Hackers' Haven, Gakunodu is a trap, not a refuge. It is the automated version of what we hackers do: it lures in dumb people looking for illegal things. It also is a way to trap hordes of dummies in fast succession rather than our apparently inefficient one-at-a-time approach.

I volunteered to build this trap with one purpose: if I built it, I'd know how to destroy it as well. And it would have to be destroyed, one way or another. It is a society killer. Or it would be if I ever got it live.

"Sir, this project has not been alpha tested; there's no telling how buggy it will be on a beta test, much less—"

Cyfib jams the sharp end of his pipe into my side, and I scream out.

"Tanto?" AldenSong whispers my name from the War floor below and his voice sounds in the Cube of Death as clearly as if he was in here with us. One screen in the Box of Death shifts from data to show a glowing circle. In that orb is Aldy.

Cyfib has the room bugged so well that he not only hears every word, but he can even automatically track the speaker.

The Cube of Death is not soundproof.

I meet my assailant's gaze. Cyfib is easily fifty to sixty pounds heavier than I am, but every inch of the bastard is pure muscle. His gray eyes stare not at me, but through me.

"Dog . . ."

I grimace but keep my gaze firm.

There was a time I'd cower. Maybe he remembers it. When I refused to hunt and went without food for six days. When he put me in solitary for a week because I blatantly let a target go. Some prisons call their solitary confinement areas holes because they are dark and damp. Others are bright, with lights that never go out.

Ours are a mixture of those hells: not only do the lights shift at unpredictable times from pitch-black to strobe-light effect, but they thrash metal music blasts at ear-bursting intensity.

Since my time in the hole, I'd gotten much better at hiding my losses. I'd even created a way to fake my wins, at least temporarily: I would submit corrupted log files to our server that created a sliver of reasonable doubt for a judge or jury over the defendant, or in other words, my target.

Back in the Cube of Death, I take a breath before responding with the obligatory, "Yes, sir." The warden yanks his pipe out of my gut and my right hand covers the bleeding wound.

I know not to immediately answer him with an agreeable response because he would change the timeline to an even sooner date. Cyfib loves to move the goalposts, to make it impossible to please him. Which is why I let him think one month to finish the project is a win for him and a loss for me.

What sucks harder than a spaceship with a hole in it is that now that I'm done stalling, I must figure out how to destroy Gakunodu without destroying myself as well.

Chapter Forty-Two

Some Choices Are More Damning than Others

M y brain is processing everything as I walk down from the Cube of Death. I'll have to wait to get stitched up, but at least the bleeding from my wound is slowing. Cyfib just took advantage of our stopping the hack and caught me when I was most vulnerable. That's what the devil does: he brings you up right before he slams you down.

Gakunodu. *Damnation.*

I thought this program was on the back burner. The team is pulling in good numbers. Something must have changed for this project to require a quick deadline. I wonder if someone above Cyfib's pay grade must've decided our current kill levels aren't enough.

Honestly, the program is 80 percent done. It only needs a working compiler. Without this part of the program, Gakunodu is like the underpants gnomes in *South Park*. The gnomes sneak in at night and steal your underpants. Their business plan goes something like: first, steal underpants. Then something happens, but they don't know what. Then, of course, they profit. How, no one seems to know, because of that missing second step.

That's when it hits me: Cyfib is in a good suit and tie.

He had a meeting. I wonder if it was a meeting with someone in the corporation who owns the facility. That would make sense. The powers that be want that piracy-enforcement money. Lance-a-Little uncovered a file a few years back that was a pay-for-play contract that was mostly redacted. In it, some company that owns this joint gets not only a bit of federal funding for housing us inmates but also a cut of the court's fines. So, the lawyers get a percentage, then the government, and finally this company. Where we hackvicts are bringing in a few drops of revenue, Gakunodu turns on the money faucet full force.

So, let's do some simple math. Whether or not I like it, I'm a resident of the Free Country of Texas. We've got around twenty-five million residents living here that range in age from babies in diapers to people in adult diapers. Surely not half of all those people are illegally downloading things, so let's say half of those are people over fifty and under eighteen. That leaves twelve point five million. Further, white people do dumb crap. I'm a fine example because I'm white and I got caught doing dumb crap, so let's just count my fellow saltines in this equation. I think we're probably 65 to 70 percent of the Texas population, so 65 percent of our number of possible perps is around eight million people.

Then let's knock it down one last time and say that only white men, the kind that scream *Hey y'all watch this* before they die, are the only ones doing illegal downloading. That splits the number in half from eight million to four million. If 50 percent of this new population has illegally downloaded or streamed a movie this year alone, and that's about right on a national average, that means two million youngish, dumb white boys are online robbing the cinemas and movie houses of their money in the Free Country of Texas.

Two million people. The maximum fine for video piracy is a hundred K, so let's halve that as well, say that the lawyers plea down the fine to fifty thousand dollars. Further, out of the fifty-thousand-dollar fine, let's say the company that owns my soul takes in only 10 percent of the booty and the rest goes to the lawyers and the government, in that order.

Finally, if the lawyers can successfully prosecute, sentence, and heavily fine one out of every ten dumb white boys out of that two million perps number, that means that, at a minimum return, one billion dollars goes straight to the company.

For doing virtually nothing but letting my code run its course.

A billion dollars.

And we're only talking about a percentage of a percentage of a percentage here.

In one state. Out of fifty.

And that's not even the part that bothers me.

What bothers me is that, if Gakunodu goes live, with its scope and reach, it will be the War on Drugs to the power of twenty.

The people downloading and streaming movies are not just ignorant. They're broke. Fifty thousand dollars of fines will destroy them. The guy downloading illegally is also working the Mc-Fryer at his McJobby-Job. He won't see fifty thousand dollars in two years, maybe three. That means bankruptcy.

For millions.

The sheer scale of social and economic consequences of that many bankruptcies is almost inconceivable.

I can't let that happen. By the Bushido Code, a warrior is not only responsible for their actions and words but also their consequences. It is the principle of *Chu*.

I need to think, and I do some of my best thinking on our roof.

The roof of our building is a half-court basketball court. You know the type, a single basket on a slab of concrete with lines on it. I'm not a sports guy, so it looks like someone drew random half circles on concrete because they love geometry. Now, a pathetic garden was here before several hackvicts pooled their units and got this sucker built. I'll admit, I chipped in, even though I'd rather eat a melon than bounce something that looks like one.

The garden was something that Lance-a-Little started with me. An escape from the screens and humming workstations. However, the Houston heat and poor irrigation only allowed us to grow leafy things that can thrive off the horrible overhead sun. It is basically the evil sun from Mario 3 that chases you around and tries to kill you.

PoBones was one of the first supporters of this change a while back. He loves the sport, though he said he plays like a drunken sailor at Mardi Gras. AldenSong enjoyed gardening, but he wants to watch people do things that make them happy, so I guess that was why he spent units on it.

When I open the door, I spot AldenSong practicing his bouncy bounces. He must've snuck out when he realized I was leaving the warden's office. Big guy must not have wanted me to notice his mother hen's level of concern about me.

Next to him is Quidlee.

"Hey, Tanto . . ." AldenSong's pronunciation of my name gets lost in a mumble as Quidlee makes a beeline straight for me. Bags are under his burning eyes and several days of stubble cover his flushed face.

He pins my head against the fence. As soon as the back of my head touches the fence, an alarm sounds. It is louder than the new prisoner siren, but higher in frequency, almost like a fluctuating air horn. Even the slightest touch or weight of anything greater than a feather on this fence alerts the guards.

Within seconds, Guard Fontana's booming voice blasts over the intercom, "Convicts, cease your aggressive behavior immediately."

We used to have a guard in the now-empty tower that is sixteen feet above us, just outside of the fence. Then the warden upgraded his anti-escape game. Now what keeps us from escaping, besides the barbed wire fence, is the motion sensor nail gun hidden atop the guard tower. It shoots carbon steel and galvanized coated nine-inch nails at speeds well over four hundred miles an hour. Now, a bullet moves at eight hundred miles an hour. However, your odds of dodging a four-hundred-mile-per-hour projectile versus an eight-hundred-mile-per-hour one is probably the same: zero.

Quidlee lets go, but still leans into my ear and hisses, "Why shouldn't I snap your neck right here and now, you coward?"

I meet his raging gaze. My father didn't teach me a lot about life, but he taught me to take compliments with a bowed head, and to face insults head-on.

It's not a pissing contest, but the rook steps back first. That's a good sign in my book.

I lean my head back as Quidlee walks away. The Houston sun is right in my eyes, interrogating me in the rook's absence. There isn't anything to say. I had wronged him, plain and simple. The way forward and possibly past this was not up to me, but him.

AldenSong rolls the basketball between his hands. "Why's everybody so touchy?"

"Excuse you, fatso?" asks Quidlee.

Aldy responds by spinning the basketball on his middle finger and angling it in front of Quidlee's face.

The rook swats the ball away. When next our eyes met, he avoids my stare and scratches at his arms.

He'd been twitching again, and not in the nervous way. While I understood his energy and rage, the underlying darkness in his eyes reminds me of another addict. This one traded the Atari I rebuilt at age nine for a pill bottle full of escapism so she wouldn't have to worry about me and the voices.

Be wary about trusting addicts because they don't trust themselves. When stressed or confronted, they have two speeds: cower or rage.

Quidlee punches the fence, grimaces, and attempts to shake the pain away. The fence alarm squawks only once, so no guards appear from the inside.

"This is all bullshit, man," says Quidlee. "We're in prison, man! I can't let you wrong me and get away with it. That's weakness. Everyone will notice, and I'll be just a chump."

Letting things slide, especially those that are unfixable, is a kindness. And, while I might counter Quidlee's rage with a dozen examples where kindness was the answer behind these walls, he is in no shape to hear them. He so reminds me of myself years ago, before I wound up in here. When I'd abandoned the real world for a cyber one. When my questionable enterprises on *dem Internets* gained me money but cost me what made me, well, me.

Quidlee is still new here, so I decide to harness what he knows about the outside world to relate to him.

"Quidlee, who do you have outside of these walls?"

"I have Screw-You is what I have."

"Scru'Que . . . is that, like, the name of your brother?" AldenSong chimes in, almost giggling, "because you're Japanese?"

"I'm Korean, you Tungan."

"And I'm Samoan, you little—"

"Neither of you are making the point you think you are," I say, knowing full well I have zero right to make any comments on race or stereotypes since I'm as white as the day is long.

Aldy counters, "Well, you're so Caucasian that your blood type is chalk."

The tiny hackvict stops pacing. His beady eyes signal to me an upcoming smart-ass response, but then his mind must've slowed his roll, because he takes a breath.

"I have a sister. Well, half-sister."

And that's a half-start. The honorable part of me wants to let him know that I still have the picture of his sister in my back pocket. I do not know why, but something about her gives me strength in a way that I cannot fully explain.

"What is her name?"

"Penny . . ." Quidlee punches the fence again, though I know there is more to this rage than what the rook is showing us. A half-chirp from the fence alarm blips.

I wait in silence.

"I messed her up, man . . ."

He paces before continuing. "Penny, you see, well . . ." Quidlee stammers and rocks side to side with the nervousness of a kid on stage at a spelling bee for close to a minute before he speaks again. "Our neighborhood wasn't exactly safe, and it wasn't exactly dangerous, if you get my drift."

The gray area of living. My mother didn't teach me much, but her actions did. She purposely chose to hang our hats in those areas. If you are the richest person in a poor neighborhood, you get broken into or mugged. However, if you're the poorest in a rich neighborhood, you get the cops at your door every Friday because of an *anonymous* caller reporting *suspicious behavior*. If you live somewhere in the middle ground, everyone keeps to themselves.

"I'd always hacked for fun. Small shit. Then these guys, the Eighth Street Bealers, approached me, offered me a job to shut down the server to a rival Memphis gang, Memphibians. They're the guys with tattoos of *The Creature from the Black Lagoon*, you know, that big-eye, scaley-looking sucker, on their necks. The Bealers told me it was a server where they were storing pictures and movies. I didn't even think to ask what type."

I knew the type. Everyone here knew. Hell, if I were out of these walls, I'd have shut that group down just because of my moral code. Then again, maybe I just tell myself that now to tolerate who I currently am.

So, Quidlee screwed up and took money for some black hat hacking. We all make mistakes, though some choices are more damning than others. Something in my gut told me that someone in the Bealers let slip that they'd forced the shutdown of the Memphibian's kiddie porn or the like. There's nothing that screws up a completed hack like someone bragging about it.

"What happened?"

"It's not what happened." Quidlee stares at the ground. "It's what is currently happening."

Chapter Forty-Three

Something I Can Actually Do

Two minutes had passed in silence as Quidlee's thoughts warred in his head. His closed eyes and bowed head, along with his bushy eyebrows trying to touch, reminded me of a level of pain I knew all too well.

Silence is key in Bushido life; many a successful warrior took time to plan how to respond to a situation. Quidlee licks his lips, and a noise rolls out of his throat that sounds like air escaping from an inner tube.

"The Memphibians found out where we lived." Quidlee rubs his palms with his fingernails and spits on the ground. "The sons of bitches didn't even hurt me . . ."

Bastards like that never do; to get to you, they hurt those around you.

A car alarm in the distance honks several times. I know the question that I must ask, but the words hurt as they slide out of my throat as if they are attached to sandpaper.

"Is Penny still alive?"

He remains silent. *Why did I ask that?* I didn't even know the girl. I instantly regret asking, but I want to know. No, I *need* to know.

"Yeah . . . she is," he takes a shaky breath. "The assault was a warning . . . they left a note stapled to her forehead."

Tears choke Quidlee as he bites his cheek, probably hard enough to draw blood.

"She's no victim," he says fiercely. "I've never known anyone as strong as her, but . . . the doctors found blood and skin cells under her nails that went through several layers of epidermis. Bruises everywhere, broken ribs . . . look, she's trained in self-defense . . . and she caused some real damage too . . . Penny just couldn't . . ."

Even the greatest warrior, one who trained and sacrificed every single day, even at their peak performance, could not survive a swarm of attackers.

"I bet she fought hard, Quidlee." Another car horn in the distance sounds and yet another follows. Houston area traffic is picking up at this point in the day. "What do the Memphibians want?"

Quidlee bites off a hangnail from his thumb and spits it through the fence. At least a little part of him has some freedom outside of this prison.

"I had a backup of the files I'd stashed in a compressed and hidden folder at the local coffee shop where I'd done the job. Until I got them their product back, they were going to make Penny mule for them. That was the day before the Feds busted my ass."

Who knows how long ago that was? They could've killed Penny the day the government made Quidlee *disappear*.

"She's posting on her blog," he says with the first note of hope in his voice. "I can't access it, of course, but I can see public posts through the dark web. In each picture there's a clue only I know about. Letting me know she's not okay, but doing okay, do you get me?"

I nod. Whether Quidlee is in front of them or as far away as Timbuktu, this gang is taking its vengeance.

I also understand his level of frustration and helplessness. Just like him, someone else was paying for my sins.

"I'd do anything to help her. Even if it means running from the Feds for the rest of my life, I'd do it to keep her safe."

I put my hand on his shoulder, and Quidlee half flinches but doesn't pull away completely. "All of us in this prison have harmed innocents."

I remove my grip and roll up my sleeve to reveal a series of names on the inside of my right forearm that I know all too well. "These are mine."

"What happened there?"

As much as I want to share my pain, to let a little of the constant weight off my shoulders, this moment is not about me.

"I'll tell you later . . . just tell me what I can do in this moment to help you."

"You got me in here." He chuckles before asking what I fear. "Can you get me out?"

With my hands on my hips, I meet his eye. I want to tell him it is impossible to get out of here without doing the work.

Yet, in a world of impossibilities, this is something I can actually do.

Chapter Forty-Four

Half

The next day I ask Guard Fontana to request a meeting with Cyfib for me. Generally, this type of request gets a baton to the stomach type of reply. However, Fontana knows I ain't a bullshitter, someone who will embarrass him by setting up this meeting, so Fontana nods without a questioning word or look. About lunchtime, the Almighty One sends his thunderous announcement from on high to summon this peasant.

"Dog, get up here."

I close out my screen and heed my master's call.

In his office, the warden clenches his white bone pipe in his teeth as he turns from his many screens to face me. He always has that pipe, but it never smells of tobacco or anything, really.

"Dog, what is the status of Gakunodo?"

Technically, this is my meeting, but this prison is his horse show, and I am only a show pony in it, so I follow his lead.

"It will be completed on time—"

"Good." He rotates back in his chair to his keyboards. "Dismissed."

"If . . ."

"Dog, do not test me."

The thin, figurative ice beneath me cracks. I almost abandon my plan. However, I take a beat and stare at the digitized floor below.

"Sir, I will complete it in time, but my workload requires a shifting of priorities to reach the benchmark. It will assist the timeline if you permit the maximum transfer of units and permit an overclocking of the Davidson Protocol for nonessential personnel."

Cyfib half turns, resting his chin on his snake-tattooed hands. What with my Indiana Jones-level fear of snakes, they've always unnerved me. Especially the copperhead tattoo on his hand, its mouth wide, about to strike.

The Davidson Protocol he was pondering was a quantitative method that originated in the Spanish Inquisition. It stated that a prison or group of prisoners could take on the sentenced time of another. In the state and federal prison systems, this procedure had never been officially adopted, but Hackers' Haven technically does not exist, so the lines are grayer here than elsewhere.

In the Double-H, any hackvict could get a maximum of ten units donated per week. That is the max I had used in my failed attempt to bribe Barca in the Davidson Protocol.

My second year in here there was a hackvict handled Regress4Progress, or R4P. He was in his mid-forties, a hardcore smoker who looked like a sober Charlie Sheen, and was married to a nice lady, apparently, who desperately needed a kidney transplant. Dialysis was no longer doing its blood-filtering magic. Turns out he'd just finished reading his blood test results when the Feds kicked down his door. The day they took him away in cuffs, R4P found out he was a donor match for his wife, and thus could have saved her.

R4P was two weeks into his stint here when he approached the warden with his dilemma, even though several of us told him that he'd have a better chance of convincing a frog to not eat flies. To everyone's surprise, Cyfib announced the activation of the Davidson Protocol: that any hackvict could donate units to any other hackvict, but only at a max of ten units per hackvict per week.

Out of nine prisoners in our joint, every single one of us donated the max units. With a few kills of his own, Regress4Progress got paroled in less than six weeks.

The week after he got out, Foshi_Taloa found an obituary. Regress4Progress's wife died the week he got out. Later, PoBones found R4P's obituary as well. Suicide.

All our units were for naught, but we had to try.

That is what my offer is: a try. If I could get the limit of ten units nixed, with all my units, along with a handful from a few others, we could parole Quidlee. I don't know if that means he can get to Memphis during his parole period, but it is a step forward. A purposeful try.

"Dog, grace me with your definition of *nonessential?*"

Even though Cyfib took the bait, the eggshells I walked on could still shatter if I misspoke.

"Sir, I am referring to inmates of Hackers' Haven who have under ten kills."

In Hackers' Haven a rookie has extraordinarily little value. It takes weeks, scratch that, *months* to get into a routine and rhythm of generating *kills*. Of course, Cyfib would know I am talking about either Quidlee or Barca, but choosing to remove this restriction could mean that veterans will spend more time here hacking and less time out or on parole. Cyfib just has to make the call for more quality hunters over quantity.

"Dog . . ." Cyfib turns in his chair as he sips out of a plain white coffee mug. "Your best course of action is to leave my office right now."

"But sir . . ."

Cyfib rises to face me, and I cower, in part for show, but partially in earnest. Dammit. I've screwed up. He's as tyrannical as he is unpredictable, but I need to get out of this room ASAP.

My first instinct is to defend my position, but it will get me nowhere. Cyfib means for his *no* to be as definitive as a bullet.

Keeping my eyes on the floor and my voice a whisper, I say, "Sir, I made an error."

"But, what kind of error, dog?"

I don't know how to answer. The warden towers over me. A whiff of burned citrus, vanilla, and coffee fills my nostrils. Apparently, the warden drinks a finer morning brew than the rest of us.

Cyfib is so close to me that the power of his body heat, and the stress of the situation, floods over me like I'm wearing a wool suit in a sauna. Sweat pours across my brow. Even though I want to run, I keep silent, searching my brain for a benevolent answer.

He leans forward, or maybe the entire world shifts under his influence enough that a twirling vertigo effect hits my inner ear. I sway. Maybe I only do this in my head. I am unsure. However, even though my body surely moves, my feet stay ten toes down.

"Answer me."

Those two words ramp up the situation in my mind. I don't have to see Cyfib's eyes to know his wheels are turning. He hears me, his most senior dog, ask to stay here for more *tool* usefulness.

"A costly one, sir." *Careful, Bushi, careful.* A penalty is coming, but the words need to soak in Cyfib's skin like a cool mist, not like a hard rain.

"I hope this waste of my time was worth half of your units," he says.

Chapter Forty-Five

Internal Hit List

H *alf.*
As I stumble out of his office in shock, it occurs to me I've lost over two hundred units of sweat and kills by trying to reason with a madman.

Getting Quidlee out the legal, or legal-ish way, was a no-go. I could protect him from Barca, at least for a bit, but even the greatest of bodyguards cannot protect one from oneself. If that didn't work, we could consider other . . . options.

I spend the next few days working on Cyfib's trap, Gakunodo. I dive face-first into the project, not to gain back any units, but to minimize his suspicions. I do not want this program to succeed, so I take time to alter the code where I can. However, that means even more time working on the project. The glare of the computer screen follows my eyes even when I'm out in daylight. Sometimes, the room even shifts 15 percent when I look at something in the distance. Hackers called it "coder eyes." I just call it a migraine in the making. When I piss, when I eat, when I close my eyes at night, there is the code, its white letters illuminated against my closed eyelids. Even when my eyes are open, every flat service projects computer code.

This software trap is simple: through a search engine optimization script that we would run through a couple of dark web hubs, Gakunodo would entice its bait with the promise of something already searched for, like free porn, or movies still in theaters, for example. After the prey willingly enters the trap, Gakunodo would track its target's movements and run multiple choices through its seventeen-point, neural net compiler, coding that is pretty close to artificial intelligence, complete with subjective insights and objective algorithms. Our digital speed bumps would make the user trip over his own greed by offering subliminal, weighted choices—weighted in our favor, of course. By pairing the prey's actions with the data of six untraceable worms, the program would gather from the target certain variables such as his age, weight, and income, for instance, to craft the perfect, individualized trap. By the end of the program, we'd know our visitor better than he knows himself.

Then, after three straight days of work, my ability to change any of the previously developed program's code no longer is an option. Cyfib has locked my handle out of root/god status, so my actions are limited to the creation of new source code right now. And after skimming the other code, it confirms some of my fears, like the benchmark and boundary for the income parameter.

Income <= 30000.

Damn. No one making that kind of money is going to even *afford* the fines of a conviction.

They also won't be able to afford a decent lawyer to fight the criminal charges. The second the unwanted thought flashes across my mind, I know it is true. He's not just generating income, he's generating inmates.

Cyfib has me securing Gakunodo's firewalls by freaking hand coding in sections that I have no idea what they relate to. There's no library that they are drawing from, so this is a self-sufficient program. That makes it extra secure. And that scares the shit out of me.

All this work is taking its toll on me. I rub my eyes and stretch. Something in my neck pops, and not in a good way. As I come out from under the programming rock, Quidlee bounces up and down, vibrating with excitement. The rook'd just gotten a kill after twenty hours of trying. Of course, his capture is a kid his own age who clicked on the wrong damn link for the wrong type of porn.

Another life ruined. But it's not up to me to bring anyone down. We are all soul-sucking vampires here, and the undead don't deserve flack for making more of their tribe out of the living.

I twist my neck from one side to another, but somehow, it's stiffer than before I stretched. I open our Alviss chat window.

[Tanto]: Look who is becoming a pro!

[Quidlee]: Ikr? It was fun!

[Barca]: I was just telling Tim here that he had some mean chops.

Shit. Barca knows Quidlee's real name. How much has Quidlee shared with Barca?

I close my eyes, take a breath, and focus on getting a capture. I probably won't get one, because my brain is mush, but who knows. It's not like I was only a few months away from parole and got robbed or anything.

Barca, a few stations over, taps his fingers on the keyboard in a non-rhythmic pattern, the kind that only irritates others. You know it, the kind where you are not actually pressing down and merely thinking of the next thing to say as fingertips skim across the top of the keys.

He's not even trying to make any kills. What's his plan?

Barca catches me looking his way. He smiles and doesn't even bother to type anything. We haven't had our *chat* yet about his attempt to kill and/or intimidate me. That will happen soon. Barca rises from his seat and walks over to the coffeepot. As he pours himself a cup, he actually chats with Guard Stevens. What floors me is that the guard chats back.

Barca wants everyone to know he is above any laws. As he walks back, he spills some of his hot coffee on my lap.

"Whoops. Sorry, Princess."

I don't know if it is the anger at his attempt to kill me, exhaustion, or both, but I stand up and get in his face. He can squash me like a piece of old fruit. I know this. He knows this. People on the moon know this. I still stand my ground.

As Barca sips coffee, he swallows and asks, "How far do you want to take this, Princess?"

My eyes sting with the desire to blink, to moisturize and wipe away the intensity of this moment. I keep them open. I've dealt with many a bully in my life, even in here. According to some psychologists, the best way to work with a bully is to ignore him. Granted, most psychologists probably haven't spent time inside a prison. I want to say something loud enough for everyone to hear. Instead, I sit down. I'm too tired to fight today.

"There ya go."

From his chair in the corner, Guard Fontana brings back up his book on learning French. After we make eye contact, he merely nods at me, and goes back to reading. I guess that is as close to a *carry on* command as I can expect from a guard.

But Barca is more than a bully. He is a team breaker, someone who brings destruction to order. As bad as Hackers' Haven is, I would rather die than let him destroy what we have built.

Barca sucks a lemon for a moment and then puts his giant mitt on my shoulder. "I can tell you're not brave enough to take me on by yourself."

Guard Fontana gets up and steps forward, unhooking his taser from his belt.

Hearing the guard's footsteps, Barca takes his hand from my shoulder. "Maybe that's why you named yourself after a little cowardly dagger."

Before the moment passes, I know that the movement is coming. It is a horrible idea, layered in hate and pride and all the bad choices before me. And yet, my mind and body conspire against me, and I back my chair right into the coffee cup, spilling the contents all over Barca.

Two of Barca's right, sharp canine teeth bite his lip so hard that blood creeps out. He sucks back in the drop. He turns his head and spots Guard Fontana a few feet away. The look Barca sends me burns my soul as his eyes narrow and he chews the inside of his cheek.

I've just gone from *passive* to *active* status on his internal hit list.

Chapter Forty-Six

Don't Know What to Believe

I don't even remember sitting down at my terminal after this. There was no way to tell how much time passed before my body stopped shaking.

Yes, Barca knew my name was taken from the small daggers that Bushido warriors kept on them. Bushido warriors used these weapons as last resorts when a Katana was dropped or if the combat went from a distanced one to one that was extremely close. The truth was that the dagger probably killed as many warriors as the sword. It just never received enough praise to be featured in movies or sold in pawnshops.

I also figured out his handle pretty easily. Hannibal Barca, also known as Chenu Bechola Barca, was the general who conquered much of the known world two hundred years before the birth of Christ. He was best known for his win at the Battle of Zama when his massive army, along with some soldiers riding their eighty elephants, took Rome. He also *lost* close to twenty times the number of soldiers than the defending Romans.

Hannibal Barca was not an outstanding leader; he was just someone in power who was willing to sacrifice anyone and everyone to win. His reign over Rome did not even last a decade—the people forced him to flee when they found him guilty of conspiring with an unknown enemy of Rome during a time of peace.

Even in victory, Hannibal Barca was not trustworthy.

I glance around and notice Barca has left the room. Probably cleaning up his shirt. Opening our group chat window, it is Aldy who brings some semblance of calm back into my life.

[AldenSong]: Anybody else think Barca's handle comes from the green dude who could electrocute other players in *Street Fighter II*?

[PoBones]: That's Blanka.

[Foshi_Taloa]: Blanka also ate people's faces. People forget that.

[Quidlee]: He didn't exactly eat them. He chomped on them.

[Foshi_Taloa]: Chomping equals eating.

[PoBones]: Naw. You can chomp gum, not swallow, otherwise it stays in your tummy for seven years.

[Quidlee]: Yes, thank you.

[AldenSong]: You poop gum out.

[PoBones]: Nope. Lives in your intestinal lining.

[AldenSong]: Your mom does.

This conversation went on for a bit. Barca never returned to the War Room that day. Maybe my brief standing up to him worked. Maybe things will get better.

And maybe monkeys will fly out of my butt.

At lunch, PoBones, Quidlee, AldenSong, and I sit together. My food tastes extra bland today, but my nerves might be more to blame than the actual food.

Barca is semi-predictable, in that he is self-serving. However, when someone is semi-predictable, it is almost worse than someone who is unpredictable or irrational. If someone is predictable, then you generally know what to expect and can relax your guard at times. If someone is irrational, you know to always put your mental armor on around them. With Barca, I'd better armor up and brace every chance I get.

During our break, Quidlee and I head to the basketball court on the roof. With the weather just right, not too humid or rainy, I get the courage to ask the rook the question I've dreaded for days.

"Quidlee, what would you be willing to do to get out of here?"

Quidlee surprises me by taking a beat. He runs his hand through his hair as the gears in his mind grind.

"I won't kill Barca for you."

I freeze in my tracks. A dryness smothers my mouth. My chest feels as if someone has shoved a vacuum head into it and is sucking all the air from my lungs. Despite minimal effort to cover it up, I'm pretty sure everyone has had more than a whiff of my dislike for the son of a bitch. It is common for new hackvicts and old to snap at each other, but to want someone dead in these walls is unheard of. Mostly.

"Hold up . . . why would you think I want anyone, but especially you, to harm Barca?" I water down the intent of the word *kill* by exchanging *harm* in its place.

"Look, I'm just saying he's threatening your territory, so that might be an option you're considering."

I'm just saying is a disclaimer, like *bless your heart.*

"But Barca told me you thought I was weak . . ."

"You're not weak."

"You used the word *fragile.*"

Any rebuttal I say may cause Quidlee to think I am trying to cover my ass. This is now Barca's side of the story for me to hear, not mine to defend.

"I apologize. Please continue."

Before Quidlee continues, AldenSong opens the door and heads our way. Something in my expression must've worked, unlike the time he punched me in the face, because Aldy's eyes raise. He stops in his tracks and heads back toward the interior.

He whistles and says, "Um, forgot something," as he reenters the building.

The natural silence from AldenSong's interruption gives me a moment to contemplate this exact wording. "So, we stopped at where Barca said I wanted you to kill him and that he thought I thought you were being weak."

"It's not like that . . ."

I worded that sentence incorrectly on purpose so that the rook might walk me through Barca's manufactured situation.

"Then what is it like? Please start at the beginning."

Quidlee grabs a handful of windblown debris, mainly empty potato chip bags and used napkins, and shoves them into the thirty-gallon steel drum anchored to the gate with a chain. I do the same. The sun hides behind a cloud, and for a second, the wind hits our faces.

"Barca's a rook here, just like me." Quidlee's head bobs side to side, a little bouncing bobblehead on a car's dashboard that is deep in thought. "I mean, sure we had an . . . altercation earlier, but he kept my spirits up with some free chips and stuff, but also, he's pointed out things that I should do better . . . scratch that, *had* to do better."

I'm biting my tongue so hard it might start bleeding. This man, who'd once beaten Quidlee's ass with zero provocation, had convinced the rook that the whole thing was a simple misunderstanding. This type of manipulation by Barca is intricate. Delicate. And it flat out sends a chill down my spine that no heat can melt.

Barca is yo-yo-ing Quidlee's emotions to establish dominance. This is a Dark Triad trait that only master manipulators excel at. I've met people like this, but never beat one. Because of that, most of my focus has been on keeping Barca out of *my* head. It never occurred to me he'd attempt the same techniques on others. *Foolish, foolish Tanto.*

Also, you can never just tell someone they're being manipulated. That's like telling a thirsty man that the water he's drinking is poisoned. To him, it is better to die of toxicity than wait for rain.

"The only thing you *have* to do is try, Quidlee. In all things, it is the intent, not the ultimate outcome."

"Barca says that since you got me captured, you're untrustworthy." Quidlee wipes a handful of sweat from his brow and flicks it on the ground. "I told him he was wrong, but he asked me what you've done to help me here. I think you're trying to help me, but Barca said you only want to help yourself. I don't know what to believe."

Barca is attempting to isolate Quidlee. *But why?*

"I told him that you've helped me from day one, but everything I told him he said didn't really matter, that you weren't really trying to help me, T."

"Then let me show you."

Chapter Forty-Seven

Hallway That Leads to Freedom

Words are just words. For Quidlee to truly believe my commitment to him, the rook requires action, even if he doesn't say it or even consciously know it.

We walk to the entryway. Right before we enter the hallway and pass underneath the doorframe, I flick my open hand against a power cord dangling from the ceiling, moving the frayed wire that connects it from the wall to one of the video cameras an inch to the left.

"This is where we first met." I point to the spot on the tile floor where we'd wrestled.

We walk toward the locked gate, which opens down the middle like in a sci-fi movie. It's secured with a basic RFID, or Radio Frequency Identification, dual sensor, like the kind they have at Disney World. If it's a system good enough to scan Mouse House tickets and wristbands, it's good enough for privatized prisons.

"Damn . . . seems so long ago, and also just feels like yesterday."

"Tell that to my thumbs." Quidlee rubs his hands together, long unbandaged but still sensitive to the memory.

I turn to face him so that we are chest to chest and only a few steps from the gate.

"Dude, what're you doing?"

"Rook, stand still. I have an idea, but this has only worked once before, so it might fail."

Quidlee raises a bushy eyebrow as we maintain eye contact.

"Behind me is a camera. I want you to look at my chest and watch my hands. This way I can give you directions without the camera getting either my hand gestures or lips on tape."

Quidlee raises the other eyebrow, but then lowers his gaze to my fingers.

"Do you see the camera directly behind my head?"

Quidlee nods.

"Do you see the camera on the far wall?" I hold my right hand to my chest and point with my index finger to the top left. "Use your peripheral vision only."

Quidlee tilts his head slightly and catches the black orb in the corner of his eye.

"Do you notice how only the one behind my head has a red light fully lit?"

The rook takes a few moments to scan between the two cameras.

"The other one is flickering . . ."

"It has a touchy power cord. The current is not consistent, so, by adjusting the cable, the camera will draw enough power to run, but not enough juice to send back an image to the server."

"How do you know that?"

"Foshi_Taloa used to work for the company that made that model of camera. He helped rig the cord. So, now the last image, an empty hallway, is all that is being transmitted, giving us a moment of privacy. But since the other camera is on, we are still visible until we step two steps to your right and out of its view. Do you understand?"

Quidlee nods.

"Quidlee, on the word *mark,* I am going to rotate to turn with my back toward the gate. You will turn right toward the gate. My right leg is going to not only come next to yours, but also move in tandem. Every time I say the word *step,* we will step at a casual pace. At one point, I probably will bump into the gate, but this is just to test a theory. Once the test is complete, we do not do anything rash, okay?"

"You're weird." Quidlee might soon steal the *Captain Obvious* title from AldenSong. "Okay, I'm ready."

I close my eyes, take a breath, open them, and straighten my back. "Mark."

Everything mostly goes according to plan. I rotate away from the gate and Quidlee faces it. Our right legs touch and Quidlee follows my orders, stepping slowly. Our legs separate, but when we reach the gate, our legs stay connected.

Upon reaching the sensor, the odd error noise that I first heard when I wrestled the rook blips. Then, the gate door rises, leading down a hallway neither of us have ever seen with unhooded eyes. The overlapping leg chips worked their magic.

Everything *mostly* goes according to plan. I do not expect Quidlee's unthinking instinct apparently kicking in. In that split second, when the gate raises, I glimpse a damned spark of an idea dancing around the rook's eyes as a smile creeps across his face.

Before I can tell him to leave it alone, I am too late. The next thing I know, I am chasing him down the hallway that leads to freedom.

Chapter Forty-Eight

Destroy the World

"**D**ammit rook!" I whisper-yell at Quidlee as he darts down the new hallway like a puppy scampering out an open door.

The gate shuts behind us as I pursue the moron. Dimmed, overhead fluorescent lights brighten; it's clearly a motion sensor reading our movements. Motion sensors mean a greater chance of security cameras being present. However, turning down the hallway, it seems there are no cameras in either ceiling corner.

It makes sense. When you have a gate that chipped prisoners cannot activate alone, why waste the money on extra security past it?

At the end of the hall, Quidlee twists the knob on a door with an electronic keypad lock on it and an exit sign above it. I grab him by the shoulders and pin him against the wall.

"Rook, quit it."

"Tanto, this is it!" Quidlee's pupils look larger in the dim light, almost like he is high on a dream and envisioning his instant escape and freedom.

"What happens when you get out, huh? Do you think that the second you get out those doors that everything will be fine, that there are no other security measures?"

"The door is just locked, Tanto. It's an electric lock. We can hack it—"

"We can. Later. First, we need to figure out the rest of the plan."

Quidlee shoves me off him and pulls his leg back to kick the door. I jump in front of him and catch the kick in my chest, cradling Quidlee's right leg and absorbing a blow that would echo down the hallway and possibly alert the guards.

"Tanto, if I don't get out soon, my sister's done for."

"You're just saying that. You don't know."

"And neither do you."

He's right. The amount of information both of us are lacking could fill a library. However, now is not the time to act rashly.

"We have to work this through . . ." I put my arm on his shoulder, but he swats it away.

"Central, open gate, over."

The voice is quiet, coming from the distance. The gate lurches open, sending echoes down the L-shaped hall. Footsteps approach. In mere seconds, whoever is walking our way will catch us. And that means an immediate transfer to the Bay.

Panicked, we dart into an empty room on the right, but a few steps into the room, the overhead lights cut on.

Dammit. I peek my head out into the hall. On the tile floor, a shadow grows.

"Rook, get to the next room's door—slowly."

I push Quidlee in front of me as he crouches and sneaks into the adjacent room. Right after Quidlee enters, Guard Stevens turns down our segment. Making a break for it, I leave the lit room and risk him spotting me out in the open.

Luckily, there is something more interesting on his smartphone because he never glances up as he stomps our way. I shoot into the still dark, empty room and flatten myself against the wall.

The footsteps stop. Maybe he's spotted my heel entering the room. Maybe he's noticed that our first hiding spot is lit up. I don't know why he's stopped, but my stomach knots up.

"Central, this is Stevens, over." A radio squawks. *He is calling it in. Dammit.*

A distorted voice comes through on his radio. "This is Central. Go ahead, over."

Squawk.

"Do we have anyone near the classroom entrance, over?"

Squawk.

I hate this guy. Why can't this guard be like guards in the movies and just stick his head in a room, look around, shrug, and then whistle as he walks over to do a crossword puzzle at his desk?

"That's a negative, over."

Squawk.

"Okay, stay with me as I check this out, over."

Squawk.

"Ten-four, over. Keep your mic live, over."

Squawk.

Keeping his mic live means that the guard has one hand on the mic button and another on his weapon. If the guard lets his hand off the button, Central will sound the alarm. It's like taking out a terrorist holding a deadman's switch: the moment the bastard lets his thumb off the depressed button, everything explodes.

From my flush position, the motion sensor—a red square box attached to the ceiling—is visible right above Quidlee's head. He's fully in the blind spot, and I am barely hidden behind the half-open door.

The door of the lit room creaks all the way as Stevens enters the other classroom.

Where is a scurrying mouse when you need one?

Over the rush of blood in my ears, Quidlee mouths the words *get him.*

I respond with stabbing eyes that are reserved for teachers who want a student to stop acting up.

No.

Yes.

No.

This right here is one of the many reasons I never want kids.

The pounding of footsteps on tiles gets louder. Stevens is back in the hallway and right outside our door. I press even harder into the cement wall, willing my body to meld with it like a chameleon on a tree stump hiding from a predator.

The guard's shock baton pushes the door open more. The overhead lights flicker, then cut on.

The guard is close enough to the door that I can smell his Speed Stick deodorant sweat and his wheatgrass smoothie breath.

Quidlee tenses, ready to pounce. Quidlee looks my way. He nods. I shake my head. If the guard looks through the square glass window of the door, he'll see the rook.

"Central, over."

Squawk.

"Go ahead, over."

Squawk.

The time between that last squawk and what happens next will run for years in my mind.

I can grab the baton, but then the guard will let go of his mic. I move my left hand further toward the doorframe but keep it against the white concrete wall. Sweat trickles down my forehead and drops splash against the tile floor.

It is now or never.

"All clear. Open gate, over."

Squawk.

"Roger, over."

Squawk.

Stevens goes back to the gate and both Quidlee and I slump to the ground. Neither of us inhale more than a half breath for close to a minute.

"So, Tanto . . ." The rook's voice quivers, which makes me wonder how badly my voice will sound after this shock. "How much poop . . . should there be . . . in one's pants . . . after a scare like that?"

"You asking . . . for a friend?"

"Yep."

"Two logs . . . minimum . . ."

"Good . . . to know."

We laugh as much as we can, considering our lungs are still at war with the rest of our bodies.

Then a siren goes off. My heart attempts to jump out of my chest.

"Shit!" Quidlee scrambles to his feet, sure we're busted. But I rest my head against the wall.

"Calm down, rook." I chuckle. Gallows humor is still humor. "Thankfully, it's just someone trying to destroy the world."

Chapter Forty-Nine

Just the Dogs I Was Looking For

There is nothing quite like an alert of an enemy attack to make everything else fade into the background. Quidlee and I sneak back in through the gate the same way we exited: feet together. Once back inside, I readjust the faulty video camera cable.

It doesn't escape my notice that this is the third alert we've had in the past six months. This many attacks this close together probably means something that only someone above my pay grade can answer.

Sadly, or not so sadly, shutting down this hack takes less time than it does to boil an egg.

We finish up and Guard Fontana tells me I have my weekly appointment scheduled with Dr. Fel.

As if I haven't spent enough time in there already.

An hour later, Dr. Fel dismisses me. I dart straight to the War Room. The Night Crew is there, the Four Horsemen: MotoRoto, a long-haired Asian guy who loves old Jerry Springer episodes, the ones where fighting is outright encouraged; MottonCather, a white former preacher turned credit card scammer; X_Marks_Da_Hot, an African American whose claim to fame is that he not only toured with some rapper named Nelly but also used some of his income to help several up-and-coming rappers get their start; and Trub_E, a dwarf with an ego the size of Mount Rushmore.

Personally, I consider my crew the "A Team," the red-hot grill you cook a steak on. That said, these guys are the reliable "B Team," the Crock-Pot that cooks at a steady heat and produces consistent results. They only garner a few *kills* a week, but you can set your watch to those captures.

The world can use more Crock-Pot people.

Before I head to the dorm I do another quick scan of the room, because there is always a chance that one of my night owls is getting a few more marks on his *kill* bingo card.

I am not five feet into the hallway when Barca rounds the corner from the latrine. For the first time since he sabotaged the Coffin's eject button, we are alone. Still, he almost runs me over as if I am nothing more than a bug on the floor.

"Whoa, Princess, didn't see your little ass there."

"I know what you did, tampering with the eject button, Barca." The words come out louder than I mean, and I am instantly worried that the sound will travel, and others will hear us. "I just don't know why."

The giant sucks on a flat sucker he probably got from Commissary. It looks like the kind you get when you visit a doctor, not the round kind you get when you leave a bank. He slurps on it loudly before he gives me an answer.

"I thought I made myself pretty clear." He takes another slurp of his lolly.

"What exactly is your game, Barca?"

Barca towers over me like a bear over a bunny. "That's a bit above your pay grade."

I hold my ground, even though craning my head back to meet his gaze makes my neck stretch and pop. "I will not let you destroy what we have here. It's not much, but this is our house."

Anyone outside these walls might interpret this statement as a desire to protect Hackers' Haven, the institution. That's wrong. Homes are not made of stone. They are made of people. This is my family, you sick son of a bitch.

"And you can't threaten me because I'm not afraid of dying." I make my stand here, but hope he keeps his crosshairs on me.

Barca sucks on his lolly as his tongue moves the stick to the right end of his mouth. "That is useful to know."

Laughter coming from Quidlee's room breaks our stalemate.

Barca walks toward the room, and I follow. AldenSong, PoBones, and Quidlee are sitting around joking.

"What's so funny?" asks Barca.

"Oh, PoBones told a joke he read in a chat room." Quidlee has his back leaning against the cement wall. Barca mimics the pose on the opposite wall.

"Well, our resident Cajun is the funniest guy here." This is mostly true. The thing about PoBones is that he can never get through a joke without cracking himself up, so even the worst knock-knock joke he tells will still make you laugh right along with his giggling, which is like that of a fifth grader.

"I like jokes." Barca takes out his lolly and points it at PoBones.

"Okay," says PoBones. "Jethro and Tull were drinking moonshine . . ."

"You named the rednecks after the band?"

"Yeah, yeah, just listen. So Jethro and Tull were drinking moonshine. After a few swallas, Jethro says, 'Time for the yearly vacation, but this year I'm gonna change it up.'"

"How's he gonna do that?"

Uh oh. The first interruption is forgivable. The second is intentional. Calculative.

"Let him tell the joke, Barca." I know that my attempt to control this situation is adding kindling to Barca's fire, but I have to try because no one else is trying.

"Hey, I'm just trying to get some background, you know what, just start over."

Since he is clearly flustered, PoBones's stutter rears its ugly head. "S-s-so Jethro and T-t-tull were drinking moonshine at the e-e-end of the d-d-day . . ."

"Hey, PoBones, take a moment, get your traction." Barca leans across from the wall and puts his hand on PoBones's leg. "You've got this."

What happens over the next few minutes is a master class in mind screwing taught by a tenured professor: PoBones starts the joke, gets a good way into it, and Barca disrupts the Cajun's flow. Whether it is by words or actions, such as when the giant lets loose a fart that brings laughter, it also destroys PoBones' train of thought. After each disruption, Barca presents some false apology. Then it all starts again. The yo-yo is a classic Dark Triad strategy for manipulation.

Barca chips away at my friend, one word at a time, and then he takes the broken piece in his hand, shows PoBones the damage, and shoves the brokenness back into place. This does not really repair the damage because part of PoBones' self-esteem is pouring out after each puncture. This is why all the king's horses and all the king's men could not reassemble Humpty-Dumpty again: when you shatter someone, there is nothing left to repair.

By the time PoBones is reaching the ultimate end of a joke about how this redneck would always go to some exotic land for vacation and, when he returned from the trip, he would discover his wife was pregnant, sweat covers my friend.

"Barca, the joke is not even that good . . ." From the angle I am sitting, I can see the tears in the corners of PoBones' eyes.

Barca puts his sucker between his front teeth and bites down, cracking it in half. The sound of the candy shattering echoes in the small cell "Finish . . . the . . . joke . . ."

PoBones swallows, stares at the ground, and rubs his hands across his jeans. "N-n-next vacation, I'm n-n-not leaving the w-w-wife at h-h-home . . ."

There is a long silence, then a barrage of deep laughs fills the room as Barca lets out a storm of guffaws. He slaps his legs and even grabs PoBones, shaking him and laughing directly in the Cajun's face.

AldenSong laughs. PoBones nervously lets out a lone chuckle in relief, sounding like air escaping from a balloon. Even I manage to squeak a laugh out.

Then, as quickly as Barca had started his laughing fit, he stops. His features drop from that of a smiling jackal to those of a flat stone.

Barca holds out the sucker and points it at PoBones. "Tell me another joke."

Something in me snaps. I reach over and grab Barca by the shirt, catching him off guard, and then drag him into the hallway with all the strength my scrawny ass can muster. My lack of a plan is about to wind up with me back in the Infirmary.

However, before either of us can do anything, the monotone voice of the devil is in our ears.

"Just the dogs I was looking for."

Chapter Fifty

A Back Door

I let go of Barca and cast my eyes toward the floor. I'm sure the warden thinks I am doing this out of respect for or fear of him, but it is to end this conflict as quickly as possible. With any luck the giant will snap and swing at me. I'll duck it, and he'll clock Cyfib, thus getting him a first-class ticket to the Bay.

Of course, that scenario will take some Three Stooges level of fortune and timing to pull off.

"With me," says Cyfib.

The warden's version of the command "heel" feels like an escape, but the command is for *both* of us. Staring at the back of Cyfib's boots as he *cha-chings* toward his office, I take a moment to breathe. Barca's hot, rabid breath moistens the back of my neck. There is no telling what would've happened if Cyfib had not accosted us when he did.

When we arrive at the Cube of Death, Cyfib points at Barca. "Stay."

I enter Cyfib's office and drop my guard a bit. After all, whatever this is cannot possibly be worse than getting a beat down by an ogre.

Right?

Wrong.

Across all the interior walls of the Cube are page after page of my code for Gakunodo. Cyfib reaches into his vest pocket, withdraws his white pipe, and points it at three lines that should never have graced his eyes.

"What the hell is this?"

Ah, well, shitty-shit-shit. With a deadline approaching, I thought for sure that Cyfib would not bother returning to areas of the code he had already run through, so that was where I hid the Randomizer.

The Randomizer is a bit of code that does three things: accesses a target's personal information; scrambles it through several free online generators; and then trades out the mash-up information with the correct info.

I am as caught as Pooh Bear with his head stuck in the honeypot. When someone catches you in prison, you can do one of two things. Confess and throw yourself down and beg for mercy or: and this is the one I'd already planned on: cover your ass.

"Sir, this code appears to be a Randomizer . . ."

"I am not blind, dog. I want to know why it is in my program."

My program. His ownership of the project both turns my stomach and gives me an avenue to pursue.

"Sir, this code should not be in this program." I commit to the role of idiot the way a drummer commits to a solo: hard and without mercy. "I'm personally insulted that anyone would work on this project without informing you . . . is there a way to see whose terminal accessed this build?"

There will be no hackers-attacking alarm saving me this time. Cyfib puts his pipe under my chin. The sharp, boney end scratches just above my Adam's apple, sending a jab of pain into my skin. Tilting my head in pain, I notice that instead of tobacco in the pipe, there's a tiny piece of paper stuffed into the bowl.

I meet his solemn gaze, two dark gray eyes boring holes into my skull.

"I've already looked into that, dog."

Of course, you have. That's why he brought Barca with us and had him wait outside. You see, when I made improvements to the actual code, such as reinforcing the parameters of variables or running script that Gakunodo needed to capture fools on the Internet, I used my log in credentials. When I made these changes, such as this compiler and few others that would get me deported, I used Barca's.

I am not sure whether Cyfib thinks my bluff is passable. His poker face is emotionless. No brows crease. No eyes break their beady lock on me, his target.

"Dismissed."

I do not take a breath until I am down the stairs and in the War Room. The Cube's door closes. Barca and Cyfib are alone.

In a perfect world, some computer in that office will malfunction and blow them both up in that box.

But we don't live in a perfect world, so maybe Barca will just get deported. That is a wonderful second place option.

Now that I am out of the danger zone, the juices that are keeping my body running in overdrive run out. Sleep crawls behind my eyes and attaches anchors to my eyelids. I crash into my bunk, fully clothed, shoes and all.

Right before I fade off into sleep, I think about how lucky I am that Cyfib only looked until he saw the first flaw in Gakunodo. I certainly made it a big enough one to catch the brunt of any prying eyes, something full of mischief and counterproductive to the source code's mission.

I'm just glad Cyfib took the bait and stopped his search there. Had Cyfib looked any deeper, he'd have discovered the real secret I was hiding in that code: a back door.

Chapter Fifty-One

A Little Exploration

After that meeting, we didn't see Barca that next day in the War Room. Or the next.

My plan worked. Sure, I had another person take a fall for my crime. But according to the Bushido Code, difficult times merit harsh tactics, especially when dealing with the greater good. The warriors of ancient Japan who followed this creed made a living by protecting people. And that sometimes required them to do things that were less than kind, such as burning homes and killing their enemies.

One cannot build a fire without first killing a tree. It is often much better if you are not said tree.

I sit alone on the rooftop, taking a minute to think about how easy it was to get rid of the monster without drawing blood. Not all Bushido warriors killed, or at least used violence as the first measure. Even though he was a master swordsman, Yamaoka Tesshū brokered peace, preventing many lives from sacrifice. And while it was his diplomacy that led Japan into the modern age, it also killed the Bushido class. He sacrificed all he believed in to save lives. I hope what I have done to Barca is one-millionth as helpful.

I don't even notice the rook next to me until the pop from his opening a can of sparkling water startles me.

"Quidlee, you 'bout scared the shit out of me. About the other day—"

"Penny got word to me."

This little bastard's interruptions, while annoying, have power behind them. He never interrupts with a comment about the weather or to ask if I ever saw this or that movie. Quidlee, whether or not he knows it, is purposeful at the most random of times. Maybe he just needs someone to break the ice first and speak, to give him the courage to say what is eating up his brain space.

I don't ask how. Message board, cryptic obituary, who knows? We all need to keep a few secrets to ourselves.

"And?"

"And . . . she's getting more threats."

I do not need to ask further. From what I know about gangs, threats are merely upcoming promises.

I look across the skyline of buildings just north of the West Pasadena Freeway. Our part of Houston, east of the big city but close enough that you can still smell the exhaust and someone smoking a brisket, is in the area called the Watershed. It's where the rain and runoff from the city flows and it makes this area mighty hard to get to when the skies open up.

Ships run through this area, about a quarter of a mile or so to the east. The buildings here mainly house industrial and petrochemical activity from refining fossil fuels.

In short, this would be the last place to find random foot traffic or a Starbucks.

In that moment, with Barca gone and the wind in our faces, I ask, "How about we clear our minds with a little exploration of ways out of here?"

Chapter Fifty-Two

Cannot Help but Smile

J ust like before, I move the cable that attaches to the hallway camera enough that the camera's signal shorts so that it cannot record us exiting the hall past the gate.

Unlike before, when we boldly walked in front of the incorruptible camera at the top of the side wall, each of us slides chest first along the wall so that we avoid any record of our exit. Quidlee goes first and makes the sliding look easy, chewing bubble gum and humming some rap song about rap things. Me, on the other hand, I wind up jamming the notepad and pen I have hidden under my shirt into my stomach as I slide into a light switch and almost recoil off the wall in pain. Luckily, common sense kicks in, and I ease over the switch and meet Quidlee at the gate.

Standing side by side with my right facing away from the gate and his right facing toward, we nod at each other.

"Mark."

Two synchronized steps later, our touching microchips enter the sensor area. The gate opens.

Five steps after that, we are walking side by side down the hallway.

I whip out the notepad and write down every detail I notice.

Ten steps from the gate until the turn in the hallway.

Thirty-two until the end of the hallway and the door out.

Total = forty-two.

We walk through each classroom together and check all the windows. Each window is dark because it has a metal sheet across it. It would be a problem to break through one since we have limited access to tools.

Quidlee steps onto one of the school desks. I hoist him up onto my shoulders. He moves one of the many stucco ceiling tiles to the side and pulls himself into the ceiling area.

In less than a minute, he's back out and shaking off like a dog straight out of the rain and sending dust and probably asbestos all over me.

"It's no use up there." Quidlee runs his hands through his bushy hair and flicks out chunks of cobwebs and gunk. "The cement walls go all the way up."

"Lone door, it is."

Both Quidlee and I take turns looking over the lock. The numeric lock on the door is a four-coder: four digits. It's probably only two attempts before the door hard locks shut until an administrator's code is inputted. I am familiar with this concept, but not this particular brand or model.

It is a standard, one-unit, gunmetal-gray handle and cover with white buttons that feature black numbers from 0 to 9. There is no number sign button or enter button, so it's a more recent model. Confusingly, someone has scraped away the name of the keypad's manufacturer on the bottom of the unit.

"You think someone did it on purpose?" Quidlee asks.

I extend my hand and Quidlee grabs me by the wrist and hoists me to my feet. "I think someone just got frustrated installing the lock and an electric screwdriver slipped out of its groove and shredded the section we need."

We still need to get a workable code.

An idea starts in the back of my skull in the area reserved for mischief and random, useless facts. The scratches are there, but underneath the scratches is something we could possibly use.

"T, can we unscrew it?"

"Negative. The boilerplate is sealed by the door code as well."

I look at Quidlee as he blows a gum bubble in my face until it pops.

"Give me your gum."

"Look, I won't blow another bubble on you, okay?"

"Give me your gum."

"I just started this piece."

"Start another."

Quidlee gets another two chews in on his existing piece before he spits the gum into my open hand and reaches into his pocket to grab another foil-wrapped chew. A spearmint smell hits my nostrils as I roll the gum around between both of my palms. Then I flatten it to about the size and thickness of a half dollar.

"Do you have the wrapper?"

"Man, you are one needy old man . . ."

Quidlee hands me the silver foil gum wrapper. I fold it end over end until it is the about twice as long and wide as the gum. Then I secure it under the half-dollar gum and place the two under the lock, rolling my index finger along the adhesion, applying some pressure, but not too much.

As PoBones says, *You gotta take time and care to butter the Turducken by hand slowly, otherwise you break its home, and don't nobody need a broken home.*

I do not want to break the home of this gum.

After a few seconds, I pull on the gum wrapper. The gum is a little more stuck to the metal than I like, but everything comes off smoothly enough to work.

It's a little like that old Detective Columbo trick of rubbing on a blank piece of paper with a pencil so you can see what someone wrote earlier. Now we have enough information to make the effort worth playing with Quidlee's saliva-drenched gum.

I take the gum in both hands, holding it by the wrapper, and then flip the gum upside down and run it along the floor.

"What're you doing?"

"Fingerprinting the suspect."

After two swipes, I lift the gum to my lips and blow. Large chunks of dust and debris fly off, but the smaller particles hold firm to the gum.

Quidlee leans over the gum. "Okay, it's backward, but once we get a mirror, we can figure out who the manufacturer is."

When we look at our work, I state the obvious. "It's not a name."

"What is it?"

"It's even better." I can't help but smile. "It's the model number."

Chapter Fifty-Three

Best You Can Hope for Is Vengeance

That next day, I make a jaunt to a great little sector of the dark web that deals with one of my favorite childhood pastimes: lock picking.

I first picked up the hobby when a buddy and I got a hold of a copy of *The Anarchist Cookbook*. This little jewel of a download was like the dark web before the dark web. In this zipped file, you could learn how to create explosives, make LSD, craft booby traps, and pick a lock with a paper clip and a bobby pin. For years, I *always* had those two items in the inside flap of my wallet.

While the Boy Scouts of America taught many a trooper how to *be prepared*, this digital masterpiece of illegal tips taught me, and many others, to be ready *in case shit happens.*

Lock picking has changed over the years, from analog to digital, and the forum I choose only takes a few minutes of perusing before I find not only the administrative code for the Model F0-FOX90 keypad but also the engineering code. The first code gives me access to open the door. The second one, the engineer's code, allows us to disassemble the lock and reassemble it the way we want.

That means that, once Quidlee is out that door, I can seal it. No one in or out unless someone has a blowtorch in their back pocket.

Over the decades, *The Anarchist Cookbook* became more of a Wiki or online collection of illegal tips and tricks. That is why I am on the dark web perusing something I never thought I'd ever need to know: how to procure a dead body.

Apparently, the key to getting a corpse is to search not the obituaries or funeral homes for someone who fits an escapee's description, such as rook Quidlee's, but the police reports over the last month for an unidentified Code Ten-Fifty-Four.

An unidentified dead body.

I know police codes pretty well. I often listened to a scanner in my childhood bedroom, just to figure out where the dangerous parts of town were. Then I would time with a stopwatch how fast police made it to a potential crime scene. At around eight years old, I might have been trying out my earliest form of hacking: tracking police patterns.

For our plan to work, not just any John or Jane Doe would fit for the rook. We needed one twenty-ish young male close enough in height and weight to fit Quidlee's description.

Most police databases run on solo systems, ones that only work within the precinct when the perp or body doesn't deal with prosecutable crimes, such as murder. Those are on a greater network, like the FBI's database. So, if you're arrested for breaking and entering, that system connects across the entire country. However, if you die of natural causes in Kansas City, Missouri, no one next door in Kansas City, Kansas, will know about it.

There is no law requiring a coroner or medical examiner to preserve unidentified bodies not associated with a crime, so disposing of a corpse is a drain on the county and up to the discretion of the county's elected coroner. Burying bodies is expensive, so they cremate most all unclaimed bodies within two weeks of arrival in a morgue.

However, there's more work in cremation than just cranking up a furnace and chucking in a corpse.

You strip the clothes off. You prep the incinerator and the body. It takes over two hours of high intensity, natural gas flowing through the incinerator to properly reduce a human being to ash. Even then, you have to gather up around seven pounds of bone matter in a plastic bag.

Factoring all that together with the coroner's time and the city's other expenses can ring up a hefty bill for a random, dead body.

Yet, just like Beanie Babies and used underwear, there is a market for these bodies.

I started this search last week with quick hidden jaunts through my backdoor access to the dark web through that little piece of code Lance-a-Little left me. Through my contacts, I started procuring fake identification for Quidlee, a phone, cash, and even a vehicle. Those sprints ultimately found us not only a workable corpse, but a coroner's assistant with a gambling problem. Those two variables go together for our little escape plan, like Jägermeister and hangovers.

Once Quidlee gets out, I have a rough idea of how he'll make sure the corpse fits enough of his description so that no one will bother questioning his "death."

The last piece of the puzzle is finding someone to meet up with Quidlee and get everything—including the corpse and some odds and ends—to him within five blocks of here.

A heated three-on-three game of basketball occurs in front of us. I am sure I could pick up the basics of this sporty game if I tried, but asking Quidlee my questions directly is a great way to pass the time.

"Quidlee, if I ask you a question, do you promise not to make fun of me?"

"If you ask me where babies come from, I'm going to lie."

"What is a free throw?"

The rook kicks his head back and chuckles, like he is about to say something, probably derogatory, but instead he takes a beat and a breath.

"Sometimes when a player fouls another player, like hits him with an elbow or pushes him out of bounds," Quidlee begins, pointing at the top of the smaller arch we've just drawn, "the wronged player gets to stand right here and take one or two uninterrupted shots to score."

"And they just let him do this and no one tries to mess it up?"

"Well, the fans do." Quidlee snickers and averts his gaze away from me. His eyes go up and to his right, which usually means a person is assembling a memory.

"There was this time that some buddies and I were at a junior college game where one of my friends—Stevie, Crazy Stevie—had a little brother who was playing ball. We had courtside seats, man. It was sweet. The visiting team had this huge guy who was pushing and elbowing everyone around him. Even knocked a guy unconscious with an elbow during a pivot left."

I do not lose the irony of this story about a bully causing chaos.

"No idea why the refs were letting him play so rough, but then the thug elbowed Crazy Stevie's brother so hard that it broke his nose. Blood everywhere. Yeah, the thug got a penalty, but there weren't enough penalties by the other team to reach the free throw range yet, just the inbound and ball turnover thing."

All of this clearly means something to Quidlee and this story about basketball. However, for me, it is like getting told VCR repair instructions in Klingon. In any case, I continue to listen intently, resting my head on my hands.

"So, we looked up this player on our phones. We found out his favorite movie, band, even what classes he was struggling with. We went onto the school's website and found the syllabi to each class the thug was in, and discovered he had a test the following day in economics that counted for 50 percent of his grade in that class."

Quidlee stumbles over his words but takes a moment and to get his bearings.

"So, we decided to help him study. I pulled up a digital copy of the textbook and every single time he either got the ball or was trying to cover another player, I read loudly from a section in the textbook as my buddies echoed key phrases. You know, help some of those big questions stick in the guy's head. A couple of fans asked us what we were doing, and we told them we were getting in Number Six's head, so everyone in our section got mouse-level quiet whenever I started reading. Now, whenever the dude would take a shot, we got the crowd to yell out together, 'Test tomorrow!' He started laying brick after brick. At the end of the game when his team lost, the dude literally ran at us, and we fled the coliseum like it was on fire!"

Quidlee laughs a good bit. His eyes trail off and look past the skyline and at a memory. In this moment, he is not a prisoner trying to escape to save his sister and make amends for his past. Right now, in his mind, he is a free man without a care in the world.

The clouds above us darken and the wind picks up. A storm is on the horizon.

"Rook, some people might view what you did to that player as bullying."

Quidlee points his finger in my face. "No! No! The refs weren't doing anything, so someone had to do something."

Rook is getting flustered. *Slow down, Tanto.*

"Which is why you actually did something remarkable. You made sure that, even though the odds, or in your case, the referees, were against your team, you made sure that Number Six was his own worst enemy."

"Yeah, that was some sweet vengeance there."

"That wasn't vengeance."

"What do you mean?"

The skies open up. Guard Fontana, leaning against the brick wall, covers his head with a clipboard as he walks inside. He gets paid to guard us, not catch a cold with us. Heavy drops smash into our heads, almost as if some higher power is sending hail and water to target us intentionally.

"Vengeance is where you get retribution on the one who has wronged you. You were not the one wronged, so you made sure this guy messed himself up, because only he could miss those shots, no matter what you did. He was causing damage to other players, and he ultimately caused damage to himself. That's justice, not vengeance."

Quidlee raises his face to the rain, getting soaked completely.

Only in a game do you get something as pure and satisfying as justice. In life, the best you can hope for is vengeance.

Chapter Fifty-Four

Watching Us

Quidlee and I wait until the shift change to enter the War Room before we do a complete practice run of the escape so that our movement in and out of the area blends with the general foot traffic. First, I move the camera's cable. Next, we scoot chest-first along the wall. Like before, we step in time through the gate. At the end of the hall, I enter the engineer's code to the lock, which causes the mechanism holding the lock to the door to loosen. With a flathead screwdriver, I pry open the lock and find the bolt that will permanently seal the door behind Quidlee once he escapes. For this run-through, I only twist the knob so that we can open the door.

The click of the bolt leaving the cylinder echoes in my bones. The door to the outside world opens. A streetlight blinds me. Five concrete steps lay before us. Before we exit, I use a handheld mirror to peep around the doorframe and scan for cameras but find none.

Although it is poor security, from a subterfuge point of view, it makes sense. To the average person, this is an abandoned warehouse next to a funeral parlor; there is no need for any active cameras or microphones. A mic would need a cover in this high-wind spot—something fuzzy, like the cover you see over a reporter's microphone, or on a boom mic in the making of a movie. That would cause suspicion and possibly prying eyes.

"Looks clear."

"T, I'm stepping out."

"Rook, don't—"

Quidlee shoots past my attempt to grab his shoulder and exits the building. He darts down the steps and skips across the sidewalk from side to side, dipping his toes in the weeds that have overtaken the lawn. The rook kicks his head back and turns around to look at our building from the outside, something I have thought about doing a million times.

"Tanto, you've gotta step out and see this place."

The kid has a point. There are no guards. No cameras. The door will not lock behind us. If there ever was a time to sample freedom, this is it.

I take three tiny steps toward the door. My right foot breaks the door-frame. Then my body locks up. I cannot put my foot down. It is as if some force is simultaneously pushing my foot away from stepping down and keeping a firm grasp on my shoulder, pulling me back into the building.

It isn't the chip in my leg. Hell, if anyone's chip should've shocked a hackvict back into the building, Quidlee's newest model gets dibs. No, this is all me. My heartbeat fills my ears. For eight years, I have hated, then tolerated, and even depended on this place.

Now I cannot even take one step outside of the place I call *home*.

The thought of life outside of these walls is so foreign to me that I never think about living, really living, away from Hackers' Haven. Sure, I think about getting better food, having sex with someone other than my hands, watching a movie in an actual movie theater, or having a private bathroom.

But these are only snippets of life, a sampling, not a full life away from my friends and routine.

I lower my leg and set it next to my other, flat on the prison-tile floor. "I'll take your word for it."

A sound behind me catches my attention, but when I look, nothing is there. My natural paranoia is kicking in and my mind is playing tricks on me. "Get back in here."

"Yes, Mother."

Quidlee returns.

I shut the door, reassemble the lock, and reenter the engineer's code. The lock whirls and the door locks.

I check my watch. Ten minutes remain until the shift change completes.

Quidlee and I step our leg-to-leg and side-by-side practiced walk through the gate. Even though I face back toward the abandoned classroom hallway, the eyes in the back of my head go wide.

I immediately know in my gut who is watching us back in the dorm.

Chapter Fifty-Five

Best Intentions

On the nights my grandparents would keep me, mainly so my mother could party with reckless abandon, my grandfather would wake up screaming. When I asked him about it, he told me it was nothing. My grandmother, on the other hand, told me that Grandaddy had demons. My grandfather was a war veteran who, I found out later, did bad things to bad people for the greater good.

Sometimes I would awaken from my spot on the sofa and find him sitting in a chair in the middle of the entire house. He'd have moved it there while I slept. The chair would swivel in circles. He would never stop turning. The moment he made it all the way left, completing a circle, he would start his rotation all the way right. He'd have his double-barrel shotgun in his lap and a Colt 45 in the magazine holder attached to the chair.

Against my better judgment, I got up the nerve to ask him one time what he was doing. He stopped swiveling and leaned forward, finger rolling along the shotgun's trigger guard.

"I'm keeping watch." Then he turned and continued. "When you turn your back, that's when the devils pounce."

Back in reality, the air in the hallway pops with each slow clap. The bare tile floors echo the mocking applause, like how thunder rolls off the mountains and reminds you just how small you really are in this big world.

"Princess, you've really outdone yourself."

No. Please, God, no. There is no way he is still here. Every offense and charge should stick. Why is he still here?

"Barca, look, nothing—"

"Ah ah ah . . ." The giant wags his index finger at my attempt to misdirect him. "Your words can't possibly undo what my eyes have seen."

There is zero reason for him to still be in Hackers' Haven. Cyfib has enough misinformation that I planted in the code for Gakunodo to deport him to Guantanamo Bay. Even so, the giant sucks on a lollipop and strolls our way.

"Whatever you are doing, I want in."

"If you had been paying attention, the fiber-optic cable that runs through the ceiling has flickered and lost connection yesterday." As Quidlee blasts these words, he walks in front of me and stands between Barca and myself. He's breaking the chain Barca has on him but, damn, does his timing for this suck. "We were fixing it. Now, just because you have the height doesn't mean you have the experience that Tanto does with our recording system."

The rook steps up with the excuse we need and, even though this monster once whooped his ass, Quidlee is taking a stand. This is his hill to die on. But I'll be beside him no matter what.

"Barca, how are you here?" I ask pointedly, hoping to put the emphasis on anything else but our transgression. "You shouldn't be here."

"You're just not getting it, are you, Princess?" Barca laughs like someone who knows a secret that he's just dying to share and points his lolly at my face. "You're the one breaking the rules now."

Damnation. My eye must've gone up and to the left. Barca has the same Kinetics training I do.

I am out of practice lying and deceiving. Even with Cyfib, I know to stare at the ground, showing this mutt is in submission and not daring to challenge the alpha in our pack.

"Get out of our way." Quidlee attempts to walk around Barca, but the big guy puts his hand around the rook's throat and shoves him to his knees.

My instinct is to grab Barca's arm, but I realize that, from where Barca is standing, his massive body blocks the working camera. Security might only see me attack Barca because Quidlee is out of frame.

I step in front of the giant and use his obscuring of the camera to my advantage. I reach into my waistband and pull out the flathead screwdriver that we used on the exit's keypad.

I hold out the sharp end toward the monster, but he only laughs.

"You use that thing, you better not come at me half-heartedly, Princess." The rook's gasps get deeper and more desperate as he claws at Barca's hand. "When you want to kill a man, you look him in the eyes . . . be a man about it."

This is my chance to rid Hackers' Haven of this threat to our home. One quick jab and in under four minutes, he'd bleed out and die. Sure, I'll go to the Bay, but this one action will keep our home safe.

I ponder the sharp, gray tip. I'd have to hit on the left side because that's the hand occupied with Quidlee's neck. There is a decent chance he'll deflect the blow or even take the screwdriver from me and stab both the rook and me.

The monster glances over and sees the instrument of his death. And he laughs.

"Do it, Princess." Barca puts both hands around Quidlee's neck and squeezes, leaning toward me and exposing his vulnerable neck even further. "You don't have the balls, and the only way to stop me is to put me in the ground for good."

I hold my attack. *Can I actually do it?*

Morihei Ueshiba, the great teacher and founder of Aikido, was not a Bushido Warrior. He did believe that you should grant your enemy every chance to find a peaceful solution as opposed to killing. Killing is permanent, but the rest is opportunity.

Curse my soul, I make a choice. I rotate the blade in toward my palm and jam the blunt handle between Barca's lower right ribs. He howls in pain, releasing Quidlee.

The rook takes advantage of the distraction to wrap his hands together in a haymaker- style punch and slam his double fists right into Barca's crotch.

The giant screams and crumples over.

Shoving Barca away, I snatch up Quidlee and hurry us away from the operable camera, hoping we stayed mostly in its blind spot. As we dart out, I hit the cable on the other camera, turning it back to record mode.

If anyone looks at the footage, they might just see Barca lounging against the wall when he is actually waiting for his balls to descend from his stomach.

Barca is wrong about the only way to stop him is for me to kill him. There is always another way. But the right way is not designed to be easy.

A problem with taking the path of the righteous is that it often has speed bumps made out of your best intentions.

Chapter Fifty-Six

Swish Thump Thump

For the next couple of days, I expect Cyfib's *cha-chings* to come for me—the executioner marching to behead me. It never happens.

Barca, for all his bluster in the hall, acts all Joe Cool. Oddly enough, he is extra chipper, and even gives both Quidlee and myself some Sun Chips from the Commissary the day after the fight. The bags are still pressurized and sealed, so he probably didn't even tamper with the snack. Probably.

My corpse contact, the coroner's assistant in gambling debt, is getting pressure to "do some spring cleaning," which probably means incinerating Quidlee's doppelgänger. I still can't find a person to courier the body and do all the paperwork for Quidlee.

Time is running out.

Who'd have thought it would be so difficult to hire someone to haul a decomposing body and fake identification papers into a major metropolitan city?

Not to mention, every day that passes is another I don't know what to do about Gakunodo, the monster for my Dr. Frankenstein.

The impact of the basketball bouncing off my knee and back toward the court brings me back. Currently playing around the basketball court is every hackvict in residency. Even the guards watch, though they do not join in. Per the employee handbook or something, they probably consider that a pickup game of any sport, with prisoners, constitutes fraternizing with the enemy.

The sport is interesting, though I can see flaws. For one, anyone my height or Quidlee's height is at a disadvantage.

That doesn't keep the rook from playing in three-on-three matches or games or whatever they are called; it just keeps him from making any points. Every time he flings the ball at the rim, someone like Barca swats it away.

The wind is especially up, giving every player an excuse for missing a shot. The rain of the other day is just a precursor to a larger storm front on the horizon.

PoBones usually joins me in spectating. Foshi_Taloa is a natural player. His quiet and calculating demeanor is perfect for this game. After an opponent takes a shot, he studies the arch of the ball. The wheels behind his eyes run at Mach speed and before the shot bounces off the backboard or rim, Foshi is under the spot wherever the ball ultimately lands. He is so accurate you can set your watch to him.

"Hey, Tanto, you want in?" AldenSong asks.

"Nope. You can miss my baskets for me."

Aldy counters my remark with one finger and a smile. I pantomime crying.

Aldy is a big body out there, which is apparently good for blocking the paths or shots or bounces of the others. There's a good mix of players on the court. There is some good trash talking between the teams. PoBones says this is part of the game: getting into the opponent's head. It makes me think about Quidlee's pop quizzing that player at the junior college game.

Apparently, there is an art to trash talking. The trash talker insults everything about the opponent, especially when he is bouncing the ball up and down and shuffling his feet. Insults range from body odor to rude things one's mother may or may not have done with wild animals. Nothing is off-limits on the court.

After several games, I am getting the hang of it all, but the term and penalty for "traveling" appears to be subjective.

The one team usually loses, mainly because Barca is on the other. I guess, in sports, when you have a giant, you use him to your advantage. During one of our games, Barca and Aldy are on opposite teams. So, when AldenSong dribbles, Barca hounds Aldy about his size.

"Hey, fat boy, you know you're just gonna choke like you did before." Barca brushes up on Aldy's turned back and swipes at the ball. "Man, you're too fat to dribble . . ."

"Your mom is . . . unless she's not and she's really good at the . . . game" AldenSong's childlike honesty is ill-suited to the trash talking element. "You ready to watch me score?"

"You're not gonna—"

Aldy pivots, leans back, and sends the ball over Barca's head, nailing a three-pointer. AldenSong raises his arms in victory, then pretends his hands are on fire. Foshi_Taloa leans over and blows out the invisible flames while Aldy makes a sizzling sound with his exhale. Barca is none too pleased with any of this.

PoBones slaps his leg and yells out, "Burn bright."

"Burn fast," Aldy responds.

"Burn down," I conclude.

"What the hell does all that mean?" Barca snaps, snatching the ball from Foshi_Taloa. "Y'all got some kinda stupid-ass prison cheer?"

"Something like that."

"Yeah, well, cut it out."

"You're just jealous." Quidlee is more intuitive than I'd given him credit for.

Barca glares at the rook until Quidlee breaks eye contact. Something is brewing between these two. Hopefully, it will not boil over.

Aldy squares off against Barca. "Barca, when you've been here longer than a month, you'll understand why we're a unit, not a bunch of felons."

Barca charges Aldy, taking several steps and fouling the big guy for good measure, yet somehow no one calls it on the giant when he scores.

Barca snatches the ball as it descends. "Oh, did I hurt your little feelings?"

"Barca," AldenSong sweeps his arms across his body. "I do big, not little, and I got big feelings in this sexy body."

"Check me, fatso." Barca passes the ball to Aldy, who checks it back to Barca. I guess our persistent bully doesn't have any comeback for our resident saint.

The game goes on. Barca's team scores, then AldenSong's scores. It is fun in its repetition. It's almost like hacking to me. Everything has a sequence, but all it takes is altering one bit of code, or faking out an opponent, and then the path to your goal clears.

"Game point, fatso." Barca blasts the ball at Aldy. The Samoan catches it with ease and shoots it back, but Barca catches it wrong.

"Dammit! Time . . . jammed my damn pinky finger."

Strangely, Barca strolls over and shows Quidlee the finger. It is jutting at an odd angle, possibly more dislocated than jammed.

Barca wraps his hand around his pinky finger and pulls, the resounding pop is so loud that even *I* flinch, and several other grunts and curses escape the lips of other players.

The giant opens and closes his hand, gritting his teeth and squinting at the already swelling joint.

"Game point." Barca shakes out his hands. "Gimme the rock."

As Barca dribbles, the wind grows in intensity. Some trash caught in wind floats all the way up to our basketball court. Just before Barca takes a shot, an empty Icee cup slams into his face.

Everyone cracks up.

Barca palms the ball with his right hand and removes the trash with his left. Glancing down at the cup, he chuckles. But not an "I'm laughing with you" chuckle. His body is here, but his mind is somewhere dangerous.

Quidlee asks, "What's so funny?"

Barca idly tosses the empty cup in the air. "I never liked Icee's. Actually, hate them. Too sugary and cold on my teeth. But Margie, well, she loved them . . ."

"Who's Margie?"

Something in my stomach turns as an almost devilish light dances across Barca's black eyes.

Curse Quidlee's question and his curiosity.

"Everyone here knows computer hacking. Computers have rules. Rules can be bent, changed, even broken. Now people, well, they're not exactly like computers. People might run on the exact same operating system—the pursuit of happiness, survival, and all that—but their firewalls and anti-virus programs, their defenses, are all different . . ."

Barca bounces the ball against the court. The echo bounces off buildings in the distance. "Margie . . . Margie . . . Margie Longfellow . . . so I'm working on this . . . project in Hays, Kansas, a little town in the middle of nowhere, the kind of place where they have an aquatic park in the middle of the freaking desert-like place. This college girl bumps into me, spilling her blue whatever flavor Icee from the Sinclair gas station off Vine Street all over my shirt and then she has the gall to blame me for the spill, and that I owed her a new drink. So, I bought her that drink . . ."

The wind's intensity dies down a bit, but the clouds overhead get darker.

"I smiled, bought her the drink, and even asked her for her number. Not surprisingly, she gave it to me. Have you seen me? So, we went out a couple of times."

Because Barca's volume stays low, either instinctively or trying to hear, the ballers step toward Barca.

"She shared things with me she hadn't shared with anyone, like how, despite wearing the prettiest clothes and always having perfect makeup on, underneath that false exterior was a girl who just wanted to be loved . . . especially by herself."

Every eye is on Barca, every ear strains to hear him over a clap of thunder in the background.

"Margie was an only child. Her father traveled, sold medical supplies with Goalton-McGregor, and her mother was a night nurse at the local hospital, I think. Some bedpan kinda job. Mother was a mousey lady. Only met her the one time. Good child birthing hips, though. Her father, well, I met him more than once. Little bastard. Talked to me like I should be afraid of his wrath or something if I broke his daughter's heart. Heh. Reminded of the kind of guy that would own a shotgun but never load it. A decorative tough, yeah. Hated me from the first time he laid eyes on me . . . good stuff. Margie's parents made good money, but they didn't spend enough time with Margie for her self-esteem to, say, prosper."

A chill in my left leg creeps up my spine and slaps my brain to say something, anything, to stop this. I open my mouth, but nothing comes out.

"You see, Margie was a cutter, just minor cuts that she could cover up. She started with the area around her nipples. Figured anyone who saw her outside of a bra wouldn't care. Sure, she'd cut around her ankles and armpits by the time she met me, but nothing too deep."

"Barca, stop." The words are past my lips before I realize my pleading will only fuel his fire.

"Don't worry, Princess, I won't leave you hanging. It's not a hanging type of story."

Barca's eyes narrow as he stares at me. No. Not at me. Through me. Almost like he is plotting something while he tells this story.

"Look, I know she wasn't a mark. There was no payday. Maybe what she did to me wasn't so wrong in your eyes, that what I was doing was vengeful. To that, I say you do not know true joy. I know you can't possibly understand what it was like to hack a person, to find the hole in their firewall, disable their anti-virus, their sense of self, and insert your malware to . . . play."

The bastard actually closes his eyes, kicks his head back, and licks his lips as a few drops from the dark cloud above sprinkle down.

"People are harder to hack, but when you do it right, there is no clean reinstallation. There is no backup file. There is only finality, and finality is a satisfying thing."

A single bolt of lightning dances sideways across a cloud in the distance. More rain comes down, but no one notices. No one even blinks.

"With me, she graduated to deeper cuts, both physically and mentally. Yeah, by the end, she was crying to me on the phone when her cuts opened the radial arteries, the ones in the wrists." In his hand, Barca rotates the Icee cup, brings the rim to his nose, and smells inside it. "When you mess with me, you will know my vengeance."

Barca opens his eyes, crushes the cup with his left hand, and takes the game-winning shot with his right.

No one moves to block it.

No one speaks in response to his story.

All he leaves us with is the sound of a leather ball full of air falling perfectly through a round hoop as it brushes against a rope net on the way down to the concrete.

Swish. Thump. Thump.

Chapter Fifty-Seven

Not a Damn Thing I Can Do About It

The slow grin starts at the corners of his mouth and his throbbing neck muscles flex, a poker-level tell that means either he is bluffing, or about to pull some stunt. It reaches Barca's face. And he bursts out into a full-toothed smile, pointing and laughing at each of us.

"Ha! I was joking you! You've should've seen your faces!"

A slow variety of chuckles fill the air as everyone disperses.

"What? Oh, come on, why's everybody so sensitive and offended by everything these days?"

Misdirection. Barca wanted to win that game so badly he filled our heads with nonsense. Part of me wonders if he told that story just to see how far he could go.

It reminds me of a psych experiment that I once took part in when I needed money right after I ran away from home. With a fake ID, experiments like that and selling my sperm for cash made up the majority of my income in those days.

This particular experiment was sexual in nature.

They put me in a sound booth and gave me a handheld buzzer, much like the one that now shocked the hell out of us here at Hackers' Haven, come to think of it. I was told I would listen to an encounter that went horribly wrong and resulted in the rape of a woman. At the point that I thought the man should've respected the woman's boundaries and not forced himself on her, I was to push the button. Also, I could leave the booth at any time.

Early into the "date," I pressed the button. I think it was around the time the girl said she didn't like the guy's hand on her thigh or something. However, to my surprise, the audio did not stop playing. As the scene played on and the date went from playful to nightmare, I guess that the experiment was never about the buzzer. Or, if it was, that was a secondary hypothesis.

The real question the researchers were after was *How long will the subject willingly listen to someone being raped before they storm out of the room?*

I never left until someone came to get me minutes after the "date" had ended. At the time, I was so worried that I wouldn't get paid if I left the room that I listened to the whole ordeal. Looking back at it, part of me wonders if they ever told me that I got paid either way, whether I stayed or went. I hope and pray this was not selective hearing.

All for a twenty-two-dollar payout.

Monsters take many forms and enact their carnage in a variety of ways. Barca had proven himself to be a master manipulator, a beast that I wish had never darkened our doors. Maybe he told this story just to see how far he could go, how long we would listen until that ultimate end that, deep down, we knew was coming.

Barca did not have to tell us he convinced a girl to commit suicide. He just had to chum the waters, baiting us for information, and then we'd all get eaten by his story.

Quidlee and I wander into the War Room. All that work on the keyboards must've re-injured one of his thumbs because his left hand is wrapped in a bandage. It makes sense—we'd worked hard—I just hope that doesn't slow us down.

After I plop down in my seat, I log into my station. Still no takers for the courier position we need for Quidlee's escape.

Getting the rook out is one thing; keeping him free is contingent on this one person. I have contacts in the right places for fake IDs, travel money, transportation, and more. Finding someone who will risk bringing a stolen body across state lines in an illegally acquired manner is a critical problem we must solve.

I think about posting on other forums, but this particular one is the best in my experience: just sketchy enough to not be controlled by a group trying to catch a predator.

I take a minute and glance around the War Room. Everything looks normal. Foshi_Taloa is sitting perfectly straight in his chair while skimming a forum of potential targets. PoBones is leaning so far back in his chair that he is daring it to break. AldenSong is walking in from somewhere, and Quidlee is next to me knee-deep in a capture.

Barca. He's sitting catty-corner from me. His screen is blank, yet he stares at it.

Something is going on.

Maybe my paranoia is flaring up, like a case of hemorrhoids that won't go away. I tell myself that this is a day like any other, but a static in the air makes my skin crawl. Maybe it is the stormy weather.

Just then, a chat window lights up my screen.

[Quidlee]: Hey, you know how you said you were going to be looking for that thing and that I shouldn't be looking for it and that it would just muddy the waters . . .

My gut curses my brain for its correct paranoia.

Don't snap. That will only make things harder.

[Tanto]: And you are writing to me to say that you did indeed do just what we talked about?

[Quidlee]: About that . . .

Son of a bitch.

Quidlee is certainly smart enough to use the safety setting to hide his screen from our system's recording software. But then there's that churning bile in my gut, like the kind that occurs when you approach a roller coaster. The attendant straps you in, and then he chuckles as the death trap lurches forward.

[Tanto]: Abort.

[Quidlee]: I'm safe, dude.

[Tanto]: Abort.

[Quidlee]: Just check out what I've found.

I get up and stroll across the room toward his terminal. Leaving my terminal is as much of a yelling match as I can get away with in the War Room. I walk to the coffeemaker, pick up the pot, and glare at Quidlee. He motions for me to come over. I can't go to his machine without rewarding his bad behavior, but if I don't do something, the rook's as good as busted. I return to my terminal and find two words on my screen.

[Quidlee]: Aborted, Mother.

[Tanto]: Thank you.

My shoulders lower from my ears and the walnut-cracking tightness in my sphincter unclenches. I glance at the rook's screen, several terminals down from mine. Whatever he has been working on is now gone. There is no telling where in cyberland this curious cat has stuck his nose.

Then, when he thinks I'm not looking, the rook shifts back to another screen, which I can see by turning my head ever so slightly.

His post is about a discussion about a deleted nude scene with Scarlett Johansson in a movie soon to be in theaters, called *Iron Man 2*. Whether there is a nude scene doesn't matter. All that matters is dangling non-entrapment-level bait.

Something in Quidlee's on-screen chat catches the corner of my eye. I turn my head and lean over.

Crap. The rook's hunting game must've gotten lax because his phrasing is borderline entrapment.

"Abort." I whisper across PoBones, who sits between us. Something in the way I say this one word causes PoBones to log out and hop out. I can't blame him. This is not his problem.

"What?" The rook clearly is not in the mood to take constructive feedback today. I slide into the empty chair.

"Now."

I find the error in his trap. Quidlee has done enough runs to avoid this blatant mistake. We all mess up; just not everyone is attempting to escape prison during these slipups. During his thread, Quidlee fails to focus on the discussion and puts a link to one of our landing page traps: a hyperlink to a section of it entitled The Best Porn You Don't Have to Pay For. Instead, he's commented, "Hey, guys, I use this site and it's free and I think you should go there," in a non-pornography related thread.

Like an alarm themselves, the *cha-chings* start.

I spit out through gritted teeth, "Abort, Quidlee."

The *cha-chings* come hard and fast, their nature more rapid than the warden's normal strides. In my mind, there is no denying their destination.

"Reboot, rook." I must think faster than Quidlee's hands because he starts closing out windows before rebooting. That will take too long.

I stand up and lean behind the computer, searching for the power strip for Quidlee's terminal, but the on/off button is way out of my reach.

The *cha-chings* get louder as Quidlee is still trying to manually log out.

Shutting your system off is the only way to keep Cyfib from keying in his administrative access code and gaining immediate access to your recent history. Yes, the warden can go through keylog files, but it will take time. In that time, we might be able to erase or at least damage those files. Might.

The clickety-clacks from the other side of Quidlee's terminal get faster.

We have no time left. The power strip has several hours of juice stored up in it to prevent data loss in a power surge, so I must yank the cord connecting the workstation to the power strip. I crane farther back and drape my body into the crevice.

There is no way to reach the power cord. The rim of the metal desk cuts into my ribs as I stretch deeper. My index finger nicks the power cord.

"Come on, come on," the rook mumbles to himself, willing the computer to shut down. With all systems programmed to back up essential files and complete their shutdown procedure, Quidlee does not have enough time. Yet he still tries.

My fingers stretch as far as they can. I get my index finger around the gunmetal-gray cord and pull. The end is firmly in the power socket. It moves a hair, but not enough to cause a power outage.

I exhale all the air from my lungs and get my middle finger around the cord as well.

Cyfib shouts, "No!" but I keep reaching.

I've lost track of all the *cha-chings*. A sharp pain shoots up my side from my right knee as Cyfib's boot stomps on it and something pops. The pain forces my hand to let go of the cord. I crumple to the floor and instinctively hold my knee.

"Bad dog!" Kick after steel-toed kick slams into my ribs as I try to protect my body in a fetal position.

From the floor, I grit my teeth until the kicking stops. I open my eyes to watch as Cyfib grabs Quidlee by the neck and tosses him away from the desk, hurling him into other hackvicts with rage-fueled strength.

From his crisp black pants, the warden withdraws his administrative flash drive, inserts it into a slot on the workstation, and types on the keyboard.

I must do something. Rush the warden? That won't do much more than delay the inevitable and send me to the Bay in the process.

Still, it's better than doing nothing. However, as I lean up, Aldy's white New Balance sneaker plants on my chest with just enough force to hold me but not hurt me.

Curse my friend. I try to move his foot with my hand, but he applies more pressure. AldenSong will not let me burn for crimes that are not mine.

Cyfib finishes his scan and turns to tower over Quidlee, who is rocking back and forth behind the warden.

"Dog, what you have done is entrapment, not enticement. By presenting something unwelcome, and encouraging admission into our trap, you are coercing the situation. Not only is this hunt ruined, but so is the site."

"Sir, I don't think it is." Quidlee's hands shoot out to his side in a wide, sweeping gesture. "The forum is just—"

Cyfib picks up Quidlee's keyboard and clocks him across the face with it. The blow knocks the rook into his workstation. After a moment, Quidlee trips and falls to the ground on top of me. A trickle of blood from his temple drips into my open mouth.

"Dog, you are not here to think." Cyfib lands a kick into Quidlee's ribs. "You are not here to question. You are here to do a task, dog. You have burned this forum for all in Hackers' Haven. You do not know the damage you have done. I think some time in solitary will serve you well."

He punctuates with a kick.

"Stay down," I whisper.

A red rage floods Quidlee's face, burning from his neck all the way up to his curly hair. My arms are pinned to my chest but luckily, AldenSong is there to hold the kid down.

Until Barca pulls Aldy off both of us.

"What're you doing, man?" asks Aldy, a hint of panic.

"Let this happen." The bastard's voice is smooth and collected.

"You are not letting anything happen." In all the confusion, I never expected the next thing before my face would be a Deringer pistol.

The gun the size of a cell phone in Cyfib's hand moves from my face to Barca's. The giant glances down at the barrel.

"Warden, you might want to reconsider . . ."

Before Barca can finish his sentence, Cyfib fires a round past Barca's ear. The small pop echoes in the room and makes all of us jump. All except Barca.

"Silence." The warden puts the gun to Quidlee's head. "Sometimes you just have to put a bad dog down."

The warden leans back, his gun eye level with Quidlee. I try to move, but my legs refuse to move.

Neither Quidlee nor Cyfib blink. Something is in the rook's hand. *Is it another shiv?*

The air in the room clings to my body as I squirm to my feet and stand between the warden, Quidlee, and a loaded gun.

"Move, dog."

No, I think, though saying the word out loud never crosses my mind. He pistol-whips me in the face. I stand firm.

Then, like I just obeyed his order and nothing happened, the warden pockets his pistol and announces, "All kills are forfeited today. Go to your cells."

Aldy knocks Barca's grip off his shoulder and moves toward Quidlee, but it is too late. Quidlee moves around me, yet knocks me to the ground in the process.

All the rage-blood drains from Quidlee's face. White splotches fill his cheeks. Losing our hard-earned work for the day, meant to take the wind from his sails, bolsters Quidlee's bravado. I don't understand why this group punishment hits him so hard; the warden's threatened it before and done worse.

But this time, it snaps something in him.

Maybe it is the upcoming stint in solitary confinement. Or the realization that we are about to lose our current window to get him out. Or maybe it really is the damage he has just caused to his fellow hackvicts' kill count.

I think it is the look on my face that he saw when I moved my leg earlier. I grimaced and bit my lip as a spasm sent red-hot lightning up my side. When I glanced up, I caught a look on Quidlee's face that was more than anger. It was that of extreme sorrow.

Tears fill his eyes. He swallows in fast succession. He knows his actions resulted in my getting hurt. Now, he wants to repay that pain somehow.

He gets in the warden's face and screams. Then he runs his fingernails across his own face, cutting four lines of crimson down his right cheek.

Slight trickles of blood drip onto Quidlee's lips, and I wait for what comes next.

It will haunt me for all of my days, and there's not a damn thing I can do about it.

Chapter Fifty-Eight

As We Flee

Quidlee lunges at the warden, but Guard Stevens intercepts him. The tears and blood on the rook's face are nothing compared to the dam inside him that just went from cracked to busted wide open. Quidlee's adrenaline gets him on top of the guard, pummeling him with childlike slaps instead of punches before Guard Fontana intercedes.

Poor Quidlee's gone mad.

Fontana's retracted baton pops as it extends. He cracks it across Quidlee's temple, knocking the rook out cold. One hit. One problem down.

I crawl up from the floor with little to do now that Fontana has ended the conflict. The new guard kicks the unconscious Quidlee and spits on him to remind everyone he is still an authority figure. Nothing says dominance like attacking a helpless human, apparently. The guards zip-tie the rook and drag him away.

The inmate we knew as Quidlee will not return to us the same man, if he even returns at all.

Solitary, especially a second stint, is usually worse than your first check-in there. Now you know what to expect. Your body fears and braces for the flashing lights and blaring noises, which means you are on edge all the time. This is a well-built, psyops level of a mind screw. In this rare occurrence, the devil you know is worse than the devil you don't.

Cyfib points at me without looking my way. "This dog seems to have tripped. Someone carry him to the Infirmary."

Of all the hands that could've lowered my way, Barca's are the last I expect. The giant extends his hand to me to help me off the ground. I knock it away, but he grabs the backside of it with his other hand and yanks me to my feet. I grunt as my bad knee sends a spasm up my spine.

"I can make it to the Infirmary on my own." It's a lie, but I will not accept help from this monster.

Barca pulls me close, close enough that the heat from his body makes my eyes water.

"You did this, Princess." Then he lets me go.

Did this? I did everything in my power to *stop* it. I shake my head in confusion.

Barca's eyes flash with fire before the pupils fade into a steady focus. Then a blankness crosses his face as he walks out of the War Room.

Before they ship Quidlee off to the Hole, then maybe the Bay, he'll have to spend time in the Infirmary.

It's a good thing too because our time is up. There is no more waiting on a courier for the fake body and identification. I will have to get Quidlee out tonight and figure the rest out as we flee.

Chapter Fifty-Nine

Oh, but Worry I Will

"Well, it's not broken. That's the good news." Dr. Fel glances at the X-ray, but then sucks his teeth. "The bad news is that your kneecap, the patella, is playing hide-and-seek from the rest of your body and can't be found right now. I mean, it is in there under all the swelling. It's not like it fell out."

The unconscious body of my friend lies on the table next to me. The rook sleeps hard, a little snore like the world's tiniest foghorn playing in his sinuses. He even sleeps through both of our quick scans in the pods.

The doc seems to be fast-tracking us to a diagnosis. My medical background is limited, but I'd think a possible concussion victim is a higher priority than one with an injured leg.

The doc must've noticed me staring at Quidlee because he sighs. "The kid's fine . . . I checked him out before you got here and gave him a sedative. Back to you and your wonky knee. Patellar subluxation. This isn't that uncommon an injury. Mainly lots of swelling and the flexibility in that leg is going to be rigid for a while. Rigid, not frigid, like my wife."

If Hackers' Haven isn't the death of me, surely the doc's jokes will polish me off.

"Some minor physical therapy and a set of crutches would help, but since this was so slight, I expect little more than soreness after I pop it back in."

Great. Then I can get back to getting us out of here. I'd hate to take Dr. Fel hostage, even if he would probably be the world's best one, helping hold doors open. Maybe he'd even wheel me out as the rook walks on.

Something in my hip burns as if someone struck a match and put it out on my side. Dr. Fel withdraws a syringe from my hip.

Oh, no.

"While you're out, I'm going to do a couple of routine procedures . . . nothing you need to worry about . . ."

"Wait . . ." The word stretches as I fall into the blackness. An invisible, weighted blanket covers my lower body, then my chest, and finally my head. The world darkens. Dr. Fel's words float to my ears from the bottom of a well.

"Gotta fix . . . then the . . . MRI . . . abnormality . . . nothing to worry . . ."

Oh, but worry I will.

Chapter Sixty

Swallows Me Whole

There is something about dreams that makes them darker and more surreal when they occur under the influence of anesthesia. The tentacles of the unconscious mind shoot out stronger and clingier, with jagged hooks that wrap around you. These are the kind that stay with you for days after you've awakened, unlike dreams that fade by breakfast coffee.

I'd taken these trips several times, only once while in a hospital or under a doctor's care. Before I could legally drink, I dabbled in the opioids and mind numb'rs of the world, anything to occasionally escape the reality I lived in. I guess you could say the pill bottle didn't fall far from the tree.

After Dr. Fel shot me up with who knows what, my consciousness found itself in a dark room with a light in the distance. It is not a glowing white light, so I am not dead, nor is it a yellow light like the sun or a standard light bulb.

It is a black light, though not one that you find in raves or in the childhood bedrooms of kids who own way too many psychedelic posters.

No, everything this light touches turns darker. And it is growing in intensity. It is heading my way.

At first, my legs will not move. Concrete fills them and, when I finally start running away from the all-absorbing black hole chasing me, each step thunders against the ground. Before that, there was only the sound of dripping water. Eventually my footsteps fade, my bare feet hitting wet ground. The mass chasing me is so powerful that it steals those sounds as well. I run faster and faster away from one void and into the lesser darkness ahead of me. It is not like the dreams where one cannot outrun the monster chasing them because they are moving so slowly or trip over every stick or branch possible.

My legs are a whirlwind. I am running faster than any Olympic track gold medalist.

And I am losing.

The darkness is just faster, more determined than me. It covers the ceiling first, then slithers around the sides of the endless hallway. My legs are moving so fast that they are a blur of motion.

Yet the darkness finally creeps under my bare feet. The bottoms of my feet go numb as they touch the darkness.

I keep running, but the darkness moves past me, first in from the side, then the top and bottom. It is five or so feet in front of me as well as above my shoulders, merely flicking against my skin. That's when I notice my legs are no longer touching the ground. I kick, but the darkness picks me up under my arms and speeds up my already rocket intensity.

As I am propelled forward, the darkness forms a human head in front of me. No, it forms two half heads. The face splits down the middle. Now a beast with two heads glares at me.

On the left side is Barca's grinning face.

On the right is Cyfib's snarl.

My two devils have united to torment me, and no amount of running away will allow me to escape their vengeance.

My ears pop from a pressure, like I'm back in the Coffin. Just like there, my breath leaves my lungs. I claw at my neck for any molecule of air hidden inside.

Barca's half face smiles at Cyfib's. The warden's snaps in return. The two half faces bark and try to bite each other, junkyard dogs fighting for alpha status. Finally, the warden lowers his head and morphs into the larger darkness behind Barca.

Only one of my beasts wants me now. The darkness' eyes narrow as the head approaches me. A wide grin stretches across its face.

Then Barca's mouth opens wide and swallows me whole.

Chapter Sixty-One

A Present

I awaken with a scream and sit straight up on the same hospital bed I'd passed out on. The doc is not there. Apparently, he's gone home.

When I rub the crust from my eyes and look around for the rook, he is nowhere. They've already taken Quidlee to the Hole. *Dammit.* Getting him out just got a lot harder.

Yanking off the blanket reveals that not only is my leg from above my knee to just below it wrapped in a bandage and ice packs, but there is also a small, taped bandage on it. Touching it shoots a dull pain up my leg. With the dryness in my mouth and pounding in my head, all sensations add to the already existing sense of dread in my gut.

I yank the IV from my left arm, tearing the tape away and squirting blood all over the room. Wrapping paper towels from the table next to me around the crook of my arm, I stand up. My good leg is fine. However, when I take one baby step, my right leg gives out, and I crumple to the floor.

From my spot on the cold tile, I spot a pair of crutches in the corner. Despite Dr. Fel downplaying my injury, it appears I'll need them to get through at least tonight.

I hobble on crutches through a haze. The effort of maneuvering the stairs using crutches burns my armpits. My equilibrium shifts like I am on a ship at sea, but I make it to the Hole, which is in the basement near the servers.

It's never guarded. However, when I get to the series of three rooms, all the doors are open. I peek in each to look for Quidlee.

He is nowhere to be found.

I make the long trek back up the stairs—no small miracle—to Quidlee's room. I lean in and look through the glass.

Again, he is not there.

I check mine and do the same. Ironically, I find my cell door locked, yet I'm standing in the hallway trying to get in. He is not there either. Finally, I go to AldenSong's and find Aldy fast asleep.

I tap on his door until he leans up out of his bunk.

"What?" A half-shout-half-mumble escapes the big guy's lips as he opens his eyes with great effort. "Hey, man, how's the leg?"

"Where's Quidlee?"

"Not...sure." I cannot tell if I am speaking to awake Aldy, full of reason, or one who is asleep, just wanting to answer any question to get back to sleep.

"He's not in the Hole or in his room."

The Samoan lets out a yawn that is so loud it would've echoed in a larger room. "Infirmary?"

"I just came from there."

"Well, give me a second to . . . get my head together . . . I'll come . . ."

And he's asleep again.

A false sense of relief sweeps through my body, but dread slaps that notion away.

They wouldn't have deported him, would they? Yes, he'd assaulted a guard. However, someone would've needed to fill out the paperwork and process orders to send him to Guantanamo Bay.

I feel sick, like I drank spoiled milk. This is the same way I feel when I dream of our Hackers' Haven victims: faceless figures either screaming at me like banshees or standing there, water streaming down from their eyes and filling the room, drowning me in the process.

This time, my gut tightens harder and will not let go.

I stumble down the hallway and pop my head into each room, knocking on doors and waking other hackvicts.

Nothing.

Then I pass Barca in the hallway with a swagger to his step.

"Barca, what are you doing out of your cell?"

He places his hand on my shoulder and sends me a smile and a wink.

"Well, since you and I are escaping soon, I really wanted to leave you a present. You'll find it in the latrine."

Chapter Sixty-Two

My Thoughts and Failures to Keep Me Company

I don't even hear the rest of what Barca says as I hobble as fast as I can to the latrine. The room is quiet. My heartbeat pounds in my eardrums.

Then I spot my "present": Quidlee's body hanging from the ceiling by a blue Ethernet cord.

Nothing is real, and yet every cell in my body hurts. The world spins and the next thing I know, I am under my friend's body.

I don't remember pulling Quidlee's body from the noose, but there it is on the white tile floor before me. I cradle him in my arms, but I genuinely think *my friend's dead body is not in my arms. This is not real. His purplish face, swollen and discolored, is not really here.*

I'm not in Hackers' Haven. My mind is not able to comprehend this moment. I am anywhere but here. It is any time but now.

I lay the still warm body of my friend out on the floor. Some of his curly hair drapes into the shower drain. I sweep it out with my open hand. *Wouldn't want his hair to get dirty.*

I don't know if I am in shock, but I must act. Something in me refuses to accept this horrible reality. Doing nothing is not an option. I tear Quidlee's shirt open. I don't know why, but maybe chest compressions work better when there is no shirt on the injured.

As soon as air hits my lungs, I expel it into my friend's lungs. Two breaths into his lungs, and then five chest compressions out as my balled-up fists press down on Quidlee's hairless chest.

Repeat.

I no longer breathe for myself.

A breath in for me. A breath out for him. Push. Pump. Pump. Pump. Pump. Do not fail.

Time eludes me. Either I do this for a minute, for an hour, or for a year. These time frames all mean the same to me right now.

A film covers my eyes. It's almost like I am a half step behind my own body. I am performing CPR, but I am also watching it over my shoulder. Everything I do is automatic. I am no longer in control of my actions. I no longer live for me, nor do I die for Quidlee.

"I'm so sorry, Tim."

No. Not Tim. I meant to say Quidlee. For some reason, his given name is all I can call him right now. Maybe in death his given name returns.

My mind travels. Through a haze, I am performing my first hack at age eight: my neighbor Rex and I hack the grocery store's intercom so that each announcement ends with a fart noise.

I return to reality-ish to discover a burning pain in my left shoulder. I'm pretty sure some muscle has torn. A river of fire burns through my upper body. My mind blasts, *keep pushing on. Ignore the pain. Fight for Tim. Don't you quit on him. You must fight for Quidlee.*

A breath in for me. A breath out for him. Push. Pump. Pump. Pump. Pump. Do not fail.

My mind again drifts from this Hail Mary work and an old scene plays out next to the body. A dim room fills with light as the memory of my mother's first overdose comes into view. There's little me, a small child with a ridiculous bowl haircut and a solid level of grime on my skin; I can't quite place how old I was when I found her like this. I do know my hand was small enough to shove down her throat and force her to vomit.

I forget now how I knew to do this. I remember I didn't even wash my hands when I returned to playing with my Legos.

Do I need to make Tim vomit? No. No! Focus.

A breath in for me. A breath out for him. Push. Pump. Pump. Pump. Pump. Do not fail.

This is not working. The CPR makes no sense, yet it makes all the sense in my madness.

As my body continues the CPR, my mind turns and spots the recent image of Barca with a smile creeping across his face.

You did this . . . I told you that you would know my vengeance.

Now, finally, everything is real. Everything hurts. Everything is breaking inside me. The cells in my body awaken and burn through each pore in my skin. My attention is fully on the chest compressions now. My arms throb and I wish they could reach into my friend's chest and pump his heart—that I could trade his lack of breath for my burning lungs.

I'd trade my life for his, not just to escape the pain in my chest that reminds me that this was my fault. I am the reason for his incarceration. The reason he is dead in my arms. This is my failure. My damned ego.

A breath in for me. A breath out for him. Push. Pump. Pump. Pump. Pump. Do not fail.

I'm here, in this room, but I'm also not here. I expel as much air as I can into my friend's lungs. Maybe it is the lack of holding in oxygen for my own body and my brain getting weaker, but my mind flashes just a few of my many horrible failures in my life and they flicker right before my eyes.

I'm twelve and in my first police lineup. Before I am old enough to drive, I will be in five more.

I'm fourteen on top of Claudia's dad's VW Bug, getting my first kiss, when her father taps on the window with his double-barrel shotgun, aims it skyward, fires it next to my head, branding and slightly deafening my left ear permanently.

I'm sixteen and hitchhiking away from my childhood home, with a handful of a dead woman's money and no plan but *to get away.*

A breath in for me. A breath out for him. Push. Pump. Pump. Pump. Pump. Do not fail.

My spirit floats back another two feet from my body. In front of me I watch a red-faced, hyperventilating version of myself count out loud during chest compressions. To the right of that scene, is eighteen-year-old me, with bloodshot eyes and foaming at the mouth, full of hard drugs and a harder hope about getting my next fix, whether it was drugs, sex, or the thrill of a hack.

Finally, to the left of my current body, I spot twenty-year-old me screwing up royally, all on a hack to impress a girl—a hack that scarred me more than any gunshot or knife ever would.

I float back to my body and transpose over it, continuing chest compressions. Maybe if I talk to my friend, he'll come back to us. *Just follow my voice back, Tim.*

"Hey . . . my tattoo . . . you wanted to know . . . about the names . . ." My voice cracks, and the words float out, as if they come from down a long, wooden hallway. "So, I was trying to impress this girl . . . you know all about that because you're . . . such a player . . . she was an ebony goddess and I thought it'd be grand . . . to crash the server that housed the KKK website and a database of membership . . ."

A breath in for me. A breath out for him. Push. Pump. Pump. Pump. Pump. Do not fail.

"Good news is I did it, crashed the whole system through the BIOS, and got mind-blowing sex . . . the kind that makes you walk funny for a week . . . heh . . . the bad news is that other databases were outsourced to that same server . . . like three hospitals' lists for those needing organ transplants . . ."

I stop. Maybe it is the story, or maybe my body needs a break. I glance down at my hands, black-and-blue from overuse and pushing them past their pain points. I attempt making a fist. Nothing happens. I think two of my fingers are dislocated.

I start CPR again.

A breath in for me. A breath out for him. Push. Pump. Pump. Pump. Pump. Do not fail.

"Six people died . . . before someone reinstalled the backups . . . the organs were even there . . . just no one could link the donor to the organ before the tissue rotted. Their names . . ."

I'm twenty-eight and continuing CPR on my long-dead friend. Something cracks in his chest on a downward compression. Maybe it is just a rib. Maybe there's no internal bleeding. Sweat covers my arms and my hands slip again.

My hand connects with Quidlee's wrapped hand. *Poor kid. I did this, too.* However, in the wrapping, I spot something metal. I pull off the bandage to reveal a metal flash drive.

That's Cyfib's administrative key.

Without another thought, I pocket it.

The CPR isn't working but stopping isn't an option. This is my failure.

You did this . . . I told you that you would know my vengeance . . .

Barca's voice pulses in my head like the bass beat on a car stereo next to you at a red light.

My sweaty arms slip again. My mind must've wandered because my weight shifts from Quidlee's sternum. I accidentally push down on Quidlee's trachea. Something in his throat pops. The sensation beneath my touch is like when a piece of celery snaps in half.

I may have punctured his larynx. *No, that's not possible,* I tell myself, a lie to keep my train of insanity chugging forward.

I move my arms back to his hairless chest and continue CPR.

"Tanto . . ."

The voice I hear is not mine, but this is not a reason for me to stop. Never stop.

A breath in for me. A breath out for him. Push. Pump. Pump. Pump. Pump. Do not fail.

"Tanto . . ." AldenSong's hand covers my shoulder. "Look, look at me!"

I don't know how long he's watched me. It must be time to get up and the cell doors are unlocked.

How long have I been here?

Maybe Aldy just walked in. I do not know, but I continue my mission. I will not fail.

"He's gone, Tanto!"

A moment of panic hits me, and I take it as an idea. I can restart Tim's heart. That will fix this situation. The key to this success is electricity. I glance around the room and spot a wall socket about six feet off the ground with a space heater plugged in.

I try to stand, but my knees buckle because my legs are long asleep. Also, one has a swollen knee the size of a damn grapefruit. My body's pain sensors must've maxed out with all the fire in my upper body. Pins and needles rush into my legs, the sensation sending a million biting ants up my thighs.

Even through the pain, I waddle to the power cord and yank it out of the socket. Using my teeth, I tear a slight rip into the cable.

I plant one foot on the base of the heater and wrap both hands around the cable. With a heave, the cable splits, tearing free of the heater and exposing the raw wiring.

I plug the damaged cable in. A slight burning smell fills my nostrils with heat. I extend the cable from the wall toward Quidlee's body.

The damn thing will not reach. It needs a conduit.

Me. I am the necessary conduit.

I stick my head under the shower and cut it on full blast.

Part of me, the rational part that is shoved deep down into a hole, couldn't interfere if he wanted to.

I am the conduit.

I can do this.

My friend does not die because of me.

I put one soaked hand on Quidlee's chest and reach for the cable.

I'm an inch away when Aldy tackles me and pins me to wall.

"Let go! Let the hell go of me!"

"Shhh . . ." His grip is kind, yet firm. "Be still . . ."

"Let go!"

"Shhh . . ." Aldy is across my front in a bear hug, pinning my arms to my chest. I slam my knee into the asshole's thigh. He holds me still. I bash again and again. Despite the occasional grunt, AldenSong holds on to me for dear life. For my life.

I say every hurtful thing I ever can about AldenSong.

I curse.

I threaten.

And I plead.

No matter what I do, Aldy holds me close.

"Be still."

"No . . . I . . . no . . ."

"Be . . . still . . ."

Just like with Barca, time passes before my body gives out and Alden-Song releases his grip. Somehow the Samoan knows exactly what to do because he pulls me into his giant chest and nuzzles me in. I punch at his kidneys, but I have no power left in my arms.

AldenSong holds me through what happens next as well.

The teakettle of events hits the boiling point in my brain. Through its tiny pinhole, everything comes out. Not just the mistake of today, nor my failure as a mentor and protector for Tim, I mean Quidlee. Everything billows forth. Years' worth of tears break free of my mental dam. I shake. I scream. I equally gasp for air and drown in what my throat catches. A wail that sounds like a coffee grinder on high vomits forth from my throat in a force and octave that I cannot pretend to control.

Throughout it all, my friend holds me so close that my own tremors come back through his giant body to me. He shakes, but he never lets up.

Tears flow from eyes that thought they knew this world and were conditioned to its hate.

All my training is bullshit.

I was wrong to think I knew hate and how to combat it.

Knowing hate without knowing about the possibility of vengeance is like understanding gasoline and not knowing what happens when it meets a lit match.

I don't know when the guards showed up, but the next thing I know, AldenSong and I are each in solitary confinement cells. Only then am I left with nothing but my thoughts and failures to keep me company.

Chapter Sixty-Three

Haunt Our Doors

For six days, I sat. I do not remember standing or sleeping or using the crapper, but I must have. The guards brought me food. They took away empty plates, so I must've eaten.

I know that, from my previous times in solitary, the warden blasts flashing lights and intermittent music to break a prisoner's psyche.

For the life of me, I do not know if any of that occurred.

For just shy of a week, I sat.

The first day I cried and struggled to accept anything that had happened in the latrine. Maybe it was all a dream. There was a chance of that. Stranger dreams had occurred. Maybe I secretly had plenty of time to get Quidlee out. Maybe each practice run was not an opportunity I had squandered.

The second day, I decided I had not dreamed Quidlee's death. I felt a scream clinging under my chin, refusing to let go of my throat and come out. If I started screaming, I was afraid I'd never stop.

I also decided that I would kill Barca. I'd failed to do it before, when I had the flathead screwdriver in my hand and Barca had taunted me for it. That failure was mine to rectify. If the big bastard wanted to talk about vengeance, I would show him vengeance.

Forget my code.

The Bushido Code was no more real than Santa Claus, a story passed down from generation to generation. *What had this code actually accom-*

plished for me? Nothing but pain. Bushis took lives. It was time for me to take one.

The third day, though, I wondered if I had the right to end a man's life. Even *this* man's life.

Who was I to kill, to end everything that a man was and ever would be? That right surely belonged to someone more hurt than me. Maybe I could sneak Quidlee's sister Penny into the prison and she could stab him in the heart. After all, it was her brother, her blood lost. But even in the best circumstances that would put her at risk—the very thing Quidlee had been fighting to save her from.

The fourth day, I cried again. I thought all the tears had left my body a couple of days ago, that the well had run dry. I was wrong.

On the fifth day, something more morphed than clicked in my mind. I remember staring at the stain on the wall that looked like the state of Idaho when the sliver of a plan formed in my noggin.

It was not in a eureka-level moment, the kind where all the pieces come together, and one sees the picture on a puzzle from overhead. No, this was an ember flickering in my mind, much like one would spot in a mostly dead fire. This ember required someone to crouch down close to it, to use one's hand to block the crosswind from extinguishing it. It required someone with patience to blow on it at just the right intensity to create a fire that would burn everything down.

If Barca was in our home, he would destroy all he touched. So, I would meet Barca's demand and get him out of this building.

And once he got out, I'd guarantee he would never haunt our doors again.

Chapter Sixty-Four

Go Big or Go Home

They release me from solitary after six days. The warden's investigation ruled the whole thing a suicide. No further investigation was necessary. How convenient for him.

Six days was enough time for an autopsy and for someone to reduce my friend's remains to something the size of a loaf of bread. My stomach churned at the thought of someone dissecting my friend.

They release AldenSong at the same time. We walk side-by-side back to our rooms. Aldy's face is pale, or as pale as his tan face gets. His sunken eyes and a week's worth of facial hair make him look more homeless and less jovial. I can only imagine how I look.

He shuffles in small steps, and I wonder how much the flashing lights and intermittent music have messed with his head. This is his fourth, maybe fifth, time in the hole. It only takes one bad stay at Hotel Solitary for your brain to crash. That was what happened to SweetThree.

Did Barca have a hand in that death as well? The thought comes unbidden into my mind.

The only thing I can figure out is that Barca wanted to get on our shift for some reason. Maybe it was because he wanted to escape the whole time.

If he was planning an escape anyway, what better time to do it than between shifts? We only have two guards then. Cyfib works partial nights;

he shows up before our shift and leaves not long after the next one begins.

My paranoia is fueling my hate, or maybe it is the other way around. If Barca wants out, I'll get him out.

Escaping with him is a bad idea, though. I can get one cadaver and a set of fake IDs, but two? *I'm good, not miraculous.*

AldenSong stumbles toward his room. I put my arm on his. He stops and looks down at it like he'd never seen a hand before. He opens his mouth.

"Aldy, are you . . ."

"I . . ."

AldenSong's eyes roll toward me, and his gaze is flat. For a second, I wonder if this trip to the Hole broke him. He's never left the place looking or acting different. His commune upbringing and unwavering faith in God and people are things I joke with him about, but secretly envy. AldenSong is stronger than his struggles, unlike me.

"I . . . need . . ."

AldenSong takes my hand in his, raises it to his face, and puts it to his lips.

"I . . . need . . . brains . . ."

Aldy's eyes flash as he kicks back his head, opens his jaw, and tries to fake bite me. I push the big lug away and get a big whiff of what one week without showering smells like.

Of course, he closes his mouth when he catches a whiff of me as well.

"T, you smell like the inside of a discarded shoe!"

"And you don't smell like a box of soap either."

"Box of soap?" Aldy chuckles. "Have they sold a *box of soap* since you were a child during the Great Depression, Grandpa?"

His laughter is infectious, and I laugh for the first time in days. Maybe weeks. Sometimes the body needs a laugh. Gallows humor is still humor.

As our laughter dies down, our thoughts return. I break eye contact with AldenSong and chew on the inside of my cheek. What are the right words to thank someone for saving your life?

Those words never come to me.

"T, I'm so sorry about Quidlee."

I nod, more out of a polite gag reflex than anything else. "I have a plan."

"I'm in."

"No." I grimace. "I've endangered enough people . . . this is my situation to fix . . . to end . . ."

"Stop." AldenSong places his giant-right-index-sausage-finger on my chest. "You don't get to go saving the world or whatever without me."

"This is not up for debate, Aldy."

"That's right . . . so just accept I'm part of this solution or part of your problem, you pick."

Damn you, you big lovable bastard.

I sigh. He is right. I can't get Barca out on my own. There are just too many variables. But with AldenSong doing something on the inside, I might have a chance at this working.

The best-case scenario is that Barca gets out.

The worst-case is that all three of us wind up in a place worse than death, the Bay.

As they say, go big or go home.

Chapter Sixty-Five

Sharp Enough to Draw Blood

That afternoon, both the day shift and the night shift follow Cyfib's orders and meet to mourn the loss of one of our own.

Earlier, during the shift change, Cyfib did his dog and pony show of holding up Quidlee's ashes in a clear plastic bag and mocking him, a lost tool whose potential was never met. Cyfib did the same word-for-word speech he said for SweetThree, complete with a bloodstained, blue Ethernet cable. Even though it was a repeat speech, the words stung harsher. They were extra pours of salt into my gaping wounds.

"I never got him out." For some reason, that thought escapes my brain and slides past my lips as Cyfib speaks. The warden sends a "hush, dogs" out to the crowd, but none of my fellow hackvicts tense up, expecting, even bracing for a correction shock from the warden. We all were hurting and, besides, what was one more shock at this point?

AldenSong puts his hand on my shoulder and gives me a squeeze. Words will not help, but he is there for me just the same.

I have one of those wavering moments where I think I can still kill Barca. While I do not know if I have the fortitude to kill someone myself, how would I know if I didn't try?

Pondering Barca's death makes me think of Yamamoto Tsunetomo's book *Hagakure*. In it, the author discusses that killing a man who would cause the suffering of tens of thousands of people is not only a just act, but a necessary one—a case where a blade designed for death actually serves a greater purpose of life.

Maybe it is time for me to become my handle's namesake.

AldenSong interrupts my train of thought by leaning down to whisper in my ear. "I can do all this through Him who gives me strength."

Of all the times for AldenSong to whisper scripture to me, it just has to be the time when I am considering taking another human's life.

While the Bushido warriors killed many a villain, the other influence in my life never harmed a soul. Mr. Lon, the *Gentleman Bandit* as the newspapers dubbed him, always treated those who he robbed, even though they were victims, with a level of respect that deserved its own criminal code.

Mr. Lon never once took wedding rings or sentimental jewelry. When questioned about this, he said that even the smallest of diamonds may contain the memory of the largest of life's joys. Not only did he respect his victims, he also would get their information from the driver's licenses, but not to haunt them or scare them like the villain in a thriller movie. No, he would wait close to a week after the crime, and then call each one of them from a different pay phone just to ensure the ordeal did not traumatize them.

Of course, Mr. Lon never met Barca or Cyfib.

I have drowned out Cyfib's last words and half-heartedly follow as the warden takes the remains of my friend with him into the Cube of Death.

Across the room, Barca teases PoBones about something and then puts the Cajun in a headlock and gives him a noogie. Even though the two are playful, I catch Barca's stare my way.

He's set his claws into his target. The predator has found its next prey.

I nod at Barca and then head back to the bathroom where he'd killed my friend. Hopefully, he will read my action to follow correctly.

However, before I leave the War Room, I snag a pen, pad, and the screwdriver I'd hidden by the coffeemaker days earlier.

One sharp enough to draw blood.

Chapter Sixty-Six

Work to Do

I take the furthest stall from the latrine's door. Barca walks in.

From the way they set up the dividers between pissers, there is no way for the bastard to tell that I am holding the screwdriver in my hand instead of my prick. The giant strolls my way with the ease of a man who's just won the jackpot at a casino: he swaggers right, then left, as if he has all the time and money in the world.

Neither of us speaks as Barca unzips his pants and pisses. I rotate the round end of the screwdriver in my sweaty right palm around and around.

Do I have what it takes to end a monster?

Yes, I will get caught. Yes, I will go to the Bay and spend the rest of my life going through who-knows-what level of interrogation and suffering, but everyone within these walls, my tribe, will be safe.

Not only a just murderous act, but a necessary one.

"Ahhhhhh . . ." the monster kicks his head back and even uses both hands to cradle his neck. He is free-hanging his piss, and a warmness on my foot tells me he's pissing on my shoe.

I turn my head and study the closed-eyed beast. There, right where Barca's shoulder meets his neck, is the spot where I will drive my weapon deep, hitting the crossroads of several crucial internal and external jugular veins.

Is this my calling in life, to rid the world of a monster?

Be still.

Those words run through my mind. The very words that AldenSong whispered to me as I was trying to become the conduit between the wall socket, an exposed wire, and a stopped heart. He saved me from electrocuting myself.

Be still.

Shut up, Aldy. There is no *being still.* There is only the here and now.

Then those two words leave my brain and run along the same veins I am going to sever on Barca. A coolness floods throughout my body. For a moment, I am not only calm. I am in control.

A sudden twinge of pain in my leg reminds me of the week I was down in the basement working on several of our servers. I banged my other knee pretty hard, crawling out from under a table. Several flies had gotten in there. I remember this because I swatted at the one that kept trying to crawl up my nose. The little sucker was vindictive and, like zombie Aldy, apparently wanted my brains.

Around day four of the work, I started trying to pry open the side of a classic POS system. It is odd that these are the machines that the warden uses. POS in this case standing for Piece of Shit because it was more of a Frankenstein machine, assembled from parts out of other dead machines. Most of our gear is from a company called Poseidon United Company, apparently a tech company I have never heard of.

When I finally got the metal cover off, what I found inside blew my mind. There, among the motherboard, fans, hard drive, and all the semi-conductors, was this intricate spiderweb, complete with a mother and her young. The little ones scurried to the corners of the unit, hiding behind dust bowls and under integrated circuits.

The mother stood her ground and even leaned back on her legs, prob-ably ready to pounce, if I made a malicious move toward her young.

As I leaned back, a damn fly landed right on my upper lip. My first instinct was to smack at the tingling sensation. Instead, I drifted my hands out from my body and blew as hard as I could from my nostrils.

The sudden whoosh of air startled the fly. As it fled my warm breath, it flew right into my outstretched right hand. In that instant, I clapped my left hand on top, trapping the fly.

I'd finally caught the brain-eating sucker. However, I took a beat and set up the best way to dispose of the fly.

Once I kicked back my rolling chair, I shook up the fly in my hands to confuse him. I felt my capture bounce all around my hands like an irritated jellybean.

At that moment, I heaved the fly forward. This little black pebble flipped end over end right into the side of that spider's web.

Once the fly knew he was trapped, he kicked and struggled. And the more he struggled, the deeper he was stuck.

One way or another, the fly was going to die there.

I will trap Barca, and he will cause his own undoing. I will get him to the security gate. Once we walk in tandem and the gate opens, I'll push him past the opening and the quick-shutting gate will slam behind him. After that, I'll pull the fire alarm.

No matter what deal or immunity Barca has with Cyfib or the corporation, if it is publicly known among the guards and hackvicts that Barca tried to escape, the warden will have no choice but to send him to the Bay for fear of losing face in front of his *dogs*.

Barca then puts his hand on my shoulder and says, "We will get through this."

Through this? Maybe I should just take the easy way out and shiv the bastard.

I take a deep breath and shake the urge off.

All that needs to happen is for him to get caught trying to escape. I just need to figure out how to make sure they catch him and not me.

Barca finishes his leak and glances over at me with a smirk. "You want to squeeze out the last few drops for me, Princess?"

He may have the power, but he is not in charge.

"Barca, we have work to do."

Chapter Sixty-Seven

This Favor is a Doozy

Despite his undefeated rank as top asshole in the galaxy, Barca is not the worst student. Sure, he interrupts me, often just to be a smart-ass, but you can't tell a dog like him he can't be a dog. All you can do is keep him on a loose leash.

Interestingly, Barca listens intently, leaning on his elbows and resting his chin in giant hands as his ears trap and his eyes juggle the pieces of our plan. I explain how the gates open when two prisoner chips go through the terminal at the same time and overload the circuit.

He interrupts with questions as often as comments and, boy, does he have questions! He wants to know why I need his exact height, weight, scars, and number of fillings. I explain why we need corpses that are close enough to us in description that they will pass a light inspection. Of course, DNA is DNA, so there is no way to hack all the databases that ours might exist on.

"So why don't we just remove both of the chips and tape them together to get through the gate, like, um, an RFID card?" he asks as we *watch* an inmate basketball game for cover.

I hate to admit it, but it's a good question.

"You see MottonCather over there?" I ask, pointing to the hackvict with one leg and no prosthetic hopping around the court, kicking everyone's ass.

"Yeah?"

"He attempted to remove the ankle implant and escape using a soldering iron. As you can see, that's why he lost a little weight."

"Ah."

Two points in one. One, if you screw up removing the microchip, the sucker causes serious damage. Two, don't underestimate people, especially those who appear weaker than you.

"I think it is possible to remove the chips, but there's just as much a chance that when you remove them, they stop working, much like a smoke detector or security alarm does when the cover to the unit is removed. We can't know until we are outside the building."

"So that's part of the plan?"

"Yes."

Barca slaps me across the back as if we are old school chums.

"Princess, I'm starting to like you."

This princess wishes there was a crown large enough to beat you with.

Between games, X_Marks_Da_Hot jogs over to our seats, tossing the basketball between his hands.

"Hey Barca, you want to tag in?"

"Naw, I'm good."

"You sure?"

"Yah."

As X dribbles off, I lean into my monster's ear. "You need to play, keep up appearances."

"Man, you don't—"

Barca holds off on his response. His eyes dart from the empty guard tower to the court. He curses under his breath. That's the thing about getting good advice from people you hate: sometimes you won't take it just to spite them, and everyone winds up losing.

Barca chuckles. "You're a smartie, Princess . . . hey, X, toss me the rock!"

As Barca takes off his shirt, his bare back reveals a tattoo of a raging elephant, one with beady eyes in mid-charge. The mammoth shimmers in the sun, probably ink that is less than a year old.

I glance down at my lone, faded tat.

Six names. When I get out, I guess I'll have to add Quidlee to the list.

Will I add his given name, or chosen handle?

Then, looking at the names, something else clicks in my head. There is a way to address the biggest gamble in our escape plan. It is a long shot, but if it works, it might be the answer to how we can get a courier.

And like an angel sent from on high, AldenSong slips into the seat next to me.

"You know when you asked to help?"

"That's vague." Aldy bobbles his head and attempts his best rich-person accent, which sounds more like a discarded Muppet than someone on the BBC. "I do try to improve the lives of my fellow man every day and require more information for a favor, if one would be so inclined to share?"

"Oh, I'm inclined." I take a breath because I am about to ask a world's work from Aldy. "Because this favor is a doozy."

Chapter Sixty-Eight

Never See You Again

For someone who loves to talk, it is equally surprising and scary to find AldenSong without words. A furrowed brow with darting eyes that bounce around the basketball court is on the Samoan's face. This is the combination of confusion, shock, intrigue, and panic that I sort of expected from overloading his brain like an overstuffed paper grocery sack.

I had just unloaded not only the plan of how to escape but also how it was meant for Quidlee—how Barca bastardized it after he killed the rook.

I also told AldenSong about the secret scripts I kept on a hidden partition on the server that allowed me untraceable access for six minutes to do whatever I pleased. Oh, and I told him about the development of Gakunodo and the fact that I had in my possession Cyfib's administrative flash drive.

Out of all that barrage of powerful details, I'm pretty sure that the ultimate piece, telling AldenSong *who* I needed him to track down and contact as our cadaver and fake ID courier, might've added too much info at once. It was like handing an anvil to a guy standing on a barely frozen pond.

The big guy sits in his confusion for a while. I give him space to process. Some things just need time to play out.

Barca scores the game-winning point and strolls over our way.

"Hey, what's with fat boy?"

"I just told him that the movie *Home Alone*, from the time that Kevin puts his head under the covers to hide from the crooks until they leave, was actually just a dream."

"What?" Barca says, successfully distracted.

A bounce pass winds up in my chest. I hurl the rock back into the middle of the court. I had read about this *Home Alone* theory on the dark web last week and was wondering when this useless information would shift to useful.

"Look at the house at the end of the movie: immaculate. When did Kevin learn to woodwork and repair a home, let alone have the tools to fix the damage from all those booby traps? He didn't even know how to shave . . ."

Barca raises a finger to say something and argue against the attack on everyone's favorite Christmas movie, but he slowly withdraws it and rubs his chin. Before I know it, he is sitting on the ground next to me.

So, on one side of me is the man I care most for in the world. On the other, the man I hate the most. Somehow, with completely different tactics and information, I've shut their brains down and overloaded their internal realities.

I can't remember which one of them cussed first, but the other echoed the statement. I wonder if AldenSong even heard me tell Barca that story.

The giant strolls to the watercooler on the other side of the court, still lost in thought. Once Barca leaves, AldenSong breaks his silence.

"For most of my life, I never touched a keyboard. Never got on the Internet. You didn't do that. Not where I grew up. We are a simpler people." AldenSong scratches his eyelids and tilts his head up toward the sky. "We believe in God, and we believe in each other. The rest is rain and wind. Then I made a . . . choice. It was not a bad choice, nor was it a good choice. It was a choice, and that landed me right here, right now, where you are asking me to make another choice."

"I understand."

"No, no, you don't, because if you did, if you truly knew me, you would know you never had to hear me answer you."

"And, since *you* know *me*, you know it wouldn't sit right with me to demand anything, especially from you." I put my hand on his back and give him a pat. "You know, Aldy, instead of telling a story, most people just answer a question."

He takes my hand from his back and places it in his. "Since when are we those people?"

After a quick squeeze, I know my answer.

Barca glares at me from across the court. He can't even let the idea of a different interpretation of a childhood movie sit. He stomps my way.

"You're wrong," he says.

"Maybe."

I should have kept in mind how much Barca needs to win at all times, even when it comes to opinions about old movies. Without warning, he puts his hands around my neck, squeezes, and shoves me against the fence.

"Say it."

It is only now that I notice the perimeter alarm blares, but no guards have rushed to my side.

"I . . . am . . ." Barca lets go and walks back toward the entrance inside.

Trub-E and Foshi_Taloa are practicing free throws. Trub-E banks a shot off the rim and the ball ricochets into the back of Barca's head. While the impact doesn't hurt him, it must've annoyed him further because Barca snatches the bouncing ball and chucks it over the fence.

The ball flies off in an arc, sailing high, before ultimately dropping below our eyeline.

I approach the fence to follow the ball's trajectory as it hits the concrete below, bounces high, and then lands at an angle, sticking in a rain gutter. Barca probably couldn't have made that shot again if he tried.

He goes inside, and I look over at AldenSong. He is scratching his palms with his fingernails, and his eyes are staring forward at a spot on the brick wall.

"What you're asking me to do . . ."

"I know . . . I understand if you want to say no . . ." I cannot blame Aldy. He is being asked to sacrifice for something that he might not believe is real. I mean, AldenSong never saw Barca kill Quidlee.

"That's not it." My friend puts his arm around my shoulders and turns his head to face mine. The corners of his eyes shimmer in the light. He is not openly crying. He has those tears that you get when you hold everything in, and the pressure forces a little water to the surface.

"What is it?"

"I don't see a way this works where I will ever see you again."

Chapter Sixty-Nine

Come Here, Tanto

I forgot about how hard a good person will work to help a friend.

One thing I asked AldenSong to do was to find this potential courier. The target was not exactly a needle in a haystack, more like a particular spoon in a drawer full of them. It would take time, so I was glad that he was on it.

Getting IDs for Barca and me was easy. Getting the cadavers was about as easy as giving an elephant an enema. Mine, being that I'm of average whiteness and weight, was easy to find. But finding a giant like Barca, that was tough. I'd started several places and realized I was overthinking it.

The answer was closer than I thought. One or two land masses over from Texas is the sports haven known as Mississippi.

I'd heard PoBones, a die-hard Louisiana State University fan, moan about "dem cheating bastards from The Sip with all their money to buy offa the refs" conspiracy theory for the past few years that I should've known that he and the band Mountain were onto something.

Mississippi Queen indeed.

Wouldn't you know it? I find three dead good ole boys and one of them will surely work for our resident monster's body. I even show Barca and let him pick his desired doppelgänger.

AldenSong makes some progress using the cloaking script, but the last time we talked about it, his target still alludes him. There are seven possibilities, and what we are asking is not something you put in an e-mail to the wrong person.

To Whom It Concerns:

Hello. We hope you are well. You do not know us, nor have we ever met. Would you be willing to journey to several states, pick up fake identification papers, grab a corpse or two that are loaded in the trunk of an automobile that was purchased using one of those fake IDs, and gather a few more odds and ends before ultimately driving everything to a hidden facility to ensure a successful prison break?

Thanks in advance for your consideration and we look forward to working with you!

Sincerely,

Three cyber terrorists

For this, you do not perform a shotgun approach and shoot your message wide, hoping that it hits someone workable. That's how you wind up shipped off to the Bay.

Of the seven possibilities, AldenSong is 90 percent sure that one or two e-mail addresses work for the target. However, he is making 100 percent sure that the target is not only in his bullseye but also willing to do what needs to be done. To achieve that level of confidence, Aldy needs more time digging up information beyond your basic social crawl and getting into deeper dirt, like fundraisers and 501(c)(3) year-end summaries.

Moreover, the big guy still gets a capture of a creep that is looking for kiddie porn that he requested have at least one, if not more, children crying in it.

It's assholes like that we all love to capture.

Speaking of monsters, Barca refuses to do a walk-through of the gate opening with our doubled-up chips when he figured out it was a literal walk-through. He laughed and told me, in his own less than subtle way that doing a practice run, with our legs side by side and touching, wasn't necessary.

"Look, if you want to pull on my hog, I'll knock your teeth down your throat, Princess."

I have so many reasons to hate Barca. His homophobia is just one more log on the fire. All it does is support the rage that is burning at a Crock-Pot level in my soul: slow, steady, dependable, yet building.

Of course, nothing turns one's plan upside down like other people.

"Attention, dogs."

I must've been *in the zone*, focused on getting a kill to keep up appearances, because I never heard the *cha-chings* of the warden's boots.

Cyfib stands in the middle of the War Room floor, his black pants, white shirt, and plain black tie against his long, flowing blond hair, looking like a boxer-turned-accountant.

For a moment, he does not speak, even though all eyes are on him, letting those potential kills lapse. Lord Odin's descent from Valhalla results in a reprieve for our targets, I guess.

Dramatic moments like this are never good news. The warden is probably about to say our numbers are down, which they are. We've lost one hunter, and three of us hackvicts are passively hunting more as a cover than anything else. I don't need to be psychic or have any schooling as a meteorologist to predict that our upcoming indoor weather is mostly cloudy with a high chance of threats in our forecast.

What I *don't* expect is for the warden to point my way.

"Come here, Tanto . . ."

Chapter Seventy

The Flaws

S *hit.*

In my eight years behind these walls, I have never heard him say a hacker's handle. We are *dogs*, nothing more. We are tools designed for capturing, not recognition.

All sound leaves the room. My nostrils clear so quickly my ears pop. My butt grips the seat like the room is about to turn upside down and my glutes are my only hope of not plummeting to my death.

"Now."

I must've stood and walked to the warden, because I am standing next to Cyfib, facing my fellow hackvicts, when he speaks next.

"Dogs, today you get to see what this one dog has learned and has brought us, a new tool with which to capture prey more . . . efficiently." That is as close to a compliment as the man can muster. He leans forward and enters a few commands on the closest keyboard. The four war screens light up with something that was never supposed to see the light of day.

"Dogs, I present to you the intelligent kill software, Gakunodo."

No. There was no way the project was fully functional; I'd stalled the program and even deleted some sections of crucial code that a debugger would not know to check or fix because it was drawing from scripts outside of the internal process.

Yet somehow, a symbol of a tent with the cursive font wording of Gakunodo with a circle-R next to it fills the four screens.

No one in the room does anything. This moment must've been like when Hugo Heiss introduced the captive bolt gun to the staff at his first slaughterhouse. I can picture the workers in their blood-spattered overalls and ragged gloves watching Heiss apply a pistol that sent a stainless-steel bolt into an animal's forehead.

Gee, thanks, Boss, we can knock the cow unconscious and slaughter it easier. However, at the end of the day, we are still killing and butchering animals for a paycheck.

I want to reach over and smash the keyboard, yet that will do nothing. It's like watching a train about to hit a car parked on railroad tracks; I can do nothing to stop the upcoming collision.

Cyfib enters the go command.

Gakunodo is now live.

Screen after screen opens. Hundreds of variables and crosschecks run against online users. These are actions that take even the best of my fellow prisoners ten or fifteen minutes. By Gakunodo, it completes them in under thirty seconds. Multiple chat windows open as the software posts on public threads in an attempt to start a false conversation with potential targets.

One such hunt happens on the screen on the far right.

[CutieBooty69]: Hey, don't tell my parents I'm online.

That one line is enough to suck in six targets.

[BigDickDan911]: No prob. How old are you?

[CutieBooty69]: Old enough to chat with you, hehehe . . .

[BigDickDan911]: What do you want to chat about, sexy thang?

[CutieBooty69]: Why don't you tell me what you desire?

We sourced the dialogue from several erotica fan-fiction websites. The script is intentionally bad; the goal is to catch those who think they are more intelligent than their prey.

The conversation gets more graphic, but not enough on our end to reach entrapment levels.

Two of the targets bail. The program is not perfect, thank God. Within one minute, the software scans, selects, and engages four targets in artificial intelligence captures. Gakunodo tosses out the same bait in different forums, dropping hooks and teasing many other creeps.

My mind cannot grasp how fast this program is going. I never designed it to perform multiple-layered interactions and work past parallel processing parameters. This program now can run all five phases—search, select, engage, lock, and pillage—at multiple sites and in multiple iterations.

It is the perfect trap, one that tracks multiple targets, preys on human behavior, and never tires.

I must stop this, which complicates things, to say the very least. But I can come up with *something*. I have a little time to work out a plan.

Or so I think.

Cyfib sucks on his white bone pipe, takes it out of the corner of his cheek, and lets out a *smile*.

The man never smiles.

The warden leans in. "I know what you are thinking. I saw the ... *flaws* ... in your code. But not to worry ..."

He lets the word *worry* hang in the air like he has just dropped a feather and I am watching it slowly arch back and forth until it rests on the ground, right before the warden stomps on it with his boot.

Then Cyfib leans back and announces to everyone the monkey to my wrench.

"Tomorrow, this dog gets paroled."

Chapter Seventy-One

Everything My One Hundred Sixty Pound Frame Allows

We have under sixteen hours for AldenSong to find the target, convince the target to complete everything necessary in case push comes to shove, and we need a courier, to get Barca out through the gate, frame him for several things, and shut down Gakunodo.

While I am at it, I might as well cure cancer, stop global warming, and out who really assassinated JFK, all before breakfast.

Of course, the *good news* of my parole sends Barca into a rage. It doesn't take a mind reader to interpret the fire that shoots from Barca's eyes. The moment the warden returns to the Cube of Death, Barca puts his hand on my neck and escorts me out to the basketball court.

He squeezes and lifts so my feet are barely touching the ground. It feels like Barca might chuck me over the fence and make fly like that basketball he'd launched.

Once outside, I swat at the monster's grip with both of my hands, but he ignores the hits. I am a ladybug attacking a dragon.

"I didn't know . . ."

"Bullshit!" He shoves me against the fence and, almost on cue, the fence's alarm sounds. My hurt knee screams in pain, but I keep my gaze on my assailant. Apparently, Barca does not care about the alarm as he shoves his sausage finger so hard into my sternum it curls my toes.

I slip away from Barca. The alarm ends mid-screech, as if it is a snuffed-out candle.

"We have twenty-four hours to get out."

Barca kicks his head back and lets out such a laugh it echoes off the empty building across the street. "There's no way you're going to pass up parole to get me out of here."

He is wrong. I do not want to leave, for several reasons. One, I have yet to pick apart Lance-a-Little's warning to stay inside. *Was he worried about leaving everyone else in Hackers' Haven unprotected from people like Barca? Was Lance so conditioned to life behind bars that the strangeness or weirdness of ex-con life on the outside was overwhelming? Or was it something completely different?*

In all this chaos, I'd forgotten to reach out to Lance and find out why he told me to stay in prison. I can't worry about that now. I think it was Masaharu Morimoto or Mencius who once said, "A man who attempts two battles at once loses three." Later problems will have to wait for a later time.

But really, my family is *here*. I have no one outside. No blood. Few friends. Here, inside this prison, I am someone, with people who care about me, even love me. Out there, who knows what I would become?

"If you get out and I don't . . ."

Barca points at me, and we both know no words will ever bring enough power to the end of that sentence. Barca will blitzkrieg everyone and everything. He is an exploding man, and no one will escape his blast zone.

"All is set up but the courier . . ."

"Oh, just that little thing!" Barca sweeps his arms out wide, and he stomps around the basketball court. No words will satiate him.

A breeze hits my face. The monster fumes and grumbles, even looking confused and helpless for a moment. He cannot threaten to take my life, but he can threaten others. However, that choice might result in my taking parole and leaving him stuck behind these bars. He has no other options but to play by my rules.

Leverage.

He may be a master manipulator, but the problem with people like that is that they look at everything that comes out of your mouth as a lie or an excuse.

The one thing Barca cannot handle is the truth.

"Barca, you don't like me." I walk up to him, his massive body blocking the light and casting me in a shadow. "And frankly, if you were on fire, I wouldn't waste the piss to put you out. But you need me."

"So here is what is going to happen. AldenSong will try to find our courier today and get them scheduled to arrive here, complete with all the paperwork. You and I are going to escape during the shift change. But before we do that, we are going to shut down that computer program that Cyfib just showed us."

"The hell we . . ."

"Shut the hell up." I put my finger in the monster's face, knowing full well that he might bite it off.

"We are going to shut down Gakunodo, and only then are we going to escape. We must stop that program at all costs. I have an idea how to do this, although it is not even a complete idea and a bad one at that, but I am willing to die right here and now and let you attempt to run this joint until Cyfib gets bored with you, as he has with me."

"Maybe you are willing to die right now, Princess." *Whew.* I intentionally moved my eyes up and to the right, a tell of a truth, when I said I would "let him run this joint," thus sacrificing my friends. "But if you cross me, I will level this place and everyone in it."

"Then let's not focus on failing."

I turn to go inside and let him follow.

As we walk into the War Room, I stop in my tracks. There are no guards in the room right now. Shift change.

Now or never.

I take a deep breath and make a terrible executive decision to get this ball rolling.

"Oh, and there's just one more thing . . ." I say loud enough that every hackvict turns away from their terminals.

Then I crouch on my good knee, take the weight off the bad one, pivot, and uppercut Barca with everything my one-hundred-sixty-pound frame allows.

Chapter Seventy-Two

Tick Tock, Princess

When I was sixteen years old, I was living on the streets of New Orleans.

You don't get a city with friendlier people and more self-pride than the Big Easy. It is like somehow red beans and rice, powdered sugar, and oysters fuel happiness. Maybe they do.

Sadly, I wasn't living in the part of the city that ran on happiness and tourism. I spent most of my time there trying to scrape out a life in Central City, home of the worst thugs the state of Louisiana offers. When you watch the ten o'clock news, you'll find that Central City has over 500 percent of the national average of violent crimes.

One of the three times someone mugged me there, I got jumped by two guys who were built like trucks and hit like them as well. They broke two ribs and nearly cracked my skull.

That mugging was a tickle fight compared to the beating Barca is giving me in the War Room.

We are on the same page about the necessary result of the altercation: we must wind up in the Infirmary for an overnight stay in order to get out of our cells because those lock for eight hours.

However, that is the extent of our mutual understanding because something snaps in both of us. The difference is one of us is clearly a battle-trained, six-eight warrior who weighs over three hundred pounds of muscle. The other is me.

My knuckles pop so hard when they connect with the giant's head that, had I not jumped and put all my weight into the punch, I doubt he would've noticed.

A sharp lance shoots up my arm and, from the elbow to my fingertips, everything goes numb. The punch catches Barca off guard, and he hits his head on the doorframe. His eyes flash as he picks me up by the neck and slams me down on the closest chair, its wheel spinning out from under me. Luckily, I get in a good headbutt to Barca's nose, bloodying his face.

Barca catches my next punch with his hand. My fist looks like a baby's in his giant hand. My dangling legs flail, but I land a kick to his crotch hard enough that he crumples over.

Our fight has progressed to the kitchenette where the coffeemaker and small fridge are located. *Good.*

I grab the coffeepot and fling some scalding-hot coffee on his leg. Barca screams in pain, grabs the pitcher from my hand, and hurls it across the room in a rage.

Next, he slams his fist into my chest, and I realize he probably has forgotten that he needs to scald me as well. That part is crucial to our escape.

I try to speak, but blood catches in my throat and I choke. I spot the broken coffeepot on the ground. Then Guard Fontana yells something. He must've just entered the room or heard the commotion.

If this plan is to work, Barca needs to burn me somehow. He needs to do it *now*. But all I can think about is the fire in Barca's eyes.

Barca crouches and lifts me by my shoulders as he charges forward. My back slams into the concrete wall and the air in my lungs abandons this sinking ship. From the corner of my eye, I watch as Fontana reaches for his remote-controlled zapper.

We are too late.

Barca winks at me, then runs my back against the concrete wall, burning my skin with a scrape that I feel from my lower back to my neck.

Before I can scream, an electric shock blasts through us. Barca drops me like I am a bag of dirty laundry. We collapse on the floor. From my fetal position, Barca sends a smile my way.

"Tick tock . . . Princess."

And, just like that, the escape begins.

Chapter Seventy-Three

Without Ever Looking Back

"**A**re you two trying to make my life a living hell?"

Dr. Fel throws down his briefcase and keys on the table as Barca and I sit on separate examination tables. My hands and feet are twist-tied to the table. Two steel chains bind Barca in a searing indictment of my comparative strength.

"Seriously. I was in the parking lot. My wife already has dinner on the table. Her folks are there, you know, and they are none too happy with waiting on my late ass."

He is clearly letting off some steam, which is fine. Until AldenSong confirms that the courier is on his way, there is no point in moving from this room. All we have to do is wait until that happens, and then we, or at least Barca, can walk straight out the gate.

Dr. Fel examines us. Besides some minor bruising and cuts, we are fine. Well, and the burns. Barca gets one tiny burn pad for his leg, and I get one the size of Mount Rushmore for my back. As Dr. Fel finishes up our examinations, a landline phone in the Infirmary rings. Dr. Fel shakes his head and cusses under his breath before answering after the fifth ring.

"Hello? No . . . don't transfer the call . . . tell her . . . look . . . tell her I am finishing up with two patients and will call . . . I don't . . . okay, yes, but, I know . . . look, don't take her side . . . just call her back . . ."

The doc sighs and puts his head in his hands. Part of me wonders if Dr. Fel wants us to knock him out so that he will not have to attend a dinner with his in-laws. If it wouldn't complicate an already complicated plan, I would offer.

"Okay . . . transfer the call in one minute . . . I'll run to the parking lot, take it, and then finish up here . . ."

Dr. Fel hangs up the phone without saying goodbye, grabs his phone, wallet, and keys, and heads out the door, leaving it open.

"I'd hate to be him." Barca says, then chuckles to himself.

"You didn't have to burn my entire damn back."

"Had to sell the fight, didn't I?"

Curse Barca.

At times, he is almost human, making jokes like that. Then his hideous side emerges, a beast that thrives on pain, death, and destruction.

"Y'all need to start calling me the Samoan Apostle, because I just performed a miracle." AldenSong, complete with a small duffel bag on his shoulder, skips into the Infirmary and performs the mark of the cross on Barca's and my forehead with his thumb. "Bless you, my child, go in peace."

Barca, our resident junkyard dog, tries to bite Aldy's thumb.

AldenSong tucks the duffel in behind a large trash can, then wags his finger in the monster's face before turning his full attention to me. "So, we're all set?"

"All set. Two hours. The basketball in the gutter is the marker."

"Even the—"

"Yep. Two hours until arrival."

"And the—"

"Courier knows only to stay one minute in order to not draw attention."

Good. If Barca bolts or screws up the last part of the plan, then I don't want our Good Samaritan to risk getting caught and wind up in the federal pen.

This moment is the difference between discussing a plan and actually following through with it. Those two things are entirely different beasts. One is hypothetical, full of what-ifs and what-abouts. The other is now-tos and chance.

There are tears in Aldy's eyes; mine are already dribbling down my cheek. This is real.

Of course, we are just preparing for the worst-case scenario. I tell myself that. There is no way I'd leave this place, my home.

However, something feels final.

The air in the room clings to Aldy and me. We lock eyes, neither of us attempting words. Then this man, whose heart is as big as his whole body and whose blood type is O-kindness, wraps me in a hug and, for a moment, the world stands still.

"If y'all just want to smash one out, I'll look away."

Even Barca's crudeness will not ruin this moment. As my chin rests on AldenSong's shoulder, a golf-ball-sized lump in my throat fights its way down along my insides all the way down to my pounding heart.

"I believe in you, and I'll be praying for you."

AldenSong's support, more than his finding of our courier, will fuel me to do what I must.

And, like that, my friend lets go of me and walks toward the door. A shiver floats across his back and he runs a hand across his face, but still walks out of the room without ever looking back.

Chapter Seventy-Four

Get Out

Within two minutes of AldenSong's departure, Dr. Fel returns to the Infirmary. He is a little flushed, and a dampness has spread under his armpits. Dr. Fel has either survived a phone call with an upset wife or just finished a five-pound dump.

"Crisis averted." The doc removes his Buddy Holly glasses and cleans them with a handkerchief already in his hands, probably covered in the sweat from his brow. "The Demons-in-Law left their casserole in the oven back home and had to go back to get it. You know, it's a whole big thing, so I'm not in trouble."

Well, goody. Out of all the things to worry about at this particular moment, Dr. Fel's relationship with his in-laws was at the top of the list.

"So, everything looks good, but just to be sure, I'm going to put both of you in our medical pods overnight. Now, does anyone need to pee? Because you're gonna have to stay in the pod."

Both of us shake our heads like small children preparing for a road trip.

"Are you sure?"

This is just getting patronizing.

"Alrighty load in."

As both Barca and I strip down to our underwear and toss our clothes into plastic bags to keep the floor from clutter, my entire upper body aches. Those two ibuprofens will not ease the beating Barca put into me.

However, when Barca bends down to grab a sock he dropped, I swear I hear him grunt.

It warms my soul that I'd at least discomforted the beast.

After we load in, Dr. Fel asks me if I want a good night story. Then he laughs to himself and shuts the hood on me. Maybe it's the rhythmic hum of the medical pod's machinery running its test that does it, but more likely it's my body's exhaustion and brokenness that sees this moment as a chance to repair itself. I blink too long, but then justify closing my eyes because both Barca and I need to lie low—for a few minutes, anyway.

Then, I awaken with a start.

How long was I out?

We had to wait to make sure the doc did not come back. However, when you're trapped in an Easy Bake Oven, tracking time isn't the easiest thing. At least Barca knew better than to leave the pod before me because if someone were to get caught, he wanted to make damn sure it was me and not him.

I push on the pod door. The lid lifts a bit, then a *chirp* sounds and I lower the lid back down.

The same alarm that got AldenSong in trouble for taking a piss is the one I'm counting on for our prison break.

I lift the lid again and inspect the lining of the casket where the lid meets the bottom. This time, I find the culprit. There, on the spot where my midsection meets the lower glass, flashes a red light when I open the lid.

It's a heat sensor, designed to make sure that one does not leave this pod. Just below the flashing red bulb is a translucent square that looks like the kind of sensor you would see in the self-checkout lane of a supermarket. My guess is that the heat sensor only sounds when the heat drops for about ten seconds. That was about how long it took until the alarm sounded when AldenSong left the pod to piss. I have not tested this theory, of course, so if I'm wrong, the entire rest of the plan dies right here.

There is no time like the present to test a bad idea. I twist my right arm behind my back and snag the corner of the burn pad. The end feels cottony yet clingy, a gooey, thin towel stuck to my strawberry burn. After a few yanks that takes some sensitive skin off with it, I get the pad free. I push open the lid. A light flashes, but no alarm sounds yet. I slam the heating pad sticky side down on the sensor.

The light flashes faster.

Dammit. I run my eyes up and down the interior of the clear plexiglass. Any of the dozens of sensors might record body heat. *But which one? What do I do now?*

I reach for the pad to move it, with only a wild guess about which sensor will work, but just as I touch it, the flashing light stops.

The pad must've needed time to seal in the heat.

I take a breath and tiptoe out into the hallway. No guards approach. I'm almost tempted to relax. Luckily, this part of the escape has gone according to plan. Then I spot the clock above the medical pods.

I rub my eyes. I must be seeing things. If not, we're screwed.

Unless I'm hallucinating, we have thirty minutes left to get out.

Chapter Seventy-Five

As If This Plan Isn't Complicated Enough

We are so far behind schedule that the clock's hands might as well spin like an airplane's propeller. But I can't help but wonder *Is it better to continue with this doomed plan, or pivot in a way that will forever change the course of my life. . . and everything I stand for?*

Should I just kill Barca here and now and put an end to all this?

I immediately realize I don't have time to contemplate the meaning of life right now. I shake my head to clear my thoughts, and I flip open the lid to Barca's medical pod.

"Move."

"Took you long enough . . ."

I don't have time for Barca's guff, so as his pod's alarm sounds, I tear the pad off his leg. As his eyes go wide in pain, I clamp down my hand over his mouth to muffle his scream. Light noises are things guards can ignore. Loud screams are a completely different animal.

I slam Barca's burn pad, covered in his leg hair and looking like the world's ugliest Brillo pad, over the heat sensor. His machine stops beeping more quickly than mine. Maybe monster fur is good for keeping in warmth.

"You're a mean one, Princess."

Neither of us speaks as we dress. I grab the duffel bag that AldenSong hid in the corner. It has supplies and a few emergency tools that we will hopefully never use. A *hope for the best, plan for the worst* type of scenario. From the duffel, I grab a wristwatch that has an active timer going that AldenSong set for me.

Twenty-eight minutes and nine seconds left until pickup.

We make our way to the War Room. Even though an hour and a half has passed, we are a few minutes away from the guards returning to their stations. I had planned our fight to coincide with the twilight period between guard changes. One would think that a prison would keep guards on duty in every area 24/7, but just like all businesses, there are downtimes when minimal personnel work the prison. But that window is closing.

Barca keeps a lookout and I ascend the stairs to the Cube of Death. Then, from my perch, I motion for Barca to join me. For a giant, the guy can sneak well because I turn my head to glance out at the War Room floor, spying the few hackvicts getting *kills* and, by the time I turn my gaze back, he is next to me.

Initially I had wanted to do this part by myself. Gakunodo is my dragon to slay. But if Cyfib is in his office, it will take Barca to subdue him.

I crack open the door.

Cyfib's office is empty.

It is an eerie sensation to look around this office without its owner there. Not quite an invasion of privacy, more like a welcoming invitation to enter and play. A warm rush spreads across my chest, the thrill of breaking the law, even if it is for the greater good. For the first time in a long while, I am hacking for me and not for the warden or the corporation.

"I'd do a damn fine job running this place from in there." I do not know if Barca is saying this to himself, to me, or as a threat. Any of those reasons turns that brief body warmth into an icy chill that runs down my spine.

Barca steps in behind me.

"No, wait!"

Click.

The giant freezes. Normally, the time you hear that sound, there is nothing you can do. Yet no explosion or alarm sounds.

"Don't . . . move . . ."

For once, Barca does not question my order. I take the duffel bag from my shoulder and put it on the floor outside of the office. From inside the bag, I withdraw a flashlight and crawl toward Barca's right foot.

There, on the edge of his boot's toe but solidly under his foot, is a button connected to something, and Barca's boot just pressed it in.

"Is it a claymore?"

A query like that answers some of the history questions I have about Barca. He has military training, and not the kind they give to people like the other residents of Hackers' Haven, those with mere technology skills.

"Negative, but we're going to treat it like one."

"Can you tell if it is weight sensitive or just pressure?"

Great question, Mister Mystery Military Man.

It occurs to me that, if there was ever a time to leave Barca and let him rot, it is now. However, I've framed him before. If I leave him here, he still might not get shipped out of here. I can't risk it.

"No . . . we're going to have to treat it like a pressure switch."

"If you're wrong—"

"Hey, I'm no carnival barker, but it doesn't take an oversized scale to guess you're over two hundred thirty pounds. We don't have time for me to guesstimate how many unplugged workstations I could stack to hold that much weight on something the size of a quarter."

I take Barca's grumble as a sign to keep with my plan. I dive in the duffel and grab some duct tape and a Phillips head screwdriver with a tip the size of the end of a piece of rice. After a quick scan for other pressure plates on the floor, I crawl behind one workstation, underneath a long desk, and find what I need.

There, on the back of the unit, are two flat metal strips that cover the unused sections of a workstation's shell. I try to remove the first plate. After a few attempts, the screw refuses to budge. Upon closer review, the threading reveals a shredded screw. This particular cover will stay here until someone decommissions the workstation.

I turn my focus on the last cover. It's tough going at first, but eventually I get both screws out. With my fingernail under the edge of the cover, I pop it free.

In an instant, it reminds me of Quidlee's first day. This is the same type of plate he made a shiv from. *What if I'd let him attack a guard? Was that punishment worse than the way he died?*

I shake the thought from my head and slide back to Barca's booby-trapped foot.

"I'm going to slide this plate under your toe." I move the flat, gray tip of the cover under the edge of his boot. However, after several attempts to slip it between the boot and button, I can't get the metal strip through.

"You're going to need to take some weight off of that foot."

"How much?"

I glance up from the floor to Barca. Apparently, the look on my face properly conveys what I want to say to such a stupid question: *Enough, dumb ass.*

Barca moves his foot up like he is easing off a car's accelerator just enough to slow down without drawing the attention of the highway patrolman following in the review mirror. I slide the metal under his foot.

Now we have to test our pressure trigger hypothesis.

"Step off on the count of three . . . and by *three*, I mean move your foot on the number. Not before or after. On."

"Okay."

"One . . . two . . . three."

As Barca moves his foot, I slide my hand across the plate. For the next few seconds, both of us wait for an alarm or explosion.

Luckily, none of that happens. The duct tape holds.

We add several strips of tape over the first, creating an asterisk on the floor, keeping whatever that button's function is from sounding.

I check my watch.

Twenty minutes and forty seconds left.

We've lost close to seven minutes on this booby trap.

The warden's monitors are off when we turn to get to work. If one was in standby mode, we could take the hint and start our search on that one. There are three workstations on the floor. Gakunodo is too valuable to install on the servers in the basement. I know it is a smaller sized program, so Cyfib would want it to run from his office.

I find Pandora's Box housed on the L-drive. With this software's ability to capture multiple idiots at once, it makes sense for it to always run. I turn on the monitor that corresponds with the workstation and am greeted with a password screen.

"You going to guess the name of the warden's childhood pet, Princess?"

"Probably Igor or Beelzebub."

I reach into my pocket and withdraw the flash drive Quidlee concealed in his bandage.

"What's that?"

"His childhood pet's name."

I pop the rectangular end of the drive into an open slot on the workstation and key in a warm reboot. It will knock Gakunodo offline and record a history of the computer restarting, which will wind up in a log file, but these are the least of my worries. I boot from the flash drive and enter the restarted system at root-user level. From there, I find three copies of Gakunodo stored throughout the network.

As I enter the commands to not only shred the files but also to force all running files associated with the program to stop so that even remnants of the program will delete, Barca puts his hand across mine.

"Copy it and copy the LODIS files as well."

In the silence that follows, a few pieces of the puzzle click into place in my mind, and now the picture of Barca gets clearer.

Once a mercenary, always a mercenary.

That is why Barca does not have to follow our rules, why he is untouchable. Someone got him in here. Barca is not in Hackers' Haven for a crime; he is here to commit one.

"That wasn't part of the deal."

"It is now."

The beast and I lock eyes. Barca, or anyone, having a copy of LODIS means he could sell this beta-tested program to the highest bidder. I am okay with that. Its application to surgeries and brain exploration might save thousands of lives.

A copy of Gakunodo, on the other hand, this world-ender, is unacceptable. However, demanding that we destroy all copies at this very moment is not the hill I am willing to die on right now. I can fix that problem later. I can do both: destroy this software and get the monster out of our house.

I can have it both ways. If I copy everything to the flash drive but keep the only copy on me, then once I push Barca out the gate, I can destroy this drive on my own. He will take the blame. However, if Barca has the flash drive on him when they catch him, it must be blank so that Cyfib cannot reinstall it.

"Fine."

With Barca breathing down my neck, I copy the files. The LODIS files are massive, but so is the flash drive. I leave a copy of the program on the system. It is, after all, a defensive, not offensive, program, one that has saved lives already.

And after a few more keystrokes, the flash drive also has a working copy of Gakunodo on it.

With the transfer complete, I delete the three other copies. I can destroy this copy later. Then, just as I log out and reach for the drive, Barca swats my hand away and snatches the flash drive from the workstation.

"Mine."

The giant tosses the drive in the air with his left hand, catches it with his right, and shoves it into his front right pocket.

As if this plan isn't complicated enough.

Chapter Seventy-Six

Everything Is Falling Apart

T he plan is getting more screwed by the second.

The two of us make our way from Cyfib's office to the gate out, my brain frantically searching for answers. Along the way, we avoid cameras and disable the one that keeps a steady gaze on our exit.

Then it hits me: Barca refused to do a practice run out the gate, because he thought it was not *manly* for us to walk with our hips touching unless absolutely necessary. He does not know the correct way to exit.

That's my chance.

"Okay, Barca, you face the gate while I face away." Barca stands at attention while I reach into the duffel bag and grab a corded computer mouse that is only in the bag, in case Cyfib's office did not have input controls. "I'm going to use these to tie together our inner thighs."

As I wrap the black cable around his upper thigh, Barca chuckles. "Yeah, I bet you just been dying to touch me, haven't you, Princess?"

I get my thigh next to his and tie the mouse loosely. If I was escaping with Barca through the gate, I would've tied our ankles together. Yes, it would've made for easier synchronized steps. However, unhooking the cable from down there the moment Barca gets near the gate without him protesting won't be easy. Finally, when you add in shoving Barca through the gate before it closes, the ankle way will prove impossible.

After we are secure, or secure enough, I lean down and grab the duffel bag. "I'm going to need you to carry this."

"Why? Because you're so weak?"

"Because I am walking backward and anything I can do to not mess up our steps, I will do."

Well, *almost* anything. When Barca tosses the bag on his shoulder, I pull my right hand in so my fingertips are between our touching legs. My other hand holds the mouse. With the bag and stepping in time as the primary focus of Barca's mind, when the gate opens, I can use that moment to shove my hand in Barca's right pocket and snag the flash drive while my other hand yanks free the mouse. Just one rotation and shove, and Barca will wind up on the gate as the door shuts behind him.

We line up four steps away from the gate. I breathe deep. *I can do this.*

In the next few seconds, Barca will wind up trapped on the other side of the gate. He has the tools in that bag to get out of a door with a keypad, so there is a decent chance he will make it outside. He might even meet with the courier in the next few minutes. Regardless, once he's outside that gate, he is someone else's problem. And if he ever gets caught by the authorities, he becomes Guantanamo's problem.

"Ready?"

"Born ready, Princess."

A calm joy fills my soul.

"Remember, I've got a bad leg, so take small steps. On the word *step.* Three . . . two . . . step."

Barca's first step is wider than my traditional gait, and I stumble a bit. Thankfully, my knee doesn't buckle, and we get in sync after the second step.

This is why some practice might have been nice.

By the third step, we are smoothly approaching the gate. Sweat drips from both my hands.

We take the fourth step. There are sensors on both of our sides as we are just about to enter the gate. I prepare to strike.

An error noise signals. However, this is not the error signal that Quidlee and I made. This one is a beeping sound, like when you hit the wrong

296

W. A. PEPPER

command when you are typing and the computer yells at you for being human.

"It's not working."

"Step back, then step forward."

Barca follows orders. After our Texas Two-Step, the gate again makes the error message.

Something is wrong. This worked with Quidlee.

"Let's step back."

"You better not have screwed this up, you little runt."

Barca does not need to add a threat to that statement. Something is horribly wrong.

We move two steps back from the gate's sensors, and I untie us. I glance down at Barca's leg. Maybe his sensor is even newer than Quidlee's. I feel his leg until I grab the sensor.

Barca's sensor is round like Quidlee's.

Then what could've . . .

Then I instinctively run my hand across the small bandage on my right leg.

Oh no.

I tear off the bandage to reveal two black stitches on my chalky white skin.

Just like a victim touches their own blood after they're shot, I have to touch this stove to prove it is hot. I must confirm what I already know in my heart.

I reach down and run my fingers across the incision and find my sensor.

My Tic Tac is now a Skittle.

Everything is falling apart.

Chapter Seventy-Seven

Plan B Relies on Finality

"**Y**ou little shit!"

"I didn't know—"

"You're lying!"

Barca's fist slams into my stomach, a hit so hard I taste what I had for breakfast three days ago. I crumple to the floor, my thoughts in equal parts disbelief and problem-solving mode.

I never thought to look under the bandage. *Why would I?* I thought maybe it was an IV spot for Dr. Fel's work.

"While you're out, I'm going to do a couple of routine procedures . . . nothing you need to worry about . . ."

The doc traded out the sensor, the one causing the duplicity error with Quidlee's, during his checkup. That might mean that these chips are easier to remove and implant than previously believed. Otherwise, Dr. Fel would've needed a surgical team with him to do the surgery.

Not that any of this matters right now. I have to think before Barca throws another bone-crushing blow to my body. For some reason, I catch a damn ant, one of those freaking crazy Russian ones, walking on the ceiling above us. And that makes me think of the quick-drying epoxy we used to keep them out.

Who would've thought that my salvation would've come from the Russians?

"I . . . can . . . still . . . get us . . . out . . ."

"How?" Barca towers over me, clearly within view of the closest camera, but not caring about anyone watching the live video of this fight. When the ship is sinking, the last thing you care about is staying dry.

"Barca, we have to get back to the Infirmary."

If we can find the chip, then we can still get Barca out the gate.

We rush back and Barca starts his rampage in the Infirmary by tearing open the medical waste containers and dumping used syringes and medical instruments onto the floor. He sifts through the piles, occasionally catching his skin on something sharp and pointy. I look through the drawers and cabinets.

"Nothing!" Barca grabs a handful of used needles and flings them across the room toward me. I duck just in time.

I don't know where the chip is. However, in the last cabinet on the end, I find heartache in the shape of a plastic bag.

There, in the top right cabinets, is a clear bag with ashes in it. The label reads Prisoner A65Q1 with a date I will never forget right below the name.

Dr. Fel somehow has the rook's ashes. Maybe he is going to dispose of them properly, with a religious burial or whatnot. Something inside of me finds strength in my dead friend's remains.

I grab the ashes and shove them into the duffel.

"Plan B."

"Bullshit . . ." Barca shakes his head, leans down, and jams his index finger to a pressure point between my left ribs, filling my side with a stabbing pain and preventing me from yelling out.

"You ain't got no *Plan B*. You're just trying to stall."

I shake my head until Barca relents.

Barca is only partially right. Walking out the gate was the cleanest way out. Plan B is a kernel of corn in my head that just popped under the pressure of the situation. I don't even bother to calculate the odds that it will work.

It is the only choice we have.

Plus, Plan B is a lot more work than either of us might pull off. I look through the trash on the ground, grab a hypodermic needle, a used cotton swab, and a paper clip.

To get Barca out of here, I'll have to go with him.

There are no half measures.

Plan B relies on finality.

Chapter Seventy-Eight

Plan B Stands for Bodies

"We need to get to the Server Room now."

"Why?"

I snatch the duffel bag and shoot out the door. There is no point in wasting time explaining. Barca follows me down the staircase to the Server Room.

As I open the door, the answer to why a guard is not always around presents itself with a fapping noise. There, in the room's corner, is the new guard, Guard Stevens, with headphones on, watching porn and masturbating so furiously that if he wore a pedometer on his wrist, it would explode.

With no bleach to wash my eyes out, I shake off the scarring image and creep over to the tool cabinet. When I get there, Barca grabs me by the shoulder.

"Stevens can get us out."

I'd wondered about that myself. Guards don't carry key cards or RFID trackers and they certainly don't have chip implants. They can only open the gate with their radios. That's what happened when Quidlee and I were scouting the abandoned classrooms for exit points.

"He'd have to call it in to get the gate open. It doesn't matter if you take him hostage, because even if they let us past the gate, they'd surround us the second our feet hit city pavement."

I take Barca's silence as unhappy agreement, so I focus on the tools. Luckily, the lock for this cabinet is the factory-made one, with just enough pins in it to count as a lock.

Lock picking is equal parts lining up the pins and harnessing the tension while building inertia. Without a true lock-picking kit, this brittle hypodermic needle and a paper clip will have to do.

I break the needle at the point where it meets the shot's plunger, then finagle the sharp end of the needle into the cotton swab. Next, I straighten the paper clip before folding the end into a tiny hook. After that, all it takes is two good insertions and a heave to the right for the tools of our escape to present themselves.

"Ahhhhh—TAKE IT YOU LITTLE SLUT!"

It wouldn't take a sexpert like Dr. Ruth to know that Stevens has climaxed and finished self-husbanding.

We need to hide. I open the door to the shed and look in. It can hold one of us, and the other one can hide under a desk. The chair under Guard Stevens's feet rolls away and I shove Barca in the shed and close the door. The sound of the guard's fly zipping back up is unnaturally loud in the silent room. I dive under the closest computer desk and scoot a computer chair in front of me.

Guard Stevens whistles as he strolls toward the room's exit. He stops and his black shoes pivot my way.

Has he seen me?

I am flat against the back of the wall with the top of the desk covering me. However, something brings him toward me.

With his shoes directly in front of me, I hold my breath.

"There you are."

Oh no.

A tissue rips from a cardboard box. A few seconds pass as Guard Stevens wipes his hands on a tissue and drops it to the floor. Floating like a leaf, the spunk rag lands right next to my face.

The only thing worse than a thin cloth soaking with a million of Guard Stevens' unborn children inches from my face is wondering if he will lean down to get it and see me.

Apparently, the postcoital bliss has kicked in because Guard Stevens leaves the tissue and heads toward the exit.

He pauses again.

Now what?

"What the—"

It is at that moment I realize the strap of the duffle bag is dangling out from under the desk.

Metal pops from Barca's hiding spot and those black shoes turn toward the shed.

Barca bursts out, slamming the guard against the closest wall. He wraps his hands around the guard's neck, lifts him in the air, and slams the back of his skull into the concrete floor with a cracking noise, as if someone has snapped a dried-out pile of sticks.

The guard's head turns my way, and his dead eyes lock with mine.

I shoot out from under the desk, unsure of what I will do, but full of righteous anger to do something, anything.

Barca leans down and stone faced answers the question I do not have the courage to ask. "You're the one who said we didn't need him."

"You could've just knocked him out."

"You can never tell how long someone will stay unconscious unless you make it a lasting nap."

Guard Stevens is dead. This is another life on my shoulders, another scar I will always carry.

Barca strolls over to the tissue, picks it up, and wipes a glob of the semen on the bottom of Guard Stevens's right shoe. Next, Barca looks at the body, takes one step over, and drops the tissue. Finally, he steps on the rag and scoots it an inch across the floor.

"If it makes you sleep better in your ivory tower, Princess, the M.E. probably will rule this head trauma from a slip and fall."

It does *not* make me feel better. Covering up this murder makes me feel worse. Barca knows that. He is showing me he can still end me at any moment.

I dive into the toolshed and survey our options. Of course, there are no useful *prison break* tools: no welding torches, bolt cutters, or the like.

Time is running out. For this miracle, we need power, so I grab one portable drill and two 18v drill batteries. Not perfect but they'll do.

Next, I snatch the portable battery tester, though it will never work again once I finish with it. Of course, I grab more duct tape, because I do not remember how much we used on that pressure plate in the Box of Death. Better to be safe than caught. Finally, I grab four cans of epoxy and a handful of screws. Explaining nothing to this murderer, I shove everything in the duffel.

I used to think Plan B stood for bullshit. I'm now realizing that Plan B stands for bodies.

Chapter Seventy-Nine

Minutes

"**W**here to?"

Barca's tone is friendly, almost like a child walking around Disneyland and asking a parent what ride is next. He's trying to draw my attention away from something, probably the Guard's murder. The callousness with which he can take a human life, as if it was the same as squashing a bug, stokes the fire in the pit of my stomach. If I can't kill him, I will keep him from killing anyone else. In here or anywhere.

We get to the roof. Once outside, I notice that a slow, yet steady rain starts. In the humidity, jabs of icy cold bounce off my sweaty skull.

I point at the basketball goal. "We need the PVC pipe that holds the backboard to get over the fence."

"No prob."

As the caveman lumbers toward the pipe, I dart between him and the most necessary tool of our escape. He is going to try the simplest method. In life, that often is the one that screws you the quickest.

"If you try to pull it down, the anchoring concrete will cause it to splinter." I turn my head to look at the entire pole. This might work. Maybe, but only if we have the entire post. If it breaks, even by a few inches, we're screwed.

"So, what, we break the concrete?"

"With a sledgehammer, which we don't have, that would take even you too long."

I dump the duffel bag on the ground and separate the tools into piles. The rest, including Quidlee's ashes, I shove back in before Barca can question anything more than he already has.

However, the picture of Penny flies out of the bag. I reach for it, but Barca gets there first.

The smile that crosses his lips is anything but kind. "That's one tasty bitch."

He pockets the picture, and even as the bile rises in my throat, I decide that now is not the time to get it. Thankfully, the picture has no identification on it.

He'll never find her . . . or will he?

As much as I want to grab it from the giant, I know I must get him out of here first.

In one pile we have one of the two fully charged 18v cordless drill batteries, the portable battery tester, duct tape, and two long screws. In the other, the drill, the last battery, the four cans of pressurized epoxy, and the rest of the screws.

I check my watch.

We have six minutes.

To meet the courier on time, everything must go right the first time.

The odds of that happening are equal to winning the lottery without buying a ticket.

"So we're going to drill through the post? That'll take hours."

"Agreed. That's why we've got to burn through it."

I hand Barca the black 18v battery and point at the plastic covering over the top.

"Break this cover." The monster's strength works in our favor. With a quick twist, the thick plastic snaps off with the ease of opening a twist-top soda.

He hands it back to me. There, through the wires, I spot the positive and negative connectors.

"Grab two screws and the electrical tape, then hand me the screws."

"Princess, if this takes any longer . . ."

"You'll what? Climb the goal and jump over the fence to your death?"

One could only hope.

I place a screw on the outside of each connector, close enough that each will link electrical current with its respective connector, but not close enough that they will touch each other.

"I'll hold, you tape around."

Barca wraps the two screws securely to the battery, and I grab the battery tester. Its ends look like tiny jumper cables, which is exactly what we need.

I yank hard on the tester's red cable. It snaps free from the device. The black one takes three pulls. Thankfully, I do not have to ask Barca for his help.

"What are you doing, Princess?"

"Making an arc welder."

"Out of this junk?"

I do not answer, instead letting my work speak for itself.

"Where'd you learn this, some nerd school?"

More like an episode of MacGyver. But I will not let him know that.

"Something like that."

I run the negative cable around the negative connector and then do the same for the positive. Then I attach the last screw in the teeth of the negative clamp's grip and then attach the positive clamp to it.

Within seconds, the screw turns red hot.

I hand both the battery and the torch to Barca. "Get as low as possible and burn through. Do not push it over at any point. We will need every inch."

"Your mom needs every inch." Barca crouches and starts his burn.

In seven minutes, the entire pipe is free from the base.

Unfortunately, those were seven minutes we did not have.

Chapter Eighty

Or Die Trying

A s Barca snatches the freed post up, he angles it toward the fence. "Don't!"

I hated screaming, but it's the only way to keep the brute from setting off the alarm and triggering the motion-sensitive nail gun. I've seen that sucker practically crucify a bird to a wall, so I hate thinking what it does to human flesh.

Barca turns and faces me expectantly, the post slung over his shoulder like an evil Paul Bunyan.

"Put it down, right here."

Barca puts it on the ground as I grab the pressurized epoxy. The rain falls harder now, more aggressively, in large blobs that usually mean strong winds are on the way.

"If we don't reinforce the hollow post, it will break under your weight." I hand over the drill and a handful of screws. "We have to put these cans on the inside of the post, then puncture them with a drilled screw."

Thank goodness this is the same rapid-drying epoxy Quidlee, Alden-Song, and I used not all that long ago. I glance down at the end of the pipe. Luckily, nothing is blocking the hollow tube, because the cans must slide to the right spot. I snatch one can of epoxy, fit it into the tube, and shove it down. It slides to just about the midpoint of the pipe. I slide another one, and they hit. The second can bumps the first one to where it is a little further down, not quite three-fourths of the way into the pipe, but close enough.

Who'd have thought learning how to play shuffleboard with my grandfather would help with a prison break?

Finally, I put the remaining cans at the openings on either side of the pipe and instruct Barca to use the screws as drill bits and use his strength and the drill to puncture each can.

As he leans into the drilling, the first can explodes with a sound like someone opening a frozen can of cinnamon rolls, catching us both off guard.

Barca knocks out the other three cans in under two minutes.

According to our limited escape window, the courier is long gone.

We've missed our window, but I still can get Barca out of my home.

Or die trying.

Chapter Eighty-One

Time to Die

B arca holds the front end of the post with the basketball goal still attached, and I swivel the base. He has the height and leverage. I oversee the aiming.

Together, we angle the goal over the fence without causing any disturbance or setting off the alarm or motion-sensitive nail gun. After a few attempts, we lay the goal, along with a foot of pipe, in the guard tower's window. The epoxy should keep the pipe from breaking—emphasis on *should.*

This is not a perfect exit, which is why it is *Plan B.*

Now comes the dilemma of who goes over the wall first.

If Barca goes first, then I can yank the post back and set off the alarm. However, I'll still get caught and get sent to the Bay, and he might still get away with a functioning version of Gakunodo and the picture of Penny, to boot.

If I go first, I can kick the post away, trapping him in the prison, but then he might somehow convince the warden that this was my idea after all. If he gets off without getting sent to Guantanamo, then I'll be outside of the prison and the monster would still be in my house.

And Guantanamo or not, he or Cyfib would still have an operating version of Gakunodo.

Not to mention, Barca probably still has some ace up his sleeve that I cannot even imagine.

Either way, I must get that flash drive from him.

"Princess, you go first."

That move makes the most sense to him. If I am thinking of ways to double-cross Barca, then my going first benefits him somehow.

I put the duffel across my shoulder. As I grab the pipe, Barca snatches the bag from my back.

"You can't carry it and not catch it on the fence." Barca drops it to the ground and points at the roughly one foot of clearance between the barbed wire and the pole.

Curse a monster for making a good point.

"Fine." I crawl underneath the post and pull my body close. "Once I get up there, toss it to me."

It bothers me that Barca does not respond. Maybe he saw that Quidlee's ashes were in that bag.

After a deep breath, I cling as hard as I can with my thighs and wrap my legs over the wet pipe.

Of course, it had to rain.

I lock my ankles and pull with my hands, like climbing a rope in gym class. *I think.* I wasn't very good at gym or climbing ropes, but now is not the time to question the instructions of my then-coach, Coach Warren.

Inch by inch, I approach the barbed wire. Sweat mixes with my soaked hands.

Curse me for forgetting gloves.

"Watch it, Princess."

"I know."

My head and shoulders go through the opening between the wire and the pipe. I'm inching my body through when my wet left leg unhooks from the right one and grazes the barbed wire.

With just the lightest touch, the nail gun's sensors activate. I try not to move, hoping that the sensor will not go off like the land mine in Cyfib's office. And, just like the office, it does not fire.

Until I try to raise my leg and catch my shoe on a lone barb.

The barrel of the gun turns and fires a round.

"Aarrg!"

"Princess, you just got—"

"Oh, trust me, I damn well know, Barca."

The nail has found a home in my left calf. Now, bleeding and shot, I must keep that leg steady. Only then will the motion sensor reset.

Luckily, no alarm blares, like when that bird kept landing on the wire until the nail gun stuck its corpse to the wall. Sure, I have more holes in me than when I started this climb, but the fact that armed guards aren't surrounding us is a silver lining.

After what seems like an eternity, the red light on the nail gun fades to black. I pull my bleeding leg up and adrenaline takes me the rest of the way to the guard tower.

Once inside, I survey the damage. The nail is big, seven inches straight through my calf muscle. Like an idiot, I try to stand on it. A lightning bolt of pain shoots through it.

Now, with two bum legs, I must catch a duffel bag and crawl down the tower.

"Toss me the bag."

"You don't need it."

"Barca, I need the duct tape to stop the bleeding, and I don't trust either of us with a target that small in all this rain."

Barca studies me with beady eyes. It is the truth, enough of it anyway. Reluctantly, the giant leans down and hurls the bag so hard into my chest that I almost fall out of the guard tower.

There's just enough tape left on the roll for two, one-inch strips. I place the remaining plastic cylinder between my front teeth to brace for the pain.

With a quick pull and a muffled scream, I yank the nail from my leg. As tears stream down my face, I tape up both ends of my wound. This will not heal a thing, but maybe it might make standing on it bearable.

By the time I finish my impromptu field medic work, Barca is dismounting in the tower.

As we descend the ladder on the other side of the guard tower in the pouring rain to the street below, I know it is time to die.

Chapter Eighty-Two

This is a Fine Death

There is an out-of-body experience that comes with impending doom. Even though my body hurts, my mind evens out. The breaths I take are not filled with pain, but with anticipation of the upcoming end.

Barca climbs down first. I am still above him. I consider dropping and grabbing him on the way down. Maybe the fall will injure him, but he probably will somehow use my body as a cushion when he lands.

Or maybe I can kick him off. Sure, both of my legs now have the combined strength of a small child, but there is a slim chance that the surprise might do the deed.

However, even knowing that my end is near, I follow each step down, carefully placing each foot on a rung as if I will live a thousand years from this point on.

Once we are on the ground, there is no fence to scale. That is obvious from just looking over the edge of our courtyard. Fences bring prying eyes. I am standing on free land, away from Hackers' Haven for the first time in the better part of a decade.

And I am about to die here.

"Alright." Barca slaps me on the back, my schoolyard chum playing hooky with me. "Where's the courier with our IDs and corpses?"

"A half a block that way."

I don't even point. There is no reason to; the courier is long gone. Even without a watch, I know we are over fifteen minutes late.

We are screwed, but only I know how badly at this point.

"Which way?"

I stumble toward the alley off to the right.

As we enter it, I walk up to the basketball that Barca had launched a while back. I lean down to touch it. Its deflated and sad shape fits this moment. The logo on it has worn away to next to nothing. Its purpose in life, the most valuable item in a game of skill, will never return. The irony of that, and me now standing outside of the building I called home for eight years, is not lost on me.

As I pat the ball, I close my eyes.

"We're here."

When I open them and turn my gaze back to the man about to kill me, the expression on Barca's face is almost worth the beating I am about to take.

Almost.

The beast charges me, lifts me by my shoulders, and slams me against the alley wall. The duffel bag is still on my left arm, so I push it between us—anything to give me a fighting chance. Barca's left hand wraps around my neck. He squeezes. My hand slips into my front pocket. I grab the flathead screwdriver, the one I almost used on Barca in the bathroom, and stab forward. He catches it right through the palm of his hand.

Barca does not even scream as he moves his right hand toward his mouth. He wraps the bloodying handle in his mouth and yanks the blade from his hand. While he focuses on that, I slip my hand into Barca's front pocket. With both hands free, Barca squeezes. Something in my throat pops. It isn't painful, so maybe it won't kill me. At least, not immediately.

I bat at Barca's hands. The giant holds tight.

"I shoulda done this a long time ago, Princess."

Still fumbling with the sad duffel blocker, my left hand finds the zipper partially open. From inside, I grab the first thing I find: Quidlee's ashes. I yank it from the bag, put it between my hands and tear a hole, then I shove that end of the bag into Barca's mouth and punch him as hard as I can in his throat.

Go get the bastard, Quidlee.

Barca gasps for air and drops me to the ground. He recoils and wheezes for air as a small portion of my dead friend's remains choke his killer. I hit the ground hard enough to knock the smile from my face.

As I hyperventilate, Barca struggles, rises to his feet, and turns his back on me. He's wounded, so maybe he's regrouping. Or worse.

My only aim before I die is to destroy that flash drive.

On damaged legs, I dive at Barca, catching my hands on his belt loops. Barca tumbles to the ground and kicks at me as I get my hand into one of his pockets. He throws an elbow into my jaw. I take blow after blow until he grabs my leg. Barca turns my calf muscle and forces a scream, then a fall, out of me. The pain, like a vice grip on my now rebleeding wound, shoots up my leg.

With my back on the ground, I find the basketball stuck in the sewer drain. Barca puts his knees in my chest and raises two fists to smash my face in. I grab the ball and deflect some of the blow, but the impact sends the ball sailing away.

I have one card left to play. As Barca grabs my neck with one hand and brings his other fist sky-high, I smile through a mouthful of blood.

"What's so damn funny, Princess?"

I show him: in my fingertips is the flash drive with the only working copy of Gakunodo. He lunges for it but, before he gets a grip, I flick it down into the drain.

"Nooooo!"

Then AldenSong's voice is in my head. *Be still.*

That is not a problem. Barca's fists are already pummeling me from my head to my chest.

I am done.

This is a fine death.

Chapter Eighty-Three

Adrenaline, Angelic Strength, or Hellfire

"**M**y assignment was simple: show the vulnerabilities in this place so my employers could make a deal for it. Who else do you think could have coordinated such perfect attacks on your weak-ass systems with a rootkit?"

The giant slams his head into mine.

"Yeah, the infection came from inside, from me. I just wanted to show how easy you were to hack, then steal LODIS, and escape."

This is met by a meaty fist in my ribs.

"That was before I knew about your pet project. A program like that. Can you imagine how much a government would pay for it? How much would the mob pay for the ability to not only steal someone's identity but also blackmail them for life?"

Now that same fist connects with my jaw.

"It was a goldmine, but you had to *complicate* everything, didn't you?"

I don't know how long Barca beats on me. I've long since floated above my body as punch after punch bashes me into the ground. I watch as this version of me, a broken body, lays there. At one point, the body spits a tooth in the monster's face.

Good for you, Tanto.

"I'll destroy everything you've ever loved." The monster backhands me. "I'll kill your fat friend; I'll find any family you have and burn them alive."

Then a voice, not mine and not Barca's, that comes from neither inside nor outside of me, whispers. No, it is not just a voice.

"Oh, and that girl in the picture? That'll be a treat."

What builds in me grows bigger than any jolt of electricity. It's an emotion strong enough to become more than a thought. It's more than a mantra—more than a belief.

"We are going to have lots of fun, Princess."

It is an eruption.

Now.

My spirit dives back into my body and brings with it either adrenaline, angelic strength, or hellfire. There is no time for pain; no time to assess the damage. There is only rage.

Through the drowning rain, with my back on the ground, I plant both of my legs in Barca's chest and, with all my might, launch the son of a bitch as far as I can.

Which is just far enough to knock him into the street as a car slams into the monster.

Chapter Eighty-Four

Now You Will Know Vengeance

Headlights engulf Barca's body as he rolls onto the hood of the car. The courier hits the brakes and sends the giant's body tumbling down.

With a moment to breathe, I notice the world hurts a whole lot more inside a beaten body than outside of one.

As the rain slows, our courier steps in front of the car lights. He moves back and forth in the light and stares at the man he's just hit.

"What the hell?" asks Barca.

Apparently, the car needs to be made of a silver bullet to stop our monster.

Barca pushes himself off the wet ground and stomps toward the courier. Even a hit-and-run from Detroit's finest can't kill the bastard.

The courier wears a fedora and trench coat that protects him from the rain. As Barca squares up with him, the small man never flinches.

I know who the courier is, or at least who he claims to be. As for Barca, I guess the monster isn't someone who remembers faces very well.

"You're late!" Barca barks at the courier.

The man motions for both of us to join him.

Broken and bloodied, I rise. As we limp to the trunk of the older model GM, Barca covers the top of his head with his hand to prevent the rain from getting in his eyes. Once we make it to the back of the vehicle that is missing license plates, our courier pops the trunk. Barca leans inside and grabs the envelope. As rain covers the paper, he opens it and dumps out our fake IDs and some cash.

He grabs his, but I leave mine there. I will not use these, not this way.

Then our courier taps on the back window of the vehicle. Both Barca and I lean in to look at the back of the car.

"There, I see the bodies in . . ." Barca's voice stops short of a full sentence, clearly taken aback by the sight before him. He looks again. I guess his eyes doubt him. I never need to look twice.

"Hold up." The monster raises an eyebrow and darts his eyes between the courier and me before shoving me against the car. "Why's there only one body? We need two."

Then the courier finally speaks. "That won't be an issue."

Barca keeps his stony gaze on me when he asks the next question. "Who the hell is this guy?"

"I'm Margie Longfellow's father."

Killing Barca was never my right. I'm hurt, not hollow. I'd lost a friend, not a child, to this monster. It was when I stepped back from my own level of importance and figured out that the one person who could not only help me kill this bastard but also help me escape was Leonard Longfellow of Hays, Kansas.

At this moment, I think about what my scripture-quoting friend Alden-Song told me long ago: *Vengeance is the Lord's.*

On this issue, we're going to have to differ.

I wouldn't trade watching Barca's face right now for all the moonshine in Tennessee.

As for *my* face, I hope it truly conveys what I want it to:

Barca, now you will know vengeance.

Chapter Eighty-Five

Wait, I'm—

S un Tzu, a great military strategist whose book *The Art of War* is on every business and military bookshelf in the world, barely discussed vengeance. His teachings involved winning the war before the first battle, or making your enemy submit without striking a single blow. However, he did say this about the topic: *It is the unemotional, reserved, calm, detached warrior who wins, not the hothead seeking vengeance.*

Nothing that is about to happen is rooted in evil. Almost everything in this moment has been calculated. Yes, a little luck was mixed in, but I smile as I take a moment to think about how Aldy tracked Margie's dad down. It wasn't through a reverse list of addresses or names. It was through donations to a Suicide Prevention hotline. The Longfellows give annually in memory of their daughter. By donating to a cause that saves lives, it resulted in Mr. Longfellow ending one.

The pop sounds more like a firecracker than a gunshot. That's a benefit of using .22 caliber pistols: firing one rarely results in a 911 call.

The first shot to the back of Barca's head fails to kill him. It must've just grazed him because I spot a trickle of blood as his eyes clench tight and his body slumps forward onto the car's roof. Then Barca turns toward his assailant and takes a swing at the air. The short Mr. Longfellow easily ducks it, though his hat gets knocked off in the process.

I want this moment to feel right and just. It does, until Barca speaks right before Mr. Leonard Longfellow, the vengeance-fueled father of a dead girl, raises his shaky hand and fires again.

"Wait, I'm—"

The round to the front of the giant's head kicks Barca's skull hard enough to drop him to the ground. As Barca's corpse lies face down, Mr. Longfellow fires the remaining rounds. Some bullets hit. Most don't. Then he drops to the ground and beats Barca's corpse as a decade's worth of pain erupts through screams and punches.

It isn't the blood splatter on my clothes that bothers me. I have enough of my own blood on me to star in a horror movie. It is the last words that the monster uttered before Mr. Longfellow landed the life-ending hit.

I wish I had only heard a few of the words he said, and not the last one. But I had, and now there is no way to come back from what Mr. Longfellow and I have just done.

As I wipe the blood from my face, Mr. Longfellow takes out a lone cigarette wrapped in a plastic container. He drops it, probably because the adrenaline in his system is pumping faster than a freight train. When he picks it up, I notice the cig is old and brittle. It will not even light in the rain until I cup my hands over it to help Mr. Longfellow light it.

"I quit when Margie died." He takes a long puff and glances at his rusty firearm. "This was my father's. I am a little surprised it and the old ammo even worked."

I nod, either at whatever Mr. Longfellow has just admitted or in final understanding of what Barca said.

"What'd the asshole say right before I shot him again?"

"I didn't catch it." My tone is flat. I hope that the shock is enough to cover the lie. Mr. Longfellow has done so much for me. There is no reason for him to carry the burden that now weighs down my soul.

As I sit on the hood of the car, I purse my lips as a darkness inhabits my body.

I glance down at Barca's body and, almost as if to repeat the shock, I swear to you I think his lips move as I hear the words play again in my head.

"Wait, I'm Agency."

We've just killed a federal agent.

Chapter Eighty-Six

Epilogue - Cry Until the Sun Comes Up

A *gency.* That's what Barca said.

Agency can only mean two things: either he is a legitimate federal agent like FBI, or something more covert, like the CIA or another branch. I do not know which. I am leaning toward the latter.

I feel like I have spent eight years staring at the same painting and have finally made out the tiniest of details about my prison. It only took killing a man to get here. Hackers' Haven does not officially exist on U.S. soil. I already knew that this watershed area doesn't even show up on a census map. However, having some agency over us explains why I could find no proof of ownership. It also means that operatives could operate without the fear of breaking 'Merica's laws because they only applied on American soil.

This also explained why Guard Stevens arrived when Barca did. I think back to when Barca removed the battery from Stevens' shock button. Maybe this explains why their relationship was anything but a guard/prisoner one. Despite what the movies show you, most undercover operations involve multiple operatives, not just a lone gunman.

But the way Barca was acting and what he was saying at the end? All that stuff about selling LODIS and Gakunodo? He was crooked. Yes, he still deserved what happened to him, but who was he crooked *for?* Who hired him to steal from us?

There must be more to this story; I just don't have all the pieces of the puzzle yet.

All I know right now is that Barca's body at my feet brings me no joy and a level of fear, like a weighted blanket of doom has just engulfed my body.

Mr. Longfellow shakes me to get my attention. The rain has stopped, but the escape is still ongoing. I tell him I am just in shock. He understands.

He goes to get the other car and I start the final stage of the escape.

I switch into robot-action mode; now is the time to act.

I reach into Barca's pocket and grab the picture of Penny. That is not his to have. I go back to the alley and grab my knocked-out tooth. Planting it near the car will help with identifying the corpse in the back seat as me. This is the only time that bleeding all over the place will actually help the criminal in a crime scene.

For some reason, my instinct is to run as fast as I can in any and all directions.

Remember the plan.

Mr. Longfellow arrives with his vehicle; the car that is actually in his name. We load Barca's body in the back. As much as I want to burn Barca's corpse to make sure he doesn't come back to life, maybe shove a stake or two into his heart for good measure, that is not my call. How Mr. Longfellow disposes of the body is up to him. Dealer's choice.

What I do need is for Barca to *appear* alive. Finding two bodies of escaped prisoners will be suspect. Finding one and the other one long gone is pretty common among escapees.

I look at the man who has just killed a monster. I don't know what I thought would happen. There is no dance in his body, no joy in his face. Apparently, vengeance does not bring forth any emotion. Maybe it is all internal. Even so, I hope to never have to do what Mr. Longfellow just did.

Mr. Longfellow hands me the nail gun, a laser level, and a black Sharpee. AldenSong coached him perfectly.

Before I knew why we needed this clunker, I'd looked up vehicles with faulty gas tanks or gas lines. This one had a recall on it because the seat and metal under it are very thin. The gas tank could get punctured if one was not careful.

Under the vehicle, I find the gas tank. I am also pleased to find that this car has not had the recalled parts installed. Then I place the laser level on the ground and angle it up so that I can mark where the tank is. Finally, I open the back door, move the laser, and mark on the stained carpet where to fire.

From outside the driver's side window, I aim the laser at the spot. I fire the nail gun. It hits the black mark. Then I toss the nail gun into the alley. It is important that the authorities find my fingerprints on that tool and link it to how I got into the parked car.

Mr. Longfellow hands me a metal bucket filled with water and a mouth guard. He plugs a modified extension cord into the junker's cigarette lighter and hands it to me as well.

Then he intelligently steps back ten feet.

I take off my right shoe, roll up my pants leg, and submerse the leg past the spot of my Skittle tracker.

Time to test my theory about Dr. Fel's tracker. I take a breath and shove the live end of the cord into the water. White-hot lightning ping-pongs through my body. I should've sat for this because my battle-weary legs give out. I lose my balance and fall over.

The first thing I notice while on the ground is that I can't move my leg. The second is a scorch mark on my ankle. I've burned out the tracker, as well as the smoking surge protector, and when I pull out my mouth guard, silver imprints fill the orange plastic. I'll worry about getting new fillings for my cavities later.

All it takes at this point is a set of tweezers to remove the shocker and drop it next to *my corpse.*

As gasoline pours out of the vehicle, I hobble a decent distance away before Mr. Longfellow lights a rolled-up newspaper and tosses it toward a stream of gasoline. In under ten seconds, the car explodes. In under thirty, the world thinks I'm dead.

An hour later, Mr. Longfellow drops me at the bus station. Before I buy a ticket out of town, I make sure I've got everything Mr. Longfellow brought for my on-the-run basics: five grand, three passports, three driver's licenses, twenty prepaid Visa cards, six burner phones, and a bare-bones laptop to customize.

One ticket and two bus stops later, I visit an all-night clinic that tells me what I already know: I have a broken nose, massive swelling in the face and hands, a knee that I should stay off of, and a few stitches in the holes in my leg. I'm right as rain if rain were piss. Next, I visit Larken, a dental hygienist with a lot of debt, working the graveyard shift of an all-night emergency dental office. He helps yank out the rest of that damaged tooth, as well as evens and smooths out my teeth a touch, to make my dental records less traceable.

Following this, I visit Rosco, a master tattoo craftsman who stretches and shortens the dermis and epidermis of my skin for new fingerprints. He's also agreed to alter the list of names I have tattooed on my arm into one symbol: a black castle-like figure with a wide base and a round top. In the game of chess, this is a rook, an often underappreciated yet dangerous piece. Many a chess master has lost their greatest matches to this one piece. For me, it too is a reminder of what I have lost.

A change of colored contacts later, I board the first bus headed to Galveston. When the bus driver asks me how I am, a spasm shoots through my hand and up my neck. I just keep walking and blame it on my nerves.

Now, I sit on a Galveston, Texas beach just before the sun rises. There's a restaurant advertising "deep fried gator" behind me, and the only people currently up are the birds. The saltwater floods my nostrils. Anyone who glimpses my Frankenstein's monsterish features will call the cops, but it is too early for anyone to be out here.

I should feel comfortable.

I stare at the crumpled picture of Penny on her bike. I will honor Quidlee. I will find her, and protect her, if I can.

With my shoes and socks on the side, I run my toes in the sand. It isn't Hawaii, but I think of AldenSong's desire to do this just one last time.

Then that comfort flushes away as I think of AldenSong. PoBones. Foshi_Taloa. All of them. Alone, yet together. I have freedom, yet they have family.

Be still.

I laugh to myself because AldenSong's words are the most opposite of what my life will be now. I am about to have to run. Consistently. Endlessly. Something in my gut tells me to never expect this calmness again.

Someone will poke a hole in my escape.

Someone will hunt me.

That will happen soon, I am sure of it.

But it does not happen now.

That is why I turn on my side, hug myself into the tightest ball I can, and cry until the sun comes up.

Burn bright.

THE END

Coming Soon

Tanto will return in 2023 in *RUNNING ON BROKEN BONES: A Tanto Thriller.*

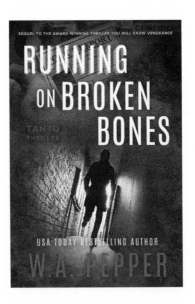

Cover may change before final publishing

Available to preorder at http://www.wapepperwrites.com/robb/

To read the first chapter of *RUNNING ON BROKEN BONES: A Tanto Thriller,*
please continue reading.

Chapter One - Dip in the Pool

While most Americans spend their Sunday mornings watching sports or listening to robed men tell magic resurrection stories, I schedule my day around an eighty-five-year-old prostitute who ensures I don't swallow my tongue. Sure, anyone can do this, but I am loyal to a fault. Plus, this bag of bones won't ask questions unless you pay her to, like I do.

At noon I check into the kind of hourly motel known for serving adultery with a side of bedbugs. "Rusty" knocks at 12:30. I swing open the door and am greeted with that yellow yet dependable Jack-o-Lantern grin. What ticks me off is that she travels in a cloud of nicotine, so my sensitive nostrils burn. Alas, Shakespeare never wrote a recall for "Stop smoking menthols before my session, whore," so I tolerate her impersonation of Pig Pen from Peanuts.

She greets me the way all in her profession welcome clients: with an open hand. I insert two bills featuring a man smart enough to avoid the presidency. She shoves them portrait-first into her lacy and ragged bra. Benny Franklin probably would've loved motorboating Rusty.

My pants drop to the floor. I slip on a man's diaper. Its smooth, lacy feel comforts my junk and inner thigh. This brand can also take the damage. Truthfully, I have browned my pants during "therapy" with Rusty before.

Diapers cost less than thrift shop jeans.

I stretch out on top of a paramedic's backboard on the bed. Rusty knows the routine: strap my head, chest, right arm, left arm, waist, right leg, and left leg firmly to the board, and then shove a pillow under my ass and one between my legs.

Rusty whips out my laptop and more safety tools from my red-leather suitcase. From my position on the board, I am too nervous to complain when she sanitizes the Shock Doctor Adult Pro Strapless Mouthguard, known for handling internal impact absorption, by breathing on it and then rubbing it on her torn jeggings before shoving it in my mouth.

Great. If therapy doesn't kill me, gingivitis will.

As I stare at the watermark in the stucco ceiling that looks like a whale, I hear the laptop chime. Rusty is now plugged into the Interrogator: a USB connectable lie detector. She straps a sensor just under my hard nipples, then on my lower abdomen, and finally puts finger sleeves on my left hand's ring and index fingers to record the chaos.

Rusty knows not to ask questions until I signal her. The meds have flushed out of my system the day before, so it's go-time.

I nod.

Rusty asks, "Are we in a motel room?"

At first my mind hears the sentence almost like I've caught half a conversation from a TV in another room. I breathe deep and open my mouth. Nothing comes. Any answer would have sufficed. Any sound or grunt would have marked a vast improvement over the last test. Then it comes. The mouth guard rumbles as my body shakes like an earthquake. Tears roll out of my eyes and the front of the diaper shifts from white to yellow as I convulse through the small seizure.

She squeezes my hand once, lets go, and asks again.

"Are we in a motel room?"

This time, the seizures pop like short bass beats. The mouth guard flies across the room like Mike Tyson has just punched it from my face. Good ole Rusty snatches it up and shoves it back in, past my chattering teeth, saving my tongue. Not like I need it.

Even through the pain, I hear the paramedic board creak and crack like popcorn bursting. A self-made current pumps through my body for a full minute until only slight tremors remain.

Rusty wipes my brow and says, "All right, sweetie, lighten up. I can't have my favorite non-penetrator dying on me. Go to the Rote. Are we in a motel room?"

I crack a smile just a twitch short of madness and then reply the only way I know how: repeating someone else's memorized words.

For the rest of our session, I hear the madman, my former warden, Cyfib's internal voice plaguing my consciousness. Even though he is not here, he always reminds me of my continued failures.

What the hell did Cyfib do to me in Hackers' Haven to cause this?

How do I fix myself when I can't even communicate?

Finally, how do I stop him from doing this anyone ever again?

Who'd have thought that the hellacious torture I experienced until a few months ago would've seemed like a brisk dip in the pool?

To be continued in RUNNING ON BROKEN BONES (coming in 2023)

Available to preorder at http://www.wapepperwrites.com/robb/

RUNNING ON BROKEN BONES: A Tanto Story

A lmost a decade has passed since a secret government agency imprisoned Tanto. Now that he has escaped and is on the run, what
is more dangerous: his degenerating body, or the criminal company that
he keeps?

Available to preorder at http://www.wapepperwrites.com/robb/

Can't wait until the sequel comes out to continue Tanto's story? If
you are interested in a prequel to *YOU WILL KNOW VENGEANCE*, please
consider reading *DoGoodR: A Tanto Thriller.*

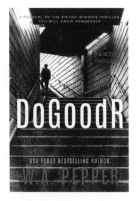

Tanto and his team of hackers must beat a ticking clock to save a
stranger from a lifetime jail sentence. How far will Tanto risk his own
freedom to protect a kid who made a mistake?

Available at wapepperwrites.com/dogoodr

Acknowledgments

Too many of us, when we accomplish what we set out to do, exclaim, 'See what I have done!' instead of saying, 'See where I have been led.'
  – Henry Ford

First and foremost, I must thank God for blessing me with the opportunity to not only write, but to share my writing. For a large portion of my life, I was told I was not and never would be a writer. Somehow, a Higher Power kept that desire to write, an ember, burning in me. The positive influences in my life stoked that fire and helped me produce the novel you have before you.

Secondly, I would like to thank my wife Taddy. She's equally my biggest supporter and biggest stickler. She is the reason this book is more than just a bunch of incoherent random thoughts. Taddy is also the only reason I was ever brave enough to publish anything. Without Taddy, not only would there not be any stories, there would be no *Vengeance* (wow, that sounded menacing). Thank you, Babe. You are my everything.

In addition, I would like to thank the following people who contributed to this work currently in your hands:

Two developmental editors worked with me on this book. Lauren Moore helped me when Books One and Two were stuck together in one big mess. Meaghan Wagner encouraged me to make some hard (and ultimately wise) choices, which helped plug some huge plot holes and made this adventure a complete story. Our copyeditor Anne Dillon took my dirty writing and cleaned it up in places I never would've thought about. Our cover artist Damon Freeman and his team made this cover feel like a true thriller. Finally, David Sandretto's excellent eye for details caught many a mistake as our proofreader. Thank you to this amazing team.

Our team of Beta Readers pointed out details and insights I never would've caught on my own. A big thank you to Cathy T., Josi D., Kenneth M., Richard D., and Skye S.

My technology teachers over the years encouraged my desire to learn and explore. I want to thank Drs. Milam Aiken, Anthony Ammeter, and Brian Reithel. I also want to acknowledge the memory of my first computer teacher, Paul "PJ" Jones. PJ's teaching style was result-oriented no-nonsense, and he encouraged his students to "just get it done any way possible."

While my fellow author Andrew Van Wey has already published several books, he is still learning and willing to share what he learns. From late night texts to email chains to me asking many a dumb question and his answering without hesitation, Andrew has helped me avoid some pitfalls that I would have easily fallen into. Thank you, my friend.

Below is a much-too-short list of people (and influencers) that I would like to thank. I tried to list everyone, but at the time of writing this, I have certainly left names off. For this, I apologize in advance and appreciate your contribution to my life and writing.

Authors I would like to thank include (in alphabetical order): Tara Alemany, Lee Child, Shawn Coyne, Brett Easton Ellis, Ricardo Fayet, Meg Gardiner, Stephen King, Dean Koontz, Mark Leslie Lefebvre, Brad Melzer, Frank Miller, John Ramsey Miller, Derek Murphy, Jo Penn (who cursed at me to encourage me to publish), Kyla Sharp, Jeremy N. Smith (and his friend, a hacker named "Alien"), A.M. Strong, Nick Thacker, Ruth Ware, and Kāsie Whitener.

Others I would like to thank include (in alphabetical order): Dan Alexander, Pam Burleson, Frank Darabont, Sam Esmail, Tom Fontana, Bryan Fuller, Jorge Garcia, Zach Gilford, Larry Gordon, Jim Jarmusch, Akira Kurosawa, Rami Malek, Jason Momoa, Lon Perry, Sonya Sargent-Strong, Jimmi Simpson, Forest Whitaker, Matt Willig, and Beau Willimon.

And to everyone in the 20BooksTo50K community. Your insights, in both writing and life, are gold.

Glossary (aka Jargon)

The following is a glossary of technical terms in this book. Some of these terms exist in the real world. Their definitions are drawn from multiple sources on the Internet (Wikipedia, Techopedia.com, Dictionary.com, HowToGeek, etc.) Other terms only exist in this book series. This is not an all-inclusive list and will continue to grow. For further definitions, please visit our website at HustleValleyPress.com.

Alviss – a proprietary private messaging application (also the name of the author's favorite locksmith).

Anti-Virus – (of software) designed to detect and destroy computer viruses.

Basic Input Output System (aka BIOS) – code that instructs a computer on how to perform basic functions such as system booting and input controls.

Bay, The – historically, Guantanamo Bay was a place where people viewed by the United States of America as "enemies of the State" or "combatants" were incarcerated and interrogated. The author is unsure if this site officially continues its prior function.

Blog – a regularly updated website or web page, typically one run by an individual or small group, that is written in an informal or conversational style.

Bot (aka Robot) – an autonomous program on the internet or another network that can interact with systems or users.

Buffer (aka Buffering) – a temporary memory area in which data is stored while it is being processed or transferred, especially one used while streaming video or downloading audio.

Bug – an (intentional or unintentional) error in a computer program or system.

Bushi – a practitioner of the Way of the Samurai or the Bushido Code.

Bushido Code – the historic code of conduct for Japan's warrior classes, and the word "bushido" comes from the Japanese roots "bushi" meaning "warrior," and "do" meaning "path" or "way."

Captures – the successful online trapping of individuals on the Internet.

CDs (aka Compact Discs) – a way to store data and music.

Chicken-Choker trap – an online trap where the victim is teased with something enticing and leads to his own capture by following his own (morbid) desires.

Coder eyes – a symptom of eye strain that occurs when the user spends too much time staring at a computer.

Compiler – a program that converts source code written in a programming language.

Dam Breaker – someone who breaks through firewalls.

Damascus – the forging of steel by heating, breaking, and reforming many times.

Dark Web – the part of the World Wide Web that is only accessible by means of special software, allowing users and website operators to remain anonymous or untraceable.

Davidson Protocol – a set of rules that allow prisoners to donate work/time off to another prisoner.

Disciplinary chips – devices that are installed into a human body, gain their power from the same source, and provide electrical shocks via remote control.

Emulator – software that enables one computer system (called the host) to behave like another computer.

Faraday (aka Faraday Bag) – a device that removes the ability to receive or transmit data from a device.

Firewall – a part of a computer system or network which is designed to block unauthorized access while permitting outward communication.

Flash drives – finger-sized devices that connect to a computer and have room for storage.

Gig – a job or task to which someone is promised something in return for completion.

Hack – use of a tool (such as a computer, person, device, or situation) to gain unauthorized access to data in a system.

Hacker – a person who uses computers to gain unauthorized access to data.

Hackers' Haven (aka Double-H) – a privatized prison that forces imprisoned hackers to hunt and secure other lawbreakers.

Hackvict – a convict that believes in using policy, action, or various forms of media to bring about political, economic, or social change.

Handle (aka Callsign or Username) – a person's identifier when they log into a computer and how the prisoners of Hackers' Haven are labelled.

HoneyBadger – a propriety operating system that uses components from both Linux and Windows operating systems.

Gakunodo – the tent where Bushido warriors rested; also, an efficient software that entices individuals online and records their (illegal) footsteps.

Internet Relay Chat (aka IRC) – a group communication device that uses text-based chats or instant messaging to correspond with individuals and share files.

IP Address – a unique string of characters that identifies each computer using the Internet Protocol to communicate over a network.

Keylogger – a computer program that records every keystroke made by a computer user, especially in order to gain fraudulent access to passwords and other confidential information.

Kills – see "Captures."

Kilobyte (aka KB) – a unit of memory or data equal to 1,024 (2^{10}) bytes.

Lap count – an interval between online pings.

Linux – an open-source operating system modelled on Unix.

Liquid Ocular Display Interceptor System (aka LODIS) – a device that records human eye and body movement through a watery substance.

Log file – file extension for an automatically produced file that contains a record of events (such as user choices) from certain software and operating systems.

Loopback – a static IP address used for testing integrated microchips.

Looping – the ability to copy files of a target computer without slowing down noticeable bandwidth or computing speed.

Malware – software that is specifically designed to disrupt, damage, or gain unauthorized access to a computer system.

Megabyte (aka MB) – a unit of information equal to 2^{20} bytes or, loosely, one million bytes.

Memory – the part of a computer in which data or program instructions can be stored for retrieval.

Neural Net – a computer system modeled on the human brain and nervous system.

Nintendo Time – when using an electronic device, this is the sensation that time is going slower than it actually is in the real world.

NumLk – the number lock key is a part of a keyboard that allows the user quick access to numbers.

Omni-Viewer – the (monitored) software that allows the prisoners of Hackers' Haven access to the Internet and Dark Web.

Paratrenicha (aka "Crazy Russian Ants") – Paratrenicha species near pubens. Ants that eat electronics (they really exist).

Ping – query (another computer on a network) to determine whether there is a connection to it.

Pods (aka Med Pods) – full body sized machines that detect abnormalities and illnesses in individuals.

Portable Document Format (aka PDF) – a versatile file format created by Adobe that gives people an easy, reliable way to present and exchange documents – regardless of the software, hardware, or operating systems being used by anyone who view them.

POS – stands for piece of shit, and is a computer made from scrap parts.

Program Lidocaine – A computer worm that, once entered into a computer system, slows the system down until the system crashes.

Radio Frequency Identification (aka RFID) – denoting technologies that use radio waves to identify people or objects carrying encoded microchips.

Random Access Memory (aka RAM) – a type of data storage used in computers that is volatile and erased when a computer is turned off.

Randomizer – a piece of software that scrambles data or information.

Root – a user account with full and unrestricted access to a system.

Rootkit – a set of software tools that enable an unauthorized user to gain control of a computer system without being detected.

Scanner – a device that scans documents and converts them into digital data.

Scripts – slang for computer code.

SkipTrace – a piece of software that takes the actual distance from the ping's source, the time at each occurrence, the bandwidth downloaded and uploaded to various IP sources, and strength and number of Internet connected devices in a known area as well as the draw of power from the utility company to calculate a user's location.

Software Patch – a downloaded series of files that fix a bug in a piece of software.

Solo – a piece of software that does not interact with other software; a hack involving software (or a software system) that forbids the use of additional software.

Tamahagane – a way of making a Japanese sword. The word tama means "round and precious," like a gem, while the word hagane means "steel."

Terabyte (aka TB) – a unit of information equal to one million million (10^{12}) or, strictly, 2^{40} bytes.

Terminal – see workstation.

Test Program Set (aka TPS) Report – "a document describing the step-by-step process in which an engineer tests and re-tests software or an electronics system." This definition is courtesy of Mike Judge, former engineer and programmer for a subcontractor working on military jets and the creator of *Office Space.*

Theia – software that allows residents of Hackers' Haven access to the Dark Web.

Timed out – a period of inactivity has passed that causes a software program to shut down.

Torrent – a file-sharing protocol based on peer-to-peer (P2P) technology that allows vast numbers of users to connect and share content without having to rely on a single source for downloads.

Tracer bullet – a piece of computer code that follows the trail of another piece of computer code and estimates possible objectives.

Units – rewards for successful captures, can be redeemed for food, non-essentials, or parole.

Unix – a widely used multiuser operating system.

Virtual Private Network (aka VPN) – an arrangement whereby a secure, apparently private, network is achieved using encryption over a public network, typically the internet.

Virus (aka Computer Virus) – a piece of code which is capable of copying itself and typically has a detrimental effect, such as corrupting the system or destroying data.

War Room – a classroom-style arrangement of computer workstations where captures and the prevention of hacks occur.

Windows – a widely used single user operating system.

Workstation – a computer monitor, keyboard, mouse, and computer connected to the servers and Internet.

Worm – a standalone malware computer program that relies on security failures and replicates itself in order to spread to other computers.

Zipped – a compressed file that consists of one or several other files.

Book Club Section

Hustle Valley Press, LLC Presents
   A Group Discussion Guide to *You Will Know Vengeance* by W. A. Pepper

If you or your book club would be interested in the author meeting with you (either virtually or in-person, where possible), please reach out to him at wapepper@hustlevalleypress.com

Introduction and a Brief recap

Incarcerated Bushido Code-following hacker Tanto lives as good of a life as he can, capturing others online and trying to avoid his warden's wrath. However, when a pair of new inmates arrive, one frail and the other fearsome, Tanto's world gets turned upside down.

(Starter questions for your book club begin on the next page).

Book Club Questions

Possible Starter Questions for Your Book Club

1. Would you have given the book a different title? If yes, what would your title be?

2. Are there any books that you would compare this book to?

3. Did your opinion of this book change as you read it? How?

4. Did you have a favorite character? If so, why? Would you be friends with that character in real life? If so, what would you two do for an activity together?

5. Which character or moment prompted the strongest emotional reaction for you? Why?

6. The character of Tanto is one who believes in the "greater good," yet often is full of pride. How do you think his pride benefits him in the novel? How does it hurt him?

7. Were there times you disagreed with a character's actions? What would you have done differently?

8. How did you feel about the ending? Would you change it? How?

9. What do you think happens to the characters in Hackers' Haven after the warden discovers that two prisoners have escaped?

About the Author

W. A. Pepper writes suspenseful thrillers. *You Will Know Vengeance* is his debut novel. He is an awarding-winning *USA Today, Wall Street Journal,* and *Amazon* Bestselling Author for his contribution to the business anthology *Habits of Success.* Under different names (and his real one of Will Pepper), he has published in multiple academic journals, interactive e-books, anthologies, and online. During the COVID-19 pandemic, he and his wife Taddy (plus their dog Danger) started the publishing house Hustle Valley Press, LLC. Through it, they published four e-books that have amassed over one hundred five-star reviews. Further, the husband-and-wife team donated the first six months of revenue from the sale of each of those books to charity; this resulted in thousands of dollars raised for the reader-selected charities that support racial equality, COVID-19 relief, veteran affairs, and St. Jude Children's Hospital. He has a PhD in Management Information Systems or, as he calls it, Business Computing, from The University of Mississippi. Finally, he, his wife Taddy, and their dog Danger split their time between Colorado and Mississippi.

CONTACT INFORMATION

♪ tiktok.com/@wapepperwrites

f facebook.com/wapepperwrites

g goodreads.com/wapepper

⊙ instagram.com/wapepperwrites

a amazon.com/author/willpepper

Made in the USA
Monee, IL
29 September 2022

29e00aa0-82b9-46d1-aa21-084458a0da04R01